Also by Pierre Pevel from Gollancz:

The Cardinal's Blades
The Alchemist in the Shadows

The Cardinal's Blades

PIERRE PEVEL

Translated by Tom Clegg

The right of Pierre Pevel to be identified as the author of this work
and of Tom Clegg to be identified as the translator of this work has
been asserted by them in accordance with the
Copyright, Designs and Patents Act 1988.

First published in Great Britain in 2009 by
Gollancz
An imprint of the Orion Publishing Group
Orion House, 5 Upper St Martin's Lane, London WC2H 9EA
An Hachette UK company

This edition published in Great Britain in 2010 by Gollancz

1 3 5 7 9 10 8 6 4 2

A CIP catalogue record for this book is available
from the British Library.

ISBN 978 0 575 08439 1

Typeset at The Spartan Press Ltd,
Lymington, Hants

Printed and bound in Great Britain by
Clays Ltd, St Ives plc

The Orion Publishing Group's policy is to use papers that
are natural, renewable and recyclable products and made
from wood grown in sustainable forests. The logging and
manufacturing processes are expected to conform to the
environmental regulations of the country of origin.

www.orionbooks.co.uk

This book is dedicated to Jean-Philippe,
my brother who fled too soon.

1. Porte de la Conférence
2. Porte Saint-Honoré
3. Porte de Richelieu
4. Porte Montmartre
5. Porte de la Poissonnerie
6. Porte Saint-Denis
7. Porte Saint-Martin
8. Porte du Temple
9. Porte Saint-Antoine
10. Porte de Nesle
11. Porte de Buci
12. Porte Saint-Germain
13. Porte Saint-Michel
14. Porte Saint-Jacques
15. Porte Saint-Marcel
16. Porte Saint-Victor
17. Porte de la Tournelle

A. Palais-Cardinal
B. Palais des Tuileries
C. Louvre
D. Église Saint-Eustache
E. Les Halles
F. Cimetière des Saints-Innocents
G. Le Châtelet
H. Abbaye Saint-Martin
I. Enclos du Temple
J. Place Royale
K. La Bastille
L. Arsenal
M. Pont-Neuf
N. Place Dauphine
O. Palais
P. Hôtel-Dieu
Q. Notre-Dame
R. Les Écailles
S. Hôpital de la Charité
T. Abbaye de Saint-Germain-des-Prés
U. Foire Saint-Germain
V. Palais du Luxembourg
W. Place Maubert
X. Abbaye Saint-Victor
Y. Jardin des Plantes
Z. Val de Grâce

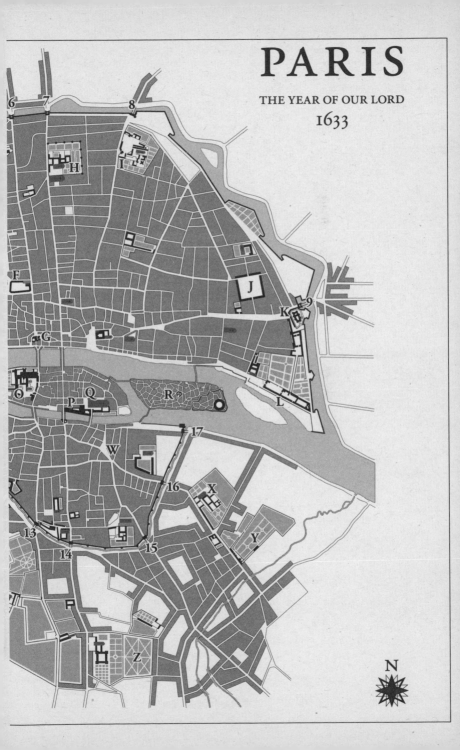

PARIS

THE YEAR OF OUR LORD
1633

A Call to Arms

1

Long and high-ceilinged, the room was lined with elegantly gilded and bound books which shone with a russet gleam in the half-light of the candle flames. Outside, beyond the thick red velvet curtains, Paris slept beneath a starry sky and a deep tranquillity had settled on the dusky streets which penetrated even here, where the scratching of a quill barely troubled the silence. Thin, bony and pale, the hand which held the quill traced fine, tight writing, delicate yet steady, making neither mistakes nor blots. The quill paused regularly to take a fresh load from the inkwell. It was guided with precision and, as soon as it returned to the paper, continued to scratch out an unhesitating thread of thought. Nothing else moved. Not even the scarlet dragonnet which, curled in a ball, its muzzle tucked under its wing, slept peacefully by the thick leather blotter.

Someone knocked at the door.

The hand wrote on without pause but the dragonnet, disturbed, opened one emerald eye. A man entered wearing a sword and a fitted cape of red silk blazoned, on each of its four panels, with a white cross. His head was respectfully uncovered.

'Yes?' said Cardinal Richelieu, continuing to write.

'He is here, Your Eminence.'

'Alone?'

'As you instructed.'

'Good. Send him in.'

Master Saint-Georges, Captain of His Eminence's Guards, bowed. He was about to withdraw when the cardinal added:

'And spare him the guards.'

Saint-Georges understood, bowed again and took care to close the door silently as he left.

Before being received in the cardinal's apartment visitors normally had to pass through five rooms throughout which guards were stationed on continuous watch, day and night. Each carried a sword at their side and pistol in their belt, remaining alert to the slightest hint of danger and refusing let anyone pass without a direct order to that effect. Nothing escaped their scrutiny, which could shift at a moment's notice from merely probing to actively threatening. Wearing their celebrated capes, these men belonged to the company of His Eminence's Guards. They escorted him everywhere he went, and wherever he resided there were never less than sixty men to accompany him. Those not on duty in the corridors and antechambers killed time between their rounds, their short muskets always near to hand. And the Guards were not the only troops detailed to protect Richelieu: while they ensured his safety inside, a company of musketeers patrolled outside.

This constant vigilance was not a simple, ostentatious show of force. They had good reason to guard him; even here in the heart of Paris, in the ornamental palace the cardinal had built just a few steps from the Louvre.

At forty-eight years old, Armand-Jean du Plessis, Cardinal de Richelieu was one of the most powerful men, and one of the most threatened, of his time. A duke and peer of the realm, member of the Council and principal minister to His Majesty; he had the ear of Louis XIII – with whom he had ruled France for a decade. That alone accounted for the numerous adversaries he reckoned with, the least of whom only plotted to disgrace him, while others made detailed plans for his assassination – for if the cardinal were forced into exile he could still act from abroad, and if imprisoned there was always the possibility of his escape. Such plots had come close to succeeding in the past, and new ones were no doubt being prepared. Richelieu had to guard himself against all those who hated him out of jealousy, because of his influence over the king. But he also had to be wary of attacks orchestrated by the enemies of France, the first and foremost being Spain, and her Court of Dragons.

It was about to strike midnight.

The sleepy dragonnet heaved a tired sigh.

'It's very late, isn't it?' the cardinal said, addressing the small winged reptile with an affectionate smile.

He looked drawn himself, both from fatigue and illness, on this spring night in 1633.

Normally he would have been in bed soon. He would sleep a little if his insomnia, his migraines and the pain in his limbs allowed it. And especially if no one woke him with urgent news requiring orders to be drawn up hastily, or worse still, a meeting in the dead of night. No matter what occurred, he rose at two in the morning and was promptly surrounded by his secretaries. After quick ablutions, he would eat a few mouthfuls of broth and then work until six o'clock. Then perhaps he would allow himself one or two hours of additional sleep, before beginning the most challenging part of the day – the rounds of ministers and secretaries of state, ambassadors and courtiers. But tonight, Cardinal Richelieu had not yet finished with the affairs of France.

Hinges squeaked at the other end of the library, then a firm step sounded against the parquet floor, followed by a clatter of spurs, as Cardinal Richelieu reread the report he intended to present to the king concerning the proposed policies against Lorraine. Incongruous at this hour and echoing loudly beneath the library's painted ceiling, the growing noise woke the dragonnet. Unlike its master, it raised its head to see who had arrived.

It was a gentleman, his features marked by long service in times of war.

Large, energetic, still strong despite his years, he had high boots on his feet, and carried his hat in his hand and his rapier at his side. He wore a grey doublet slashed with red and matching hose the cut of which was as austere as the fabric itself. His closely trimmed beard was the same silver-grey as his hair. It covered much of his severe-looking face, rendered gaunt by battle and long hours of riding, and perhaps also by old regrets and sadness. His bearing was martial, assured, proud, almost provocative. His gaze was that of a man who would never look away first. And he wore a tarnished steel ring on his left hand.

Letting a silence settle, Richelieu finished his perusal of the report while his visitor waited. He initialled the last page, sanded it to help the ink dry, and then blew the grains away. They rose into the air, tickling the dragonnet's nostrils. The little reptile sneezed, raising a smile on the cardinal's thin lips.

'Apologies, Petit-Ami,' he murmured to it.

And finally acknowledging the man, he said:

'A moment, if you will?'

He rang a small bell.

The chimes summoned the faithful and indefatigable Charpentier, who had served His Eminence in the capacity of private secretary for twenty-five years. Richelieu gave him the initialled report.

'Before I present it before His Majesty tomorrow, I want Père Joseph to read it and add those biblical references which His Majesty likes so much and serve the cause of France so well.'

Charpentier bowed and departed.

'The King is very pious,' the cardinal explained.

Then, speaking as if his guest had only just arrived:

'Welcome, Captain La Fargue.'

'Captain?'

'That's your rank, isn't it?'

'It was, before my commission was taken from me.'

'We wish that you return to service.'

'As of now?'

'Yes. Did you have something better to do?'

It was an opening sally, and Richelieu predicted that there would be more to follow.

'A captain must command a company,' said La Fargue.

'Or a troop, at the very least, which may be more modest in size. You shall reclaim yours.'

'It was dispersed, thanks to the good care and attention of Your Eminence.'

6

That comment raised a spark in the cardinal's eye.

'Find your men. These letters, intended for them, are ready to be sent.'

'They may not all answer the call.'

'Those who respond will suffice. They were the best, and they should still be. It has not been so long . . .'

'Five years.'

'. . . and you are free to recruit others,' Richelieu continued without permitting an interruption. 'Besides, my reports indicate that, despite my orders, you have not severed all of your connections with them.'

The old gentleman blinked.

'I see that the competence of Your Eminence's spies has not faltered in the least.'

'I believe there are few things concerning you of which I am unaware, captain.'

His hand poised on the pommel of his sword, Captain Etienne-Louis de La Fargue took a moment to think. He stared straight ahead, over the cardinal's head who, from his armchair, observed him with patient interest.

'So, captain, you accept?'

'It depends.'

Feared because he was influential and all the more influential because he was feared, Cardinal Richelieu could ruin a destiny with a stroke of his quill or, just as easily, propel a career towards greatness. He was believed to be a man who would crush all those who opposed him. It was a significant exaggeration but as he himself was fond of saying, 'His Eminence has no enemies other than those of the State. But towards them, he is utterly without mercy.'

Cold as marble, the cardinal hardened his tone.

'Is it not enough for you, captain, to know that your king recalls you to his service?'

The man unflinchingly found and held the cardinal's gaze.

'No, monseigneur, it is not enough.'

After a pause, he added:

'Or rather, it's not enough any more.'

*

For a long moment, nothing but the hissing breathing of the dragonnet could be heard beneath the rich panelling of the Palais-Cardinal's great library. The conversation between the two men had taken a bad turn, with one of them still seated and the other standing, each taking the measure of the other, until La Fargue gave in. But he did not lower his gaze. Instead he lifted it, looking straight ahead again and focusing on a precious tapestry behind the cardinal.

'Are you demanding guarantees, captain?'

'No.'

'In that case, I'm afraid I do not understand you.'

'I want to say, monseigneur, that I demand nothing. One does not demand that which one is due.'

'Ah.'

La Fargue was playing a dangerous game, opposing the man said to be in greater command of France than the king himself. His Eminence knew that not all battles were won by force of arms. As the old soldier stood at unwavering attention, no doubt ready to be incarcerated in the deepest, grimmest prison for the remainder of his days, or swiftly dispatched to fight savages in the West Indies, Richelieu leaned on the table and, with a gnarled index finger, scratched the dragonnet's head.

The reptile closed its eyes and sighed with pleasure.

'Petit-Ami was given to me by His Majesty,' said the cardinal in a conversational tone. 'It was he who named it, and it seems these creatures become accustomed very quickly to their nicknames . . . In any case, it expects me to feed it and care for it. And I have never failed in that, just as I have never failed to serve the interests of France. Nevertheless, if I suddenly deprived it of my care, it would not take Petit-Ami long to bite me. And this, without any consideration for the kindnesses I had lavished upon it previously . . . There's a lesson to remember here, don't you think?'

The question was rhetorical. Leaving the dragonnet to its slumber, Richelieu sank back into the cushions of his armchair, cushions which he piled on in a vain attempt to ease the pangs of his rheumatism.

He grimaced, waiting until the pain lessened before continuing.

'I know, captain, that not so long ago I let you down. You and your men served me well. In view of your previous successes and your value, was your disgrace justified? Of course not. It was a political necessity. I grant you that your efforts were not entirely unworthy and that the failure of your delicate mission during the siege of La Rochelle was in no way your fault. But considering the tragic turn taken by the events in which you were involved, the French Crown could do nothing but disown you. It was necessary to save face and condemn you for what you had done, secretly, by our order. You had to be sacrificed, even if it heaped dishonour upon the death of one of your men.'

La Fargue agreed, but it cost him to do so.

'Political necessity,' he said in a resigned tone while his thumb rubbed the steel signet ring against the inside of his fist.

Suddenly seeming very tired, the cardinal sighed.

'Europe is at war, captain. The Holy Roman Empire has known nothing but fire and blood for the last fifteen years, and France will no doubt soon be drawn into the fighting there. The English threaten our coasts and the Spanish our borders. When she is not taking up arms against us, Lorraine welcomes all the seditious elements in the kingdom with open arms while the queen mother plots against the king from Brussels. Revolts blossom in our provinces and those who foment and lead them are often placed at the highest levels of the State. I shall not even mention the secret factions, often funded from abroad, whose intrigues extend all the way into the Louvre.'

Richelieu looked La Fargue firmly in the eye.

'I cannot always choose the weapons I employ, captain.'

There was a long silence, and then the cardinal spoke again:

'You seek neither fortune nor glory. And in truth, I can promise you neither. You can rest assured that I am as ready now as yesterday to sacrifice your honour or your life if reasons of State demand it . . .'

9

This frank admission surprised the captain, who raised a sceptical eyebrow and returned Richelieu's gaze.

'But do not refuse the hand I extend to you, captain. You are not one of those who shirk their duty, and soon the kingdom will have great need of a man like you. A man capable of gathering together and commanding honest, courageous and expert swordsmen, adept at acting swiftly and secretly, and above all, who will kill without remorse and die without regret in the service of the king. Captain, would you still be wearing your signet ring if you were not the man I believe you to be?'

La Fargue could not answer, but for the cardinal the business had been settled.

'You and your men liked to call yourselves the "Cardinal's Blades", I seem to recall. The name was never whispered lightly amongst the enemies of France. For that reason, among others, it pleased me. Keep it.'

'With all the respect that I owe you, monseigneur, I have not yet said yes.'

Richelieu stared at the old man for a long time, his thin angular face expressing only coldness. Then he rose from his armchair, opened a curtain a little to look outside and said carelessly:

'And if I said it could affect your daughter?'

Suddenly growing pale, and visibly shaken, La Fargue turned his head towards the cardinal who seemed absorbed in the contemplation of the night-time garden.

'My . . . daughter? . . . But I don't have a daughter, monseigneur—'

'You know very well that you do. And I know it as well . . . But don't be alarmed. The secret of her existence is one guarded by a few trustworthy people. I believe that even your Blades are unaware of the truth, is that not so?'

The captain surrendered, abandoning a battle he had already lost.

'Is she . . . in danger?' he asked him.

At that moment Richelieu knew he had won. His back still turned to La Fargue, he hid a smile.

'You shall understand soon,' he said. 'For now, gather your Blades in preparation to receive the details of your first mission. I promise you that these shall not be long in coming.'

And at last rewarding La Fargue with a glance over his shoulder, he added:

'Good night, captain.'

2

Agnès de Vaudreuil woke with a scream in her throat, her eyes wide and filled with the terrors which haunted her every night. She had sat up in a panic, and remained dazed for a moment watching the shadows around her bed. She was forced to wait while the furious pace of her heart slowed. Wait until her breathing, almost panting, finally calmed. Wait for the sour sweat to dry on her skin.

The terror left her little by little, with regret, like a pack of dogs frustrated not to have triumphed over their wounded yet tenacious prey.

The young woman sighed.

A peaceful silence reigned inside as much as it did without, a clear shimmering light falling from the cloud-flecked sky and through the open window as far as the four-poster bed. Elegant and spacious, the room was richly furnished, decorated with heavy hangings, valuable miniatures, delicately painted woodwork and gilded mouldings. A certain disarray disturbed this tableau of luxury, however. A chair had toppled over. A man's hat perched at a jaunty angle atop an antique statuette. Candles had burned down into wax stalagmites clinging to the candlesticks. The remains of a fine supper stood on an inlaid table and an assortment of clothes were strewn across the carpet.

Leaning forwards, Agnès pulled her knees up under the bedclothes, leaned her elbows on them and slid her fingers through her thick hair, running them from the front to the back of her skull. Then she slowly raised her head, letting the palms of her hands smooth her cheeks. She felt better but the fear was only postponed, not gone for good. The pack would return, always hungry and perhaps more ferocious than ever. There was nothing to do but accept it.

And live.

Agnès pulled herself together.

She rose without disturbing the man sleeping beside her, pulling a rumpled sheet with her and wrapping herself in it. Taller and considerably thinner and more muscular than her peers, who took care to remain plump in order to entice men, she was not, however, without charm. She had an elegance of gesture, a nobility of movement, and a severe and savage kind of beauty, provocative and almost haughty, which promised failure to any who attempted to conquer her. Thick with ample curls, her long black hair framed a slender but forceful face and underlined her paleness. Her full, dark lips seldom smiled. Nor did her emerald green eyes, in which burned a cold flame. Had they shown any sign of joy, she would have been, all in all, absolutely radiant.

Her left fist holding the cloth tight against her chest, Agnès trampled over the dress and the ruffled underskirts she had worn the day before. Her white stockings still sheathed her long legs. With her free hand she lifted and shook a number of wine bottles before finding one that wasn't empty. She poured the dregs into a glass and carried it to the window, letting the warm May breeze caress her. From the first floor she had a view over the courtyard of her manor and the surrounding countryside, reaching as far as the distant glimmer of the Oise river.

Agnès sipped her wine and waited for dawn to come.

By daybreak the sheet had slipped a little, revealing a mark on her shoulder blade – a mark which worried some of her lovers and prompted a few to comment that Agnès had something of a witch about her. Remaining at the window, she toyed distractedly with a signet ring she wore around her neck. The jewel, set in tarnished steel, was etched with a Greek cross with arms capped by fleur-de-lys, and crossed by a rapier. Agnès heard the man rise from the bed behind her. She released the ring and thought of covering her shoulder but didn't turn as he dressed and left the room without a word. She saw him appear in the courtyard and wake the coachman sleeping beneath the harnessed carriage. The whip cracked, the horses snorted, shaking their heads, and the vehicle of this already-forgotten gentleman was soon nothing more than a cloud of dust on the stony road.

Life soon began to stir in the manor, as the surrounding village bell-towers signalled the first mass of the day. Agnès de Vaudreuil finally left the window when she saw a valet taking orders from the ostler outside the stable. She performed a rapid toilette and hastily braided her long hair. She changed her stockings, did up her breeches, pulled on a wide-collared shirt and, over it, an old red leather corset. She chose her best riding boots, then belted on the baldric and sheathed rapier which hung by the door.

The blade had been made for her especially, forged in Toledo from the best steel. She unsheathed it to admire its perfect straightness, its beautiful shine, its suppleness and keen edge. She sketched a few feints, parries and ripostes. Finally, with her thumb, she made a spike as long as her hand spring from the pommel, fine and sharp-edged like a Florentine dagger, which she admired with an almost loving gleam in her eye.

3

On its completion, the Palais-Cardinal would comprise a splendid main building, with two long wings, two courtyards and an immense garden which stretched between rue de Richelieu and rue des Bons-Enfants. But in 1633, it was still little more than the original Hôtel d'Angennes, acquired nine years earlier, although its new, illustrious owner, determined to have a residence in Paris appropriate to his station, was busy having it enlarged and embellished. He was so determined, in fact, that when he was put in charge of the city's new fortifications he seized the opportunity to extend his domain into the vast area which the old ramparts had occupied, rebuilding the walls further to the west from the Saint-Denis gate to the new gate of La Conférence. The capital gained as much as the cardinal from this enlargement: new streets were laid out and new districts were born where only wasteland and ditches had existed before, including the creation of a renowned horse market and the beginnings of the neighbourhoods of Montmartre and Saint-Honoré. But Richelieu was condemned to live with the builders a while longer in the Hôtel d'Angennes. The imposing façade of his palace, on rue de Saint-Honoré, would still take years to complete.

Thus it was that, at eight o'clock in the morning, Ensign Arnaud de Laincourt entered the Palais-Cardinal by passing beneath a large scaffold which was already loaded with workmen. The musketeers who had just opened the wrought iron gates recognised him and gave him a military salute to which he responded before entering the guard room. This area, with its one hundred and eighty square metres of floor space and its monumental chimney, was where ordinary visitors waited to be summoned. There were already a score of them in attendance, but above all the room was crawling with men in red capes, as it was here that guards who had ensured the safety of His Eminence all night were relieved by those who, like Laincourt, had arrived to take their shift. Rows of muskets – loaded and ready to fire – were arranged on the racks. The light fell from high south-facing windows and conversations blended into a hubbub which echoed beneath the wainscoting.

Slender and athletic, Arnaud de Laincourt was approaching thirty. He had dark eyebrows, crystalline blue eyes, a straight nose, smoothly-shaven cheeks and pale skin. His fine features had a strange charm, youthful yet wise. It was easier to imagine him studying philosophy at the Sorbonne than wearing the uniform of the cardinal's horse guards. Nevertheless, he carried the plumed felt hat and the white gloves, and wore the cape blazoned with a cross, along with the sword hanging from the regulation leather baldric which crossed his chest from his left shoulder. Moreover, as an ensign he was an officer – a junior officer according to the military hierarchy then in force, but an officer nonetheless, and one who was promised a lieutenancy, so highly did Richelieu regard him.

He was saluted again and, as was his habit, he courteously returned the salute with a personal reserve which discouraged idle chatter. Then he took one of the small books known as sextodecimos from his russet-red leather doublet and, intending to read, went to lean against a pillar close to two guards sitting by a pedestal table. The youngest, Neuvelle, was only just twenty-six and had not been with the guards for more than a few weeks. His companion, on the other hand, was turning grey. He was called Brussand, was a good forty years of age, and had served with the Cardinal's Guards since the formation of the company seven years earlier.

'Still,' said Neuvelle in a lowered voice, 'I would love to know who the man His Eminence received in such secrecy last night was. And why.'

When Brussand, leaning on the card table, did not react, the young man insisted:

'Think about the fact that he did not pass through the

antechambers. The musketeers who guard the little gate were ordered to do nothing but announce his arrival, and not ask questions. All the other guards were kept away. And it was Captain Saint-Georges in person who escorted him to the cardinal's apartments and accompanied him back!'

'Our orders' Brussand finally replied, without raising his eyes from his game of patience, 'were to be deaf and blind to all that concerned this gentleman. You should not have watched the doors.'

Neuvelle shrugged.

'Pff . . . What harm did I do? . . . And anyway, I only caught a brief glimpse of a silhouette in the corner of a very dark corridor. He could have shook hands with me without my recognising him.'

Brussand, still absorbed by his game, smoothed his salt-and-pepper moustache without comment, then with an air of satisfaction laid the wyvern of spades, which had appeared at the opportune moment, upon the previously troublesome knave of hearts.

'All these mysteries intrigue me,' Neuvelle blurted.

'They shouldn't.'

'Really? And why is that?'

Although he gave no sign, Brussand, unlike his young companion, had noticed Laincourt's discreet arrival.

'Would you explain it to him, monsieur de Laincourt?'

'Certainly, monsieur de Brussand.'

Neuvelle watched Laincourt, who turned a page and said:

'Accept that there are secrets into which it is better not to pry, nor even to pretend to have stumbled across. It can prove to be harmful. To your career, of course. But also to your health.'

'You mean to say that—'

'Yes. I mean to say exactly that.'

Neuvelle mustered a weak smile.

'Go on! You're trying to frighten me.'

'Precisely. And for your own good, believe me.'

'But I'm a member of the Guards!'

This time, Laincourt lifted his eyes from his book.

And smiled.

Neuvelle wore his scarlet cape with a mixture of confidence and pride, convinced, not without reason, that he was protected to the same degree that he had been promoted. Because he entrusted his life to them, Richelieu chose all his guards personally. He wanted them to be gentlemen of at least twenty-five years in age, and required most of them to have served for three years in the army. Perfectly trained and equipped, subjected to an iron discipline, they were a company of elite horsemen. The cardinal preferred them by far to the company of musketeers – foot soldiers – that he also maintained and which recruited professional soldiers from the ranks of ordinary folk. And he rewarded his guards for their devotion by extending his protection to them in turn.

However . . .

'To be in the Guards, Neuvelle, is an honour which particularly exposes you to dangers that the common run of people do not even suspect – or which they exaggerate, which amounts to the same thing. We are like the fire-dogs before a hearth which holds an eternal flame. This blazing fire is the cardinal. We defend him, but if you draw too near, you risk being burned. Serve His Eminence faithfully. Die for him if circumstances require it. Nevertheless, only listen to what he wishes you to hear. See only that which you are given to see. Guess only at what you are supposed to understand. And be quick to forget the rest.'

His tirade complete, Laincourt peacefully returned to his reading.

He believed the matter was settled, but still Neuvelle persisted.

'But you—'

The ensign frowned.

'Yes?'

'I mean . . .'

Searching for words, Neuvelle's eyes implored for help from Brussand, who rewarded him with a black look in reply. The young guard suddenly understood that he had ventured into territory which was delicate, if not dangerous.

18

He would have given a great deal to have been suddenly transported elsewhere and was very relieved when Laincourt chose another target.

'Monsieur de Brussand, have you spoken to monsieur de Neuvelle about me?'

The interested party shrugged his shoulders, as though excusing himself.

'We're often bored, when we're on guard.'

'And what have you said?'

'On my word, I said what everyone says.'

'Which is?'

Brussand took a breath.

'Which is that you had intended to become a lawyer, before the cardinal noticed you. That you joined the ranks of his personal secretaries. That he soon entrusted you with confidential missions. That on one of these missions you left France for two years and, when you returned, you took the cape and the rank of ensign. There. That's everything.'

'Ah . . .' said Arnaud de Laincourt without betraying any emotion.

There was a silence in which he seemed to reflect on what he had heard.

Finally, with a vague glance, he nodded.

Laincourt returned to his reading while Neuvelle found other things to do elsewhere and Brussand began a new game of patience. A few minutes passed, and then the veteran guard blurted out:

'To you, and you alone, Laincourt, I would say—'

'What is it?'

'I know who His Eminence received last night. I saw his outline as he was leaving, and I recognised him. His name is La Fargue.'

'This name means nothing to me,' said Laincourt.

'At one time, he commanded a troop of highly trusted men and carried out secret missions on the cardinal's behalf. They were called, in a whisper, the Cardinal's Blades. Then there was some nasty business during the siege of La Rochelle. I don't know the details but it brought about the disappearance of the Blades. Until last night, I had believed they were permanently disbanded. But now—'

Arnaud de Laincourt closed his book.

'The same prudent advice I gave to Neuvelle also applies to us,' he said. 'Let us forget all of that. Without doubt we shall be better off for having done so.'

Brussand, thoughtful, nodded.

'Yes. You are right. As always.'

At that moment, Captain Saint-Georges summoned Laincourt. Cardinal Richelieu wished to go to the Louvre with his entourage, and his escort needed to be prepared. Saint-Georges was taking command and Laincourt, in his capacity as an officer, was to watch over the cardinal's palace during his absence.

4

Two coaches sat at some distance from each other in a meadow by the road to Paris. Three elegant gentlemen surrounded the marquis de Brévaux by the first coach while, by the second, the vicomte d'Orvand paced alone. He went backwards and forwards, sometimes stopping to watch the road and the horizon as he nervously stroked his thin, black moustache and the tuft of hair beneath his lower lip and sent impatient looks towards his coachman, who remained indifferent to the entire proceedings but was beginning to feel hungry.

At last, one of the gentlemen detached himself from the group and walked towards d'Orvand, passing through the soft, damp herb grass with a determined step. The vicomte knew what he was going to hear and struck as appropriate an attitude as possible.

'He's late,' said the gentleman.

'I know. I'm sorry, believe me.'

'Will he come?'

'I believe so.'

'Do you even know where he is, right now?'

'No.'

'No?! But you're his second!'

'Ah . . . well, that is to say . . .'

'A quarter of an hour, monsieur. The marquis de Brévaux is willing to be patient for a little longer — for another quarter of an hour, by the clock. And when your friend arrives, if he arrives, we—'

'Here he is, I believe . . .'

*

A richly decorated coach arrived. Drawn by a splendid team of horses, it stopped in the road with a spray of dust and a man climbed out. His doublet was entirely undone and his shirt hung half out of his breeches. His hat in his right hand and his left resting on the pommel of his sword, he kept one boot on the footplate in order to embrace a pretty young blonde leaning towards the open door. This spectacle did not surprise d'Orvand, who did, however, roll his eyes when he saw another farewell kiss exchanged with a second beauty, a brunette.

'Marciac,' murmured the vicomte to himself. 'You never change!'

The gentleman charged with conveying the marquis de Brévaux's complaint returned to his friends while the luxuriously gilded coach made a half-turn in the direction of Paris and Nicolas Marciac joined d'Orvand. He was a handsome man, attractive despite, or perhaps even because of, the disorder of his attire. He was in need of a razor and he bore a wide grin on his face. He tottered only slightly and was the very image of a society-loving rake enjoying his evening, entirely heedless of the morrow.

'But you've been drinking, Nicolas!' exclaimed d'Orvand, smelling his breath.

'No!' insisted Marciac, shocked . . . 'well . . . a little.'

'Before a duel? It's madness!'

'Don't alarm yourself. Have I ever lost before?'

'No, but—'

'All will be well.'

By the other coach, the marquis de Brévaux was already in his shirtsleeves and executing a few feints.

'Good, let us finish it,' Marciac declared.

He removed his doublet, threw it on the vicomte's coach, greeted the coachman and asked after his health, was delighted to learn it was excellent, caught d'Orvand's gaze, adjusted his shirt, unsheathed his sword and set out towards Brévaux, who was already walking to meet him.

Then, after a few steps, he changed his mind, turned on his

heel without fear of further exasperating the marquis, and pitched his words for his friend's ear alone:

'Tell me just one thing . . .'

'Yes?' sighed d'Orvand.

'Promise me you will not be angry.'

'So be it.'

'Well then, I have guessed that I am to fight the man in his shirtsleeves who is watching me with that rough gaze. But could you give me some idea as to why?'

'What?' the vicomte exclaimed, rather louder than he had intended.

'If I kill him, I should know the reason for our quarrel, don't you think?'

D'Orvand was initially lost for words, then pulled himself together and announced:

'A gambling debt.'

'What? I owe him money? Him too?'

'Of course not! Him! . . . It's he who . . . Fine. Enough. I shall cancel this madness. I shall tell them you are unwell. Or that you—'

'How much?'

'What?'

'How much does he owe me?'

'Fifteen hundred livres.'

'Good God! And I was going to kill him . . . !'

Light-heartedly, Marciac continued to walk towards the furious marquis. He assumed a wobbly *en garde* stance and declared:

'I am at your disposal, monsieur le marquis.'

The duel was speedily concluded. Brévaux took the initiative with assertive thrusts which Marciac nonchalantly parried before punctuating his own attack with a punch that cut his adversary's lip. Initially surprised, then enraged, the marquis returned to the fray. Once again, Marciac was content to merely defend, feigning inattentiveness and even, between two clashes of steel, stifling a yawn. This offhandedness left Brévaux crazed with anger. He howled, struck a foolish two-handed blow with his rapier and, without understanding how, suddenly found himself both disarmed and wounded in the shoulder. Marciac pressed his advantage. With the point of his blade, he forced the marquis to retreat to his coach, and held him there.

Pale, breathless and sweating, Brévaux clutched his shoulder.

'Very well,' he said. 'You win. I'll pay you.'

'I am afraid, monsieur, that a promise is not enough. Pay me now.'

'Monsieur! I give you my word!'

'You have already promised once, and you see where we are now . . .'

Marciac tensed his arm a little and the point of his rapier approached the marquis's throat. The gentlemen of Brévaux's retinue took a step closer. One of them even began to draw his sword while d'Orvand, worried, came forward and prepared to assist his friend if necessary.

There was a moment of indecisiveness on both sides, but then the marquis removed a ring he wore on his finger and gave it to Marciac.

'Are we now even?'

He took it and admired the stone.

'Yes,' he said, before sheathing his sword.

'Damned Gascon!'

'I hold you in high esteem as well, monsieur. I look forward to seeing you again.'

And as he turned towards d'Orvand, Marciac deliberately added:

'Splendid day, isn't it?'

5

In a small study to which she alone possessed a key, the very young, very blonde and very charming vicomtesse de Malicorne removed the black silk cloth protecting the oval mirror before which she sat. With only two candles burning, one to either side of the mirror, the room was shrouded in a half-light.

In a low voice, with her eyes closed, the vicomtesse chanted words in the ancient, dread language of the Ancestral Dragons, the language of magic. The surface of the precious silver mirror rippled, moving like a puddle of mercury disturbed by movement deep within it, then solidified again. A dragon's head appeared in the ensorcelled mirror – all blood red scales, gleaming black eyes, a bony crest and pale, large and prominent fangs.

'Greetings, my sister.'

'Greetings, my brother.'

Someone, thousands of leagues distant, had answered the vicomtesse's call. Wherever he was, he must have been human in outward form. But the mirror did not lie: the images it portrayed were an accurate reflection of the true nature of those who used it, so that the pretty young woman also presented a draconic appearance to her faraway contact. For although neither of them were Ancestral Dragons, they were both descendants. In their veins ran the blood of a race which had evolved over centuries and millennia, a race which had given up the superior draconic form to become part of mankind. But their race was no less feared for having changed, and with good reason.

'There is some concern about your progress, my sister.'

'Who is concerned?'

'I am, in the first instance. But there are others as well who, unlike me, are not favourably inclined towards you. Not everyone within the Black Claw is your ally.'

'I would have thought the Black Claw would be delighted by the prospect of my forthcoming success. A success which shall also, incidentally, be theirs.'

'Here, in Spain, there are brothers who are jealous of your foreseeable triumph. You will prevail where some of them have failed—'

'Should they not be reproached for that, rather than blaming me?'

The dragon in the mirror seemed to smile.

'Ah, my sister. You are not so naïve—'

'Certainly not!'

'You're aware that failure shall not be forgiven.'

'I shall not fail!'

'Under the pretext of assuring themselves of this, certain Masters of the Grand Lodge have decided to assign one of their initiates of the first order to assist you. A certain Savelda. You know of him?'

'Enough to guess that his mission is less to help me than it is to keep count of every conceivable error. So that if I do fail, my enemies are as well armed as possible to denounce me . . .'

'At least you know what awaits you. Savelda is already on his way and shall present himself to you soon. His duplicity with respect to you is certain, but the man is capable and he has the interests of the Black Claw at heart. Politics is likely to be of no importance to him. Employ him advisedly.'

'So be it.'

A ripple crossed the surface of the mirror and, as the vicomtesse struggled to focus her will, the phantom dragon head facing her began to waver.

'You are tired, my sister. If you wish to continue this later—'

'No, no. It will pass . . . Continue, please.'

In the dark close room, the young woman nimbly wiped away the black droplet that had beaded on her nostril.

'We have,' said the dragon, 'introduced a spy into the upper levels of the Palais-Cardinal.'

'I know. He—'

'No. It's someone other than the spy who keeps you informed. As yet, you do not know of the spy of whom I speak. Or, at least, not in this capacity. He is one of your future initiates.'

The vicomtesse was visibly surprised.

The Grand Lodge of Spain had an agent close to the cardinal, an exclusive agent, of whose existence she had only just learned. It was common practice for the Black Claw, and the Grand Lodge in particular, to proceed in this manner. The Spanish Lodge had been the very first to be founded and it traditionally predominated over the other lodges of Europe, welding together an empire of which it became all the more jealous as its authority began to be questioned. It was rightly criticised for being stifled by the crushing weight of tradition and guided by masters primarily concerned with preserving their privileges. Against its influence, in the very heart of the Black Claw, there was a growing plot involving dragons who secretly dreamed of renewing – if not cutting down – the old idols. The vicomtesse de Malicorne was one of these ambitious rebels.

'So?' she said.

'Our spy has informed us that the cardinal has a project afoot to recall one of our old enemies. Given the time it took this news to reach us in Spain, it is perhaps already done.'

'One of our old enemies?'

'La Fargue.'

'La Fargue and his Blades.'

'Without a doubt, yes. I don't know if their sudden return relates to your business, but guard yourself against these men, and especially against their captain.'

6

Jean Delormel's fencing school was situated on rue des Cordières, close to the Saint-Jacques gate. It could only be reached by entering a small courtyard which was unevenly but solidly paved, and was almost entirely concealed by the foliage of an apple tree which grew up from its centre. At the bottom to the left the beautiful main building met the stable, which was adjoined at a right angle to a small forge. The feet and gaze of visitors, however, were naturally drawn towards the house on the right, which could be recognised for what it was by the traditional sign which decorated the threshold – an arm holding a sword.

Sitting on a stone bench under the apple tree, a small six-year-old girl was playing with a doll – its body made of rags and with a painted wooden head – when Captain La Fargue arrived on horseback. Neatly dressed and with curly red hair, little Justine was the youngest child of Delormel, the fencing master, and one of seven offspring his wife had given him, three of whom survived. As an old friend of the family, La Fargue had witnessed Justine's birth just as he had witnessed the births of her elder siblings. But during his lengthy absence the infant had become a pretty child, full of seriousness, who listened more than she spoke, and thought even more. This metamorphosis had seemed sudden to the captain, the evening before, on his return after five years. Nothing showed the passage of time better than children.

Rising, Justine dusted down the front of her dress in order to offer a most formal curtsey to the rider, who had just got his feet on the ground and, to tell the truth, took little notice of her now as he walked towards the stables.

'Good morning, monsieur.'

Reins in hand, he stopped.

His cold glance, severe expression, grey beard and patrician neatness, the austere elegance of his attire and the proud assurance with which he carried his sword, all impressed adults and intimidated children. This little lady, however, did not appear to fear him.

Somewhat disconcerted, the old captain hesitated.

Then, very stiffly, he greeted her with a nod of his head and the pinch of his thumb and index finger to the rim of his hat, before walking on.

Busy in the kitchen, Justine's mother had observed the scene through an open window in the main building. She was a young woman, pretty and smiling, whose successive pregnancies had done surprisingly little to enlarge her slender waistline. Her name was Anne, and she was the daughter of a renowned fencing master who gave lessons on Ile de la Cité. La Fargue also greeted her as he approached, this time doffing his hat.

'Hello, madame.'

'Good morning, captain. A beautiful day, isn't it?'

'Indeed. Do you know where your husband is?'

'In the practice room. He's waiting for you, I believe . . . Will you dine with us?'

It was common to breakfast in the morning, dine at midday and eat supper in the evening.

'With pleasure, madame. I thank you.'

La Fargue tethered his mount to a ring in the stable when he heard:

'Monsieur, my papa is going to scold you.'

He turned and saw Justine, who loitered right at the threshold of the stable but did not enter, almost certainly because she was forbidden to approach the horses.

Intrigued, the old gentleman's brow wrinkled. It was difficult to imagine anyone 'scolding' a man of his temper. But, the little one was still at the age when a daughter would not for a moment doubt the invincibility of her father.

'He will scold me? Truly?'

'My father was very anxious. So was my mother. They waited for your return until very late last night.'

'And how do you know this?'

'I heard them talking.'

'Were you not in your room?'

'I was.'

'And weren't you asleep at that hour, as is appropriate for young ladies of your age, if they are well-behaved?'

Caught out, Justine paused for a moment.

'Yes,' she said.

La Fargue stifled a smile.

'Very well then, you were asleep in your room, yet you heard my friend your father speaking . . .'

The little one replied in a flash:

'I happen to have very good ears.'

And, full of dignity, she turned on her heel.

La Fargue left the stable a few moments later.

Beneath the apple tree, Justine was only interested in her doll, with whom she seemed to be arguing. The morning was over. The sunshine was warm and the thick foliage gave the courtyard a pleasant freshness. From here the bustle and racket of the Paris streets were just a distant murmur.

In the practice room, La Fargue found Martin – a young man, the eldest son and senior instructor in Delormel's school – dispensing a private lesson while a valet gave the earthenware floor a thorough scrubbing. The room was almost empty, with bare walls and furnished with nothing but three benches, a rack of swords and a wooden horse for teaching students mounted swordplay. There was a gallery which could be reached by a staircase on the right, from which one could comfortably observe the action below. The fencing master was at the balustrade. He adopted an air of great satisfaction on seeing the captain enter. La Fargue climbed the steps to meet him, exchanging a friendly smile with Martin on the way, the young red-haired slender man beating time for his pupil's movements by striking the ground with a large stick.

'Glad to see you, captain. We've been waiting for you.'

In spite of events, Delormel had never ceased to address La Fargue by his rank. Out of habit, no doubt. But also to make the point that he had never acknowledged that La Fargue had been stripped of his commission.

'For most of the night, yes, I know. The news reached me. I am sorry.'

Delormel was astonished.

'That news reached you? How?'

'Your daughter. The youngest.'

The fencing master smiled affectionately.

'The little devil. Nothing gets past her . . .'

Tall and broad across the shoulders, Delormel was a fencing master who had been a soldier and who regarded fencing as more of a practical experience than a science. A thick scar scored his neck; another traced a pale furrow down his face. But what one noticed first was his thick russet-red hair, which he had inherited from his father and passed on to all his children: a Delormel was a redhead, or they weren't a Delormel. Well-groomed, he wore a modestly cut and perfectly pressed doublet.

'However,' said La Fargue, 'you are more correct than you believe in addressing me as "captain".'

'I beg your pardon?'

'The cardinal has secretly returned my rank to me. He wants the Blades to return to service. Under my command.'

'All of them? That is: all of the Blades?'

The captain shrugged.

'All those who are left and would like to serve, at least. And for those who do not, I have no doubt that the cardinal shall find some persuasive leverage. Letters summoning them have already been sent out.'

Reading the concern on La Fargue's face, Delormel hesitated, and then asked:

'And this isn't good news?'

'I've yet to form an opinion on the subject.'

31

'Come, captain! The Blades are your life! And here you are! Soon those five years will be—'

But he did not complete the sentence.

Suddenly nervous, he looked to the left and right and then murmured:

'I beg you, do not tell me you said no to the cardinal! No one says no to the cardinal, do they? Nobody. Not even you, eh?'

La Fargue had no reply.

His eyes flicked toward Martin and his student below and he said:

'I thought you only opened your practice room after dinner.'

'It's only a private lesson,' specified Romand. 'That braggart you see there pays in gold.'

Calling him a braggart spoke volumes. The old gentleman, however, asked:

'And how is he doing?'

The fencing master made a disdainful face.

'He can't tell his right from his left, holds his sword like a shovel, believes he knows everything, understands nothing and constantly complains, claiming that everything is badly explained to him.'

'His name?'

'Guérante, I believe. If I was Martin, I would have slapped him ten times by now.'

'And you would have lost your client.'

'No doubt, yes . . .'

La Fargue did not take his eyes from Martin's student. He was a young man, very richly dressed and everything about him, especially his attitude, indicated that he was a wealthy scion with a head swollen by his family's title and fortune. He lacked patience as much as he lacked talent, became irritated over nothing, and found a thousand excuses for his awkwardness. He was out of place here, where serious, practical fencing was taught; fencing which demanded hard work without sparing the ego.

'I didn't say no,' the captain suddenly announced. 'To the cardinal, last night. I did not say no to him.'

Delormel's face split into a broad smile.

'Praise be! You are never truly yourself unless you're serving the king and, no matter what you think, you never served him so well as you did during the years when you commanded your Blades.'

'But to what end? One death, and the treachery of a friend—'

'You are a soldier. Death comes with war. As for treason, it comes with life.'

La Fargue nodded, but it lacked the vigour that would suggest he truly agreed.

Clearly anxious to change the subject, Delormel took the captain by the elbow and, limping a little because of an old wound, drew him away from the balustrade.

'I do not ask you what your mission is, but—'

'You can,' interrupted La Fargue. 'At the moment, all we have to do is arrange, with all speed and without attracting too much attention, the recall of the Blades. And perhaps find others . . . It seems clear that the cardinal has precise plans, which I shall soon learn. But why is he recalling the Blades? Why them, when he does not lack other devoted agents? Why me? And most importantly, why now, after all these years? There is a mystery behind all of this.'

'These are troubled times,' suggested Delormel. 'And contrary to what you said, perhaps His Eminence does lack men capable of doing the things you and your Blades have achieved in the past . . .'

Below them there was a sudden outburst which drew them, surprised, back to the balustrade.

Guérante had just fallen, entirely through his own fault, and, furious, he hurled insults at the younger Delormel. Pale, the other withstood the outburst without responding: he was only a commoner while his student was of the nobility, and therefore both protected and permitted to do as he pleased.

'Enough,' said La Fargue after a moment. 'That will do.'

He walked down the staircase with a determined step while the gentleman struggled back to his feet and continued to howl. La Fargue seized him by the collar, forced him out of the room ignoring his thrashings, dragged him across the courtyard in front of Justine, who watched with huge round eyes, and threw him out into the street. Guérante measured his length in a patch of mud through which one would hesitate to walk, to the great delight of passers-by.

Livid, stinking and dripping with muck and urine, the braggart pushed himself up and would have stripped off his soiled outer layers ready to fight. But La Fargue froze him in place with a movement of an index finger, pointing at Guérante's chest.

'Monsieur', he said to him, in too calm a voice not to be threatening. 'I am a gentleman and therefore do not have to put up with either your whims or your poor temper. If you would draw your sword, do so, and you shall learn with whom you speak.'

Guérante hesitated, changed his mind, and returned the two inches of steel he had drawn in the heat of the moment to their scabbard.

'Another thing, monsieur,' added the captain. 'If you are religious, pray. Pray that my friend Delormel does not come to any misadventure. Pray that no one bothers either his clients or his family. Pray that petty thieves do not come in the night and plunder his school or his home. Pray that he does not receive a beating on a street corner . . . Because I shall learn of it. And without any further consideration, I shall find you and I shall kill you, monsieur de Guérante. Do we understand each other?'

Mortified and covered in slurry, the other made an effort to recover his dignity. There were spectators watching and mocking him, and he did not want to lose face entirely.

'This business,' he promised, puffing himself up . . . 'This affair does not end here.'

'It does,' La Fargue shot back, harsh and inflexible.

'We shall see!'

'This business is finished here and now if you do not draw your sword, monsieur . . .'

His terrible gaze plunged Guérante into the deepest pit of fear.

'Well?' he demanded.

Delormel and his son waited for La Fargue in the courtyard. His wife, pale and worried, watched from the threshold of the main building, Justine pressed against her skirts.

'Let's eat,' said the captain, as he returned.

His rapier had never left its scabbard.

7

In the kitchen of the Vaudreuil manor, a woman in an apron and a large serge skirt scrubbed a series of copper saucepans.

Her name was Marion.

Sitting at the end of a large oak table worn smooth by old age and hard use, she turned her back to the hearth where small flames gently heated the blackened bottom of a pot. Drying herbs, a string of garlic and some earthenware pots decorated the chimneypiece. A door which stood open onto the courtyard allowed tiny dust particles to enter which, carried by a light breeze, sparkled in the spring air. Pieces of straw were scattered on the floor as far as the threshold.

A horse could be heard approaching at a fast trot. It frightened the hens, which squawked and fluttered their wings, and when it neighed a dog responded excitedly, barking from the end of its chain. Iron-shod boots struck the hard earth with a jingle of spurs. Steps approached and Agnès de Vaudreuil ducked her head as she came through the low door.

Seeing the young baronne arrive, Marion greeted her with a warm smile and a disapproving glance, a subtle combination which she had perfected through long practice over the years. Dressed for riding, her rapier thumping against her thigh, Agnès was covered in dust from her riding boots to the top of her breeches, and she was still wearing that infernal red leather corset which, rough and waxed and buckled on tight like armour, was as much a warrior's talisman to her as an item of clothing. Her face glistened with sweat. As for the heavy braid which fell from the nape of her neck, it only managed to confine half of her hair, allowing the rest to hang free.

'I have left Courage tethered outside,' the young woman said breathlessly.

Marion nodded to show that she was listening.

'I pushed him a little in the lower valley and I really believe he is perfectly recovered from his injury.'

The maidservant had no reply to that either.

'Damnation! I'm dying of thirst.'

Agnès went over to the brass water tank which, set up at an angle, released water through a small tap. She leaned over it, cupping the palms of her hands, and splashing water over the stone floor slabs as she drank. Then she grabbed a crusty heel of bread lying on the sideboard and, ripping it open with her fingers, proceeded to nibble at its soft interior.

'Have you eaten anything today?' asked Marion.

'No.'

'I'll make you something. What would you like?'

She was about to rise, but the young woman halted her with a gesture.

'Don't trouble yourself. I'm fine.'

'But—'

'I said I'm fine.'

The servant shrugged and returned to her work.

Standing up, leaning against door to the salting room and putting a foot up on a bench, Agnès looked at Marion. She was still attractive, with an ample bosom and small greying locks of hair twisting themselves free between the nape of her neck and her linen bonnet. At one time she had been much courted by men, and she continued to be on occasion. But she had never married, a fact that intrigued other local inhabitants of this area of the Oise valley.

A silence settled over the room, and lingered.

Finally, when she could restrain herself no longer, Marion said:

'I heard a coach leave early this morning.'

'Good. Then you're not deaf.'

'Who was it?'

Agnès threw the piece of bread, reduced to no more than an empty crust, onto the table.

'What does it matter? I remember only that he was well built and knew what he was doing between the sheets.'

'Agnès!' Marion exclaimed.

But there was more sadness than reproach in her voice. With an air of resignation, she gently shook her head and started to say:

'If your mother—'

'None of that!' interrupted Agnès de Vaudreuil.

Suddenly frosty, she became absolutely rigid. Her emerald green eyes gleamed with contained anger.

'My mother died giving birth to me and it's futile for you to tell me that she might say this or that. As for my father, he was a pig who shoved himself between every pair of thighs he could snuffle out. Including your own, as I well know. So do not preach to me about the way in which I occasionally fill my bed. It's only in such moments that I feel even remotely alive, ever since . . .'

Trembling, with tears in her eyes, she couldn't finish the sentence.

Marion was visibly shaken by this outburst, and returned ashen-faced to her scrubbing with more energy than was strictly necessary

Now in her forties, Marion had witnessed Agnès' birth and the accompanying agony of her mother, who had lain in labour for five days. After fighting at the side of the future King Henri IV during the Wars of Religion in France, the baron de Vaudreuil was always too busy serenading the beautiful ladies at the royal court or stag hunting with the French monarch to interest himself in the fate of his spouse. And upon learning that the child was female, he had not even bothered to attend his wife's funeral. Entrusted – or rather abandoned – to the care of Marion and a rough soldier by the name of Ballardieu, it was seven years before the little girl met her father. This occurred during a brief stay on his domain, when he had also dragged Marion into his bed. Although she might have offered herself freely to him, if she had had any say in the matter. But the baron was not one to brook refusal from a servant, and would have dismissed her without further ado if denied. Marion could not bear the thought of being separated from Agnès, who adored her and had almost no one else in the world to look after her. The baron had been highly amused to discover that his latest conquest, although by no means a young woman, was still a virgin. Delighted, after it was done he left her to go sleep elsewhere, saying that he deserved her gratitude.

Calmer now and beginning to feel ashamed of herself, Agnès walked around the table to stand behind the woman who had raised her, and bent to embrace her, resting her chin against Marion's head.

'Forgive me, Marion. I'm mean and stupid . . . Sometimes, I think I'm going mad . . . But it's not you who's making me so angry. You realise that, don't you?'

'Yes. But who is it, then?'

'I think . . . I'm angry at myself. All these memories I have, that I would just as soon forget. Things I've seen and done . . . And things which were done to me . . .'

She straightened up, sighed, and added:

'One day, perhaps, I shall tell you all.'

8

As they travelled back to Paris by coach, Nicolas Marciac and the vicomte d'Orvand enjoyed a light red wine designed to sharpen their appetites. A wicker basket filled with food and some good bottles of wine stood between them on the bench. They drank from small engraved silver goblets, half-filled so that the bumps and jolts of the road, which shook them violently and without warning, soaked neither their chins nor their laps.

'You hadn't been drinking,' said d'Orvand, referring to the duel.

Marciac gave him a wicked, amused glance.

'Just a mouthful for my breath. Do you take me for a complete idiot?'

'Then why this comedy?'

'To make sure Brévaux was overconfident and lowered his guard.'

'You would have defeated him without that.'

'Yes.'

'Moreover, you could have let me in on it—'

'But that would have been much less fun, wouldn't it? If you could have seen your face!'

The vicomte could not help but smile. His friendship with the Gascon had accustomed him to this kind of joke.

'And who were the two charming ladies whose coach you borrowed to make your entrance?'

'Now, vicomte! I would be the very lowest of gentlemen if I told you that.'

'In any event, they seemed to have a great deal of affection for you.'

'What can I say, my friend? I am well liked— Since you are so curious, then know that one of them is the very same beauty upon whom the marquis de Brévaux, it seems, has set his sights. I'm sure he recognised her . . .'

'You are reckless Nicolas. No doubt the marquis's anger grew and his skill as a fencer proportionately decreased when he saw you kiss the woman. But by doing so you gave him a reason to demand another duel. Not content to defeat him, you had to humiliate him. For you it's a game, I know. But for him . . .'

Marciac thought for a moment about the prospect – which had not crossed his mind until now – of a second duel against the marquis de Brévaux. Then he shrugged.

'Perhaps you're right . . . We shall see.'

And extending his empty goblet, he added:

'Before we start on the pork, it would be my pleasure to drink a little more of your wine.'

As d'Orvand poured for his friend, risking his clean, beautifully cut breeches in the process, Marciac held the prize he had won from the marquis up to the light. Admiring the ruby, he slid it onto his finger, where it came to rest against a signet ring. But it was the signet ring itself which caught the vicomte's eye – made of tarnished steel, it was etched with a rapier and a Greek cross capped with fleur-de-lys.

'There,' said Marciac admiring the shine of the stone, 'that should keep Madame Rabier satisfied.'

'You borrowed money from La Rabier?' exclaimed d'Orvand in a tone of reproach.

'What else could I do? I have debts and it is necessary that I honour them. I am not the marquis de Brévaux.'

'Still, La Rabier . . . Borrowing money from her is never a good idea. I would have been happy to advance you a few écus. You should have asked me.'

'Asked you? A friend? You're joking, vicomte!'

D'Orvand slowly shook his head in silent reproof.

'All the same, there is one thing that intrigues me, Nicolas . . .'

'And what would that be?'

'In the nearly four years during which you have honoured me with your friendship, I have often seen you impoverished – and even that word is a poor description for it. You have pawned and redeemed your every possession a hundred times over. There were times when you were forced to fast for days, and you would doubtless have let yourself die of hunger if I hadn't invited you to my table under one pretext or another. I even remember a day when you had to borrow a sword from me in order to fight a duel . . . But never, ever, have you agreed to be separated from that steel signet ring. Why is that?'

Marciac's gaze became vague, lost in the memories of the day when he first received the ring, until a sudden bump in the road jolted the two men perched on their stuffed leather bench.

'It's a fragment of my past,' replied the Gascon. 'You can never be rid of your past. Not even if you pawn it . . .'

D'Orvand, who found that melancholy did not suit his friend, asked after a moment:

'We will soon be in Paris. Where would you like to stop?'

'Rue de la Grenouillère.'

The vicomte paused a moment, then said:

'Did you not have enough of duelling for one day?'

Marciac replied with a smile, and muttered, almost to himself:

'Bah! . . . When I die, I want to be certain at least that I have truly lived.'

9

Paris at midday was packed with working, bustling and gossiping people, but in contrast, at the Palais-Cardinal, the guards on duty seemed to be sentries of some luxurious necropolis. Accompanied by his large entourage of advisors and his armed escort, Richelieu was at the Louvre, and in his absence, life at his residence carried on slowly, almost as though it was night. Men in capes were barely to be seen. More lowly servants moved along dark corridors without haste or noise, carrying out routine menial tasks. The crowd of supplicants had thinned out considerably when they heard that the master of the palace had left, and only a few persistent souls decided to wait for his return, making do with an improvised repast on the spot.

Alone in a small study, Ensign Arnaud de Laincourt made use of this lull in activity to carry out a task which came with his rank: filling out the log-book of the Cardinal's Guards. The rule was that the officer on duty must scrupulously record all the day's events, whether they were ordinary or unusual, from the hour when guards were relieved at their posts to possible lapses in discipline, and detailing every occurrence or incident which might affect His Eminence's security. Captain Saint-Georges consulted the log at the end of each shift, before communicating anything noteworthy to the cardinal.

'Enter,' said Laincourt, on hearing a knock at the door.

Brussand entered.

'Monsieur de Brussand. You're not on duty . . . Would you not be better off at home, resting after your long night on watch?'

'Of course, but . . . Would you grant me a minute?'

'Just allow me to finish this task.'

'Certainly.'

Brussand sat down in front of the desk at which the young officer was writing by candlelight. The room had only a high, bevelled window opening onto a light well into which the sun barely peeped. There were, without a doubt, dungeons in the Bastille or in the château de Vincennes that were better lit.

Laincourt finished his report, checked it, wiped his quill on a rag and then slipped it between the pages of the thick log-book before he closed it.

'There,' he said. 'I'm all yours.'

And turning his crystal blue eyes upon Broussard, he waited.

'I have come to assure myself,' said the other, 'that you do not hold anything against me.'

'Regarding what?'

'Regarding confidences about you that I repeated to young Neuvelle. Concerning your past. And the circumstances under which you joined the Cardinal's Guards.'

Laincourt gave an amiable smile.

'Did you say anything slanderous?'

'Certainly not!'

'Anything untrue?'

'No. At least, not unless I've been misled myself.'

'Then you have nothing to reproach yourself for. And therefore, neither do I.'

'Of course. But . . .'

There was a silence during which the officer's smile did not waver.

His courteous mask, ultimately, proved to be a perfect defence. Because it expressed nothing but polite interest it left others to carry the conversation, so that, without any effort on his part, they little by little became less self-assured. Rarely failing, this strategy was proving particularly effective against Brussand, who was growing more embarrassed by the moment.

But the old guard was a soldier, and rather than remain exposed in this manner, he instead charged forward:

'What can I say? There are certain mysteries surrounding you that encourage rumours—'

'Indeed?'

'Your famous mission, for example. The one which, it is whispered, detained you for two years in Spain. And for which, no doubt, you were promoted to the Cardinal's Guards with the rank of ensign . . . Well, you can imagine what is said about all that, can't you?'

Laincourt waited without making any reply, the same indecipherable smile on his lips.

Then, a clock sounding half past one, he rose, picked up his hat and tucked the heavy log-book under his arm.

'Forgive me, Brussand, but duty calls.'

The two men walked together to the door.

As he allowed the officer to go first, Brussand said to him in a conniving tone:

'Strange country, Spain, isn't it?'

Laincourt walked on, leaving Brussand behind him.

With the air of a man who knows exactly where he is going, Arnaud de Laincourt strode through a series of salons and antechambers, paying no heed to either the servants or the guards on duty who snapped to attention as he passed. Finally, he entered an empty service corridor and, at its intersection with another, paused a few seconds before turning right towards the cardinal's private apartments.

From that point, he moved as quickly and silently as possible, although taking care not to appear furtive: there was no question of making his way on tip-toe, or hugging the walls, or glancing anxiously around. If someone was to surprise him, it was best to behave in a manner unlikely to arouse suspicion. His rank and his cape, certainly, protected him. But then, suspicion was the rule in the Palais-Cardinal.

He soon pushed open a door which, seen from the room within, merged seamlessly with the decorated wooden panels. This was the study where monsieur Charpentier, Richelieu's secretary, normally worked. Functionally but elegantly furnished, it was filled to the point of overflowing with papers.

Daylight filtered in through the closed curtains, while a candle guttered weakly. It was not there to provide light, but its flame could be transferred to numerous other candles at hand, and thus, in an emergency, fully illuminate the study in the middle of the night if required. Just one of the many precautions taken by those in the service of His Eminence, who demanded readiness at all times of the day or night.

Laincourt set the log-book down.

He drew a key from the pocket of his doublet and opened a cupboard. He had to be quick, as every minute now counted. On a shelf, a box sat between two tidily bound manuscripts. This was the object of his search. Another key, a tiny one, opened its secrets to him. Inside were letters waiting to be initialled and sealed by the cardinal. The ensign thumbed through them impatiently, and took out one which he perused more closely.

'That's it,' he murmured.

Turning, he brought the letter closer to the candle and read it twice in order to memorise its every comma. But as he refolded the document, he heard a noise.

The squeak of a floorboard?

The ensign froze, heart thumping, with all his senses alert.

Long seconds passed . . .

Nothing happened. No one entered. And, almost as if it had never occurred, the sound was not repeated.

Pulling himself together, Laincourt replaced the letter in the box and the box in the cupboard, which he relocked with his key. He assured himself that he had disturbed nothing, and then departed silently, taking his log-book with him.

But Laincourt had barely gone when someone pushed open another door, left ajar and hidden behind a wall hanging.

Charpentier.

Returning in haste from the Louvre to fetch a document which Cardinal Richelieu had not thought he would need, he had seen everything.

10

Having saddled his horse, La Fargue was strapping on the holsters of his pistols when Delormel joined him in the stable, amidst the warm smell of animals, hay and dung.

'You'll come see us again soon?' asked the fencing master. 'Or, at least, not wait another five years?'

'I don't know.'

'You know you are always welcome in my home.'

La Fargue patted his mount's neck and turned round.

'Thank you,' he said.

'Here. You left this in your room.'

Delormel held out a small locket on a broken chain. The old gentleman took it. Worn, marked, scratched and tarnished, the piece of jewellery seemed worthless, lying there on his big gloved hand.

'I didn't know you still kept it after all this time,' added the fencing master.

La Fargue shrugged.

'You can't give up your past.'

'But yours continues to haunt you.'

Rather than answer, the captain made to check his saddle.

'Perhaps she didn't deserve you,' Delormel commented.

His back turned, La Fargue went rigid.

'Don't judge, Jean. You don't know the whole story.'

It wasn't necessary to say anything more. Both men knew they were speaking of the woman whose chipped portrait was to be found inside the locket.

'That's true. But I know you well enough to know that something is eating at you. You should be delighted by the prospect of reuniting the Blades and serving the Crown once again. So I'd guess that you only accepted the cardinal's proposal under duress. You yielded to him, Étienne. That's not like you. If you were one of those who yielded easily, you would already be carrying a marshal's baton—'

'My daughter may be in danger,' La Fargue said suddenly.

Slowly, he turned to face Delormel, who looked stunned.

'You wanted to know the whole truth, didn't you? There, now you know.'

'Your daughter . . . ? You mean to say . . .'

The fencing master made a hesitant gesture towards the locket which the captain still held in his fist. La Fargue nodded:

'Yes.'

'How old is she?'

'Twenty. Or thereabouts.'

'What do you know of the danger she's in?'

'Nothing. The cardinal simply implied there was a threat against her.'

'So he might have lied to you in order to secure your services!'

'No. I doubt he would have played this card with me without good reason. It is—'

'—despicable. And what will you say to your Blades? These men give you their blind trust. Some of them even look on you as a father!'

'I shall tell them the truth.'

'All of it?'

Before mounting his horse, the old captain admitted, at some cost:

'No.'

11

Fiddling distractedly with his steel signet ring before returning it to the third finger on his left hand, Saint-Lucq watched
the everyday drama on display in the crowded tavern.

Located on a miserable-looking courtyard in the Marais
neighbourhood, tucked away from the beautiful private mansions with their elegant façades being built in the nearby Place
Royale, *The Red Écu* was a cellar tavern whose poor-quality
candles gave off more soot than light, in an atmosphere
already poisoned by sweaty bodies, bad wine-soaked breath,
tobacco smoke and a potent whiff of the muck picked up by
shoes walking the streets of Paris. Here, everyone spoke
loudly and forced others to raise their voices in turn, creating
an infernal uproar. The wine being drunk had something to
do with this. Loud laughter burst out, as did the occasional
sharp quarrel. A hurdy-gurdy played songs on demand. From
time to time, cheers and applause greeted a lucky throw of the
dice, or the antics of a drunkard.

Saint-Lucq, without appearing to do so, kept a close eye on
all.

He observed who entered and who left through the small
door at the top of the stairs, who used that other door normally reserved to the tavern keeper and the serving girls, who
joined someone else and who remained alone. He stared at no
one, and his gaze slid away whenever it met that of another.
But those present barely took any notice of him. And that was
exactly as he liked it, in the shadowy corner where he had
chosen to sit. He was constantly on the lookout, keeping
track of any anomalies that might indicate a threat. It could
be anything: a wink between two people who otherwise

pretended not to know one another, an old coat concealing new weapons, a faked fight designed to distract attention. Saint-Lucq was always wary and watched for such things automatically, out of sheer force of habit. He knew that the world was a stage filled with deception, where death, disguised in everyday rags, could strike at any moment. He knew this all the more, for it was often he who delivered the mortal blow.

Upon his arrival, he had ordered a jug of wine, none of which he drank. The young woman who served him offered to keep him company, but he declined the offer with a calm, cold, definitive 'No'. She went off to talk with the other two serving girls, who had watched her approach the new customer. From their reaction, it was obvious that they found Saint-Lucq both attractive and intriguing. He was still young, well-dressed, and a handsome man in a dark way which hinted at sinister and exciting secrets. Was he a gentleman? Perhaps. In any case, he wore his sword naturally, his doublet with elegance, and his hat with a quiet, gallant confidence. His hands were exquisite and his cheeks freshly shaven. Of course, his boots were muddied, but despite that they were made from excellent leather, and who could go unsullied by the disgusting muck of Paris, unless they travelled by coach? No, clearly, this cavalier dressed in black had plenty of pleasing assets. And then he had those curious spectacles with red lenses perched on his nose, which concealed his eyes and rendered him still more mysterious.

Since Saint-Lucq had turned away a slim brunette, a busty blonde tried her luck. And met with the same lack of success. The serving girl returned to her friends, irritated and disappointed, but she shrugged and said to them:

'He just left a brothel. Or he has eyes only for his mistress.'

'I think he prefers men,' added the brunette, with a pout which betrayed her hurt feelings.

'Perhaps . . .' the third trailed off. 'But if he does not touch his glass and he is not seeking company, what does bring him here?'

The other two agreed, in any case, that there was little point in persisting with their advances, and Saint-Lucq – who was watching their debate out of the corner of his eye – was led to hope that they would now leave him in peace.

He returned to his surveillance.

A little after midday, the man Saint-Lucq had been expecting to appear entered the tavern.

He was tall and badly shaven, with long greasy hair, a sword at his side and a surly air about him. He was called Tranchelard and, as was his habit, he was accompanied by two scoundrels, no doubt hired for their brawn rather than their brains. They picked a table – which emptied as they approached – and did not have to order the wine jugs the tavern keeper brought to them with an apprehensive look.

The third serving girl, whose eyes had remained fixed on Saint-Lucq, chose this moment to act.

She was red-haired and pale-skinned, very pretty, no more than seventeen and knew – from experience – the effect that her green eyes, rose-coloured lips and young curves had on men. She wore a heavy skirt and, beneath her bustier, her open-necked blouse left her shoulders bare.

'You do not drink,' she said, suddenly standing in front of Saint-Lucq.

He paused before replying:

'No.'

'No doubt because you don't care for the wine you have been served.'

This time he said nothing.

'I could bring you our best.'

Silence again.

'And at the same price.'

'No thank you.'

But the girl wasn't listening. Adolescent pride dictated that, after the unsuccessful attempts of her two colleagues, she could not fail.

'In return, I shall ask you only to tell me your name,' she insisted with a smile full of promise. 'And I shall give you mine.'

Saint-Lucq held back a sigh.

Then, expressionless, he slid his red spectacles down his nose with an index finger and gazed back at the young girl . . .

. . . who froze when she saw the reptilian eyes.

No one was unaware of dragons, of the fact that they had always existed, that they had adopted human form, and that they had been living among men for centuries. To the misfortune of all of Europe, a great number of them were now to be found within the royal court of Spain. And their distant racial cousins, the wyverns, served men as winged mounts, while the tiny dragonnets made valued pets and companions. Despite that, a half-blood always made a powerful impression. They were all born of the rare love between a dragon and a human woman, provoking a malaise which became hatred in certain people, horror in others, and in the case of a few men and women, an erotic fascination. Half-bloods were said to be cold, cruel, indifferent and scornful of ordinary human beings.

'I— I'm sorry, monsieur . . .' the serving girl stammered. 'Forgive me . . .'

She turned on her heel, her lower lip trembling.

Saint-Lucq pushed his spectacles back to the top of his nose and interested himself anew in Tranchelard and his bodyguards. As they had only come to drink a glass of wine and extort their protection fee from the tavern keeper, they soon left. The half-blood drained his glass, rose, left a coin on the table and followed them out.

Tranchelard and his men moved steadily through the packed streets where their ill manner alone was enough to open a path for them. They chattered and laughed, unaware of any danger. The crowd protected them, although it also provided cover for Saint-Lucq as he tailed them discreetly. As luck would have it, they soon turned off into a winding alley, as rank as a sewer, which offered a shortcut to the old rue Pavée.

It was too good an opportunity to miss.

Suddenly pressing forward, Saint-Lucq caught up with them in a few strides and took them totally off-guard. They barely had time to hear the scrape of the steel leaving its scabbard. The first man fell at once, knocked out by a blow from Saint-Lucq's elbow which also broke his nose, Tranchelard was held immobile by the caress of a dagger blade at his throat, and the third man had barely moved his hand towards his sword when a rapier point, an inch from his right eye, froze him in mid-gesture.

'Think twice,' the half-blood advised in a quiet voice.

The man did not delay in taking to his heels, and Saint-Lucq found himself alone, face-to-face with Tranchelard. Continuing to threaten him with the dagger, Saint-Lucq pressed him back up against a grubby wall. They were so close that their breaths blended together; the street thug stank of fear.

'Look at me carefully, my friend. Do you recognise me?'

Tranchelard swallowed and nodded slightly to the man with red spectacles, sweat beading at his temples.

'Perfect,' Saint-Lucq continued. 'Now, open your ears and listen . . .'

12

As his feet touched ground in the courtyard of a beautiful mansion recently built in the Marais quarter, near the elegant and aristocratic Place Royale, the gentleman entrusted his horse to a servant who had rushed up at once.

'I'm not staying,' he said. 'Wait here.'

The other nodded and, reins in hand, watched out of the corner of his eye as the marquis de Gagnière climbed the front steps with a quick and supple step.

Sporting a large felt hat with a huge plumed feather, he was dressed in the latest fashion, with such obvious care for his appearance that it bordered on preciousness: he wore a cloak thrown over his left shoulder and held in place beneath his right arm with a silk cord, a high-waisted doublet of grey linen with silver fastenings, matching hose decorated with buttons, cream lace at his collar and cuffs, beige suede gloves and cavalier boots made of kid leather. The extreme stylishness of his manner and attire added to the androgynous character of his silhouette: slender, willowy, and almost juvenile. He was not yet twenty years old but seemed even younger, his face still bearing a childish charm and softness which would take a long time to mature, while the blond hair of his moustache and finely trimmed royale beard preserved a silky adolescent downiness.

An ancient maître d'hôtel greeted him at the top of the steps and, eyes lowered, accompanied him as far as a pretty antechamber where the marquis was asked to wait while he was announced to the vicomtesse. When the servant finally returned he held a door open and, with a bow, ushered the marquis through. Remaining by the door, he again avoided

meeting the young man's gaze as though something dangerous and troubling emanated from him, his elegance and
angelic beauty nothing but a façade disguising a poisonous
soul. In that respect, the young marquis resembled the sword
which hung from his baldric: a weapon whose guard and
pommel had been worked in the most exquisite manner, but
whose blade was of good sharp steel.

Gagnière entered and found himself alone when the maître
d'hôtel closed the door behind him.

The luxuriously furnished room was plunged into shadow.
Drawn curtains shut out the daylight and the few scented
candles that burned here and there created a permanent
twilight. The room was a study for reading. Shelves full of
books covered one wall. A comfortable armchair was installed
next to a window, by a small side table which bore a
candelabrum, a carafe of wine and a small crystal glass. A
large mirror in a gilded frame hung above the mantelpiece,
looming over a table and an old leather-backed chair with a
patina of age.

Upon the table in the middle of room, supported by a
delicate red and gold stand, reposed a strange globe.

The gentleman approached it.

Black, gleaming and hypnotic, it was as though the globe
was filled with swirling ink. It seemed to absorb the light
rather than reflect it. One's eye soon became lost in its deep
spirals.

And with it, one's soul.

'Don't touch it.'

Gagnière blinked and realised he was leaning over the
table, his right hand stretched out towards the globe. He
pulled himself back and turned, feeling perturbed.

A young woman dressed in black and purple had made her
appearance through a concealed door. Elegant yet severe in a
gown with a starched bodice, her low neckline was trimmed
with lace and decorated with a grey mother-of-pearl brooch
representing a unicorn. She was beautiful; blonde and slender,
with a small sweet face that seemed to have been designed to
be adorable. Her sparkling blue eyes, however, showed no

sign of any warm emotions, any more than her pretty, but unsmiling, lips.

The vicomtesse de Malicorne took a slow but assured step towards the gentleman.

'I . . . I'm sorry,' he said, '. . . I have no idea what—'

'There is no need to reproach yourself, monsieur de Gagnière. No one can resist it. Not even me.'

'Is it . . . Is it what I think it is?'

'A *Sphère d'Âme*? Yes.'

She spread a square of brocaded golden cloth over the ensorcelled globe, and it was as though an unhealthy presence had suddenly deserted the room.

'There. Isn't that better?'

Straightening up, she was about to continue when the marquis's worried expression stopped her.

'What is it?'

Embarrassed, Gagnière pointed a hesitant finger towards her, and then indicated his own nose:

'You have . . . there . . .'

The young woman understood, touched her upper lip with her ring finger and found its tip fouled by a blackish fluid that had leaked from her nostril. Untroubled, she took an already-stained handkerchief from her sleeve and turned away to press it to her nose.

'Magic is an art which the Ancestral Dragons created for themselves alone,' she said, as though that explained everything.

She faced the large mirror above the mantelpiece and, still dabbing at her lip, spoke in a conversational tone:

'I recently charged you with intercepting a covert courier between Brussels and Paris. Have you done as I required?'

'Certainly. Malencontre and his men have undertaken the task.'

'With what result?'

'As yet, I don't know.'

Her pretty face now clean of all foulness, the vicomtesse de Malicorne turned from the mirror and, with a half-smile, said:

'Allow me to enlighten you then, monsieur. Despite all the

opportunities he has had to lay an ambush, Malencontre has already failed twice. First at the border, and then close to Amiens. If the rider he pursues continues at the same pace, Malencontre's only hope of catching him is at the staging post near Clermont. After Clermont, he will proceed straight on to Paris. Is it truly necessary to remind you that this letter must under no circumstances reach the Louvre?'

The gentleman didn't ask how she knew so much: the globe, with all the secrets it deigned to reveal to any who sacrificed part of themselves to it, was sufficient explanation. He nodded in reply:

'I remain confident, madame. Malencontre and his men are quite used to these missions. They shall succeed, no matter what the cost to themselves.'

'Let us hope so, monsieur le marquis. Let us hope so . . .'

With a gracious, urbane gesture the vicomtesse invited Gagnière to take a seat and took one herself, opposite him.

'Right now, I would like to speak with you on an entirely different matter.'

'Which is, madame?'

'The cardinal is about to play a card of great importance, and I fear that he means to play it against us. This card is a man: La Fargue.'

' "La Fargue"?'

'An old captain and one of the king's most faithful swords-men. Believe me, his return does not bode well for us. Alone, this La Fargue makes a formidable opponent. But in the past he commanded the Cardinal's Blades, a secret company of devoted and reliable men, capable, with La Fargue, of achieving the impossible. If they have been reunited . . .'

Pensive and worried, the young woman fell silent.

'Do you know the cardinal's intentions?' Gagnière asked cautiously.

'No. I merely guess at them . . . Which is why I want you to make inquiries into this matter. Speak with our agent in the Palais-Cardinal and learn everything you can from him. Can you meet him soon?'

'Yes.'

'Perfect.'

Having received his orders, and believing the interview to be over, the gentleman rose.

But the vicomtesse, looking elsewhere, continued:

'All this comes at the worst possible moment. We are about to achieve everything the Black Claw has been so desperate to accomplish for so long: to firmly establish itself in France. Our Spanish brothers and sisters have long since concluded that this goal is impossible, and although we are but a few hours from proving them wrong, I know that the majority are still doubtful. As for those who no longer doubt us, they already envy our forthcoming success – which amounts to saying that they too secretly hope for our failure.'

'You think that—'

'No, no . . .' said the vicomtesse, her hand brushing away the theory the marquis was about to propose. 'Those who are envious will not try to harm us . . . But they will not forgive the slightest shortcoming on our part and will seize any pretext to speak ill of us, of our plans and of our competence. They will be only too happy to claim they would have succeeded where we might still fail . . . These envious persons, moreover, have already begun to set their pawns in motion. I have been informed of the imminent arrival of a man sent to us by the Spanish lodge.'

'Who?'

'Savelda.'

From the corner of her eye, the vicomtesse de Malicorne detected Gagnière's dubious grimace.

'Yes, marquis, I share the sentiment. I've been told that Savelda comes to help us put the finishing touches to our project, but I know that his true mission is to observe us and take note of our mistakes, in case someone wishes to reproach us—'

'We should keep him in the dark, then.'

'Absolutely not. But we shall be beyond any reproach . . . Now you understand why it essential that we foresee and fend off every blow the cardinal might like to strike against us, don't you?'

'Indeed.'

'Then start by catching that courier from Brussels. Then we shall take on the Cardinal's Blades.'

13

Located at the entrance to a hamlet, which had no doubt risen up in its shadow, the inn was a typical example of the staging posts to be found across the country. In addition to the main building capped with red tiles it comprised a stable, a barn, a forge, a hen house, a loading area for coaches and a small pig pen, all of which was enclosed by a high wall whose grey and white stones were warmed by the afternoon sun. A river flowed past nearby, turning the wheel of a small mill. Beyond, the meadows and fields where cattle grazed stretched away to the east until they met the edge of a verdant forest. The weather was splendid, and the light from the great clear sky shone so brightly that one was obliged to squint.

A dog barked as a rider arrived.

Hens were pecking away in the courtyard, where the wheel of a stagecoach was being changed. Once it was repaired the coach would be harnessed with fresh horses and reach Clermont by evening. The coachman was lending the blacksmith and his assistants a hand while the passengers watched or took advantage of this opportunity to stretch their legs. Coaches generally offered a reliable and rapid service, barring accidents and taking into account the state of the roads – for the most part dust tracks in summer and turning boggy after the first autumn rains. Passengers had to put up with the unpleasantness of travelling in a jouncing and noisy vehicle, open to the wind, squeezed together in fours on opposing wooden benches, shoulder to shoulder and knees pressed together.

As soon as he dismounted, Antoine Leprat d'Orgueil held out the reins to a stable boy, no more than twelve years old, who was dressed in rough serge and ran around barefoot.

'Groom him and feed him with good oats. But don't let him drink too much. I leave again in an hour.'

The rider spoke like a man accustomed to being obeyed. The child nodded and headed towards the stables leading the horse behind him.

Indifferent to the sidelong glances sent in his direction, Leprat spied a water trough into which, his hat in hand, he plunged his head. Then he rubbed his face and the back of his neck with fresh water, rinsed his mouth, spat, smoothed back his chestnut hair, and finally replaced his black hat with its grey plume and rim raised on the right-hand side. His dust-covered doublet, worn open over his shirt, had seen better days but it was made of fine cloth. His riding boots, dirtied and softened by use, also seemed to be well made. As for the rapier, ensconced in its scabbard which hung from his leather baldric, it was of a kind that no one, here or anywhere else, could boast of ever having seen the like. He carried it on the right, being left-handed.

Leprat slowly climbed the steps to the main building, fronted by a gallery with ivy clinging to its beams. Having pushed the door to the building open he stood on the threshold for a moment, silence falling within the room as he looked over the ordinary travellers seated at several tables, and they observed him in return. Tall, well-built, with stubbled cheeks and a stern gaze, he exuded a masculine charm which was reinforced by the warlike garb of a weary courier. A first glance suggested that here was a man who smiled little, spoke less, and did not seek to please others. He was between thirty-five and forty years old. His face had the lined features that indicate the iron will of a man of honour and duty who can no longer be moved or upset by anything, because he has already witnessed all the evils of this world. He did, however, spare a brief but tender look for a little girl who was sitting on her mother's knee, dipping her chubby fingers into a bowl and smearing herself with jam.

Leprat let the door close behind him. Conversations picked up again as he came inside, his iron-tipped boots thudding against the rough floor with a rattle of spurs. As he passed, a few noticed the sword he carried at his side. Only the pommel and guard could be seen above the scabbard, but they seemed to be carved from a solid block of a material which shone like polished ivory.

A white rapier.

That was enough to be intriguing, even if no one knew exactly what it implied. Elbows were nudged discreetly, and uncertain expressions were exchanged with looks of puzzlement.

Having chosen a small empty table, Leprat sat with his back to a window through which, with a mere glance over his shoulder, he could cast an eye over the courtyard. The landlord, with greasy hair and a stained apron wrapped around the curve of his enormous belly, hastened towards him.

'Welcome, monsieur. How can I be of service?'

'Wine,' said Leprat, placing his hat and sheathed rapier on the table.

Then, eyeing the bird roasting on a spit over the hearth, he added:

'And the chicken, there. And bread.'

'Immediately, monsieur. Hard travelling in this heat, isn't it? You'd think it was already summer!'

'Yes.'

Understanding that the conversation would go no further, the landlord passed his order to a serving girl.

Quickly served, Leprat dined without lifting his eyes from his plate. He had not unsaddled his horse since the previous evening and found himself more famished than tired. In fact, he did not even feel the aches and pains plaguing his back until he was finally sated. He had been riding hard on the road between Brussels, which he had left in the middle of the night almost three days previously, and Paris, where he hoped to arrive that very evening.

The dog that had welcomed him barked again.

Turning his head towards the window, Leprat saw the riders arrive in the courtyard. He'd thought he'd succeeded in leaving them behind in Amiens, after the first ambush which he had eluded on the border between France and the Spanish Netherlands.

Evidently, he had been mistaken.

He summoned the serving girl with a calm gesture. An overly plump brunette of about twenty, she resembled the innkeeper so strongly she had to be his daughter.

'Monsieur?'

'Could I ask that you close the window curtains, please?'

The young girl hesitated as the window in question was the only source of light in the room.

'If you please,' Leprat insisted.

'Certainly, monsieur.'

She closed the curtains, blocking all view of the new arrivals who were dismounting outside. Inside the inn, there was some surprise at being suddenly pitched into shadow. But seeing who had made this request to the serving girl, all those present held their tongues.

'There, monsieur.'

'Now, do you see the woman with the white bonnet? The one with the little girl on her knee?'

'Yes.'

'Take them both out of here, without delay. Whisper in the mother's ear that they are in danger, and tell her she must leave for her own safety and that of the child.'

'Excuse me? But, monsieur—'

'Do it.'

The young woman obeyed, looking worried. Leprat watched while she spoke quietly with the woman in the white bonnet. The woman frowned, and although she displayed some signs of concern, she seemed disinclined to move . . .

. . . at least, not until the door opened.

On seeing who it was, she hurried ahead of the serving girl into the kitchen, her little girl in her arms.

Relieved, Leprat edged his chair back without rising.

The freebooters entered with a swagger, as thugs everywhere enter a room when they are certain they are danger personified. Armed with rapiers and wearing thick leather doublets, they were grubby, sweaty, and stank of the stable. A tall thin man with long flaxen hair was in the lead – he wore a leather hat and had a scar across the corner of his lips which drew them into a strange, smiling rictus. The other three, each with a sinister bearing, escorted him closely and had the almost ordinary faces of conscienceless mercenaries who would cut a throat for a mouthful of bread. And then the last of the riders entered, and with his appearance alone managed to congeal the already apprehensive silence. He was a drac: a member of a race spawned by the dragons in order to serve them, known for its cruelty and violence. A grey drac, as it happened. Fine slate-coloured scales covered his jowled face, and his clawed hands had four fingers. He, too, was dressed as a hired killer.

Dumbstruck, the patrons in the inn made a show of paying no attention to the freebooters, as if this ploy could somehow dispel their menacing presence. The innkeeper hesitated over whether or not to go up to them, hoping against all odds that they would desire neither food nor drink. In the end, his courage deserted him entirely and he decided to remain close by the door leading to the kitchen.

The mercenaries slowly swept the room with inquisitorial gazes as their eyes adjusted to the half-light. When they saw Leprat, sitting with his back to the window and its closed curtains, they knew that they had found their man.

They approached him without crowding one another and took up position before his table. The drac remained by the door, and when customers tried to rise discreetly in order to leave, he was content to simply turn his head towards them. His vertical, membranous eyelids closed briefly over his expressionless reptilian eyes. Everyone resumed their seat.

The flaxen-haired man settled himself at Leprat's table, sitting opposite him, without provoking any reaction.

'May I?' he asked, pointing a finger at the chicken Leprat had been eating

Without waiting for permission, he tore a wing from the plump carcass, bit into it and gave a sigh of satisfaction.

'This is truly an honour,' he said conversationally. 'Now I can say I have shared a meal with the famous Antoine Leprat, chevalier d'Orgueil . . . Because that's who you are, are you not? No, no, don't answer. Seeing that is proof enough.'

With his chin he indicated the white rapier lying, in its scabbard, on the table.

'Is it true that it was carved in one piece from the fang of an ancient dragon?'

'From the point to the pommel.'

'How many others like that do you think there are in the world?'

'I don't know. Perhaps none.'

The mercenary chief put on an admiring expression that might have been quite sincere. Half turning, he called out:

'Innkeeper! Wine for the chevalier and I. Be sure it's your best!'

'Yes, monsieur. At . . . at once.'

The two men locked eyes until the innkeeper came to serve them with a trembling hand, then scurried away leaving the wine jug. Leprat remained impassive as the other lifted his glass; upon seeing that his gesture was not imitated, the mercenary shrugged and drank alone.

'And me. Do you know who I am?'

The chevalier eyed him with contempt and did not reply.

'I am called Malencontre.'

Leprat smiled faintly.

Malencontre.

In other words: mishap. Or ill met.

Yes, that name did indeed fit this character.

14

'Do I know enough?'

'You will always know enough, if your adversary knows less than you.'

'But would you say I've progressed?'

Having counted up his meagre salary, Almades tightened the strings of his purse and raised his eyes towards the very young man who, still sweaty and out of breath from his latest fencing lesson, was watching him anxiously. He knew that look. He had seen it often in the past year, and he was astonished that he was still moved by it.

'Yes, monsieur. You have indeed made progress.'

It was no lie, considering that a week earlier the man had never held a sword in his life. He was a law student, who had come one morning to this inn, located in the outlying district – known as a *faubourg* – of Saint-Antoine, seeking the courtyard where Almades received his clients. He had a duel to fight, and wanted to learn how to cross blades. Time was short. But wasn't it said that this backyard, where the Spaniard taught, was a better school than the finest fencing halls in Paris? Paid for in coin, no doubt a few lessons, properly learnt and applied, would suffice. After all, he only needed an unstoppable flurry of two or three clever thrusts to kill his man, didn't he?

Almades frequently asked himself, when faced with students like this, if these young men truly believed in the existence of such 'deadly thrusts' which, once their secrets were mastered, were capable of guaranteeing success without any need for fencing talent. And even if there were such a thing, did they imagine this mysterious knowledge could be had for a mere fistful of pistoles? But it was highly likely that this student, terrified by the prospect of risking his life, sword in hand, would want to believe it to be true. Like all the others, he would be led by honour, pride, or stupidity to the meadow tomorrow. He was afraid and, now that he was committed to this duel, hoped for salvation from a miracle worker.

Almades had carefully explained that in the time available to them he could not do more than impart the basic rudiments of fencing, that the greatest swashbuckler ever born was never certain to carry the day, and that it was always better to renounce a bad duel than one's life. But faced with the student's insistence he had accepted taking him on as a pupil, for a week, on condition that he paid the greater part of the agreed fee in advance. Experience had taught Almades that novices, put off by the difficulty of actually learning to fence, were quick to abandon their lessons, and with them, payment of any tuition.

This one, however, had not yet given up.

'I beg you, monsieur, tell me if I am ready,' the young man pleaded. 'I must fight tomorrow!'

The fencing master stared at him for a long while.

'Above all else,' he finally said, 'what truly matters is whether you are ready to die.'

His full name was Anibal Antonio Almades di Carlo. He was tall and thin, clearly of a naturally slender build, but had grown gaunt due to long periods of hunger. He had dark eyes and hair with a pale complexion and a grizzled but still tidy moustache. His doublet, his shirt and his shoes were clean, although discreetly patched in places, and the lace at his collar and cuffs had seen hard use. His hat was missing its plume and the leather of his fold-over boots was unpolished. But even if he had nothing but rags to wear, Almades would have worn them well. Old Andalusian blood ran in his veins, nourishing his entire being with a haughty austerity which shone forth from him.

Brutally confronted by the prospect of his own death, the student blanched.

'Your duel,' asked the fencing master to lessen the blow, 'Is it to first blood?'

'Yes.'

'Well, that's for the best. Rather than employing this science to kill your adversary, use it to ensure you're only slightly wounded. Stay on the defensive. Take breaks to conserve your strength and catch your breath. Wait for a mistake; it's always possible that your adversary will make a clumsy move. But don't be in too much of a hurry to finish him off, as you risk exposing yourself. And hold your left hand high enough to protect your face if necessary: it's better to lose a finger than an eye.'

The young man nodded.

'Yes,' he said . . . 'Yes, I will do exactly as you say.'

'Goodbye, monsieur.'

'Goodbye, master.'

They parted with a handshake.

Leaving the gloom of the inn, Almades went out into the open courtyard at the rear, a simple square of beaten earth where he supervised the exercises of his rare students. Hens squawked nearby; a horse neighed; a cow could even be heard lowing in the distance. The faubourg Saint-Antoine was a recent addition to the city, still very rural in character, made up of new dwellings and manors whose façades along both sides of the dusty roads converging on Paris hid the surrounding farms, fields and pasture land from travellers' sight. The faubourg began in the shadow of the Bastille, just beyond the Saint-Antoine gate and the city's defensive moat, and the buildings progressively thinned out as one moved away from the capital and its stink.

At a table which had been left outside, exposed to the elements, Almades took out the rapier he kept for his clients' use. Along with the sword which hung at his side, this comprised his sole teaching aid, and his entire fortune. It was an iron rapier of poor quality, doubtless too heavy, and in danger from rust. Sitting on a wooden stump, he began to patiently clean the notched blade with an oiled rag.

Footsteps could be heard in the courtyard. A group of men approached him, stopping a few metres away, remaining silent and waiting to be noticed.

Almades examined them from beneath the brim of his hat.

There were four of them. A provost and three apprentices. The first was armed with a sword, while his seconds carried iron bars. And they had all been sent by a fencing master who maintained a school close to the Bastille, and who simply could not bear the thought of anyone benefiting from fencing lessons illegally dispensed by the Spaniard.

His iron rapier across his knees, Almades raised his head, squinting in the sunlight. He observed the four men with an inscrutable expression, and as he did so, idly fiddled with the steel signet ring he wore on his left finger, twisting it around three times.

'Monsieur Lorbois, isn't it?' he said to the provost with a slight accent.

The other nodded and announced:

'Monsieur, my master has warned you a number of times to cease laying any claim to the title of "fencing master", without which the practice of teaching fencing is illegal. You have persisted in spite of those warnings. My master has sent us today to assure ourselves that you will leave Paris and the surrounding area within the hour, never to return.'

Like any other trade, that of fencing masters was regulated. Formed in 1567 under the patronage of Saint Michel, the guild of Parisian fencing masters organised and oversaw the practice within the capital, and the status of its members was confirmed by letters of patent. None who lacked such a letter could instruct another in the art of fencing.

Almades rose, the iron rapier in his left hand.

'I am a fencing master,' he said.

'In Spain, perhaps. But not in France. Not in Paris.'

'Spanish fencing is as worthy as French.'

'Do not force us to deal with you, monsieur. There is to be no question of a duel here. We are four, and you are alone.'

'Then let us even the odds.'

Under the gaze of the provost, who did not understand the

implications of this sentence, Almades placed himself in the centre of the courtyard, still holding the old iron rapier in his left hand . . .

. . . and unsheathed his own steel rapier with his right.

'I await you, messieurs,' he said, whipping both his blades around and up to the vertical three times.

Then he placed himself *en garde*.

The provost and his three apprentices deployed themselves in a semi-circle and pressed their attack at once. In a single flurry Almades pierced the shoulder of the first apprentice, the thigh of the second, ducked to avoid the iron bar of the third, straightened up and slashed the armpit of this last assailant while turning, and completed his move by crossing his rapiers to seize the provost's throat in the scissors formed by his two sharp blades.

No more than a few heartbeats had passed. The apprentices were out of the fight and their provost found himself at the Spaniard's mercy, paralysed by shock and fear, hesitating to even swallow with the blades placed against his throat.

Almades allowed a handful of seconds to pass and allow the provost to take full stock of the situation.

'Tell he who sent you that he is rather a poor fencing master and that what I've seen of his science, as displayed by your performance, makes me laugh . . . Now, get out.'

The humiliated provost retreated from the courtyard, along with his entourage of apprentices, one of whom, his thigh drenched in blood, had to be supported by the other two. The Spaniard watched them limp away, sighed, and heard a voice behind him say:

'My congratulations. The years have not dulled your skills.'

He turned to discover captain La Fargue standing there.

A twitch of the eyelid was the only sign that betrayed Almades's surprise.

They took a table in the near-empty inn. Almades ordered and paid for a jug of wine, which would deprive him of dinner later, then filled their glasses, pouring three times in each case.

'How did you know where to find me?' he asked.

'I didn't.'

'The cardinal?'

'His spies.'

The Spaniard swallowed a mouthful of wine while La Fargue slid a letter towards him. Richelieu's seal was stamped into the red wax seal.

'I have come,' said the Captain, 'to bring you this.'

'What does it say?'

'That the Blades have returned to the light of day and they wish for your return.'

Almades took in the news with a slight movement of his head.

'After five years?'

'Yes.'

'Under your command?'

The captain nodded.

Almades mulled this over, keeping his silence while twisting his signet ring around, over and over, in series of threes. Memories, not all of which were happy, flooded into his mind. Then he gave his current surroundings a long sweeping glance.

'You'll need to buy me a horse,' he said finally.

15

In Paris, the vicomte d'Orvand's coach left Marciac, as he requested, on rue Grenouillère, or more precisely, in front of a small, cosy house which had no real distinguishing features compared to the rest except that it was known to locals as *Les Petites Grenouilles* ('The Little Frogs'). Being familiar with the neighbourhood, the Gascon knew he would find the front door closed at this hour of the afternoon. So he went around to the rear and climbed over a wall, before crossing an attractive garden and entering the house through a low door.

He walked soundlessly into the kitchen where a very plump woman dressed in a skirt, apron and white bonnet had her back turned to him. He approached her on tiptoe and surprised her with a sound kiss on the cheek.

'Monsieur Nicolas! Where did you spring from? You almost scared me to death!'

'Another kiss, to win your forgiveness?'

'Be off, monsieur. You know very well that I have passed the age where such gallantries—'

'Really? And what about that handsome, strapping carpenter who curls his moustaches on the doorstep every time you go to the market?'

'I don't know of whom you speak,' replied the blushing cook.

'Now, now . . . Where are the young ladies?'

'In the next room.'

Moments later Marciac made his appearance in a bright and elegantly furnished room, where he immediately attracted the notice of four pretty young ladies who were sitting about in casual dress. The first was an ample blonde; the second a slim brunette; the third was a mischievous redhead; and the last was a Jewish beauty with green eyes and dusky skin. The blonde read from a book while the brunette embroidered and chattered with the other two.

Armed with his most roguish smile, Marciac bowed, doffed his hat with a flourish and exclaimed:

'Greetings, mesdemoiselles! How are my charming little frogs?'

He was welcomed with fervent cries of joy.

'Monsieur Nicolas!'

'How are you—?'

'It's been so long—!'

'Do you know how much we've missed you—?'

'We were worried—!'

The eager young women, relieving Marciac of his hat and sword, made him sit on a divan.

'Are you thirsty?' asked one of them.

'Hungry?' asked another.

'Desire anything else?' asked the most daring of the lot.

Marciac, delighted, accepted both a glass of wine and the demonstrations of affection that were lavished upon him with such good grace. Teasing fingers roamed over his chest and toyed with his shirt collar.

'So, monsieur Nicolas, what do you have to recount for us after all this time?'

'Oh, not much, I'm afraid . . .'

The young women made a show of profound disappointment.

'. . . merely that I fought a duel today!'

This news produced rapture.

'A duel? Tell us! Tell us!' the redhead cried, clapping her hands.

'Before anything else, I must describe my adversary, because he was rather formidable—'

'Who was he? Did you kill him?'

'Patience, patience . . . If memory serves me, I believe he was almost four measures tall.'

A measure was equal to two metres. They laughed.

'You're mocking us!'

'Not at all!' Marciac protested in a joyful tone. 'He even had six arms.'

More laughter.

'And to complete his portrait, I should add that this demon came straight from hell, had horns and breathed fire from both his mouth and his ars—'

'And just what is going on here?' demanded a voice which rang with authority.

A heavy silence fell. Everyone froze, while the temperature in the room seemed to fall by several degrees. Marciac, like some Levantine pasha in the midst of his harem, found himself caught with one little frog on his right, one to his left, another kneeling at his feet and the last perched on his knee. He attempted a smile, which only worsened the delicate situation in which he had been surprised.

Gabrielle had just made her entrance.

She had shimmering strawberry-blonde hair and was one of those women who are less striking for their beauty – however great – than for their imperious presence. A gown of silk and satin emphasised the perfection of her skin and the spark of her royal blue eyes. Tiny wrinkles had begun to appear at the corners of her eyelids over the passing years – lines which usually denote experience, as well as a certain penchant for laughter.

But Gabrielle neither laughed, nor even smiled.

Icily, she took in each detail of the Gascon from head to toe, as though he were a muddy dog who threatened to ruin her carpets.

'What are you doing here?'

'I came to pay my respects to your little frogs.'

'Have you?'

'Uh . . . yes.'

'Then you can go. Goodbye.'

She turned on her heel.

Marciac extricated himself, not without difficulty, from the divan and its little frogs. He caught up with Gabrielle in the corridor and detained her by the elbow, but, when skewered by her deadly stare, promptly released his hold.

'Gabrielle, my beauty, please . . . One word—'

'Don't you dare speak to me. After that nasty trick you played, I should have you beaten! . . . Ah, actually, that's an idea.'

She called out:

'Thibault!'

A door – leading into the front hall through which visitors to the house normally passed – opened. A giant dressed as a lackey appeared, who seemed at first astonished and then delighted to see Marciac.

'Hello, monsieur.'

'Hello, Thibault. How is your son, the one who broke his arm in a fall?'

'He has recovered, monsieur. Thank you for your concern, monsieur.'

'And your littlest one? How is she?'

'She cries a great deal. She's teething.'

'Just how many children do you have, exactly?'

'Eight, monsieur.'

'Eight! Well, well, you know your business, my lusty chap!'

Thibault blushed and dropped his gaze.

'Have you finished?' Gabrielle asked in a frosty voice. 'Thibault, I am not pleased.'

When he looked at her without comprehension she had to explain:

'He waltzed in here as though we live in a barn!'

Thibault turned towards the front hall and the main entrance.

'But he didn't. The door is shut tight and I swear to you I never left my stool. Although I wouldn't say no to a cushion, due to the pains which—'

Marciac made an effort not to laugh.

'That's enough, Thibault,' Gabrielle decreed. 'Return to your stool and your tightly shut door.'

And, catching sight of the little frogs peeping at them from the salon door, she ordered:

'And you! Off with you! Now! And close the door.'

Swiftly obeyed, but still dissatisfied, she added:

'Well, there's never a moment's peace in this house. Come.'

Marciac followed her into an antechamber, one adjoining her bedroom, whose delicious pleasures he remembered well. But the door to that retreat remained closed and Gabrielle, standing very stiff with her arms folded, prompted him:

'You wanted a word with me? Very well. Go ahead, I'm listening.'

'Gabrielle,' the Gascon began in a conciliatory tone—

'There. A word. You've said it. Now, goodbye. You know the way . . . And do not make me ask Thibault to accompany you.'

'Under these circumstances,' Marciac said contritely but gamely, 'I wager that even a chaste kiss would be too much to ask—'

'A kiss from Thibault? I'm sure you can arrange that.'

His shoulders lowered, Marciac made a show of leaving. Then he turned and proffered, as a peace offering, the ring won in his duel against the marquis de Brévaux.

'A gift?'

Gabrielle made an effort to remain unmoved. In her eyes, however, there was a gleam with the same sparkle as the ruby in its setting.

'Stolen?'

'You wound me. Handed over willingly by its former owner.'

'Before witnesses?'

'Yes. D'Orvand. You can ask him.'

'He no longer visits me.'

'I'll make him come see you again.'

'It's a man's ring.'

'But the stone is still beautiful.'

She softened somewhat.

'That's true.'

'And it has no regard for gender.'

With a shrug of her shoulders, Gabrielle took the ring with

a swift gesture and, pointing her finger menacingly, she snapped:

'Don't believe that all is forgiven because of this!'

Marciac, now happy and seeking to endear himself further, gave her a knowing look and replied:

'But it's a start, no?'

16

Inside the inn on the road to Clermont, no one had dared to speak or move since the five mercenaries had entered.

'Malencontre,' their leader repeated, tucking his flaxen hair behind his ear. 'It's a memorable name for a warrior, isn't it?'

He was still seated at Leprat's table and, having ordered wine, made conversation in a tone that was too self-confident to be at all innocent. Three of his men gathered together behind him while the last of the band, the drac with slate grey scales, guarded the door and kept an eye on everything.

'And yet,' continued Malencontre, 'My name means nothing to you. Do you know why?'

'No,' said Leprat.

'Because all those who have heard it from my mouth, without being my friends, soon met their end.'

'Ah.'

'That doesn't worry you?'

'Hardly.'

Malencontre scraped the scar at the corner of his mouth with a fingernail, and forced himself to smile.

'You're right. Because you see, today, I happen to be in a merciful mood. I am ready to forget the numerous difficulties which you have created for us. I am even disposed to forgive you for the two bodies you left on the bridge at the border. Not to mention that trick you played on us in Amiens. But . . .'

'But?'

'But you have to give us what we seek.'

The mercenaries scented victory. They were five against a single adversary who had no hope of reinforcements. They smiled, anticipating the moment when they would draw swords and let blood spill.

Leprat appeared to take stock of his situation, and then said:

'Understood.'

He slowly plunged his left hand into his dusty doublet and withdrew a letter sealed with a blob of red wax. He placed the document on the table, pushed it in front of him, and waited.

Malencontre watched this, frowning.

He made no move to pick up this missive which had already cost two lives.

'That's all?' he said in surprise.

'That's all.'

'You simply comply? Without even making a show of resistance?'

'I've already done enough, it seems to me. I will no doubt be held accountable for my actions, but it does not serve me at all if, in the end, you pluck a piece of paper from my corpse, does it? In any case, I must have been betrayed for you to have found me so quickly. Someone told you which route I would follow. I believe that this authorises me to take a few liberties as far as my masters' orders are concerned. One owes nothing to those who prove unworthy of one's trust.'

When the other continued to hesitate, Leprat insisted:

'You want this letter? Take it. It's yours.'

In the shadowy room, lit only by the faint red flames of the hearth, the silence grew as it does just before the fall of an executioner's axe, when the upraised blade catches a ray of sunlight and the crowd holds its breath.

'So be it,' said Malencontre.

Slowly, he extended a dirty-nailed hand towards the letter.

And if he glimpsed, at the last moment, a gleam awaken in Leprat's eye, he was too slow to react to it.

The mercenaries were caught short by their leader's screams: Leprat had nailed his hand to the table with the greasy knife he had used to slice up the fowl. Malencontre freed his tortured hand and spat:

'KILL HIM!'

On his feet, Leprat had already seized his sheathed rapier.

With a violent blow from his heel, he propelled the table into his attackers' legs and added to the confusion by forcing them to spread out before they could draw their swords. Malencontre, his bloody hand held tight against him, jostled them in order to reach the drac who was coming to his rescue. Backed against the curtained window, Leprat was forced to retreat. But he still had enough space to fight. Calmly, he slashed the air with his sword and managed to dislodge its scabbard, which slid across the floor.

Then he placed himself *en garde*.

And waited.

The tables around them finished emptying in a clatter of moving furniture. Silent and anxious, the inn's patrons huddled tight against the walls or on the steps of the staircase leading to the first floor. No one wanted to receive an ill-judged blow. But they all wanted to watch. The innkeeper himself had taken refuge in the kitchen. It seemed he lacked the stomach for this type of entertainment.

In a corner, the drac wrapped up Malencontre's hand with shreds torn from the first handy piece of cloth. The other three, finally untangled and ready to fight, prudently deployed themselves in a semi-circle. Without taking his eyes off them, the chevalier d'Orgueil allowed them to approach.

Closer.

Much closer.

In reach of a blade.

That should have worried them, but they realised it too late.

Leprat suddenly thrust his right hand behind him and pulled open the curtains. Brilliant daylight burst into the darkened room, clearly revealing his dark silhouette and striking the mercenaries in the face. Without waiting, he struck. The ivory rapier found one blinded freebooter's throat and produced a scarlet spurt which the villain tried in vain to staunch with his fingers. He fell, blood bubbling from his mouth and nostrils. Leprat broke off his attack immediately and dodged a clumsy lunge from another mercenary, who was still protecting his eyes from the sun with his elbow. Leprat doubled him up with a blow from his knee and sent him smashing, head first, into the mantelpiece. The man's skull cracked. He fell face-first into the hearth and began to burn; the smell of scorched hair and cooking meat quick to impregnate the room. The third brigand, who could now see better, was already charging him from behind, brandishing his sword. Leprat didn't turn. In one movement he reversed his sword and wedged it beneath his armpit, took a step back and dropped to one knee, allowing his attacker to impale himself on the ivory blade. The man stiffened, arm raised, face incredulous and lips dribbling pink spit. Leprat slowly returned to his feet, pivoted and finished driving his blade into the body, up to the hilt. He stared deeply into the dead man's eyes, and then pushed the corpse away, to fall backward to the floor.

Less than a minute had passed since he had opened the curtain, and three assassins were already lying dead beneath blows from the chevalier d'Orgueil. He was well known in Paris, in the Louvre as well as in all the fencing schools, as one of the best swordsmen in France. Evidently his reputation was not undeserved.

Malencontre was in no state to fight, but the drac was still waiting to enter the fray.

Leprat sized him up. He snapped out a sharp movement with his rapier which spattered the floor with red droplets, drew a dagger from its sheath over his kidney with his left hand, and resumed the *en garde* position. The drac seemed to smile. In his turn, he crossed his arms before him and simultaneously drew a straight sabre and a dagger.

He would also fight with two weapons.

The duel was furious from the very first exchange. Tense and concentrated, the drac and Leprat exchanged attacks, parries, counterattacks and ripostes without holding back. The reptilian understood who he was fighting and the chevalier quickly realised the worthiness of his opponent. Neither seemed to have the upper hand. When one of them retreated a few paces, he was quick to reclaim the advantage. And when the other was forced to parry a flurry of blows, he always managed to take the initiative with his next attack. Leprat was an experienced and talented swordsman, but the drac had greater strength and endurance: his arm seemed indefatigable. Steel against ivory, ivory against steel, the blades spun and clashed together faster than the eye could see. Leprat was sweating, and could feel himself tiring.

He had to finish it quickly.

Finally daggers and swords crossed at the guards. Pushing one against the other the drac and Leprat found themselves nose-to-nose, their arms extended above them like a steeple. With a mighty bellow, the drac spat a mouthful of acid into the chevalier's face, who replied with a powerful head butt. He managed to stun his opponent and, seizing the moment, wiped his burning eyes on his sleeve, but the drac was already rushing at him with foaming mouth and bloody nostrils. It was a weakness of dracs: they were impulsive and quick to abandon themselves to blind rage.

Leprat saw an opportunity that wouldn't present itself a second time.

With one foot, he slid a stool into the drac's path. The reptilian stumbled but continued his charge, half running, half falling as he came. His attack was fierce but inaccurate. Leprat stepped aside and pivoted towards the left as the reptilian passed him on the right. He managed to turn and slash, arm extended horizontally.

The ivory rapier sliced neatly through its target.

A scaly head spun and, at the end of a bloody arc, bounced against the floor and rolled a considerable distance. The decapitated drac's body fell, releasing a thick jet of liquid from its neck.

Leprat immediately looked for Malencontre. He didn't find him, but heard cries and the sound of hoof beats out in the courtyard. He rushed to the door in time to see the man escaping at a gallop, watched by those who had remained outside and were only now emerging from their hiding-places.

Stained with the blood of his victims, the remains of the acidic reptilian spit still clinging to his cheeks, Leprat went back inside the inn. He was the focus of attention of all those present, whose reactions wavered between horror and relief. So far no one was inclined to move, and certainly not to talk. The soles of nervous feet scraped against the raw wooden floor.

Weapons in hand, Leprat contemplated the carnage and disorder with a tranquil air. Amidst the upturned furniture, the broken plates and the trampled food, three bodies lay in thick pools of blood, while the fourth continued to burn in the hearth, the greasy flesh of his face crackling in contact with the flames. The smell, a mixture of blood, bile and fear, was appalling.

A door creaked open and the innkeeper came out of the kitchen brandishing an antique arquebus before him. The fat man wore a ridiculous-looking helmet on his head and a breastplate whose straps he was unable to fasten. And due to the trembling of his limbs, the barrel of his weapon – gaping open like an incredulous mouth – seemed to be following the erratic path of an invisible fly.

Leprat almost laughed, but succeeded only in smiling wearily.

It was then he saw the blood running from his right hand and realised that he had been wounded.

'All's well,' he said. 'In the king's service.'

17

'What?' exclaimed a merchant. 'That Amazon with the flying hair who galloped past us this morning? A baronne?'

'God's truth!' confirmed the old soldier. 'Just as I told you!'

'It's beyond belief!' blurted another merchant.

'And yet,' added a pedlar who knew the region well. 'Nothing could be truer.'

'And since when did baronnes carry swords, around here?

'Why, since it pleased them to—'

'It's simply extraordinary!'

'The baronne Agnès de Vaudreuil . . .' sighed the first merchant dreamily.

'It's said she's of excellent birth,' said the second.

'Old nobility of the sword,' declared the veteran of the Wars of Religion. 'The best. The true . . . Her ancestors went on the crusades and her father fought beside King Henri.'

This exchange took place at *The Silver Cask*, a village hostelry on the road to Paris. The two merchants had stopped there after concluding their business at an excellent market in Chantilly, which explained their shared good humour. Two more men had invited themselves to join their table. One was a quaint, garrulous local, an old soldier with a wooden leg who lived on a meagre pension, passing the greater part of his days drinking, if possible at someone else's expense. The other was a pedlar who seemed not at all eager to resume his rounds, carrying his heavy wicker pannier on his back. It was an hour after dinner and, with the afternoon rush over, the tables had quickly emptied. With the aid of wine, the conversation rolled along freely and vigorously.

'She seemed very beautiful to me,' said a merchant.

'Beautiful?' repeated the veteran. 'She is more than that . . . Her firm tits. Her long thighs. And her arse, my friends . . . that arse!'

'The way you speak of her arse I would swear you'd seen it?'

'Bloody hell! I've not had that good fortune . . . But others have seen it. And felt it. And enjoyed it. For it's a very welcoming arse, indeed . . .'

The drinkers were talkative, the subject ripe for discussion and the wine pitchers quickly emptied, all to be replaced immediately. However, the prospect of a handsome profit was not enough to gladden the heart of master Léonard, owner of *The Silver Cask*. Anxious, but not daring to intervene, he kept an eye on another customer sitting all alone at a table, visibly fuming.

The man wore sagging funnel-shaped boots, brown leather trousers and a large red velvet doublet left open over his bare chest. His body was of a robust build but weighed down with fat – large thighs, broad shoulders, and a thick neck. He might have been fifty-five years old, perhaps more. Beneath a close-cut beard, his lined face was that of an old soldier who had grown soft over the last few years, and interlacing crimson veins – which would soon blossom into blotches – decorated his cheeks. Nevertheless, his eyes remained sharp. And the impression of strength which emanated from his person was unmistakable.

'And where are they, these happy arse-samplers?' gaily demanded the most cheerful, and most drunk, of the merchants. 'I would like to hear more from them!'

'They're all about. This beauty is not shy.'

'It's said she kills her lovers,' interjected the pedlar.

'Nonsense!'

'You might better say that she exhausts them!' corrected the veteran with a bawdy wink of the eye. 'If you know what I mean . . .'

'I see, yes,' nodded the merchant. 'And I say, myself, that there are worse deaths than that . . . I'd gladly flirt with her myself, the naughty wench!'

Hearing that, the man who had been listening to them unnoticed rose with the air of someone resolved to carry out a necessary task. He advanced with steady steps and was half-way to the table when master Léonard nimbly barred his path, a somewhat courageous act, since he was two heads shorter and only half the other man's weight. But the safekeeping of his establishment was at stake.

'Monsieur Ballardieu, please?'

'Don't be alarmed, master Léonard. You know me.'

'Precisely. With respect . . . they've been drinking. No doubt, too much. They don't know what they're—'

'I tell you, there's no cause for concern,' the man said with a friendly and reassuring smile.

'Just promise me you won't start anything,' begged the innkeeper.

'I promise to do everything possible to that end.'

Master Léonard stepped aside with regret and, wiping his damp hands on his apron, watched Ballardieu continue on his way.

On seeing him, the veteran with the wooden leg turned pale. The three others, in contrast, were taken in by his easy manner.

'Please excuse me, messieurs, for interrupting you . . .'

'Please, monsieur,' replied a merchant. 'What can we do for you? Would you care to join our table?'

'Just a question.'

'We're listening.'

'I would like to know which of your four heads I shall have the honour of breaking first.'

18

A sound disturbed the drowsing Saint-Lucq.

It was a repeated, irregular scratching, which sometimes seemed to have stopped only to promptly begin again. A scrape of a claw. Against wood.

The half-blood sighed and sat up under the bedclothes. The afternoon was drawing to a close.

'What is it?' asked the muffled voice of the young woman lying beside him in bed.

'You can't hear it?'

'I can.'

'What is it?'

'Nothing. Go back to sleep.'

And she turned over, pulling the bedcovers round her.

Having two or three hours to kill during the day, Saint-Lucq had approached her on rue de Glatigny, an alley in the city where ladies of pleasure had plied their trade since the Middle Ages. He had offered to pay her handsomely on the condition that he could also take rest in her dwelling. The deal concluded, she had led him into the little attic room where she lived, close to the law courts. 'You're not my first', she had said, on seeing the half-blood's reptilian eyes.

Then she'd undressed.

An hour later, she was asleep. As for Saint-Lucq, he had remained awake for a moment, looking at the stripped plaster ceiling. He had no preference for the company of prostitutes but their bought hospitality had its advantages — one being that, unlike hoteliers, they did not keep a guest register.

The scratching continued.

Saint-Lucq rose, put on his breeches and his shirt, listened carefully, and drew back the nasty brown rag which served as a curtain to the sole window. The sound was coming from there. Daylight entered, and the silhouette of a black dragonnet was clearly visible behind the pane of glass.

The half-blood was still for a moment.

'Is he yours?'

The young woman – she claimed to be called Madeleine, 'like the other Magdalene' – sat up and, squinting in the light, grumbled:

'No. But it seems to think so . . . I made the mistake of feeding it two or three times. Now it won't stop coming here to beg for more.'

Truly wild dragonnets had almost disappeared in France. But those that were lost, had escaped or been abandoned by their masters, lived in the cities like stray cats.

'Find me something to feed him,' ordered Saint-Lucq as he opened the window.

'Oh, no! I want to persuade him to go elsewhere. And it's not—'

'I'll pay for it as well. Surely you have something he'll eat?'

Madeleine rose, naked, while the half-blood watched the dragonnet and the dragonnet watched the half-blood, with equal wariness. The reptile's scales shone in the light of the waning sun.

'There,' said Madeleine, bringing in a cloth tied together at the corners.

Saint-Lucq untied the linen and found a half-eaten dried-up sausage.

'That's all?'

'That's all,' confirmed the young woman, already back in bed. 'But there's a roast-meat seller on the street corner, if you like . . .'

Hand held flat, the half-blood presented a morsel of sausage to the dragonnet. The animal hesitated, sniffed, took the food in at the tip of its pointed muzzle, and seemed to chew it with some regret.

'You prefer your victims to be alive and fighting, don't you?' murmured Saint-Lucq. 'Well, so do I . . .'

'What are you saying?' asked Madeleine from the bed.

He didn't reply, and continued to feed the dragonnet.

A wyvern – which, ridden by a royal messenger, was returning to the Louvre – passed high above them, giving voice to a hollow cry from the skies. As though responding to the great reptile's call, the black dragonnet suddenly spread its leathery wings and was gone.

Saint-Lucq shut the window, swallowed the remains of the sausage and finished getting dressed.

'You're leaving?' asked Madeleine.

'So it would seem.'

'You have a meeting?'

'Yes.'

'Who with?'

The half-blood hesitated, then offered a truth so incredible it might as well be a lie.

'With the Grand Coësre.'

The prostitute laughed loudly.

'Oh, really! Say hello for me. And to the entire Court of Miracles, while you're at it . . . !'

Saint-Lucq simply smiled.

A minute later, he buttoned his doublet, hung his sheathed sword from his belt and fitted his strange spectacles with their crimson lenses. Then, from the attic room's threshold, the door already half-open, he turned and threw two pieces of silver on to the bed.

The gesture astonished Madeleine since she had already been paid for her services.

'That's a lot for a little bit of sausage,' she teased him.

'The first coin is for you to feed the dragonnet if it returns.'

'Done. And the second?'

'It's so you don't forget what the first is for.'

19

Arnaud de Laincourt lived on rue de la Ferronnerie which ran between the neighbourhoods of Sainte-Opportune and Les Halles, extending rue Saint-Honoré, skirting the Saints-Innocents cemetery and linking up with rue des Lombards, thus creating one of the longest routes through the capital. Broad, at almost four metres across, and heavily used, it was a place of sad memories: it was here that Ravaillac had stabbed Henri IV when the royal coach was halted by the busy street traffic. But this detail aside, Laincourt's address was quite commonplace. He rented accommodation in a house similar to many others in Paris: tall and narrow, crammed in between its neighbours, with a small shop on the ground floor – a ribbon seller, as it happened. Next to this establishment, a door for residents opened onto a corridor which passed through the building and led to a lightless staircase. From there, the top floors could be reached by following a shaky wooden banister up through the fetid air well.

Laincourt had his foot on the first step when he heard the squeak of hinges behind him in the shadowy corridor.

'Good morning, officer.'

It was monsieur Laborde, the ribbon seller. He must have seen him arrive, just as he saw everyone who came and went. In addition to the shop, he rented the three rooms on the first floor for himself and his family, as well as one poor, tiny room on the second floor for their maid. He was the principal lodger in the house. Because of this, he collected the rent and claimed to keep an eye on everything, puffed up with pride, jealous of the trust placed in him by the landlord, and very concerned about the respectability of the place.

Laincourt turned to greet him, suppressing a sigh.

'Monsieur Laborde.'

Like most members of the petty bourgeoisie, the ribbon seller evinced a fearful hatred of the popular masses, despised anyone poorer than himself, envied his equals and deemed them all to be upstarts, was quick to abase himself before those with power and always felt he needed to wriggle into the good graces of representatives of authority. He dreamed of being able to count Laincourt, an ensign with His Eminence's horse guards, amongst his customers.

'I invite you to do me the honour of passing by my shop sometime, monsieur. I have received some swathes of satin which, if I am to believe my wife, would look quite wonderful on you if made up into a doublet.'

'Ah.'

'Yes. And you know as well as I do how the ladies have an eye and a taste for such things.'

Laincourt could not stop himself from thinking of Laborde's wife and the metres of coloured ribbons which adorned the least of her dresses, although in all honesty none of these could be described as 'the least' once one had seen the imposing dimensions of the lady in question.

'True elegance is in the detail, isn't it?' insisted the tradesman.

Detail. Another word which sat poorly with the enormous madame Laborde, who raised her little finger when she sipped her chocolate and gobbled up pastries as though eating for four.

'No doubt,' said Laincourt with a smile which said nothing. 'Good day, monsieur Laborde.'

The ensign climbed as far as the second floor and, passing in front of the garret door where the ribbon seller's maid slept, he entered his own rooms. His apartment was made up of two very ordinary rooms, that is to say: cold and gloomy ones, where the air circulated poorly. But he didn't have much reason to complain as each had a window – even if one looked onto a dirty courtyard and the other into an alley so narrow that one could touch the opposing wall with an outstretched arm. His furniture was meagre: a bed and a chest for clothes in the bedroom; and a table, a rickety sideboard and two chairs in the second room. This furniture, moreover, did not belong to him. With the exception of the chest, they had all been there when he arrived and would remain there when he left.

In order not to compromise the impeccable cleanliness of his rooms, Laincourt's first care was to remove his stained boots, promising himself he would soon clean off the black and stinking muck they had acquired from the Parisian streets. Then he hung his belt from the same nail which held his felt hat with its white plume, and took off his cape.

There were writing implements on the table and Laincourt set to work at once. He had to re-transcribe the letter he had read at midday in Charpentier's – Richelieu's secretary – tiny study. He copied it out from memory, only he used Latin vocabulary combined with Greek grammar. The result was a text which, while not entirely undecipherable, could not be read by anyone without a perfect knowledge of both languages – which remained the province of scholars alone. The ensign didn't hesitate even once as he filled a page with lines of cramped writing, and he didn't release the quill until he had penned the final full stop.

He was waiting, motionless and impassive, for the ink to dry, when someone knocked on the door. Laincourt turned his head towards it, frowning.

As the knocking was insistent, he resolved to go and open the door. When he did, he saw the Labordes' servant, a nice girl with pink cheeks who nursed a secret crush on the young ensign of the Cardinal's Guards.

'Yes?'

'Good morning, monsieur.'

'Good morning.'

'I don't know if you know, but a gentleman came here.'

'A gentleman.'

'Yes. He asked some questions about you.'

'Questions to which monsieur Laborde no doubt zealously replied . . .'

The servant nodded, embarrassed, as if a little of her master's abject nature reflected on her.

'Did he give his name, this gentleman?' asked Laincourt.

'No.'

'How did he look?'

'He was tall, slightly handsome, with black hair. And he had a scar on his temple . . . He did not give any cause for alarm, but he was . . . frightening.'

The ensign nodded, inscrutable.

At that moment, madame Laborde called out for her maidservant, who made haste to answer the summons.

'Thank you,' said Laincourt, as she took leave with a brief curtsey.

Having closed the door again, he returned to his writing table and slipped the transcription of the letter into a thin leather envelope. He carried it to the chair, lifted the rug, dislodged a floorboard and hid the secret document before returning everything to its normal place.

Or almost.

As he saw at once, a corner of the rug remained rolled up: an obvious discrepancy which was at odds with the perfect order of the room.

The ensign hesitated for a moment, then shrugged and prepared to leave. He pulled his fouled boots back on, strapped on his belt, took his hat and threw his folded cape over his shoulder. In the distance, the Sainte-Opportune bell-tower tolled the half-hour, almost immediately followed by the Saints-Innocents church.

20

At *Les Petites Grenouilles*, Marciac woke sated and happy in a very rumpled bed, and leaned on an elbow to watch Gabrielle as she brushed her hair, sitting half-naked in front of her dressing table. This sight made his joy complete. She was beautiful, the folds of cloth which barely covered her had all the elegance of the drapery of ancient statues, and the light of the setting sun shining through the window made the loose strands of hair at the nape of her slender neck iridescent, flattered her pale round shoulders, and outlined the curve of her satiny back in amber. It was one of those perfect moments when all the harmony of the world is combined. The room was silent. Only the faint sound of the brush caressing her smooth hair could be heard.

After a moment, Gabrielle caught her lover's gaze in the mirror and, without turning, broke the spell:

'You should keep the ring.'

The Gascon saw the prize that he had won in the duel. Gabrielle had removed it from her finger and placed it near her jewel case.

'I gave it to you,' said Marciac. 'I shall not take it back again.'

'You need it.'

'I don't.'

'Yes, you do. To repay La Rabier.'

Marciac sat up in bed. Gabrielle, her back still turned to him, continued to brush her hair, saying no more.

'You know about that?' he said.

She shrugged.

'Of course. All secrets are known in Paris. All you have to do is listen . . . Do you owe her much?'

Marciac didn't reply.

He let himself fall back onto the bed, arms opened wide, and contemplated the canopy above his head.

'As much as that?' said Gabrielle in a quiet voice.

'Yes.'

'How did you let it come to this, Nicolas?'

There was both reproach and commiseration in the tone of her voice – a tone which was, ultimately, very maternal.

'I played, I won, I lost triple,' explained the Gascon.

'Mother Rabier is a vicious woman. She can harm you.'

'I know.'

'And the men she employs have blood on their hands.'

'I know that as well.'

Laying her brush down, Gabrielle turned in her chair and fixed Marciac with a clear and penetrating gaze.

'She should be paid. Would this ring be enough?'

'It would be enough to make a start.'

'Then it's decided.'

They exchanged a smile. A smile full of affection from her, and one full of gratitude from him.

'Thank you,' he said.

'Don't mention it.'

'I should consult you over every decision I make.'

'If you merely do the opposite of whatever your whim dictates, all will be well.'

Smiling easily, Marciac rose and began to dress while his mistress drew on her stockings, another spectacle of which he missed nothing.

Then, without preamble, Gabrielle said:

'A letter arrived here for you.'

'When?'

'Today.'

'And as you were still furious with me,' guessed the Gascon while lacing his breeches, 'you burnt it.'

'No.'

'Not even tore it up?'

'No.'

'Nor crumpled it?'

'You're infuriating, Nicolas!' exclaimed Gabrielle.

She had almost shouted, and then, stiffening, stared straight ahead.

As they had often teased each other like this, he couldn't explain her reaction. His chest bare, he watched the woman he loved and detected her anguish.

'What is it, Gabrielle?'

With her index finger, she discreetly wiped a tear from the corner of her eye. He approached her and, leaning over her from behind, held her gently.

'Tell me,' he murmured.

'Forgive me. It's for you.'

Marciac took the letter she held out to him, and understood her distress when he saw the emblem stamped into the red wax seal.

It was that of Cardinal Richelieu.

'I thought . . .' said Gabrielle in a strangled voice, 'I thought that this period of your life was over.'

He had thought so too.

21

The sun was still high when Agnès de Vaudreuil arrived in sight of the village. Her doublet open and her sheathed rapier beating against her thigh, she was covered in the dust raised by her galloping horse's hooves since she left the manor with all speed. She had pink cheeks and her face shone with sweat. Thrown into disarray by the ride, her long plait was now a mess of loose braids barely held together at their ends, with many full black curls having already escaped completely. Her face, however, still expressed a combination of relentless determination and contained anger. And her gaze remained fixed on the objective towards which her foaming mount progressed without flagging.

From a mere hamlet, the village had grown up around its church at the crossroads between two roads which wound between wooded hills. It was still only a staging post on the Chantilly road and it owed its incipient prosperity to *The Silver Cask*, an inn renowned for the quality of its cellar and kitchen, and the amiable company of its serving girls. Local people went there for a glass of wine on occasion and well-informed travellers would happily sleep there – on their outward journey if their business did not require them to be in Chantilly at daybreak, or else upon their return.

Agnès slowed as she passed the first houses. In the streets her horse trod the same beaten ground as on the road, and she guided it into the heart of the village at a trot. In front of *The Silver Cask*'s porch, the villagers were dispersing. They smiled and chattered with one another, sometimes making grand gestures. One of them climbed on to a mossy stone bench and raised a laugh by miming blows and vigorous kicks up the arse. All of them seemed delighted, as though they were leaving a theatre where they had seen an exceptionally funny farce. Agnès guessed who might be behind this festive mood, which didn't bode well. Just because the spectators were delighted did not mean that the spectacle itself had been pleasant. In these times, crowds gathered to witness the public punishment of condemned criminals, and were greatly amused by the many howls and twitches of the unfortunates being thus tormented.

On seeing the horsewoman pass, some of them doffed their caps, and the clown climbed down from his bench.

'Who is that?' asked someone.

'The baronne de Vaudreuil.'

'Our Lady!'

'As you say, my friend. As you say . . .'

The Silver Cask was a picturesque sight with its crooked buildings, its old and beautiful grey stone, its façades covered with ivy and its red-tiled roofs.

Agnès dismounted just beyond the porch, her spurs jingling as the heels of her riding boots touched the cobblestones of the courtyard. She wiped her shining face with the back of her sleeve, unbound her hair and shook her head to make her heavy black curls fall into place. Then, dishevelled, dusty and yet heedless of anyone's glance, she looked around.

She recognised the innkeeper standing in front of the main building, trying to calm the impatience, if not the anger, of several patrons. Nervous and agitated, they were vying with one another for the chance to roundly scold the man, punctuating each angry point with jabs of their index fingers at his chest. The innkeeper made appeasing gestures expressing his most fawning respect, all the while preventing anyone from entering the building. But his efforts proved unsuccessful. His customers would not be soothed, and Agnès noticed that the appearance of a few of them – if not quite as disorderly as her own – left something to be desired. One had the right sleeve of his doublet, torn at the shoulder, tightly wrapped around his elbow; another, shirt hanging out from his breeches, was pressing a wet cloth against his face; a third was wearing a badly dented hat, and his lace collar hung down miserably.

Finally, remarking on her arrival, the innkeeper excused himself from the gentlemen. They grumbled while he hastened to greet Agnès. On his way, he hailed a stable boy, who abandoned his bucket and pitchfork to busy himself with the baronne's horse.

'Ah, madame! Madame!'

She walked towards him with a firm step. And as she neither slowed her pace nor changed her course when they met, he was forced to make an abrupt about-turn and trot along at her side.

'What has he done now?' asked Agnès.

The innkeeper was a small, dry, thin man, although sporting a pot-belly as round as a balloon. He wore a short waistcoat over his shirt, and his figure was squeezed by the belt of his apron, which fell to his thighs.

'Thank the Lord, madame. You're here.'

'Rather than heaven, thank the boy you sent to warn me, master Léonard . . . Where is Ballardieu? And what has he done?'

'He's inside, madame.'

'Why are all these people waiting outside?'

'Because their coats or bags are still within, madame.'

'Then why don't they collect them?'

'Because monsieur Ballardieu will not let anyone in.'

Agnès halted.

Caught unawares, the innkeeper was two steps past her before he followed suit.

'Pardon me, master Léonard?'

'It's just as I said, madame. He threatens to shoot anyone who opens the door in the head, unless it is you.'

'Is he armed?'

'Only with a pistol.'

'Is he drunk?'

Master Léonard had the air of a man who was not quite

certain he understood the question and was afraid of committing a faux pas.

'Do you mean: more drunk than usual?'

The baronne gave an aggravated sigh.

'Yes, that's exactly what I mean.'

'Then yes, madame. He is drunk.'

'Plague on the old toss-pot! Can he not indulge within reason?' she said to herself.

'I believe he never learned how, madame. Or else he has no desire to do so—'

'So how did all this start?'

'Ah, well,' the innkeeper hesitated . . . 'There were these gentlemen . . . Please note, madame, that they had enjoyed an excellent meal and that it was more the wine than themselves that was talking . . .'

'I see. And then?'

'A few of their comments displeased monsieur Ballardieu—'

'—who, in his way, let them know it. Very well, I understand. Where are they, these gentlemen?'

The innkeeper was astonished.

'They're still inside, madame!'

'So who are those three over there, covered with bumps and bruises?'

'Just those who attempted to intervene.'

Agnès raised her eyes to the sky then continued to walk towards the inn and, in addition, towards those standing outside it. Master Léonard hurried ahead of her to open a path.

Seeing that she was about to enter, an elegant officer who had only remained to be entertained by the comedy of the situation, said to her:

'Madame, I advise you against opening this door.'

'Monsieur, I advise you against preventing me,' the baronne replied in a flash.

The officer drew back his shoulders, more surprised than annoyed. Agnès suddenly understood that he had only meant to be gallant. She softened.

'Never fear, monsieur. I know the man conducting the siege inside.'

'What?' interrupted the man with the dented hat. 'You know that raving madman?'

'Have a care with your remarks, monsieur,' said Agnès de Vaudreuil glacially. 'He of whom you speak began some work upon you which I could easily complete. And it would cost you a little more than a hat.'

'Would you like me to accompany you?' the officer insisted politely.

'No, thank you, monsieur.'

'Know, nevertheless, that I shall be ready if needed.'

She nodded and entered.

Low-ceilinged and silent, the room had been thrown into an upheaval of fallen chairs, toppled tables and shattered crockery. Splatters of wine stained the walls where jugs had been broken. Several panes of glass were missing from a window. A serving platter had been cracked. In the hearth, the spit was only held up by one forked support and the counterweight mechanism designed to keep it turning clicked uselessly.

'Finally!' exclaimed Ballardieu in the tone of someone welcoming a long-hoped-for visitor.

He was enthroned in triumph in the middle of the chaos, sitting on a chair, one foot leaning against a supporting beam to balance himself. His red velvet doublet was open over his massive chest, hairy and sweating, and his smile was huge, seeming full of reckless joy despite – or perhaps because of – his split lip and swelling eye. Ballardieu was one of those who took delight in a good brawl.

He held a wine bottle in one hand and, in the other, something which looked like a wooden skittle.

'Finally?' Agnès was astonished.

'Of course! We've been waiting for you!'

' "We"? Who is this "we"?'

'These messieurs and myself.'

Tearing her incredulous gaze away from the old soldier

with great difficulty, Agnès observed the men. They were all a sorry sight to see, having received a severe chastising.

Two very richly dressed men – merchants no doubt – were piled up one on top of the other, either unconscious or pretending to be. Another – most likely a pedlar – had scarcely fared better: he was sitting with his arms and chest pinned inside a large wicker basket through the bottom of which his head had burst, the latter now swaying woozily on his neck. Lastly, a fourth member of the party was huddled up at Ballardieu's feet, and his cringing manner indicated that he feared another thump. This one the baronne knew by sight at least: he was a veteran who had lost a leg in the Wars of Religion, and henceforth, hobbling around, dedicated his days to a tour of the local inns.

'You've left them in a pretty state,' commented Agnès.

She noticed that the veteran was missing his wooden peg-leg, and suddenly realised it was the skittle-shaped object with which Ballardieu was playing.

'They deserved it.'

'Let us hope so. Why have you been waiting for me?'

'I wanted this man, right here, to offer you his apologies.'

Agnès looked at the unfortunate one-legged man who, trembling, was protecting his head with his forearms.

'Apologies? For what?'

Ballardieu suddenly found himself extremely embarrassed. How could he explain, without repeating the vulgar and abusive comments that had been made about her?

'Uhh . . .'

'I'm waiting.'

'The important thing,' continued the old soldier waving the wooden peg-leg like a sceptre . . . 'The important thing is that this lout offers his apologies. So, lout, speak up! The lady is waiting!'

'Madame,' groaned the other, still seeking about for his prosthesis, 'I beg you to accept my most sincere and respectful apologies. I have ignored all my obligations, which not even my poor nature, my neglected education and my deplorable habits can justify. I promise to mind my conduct and manners in future and, conscious of my faults, I deliver myself to your goodwill. I add that I am ugly, have a mouth like an arse and that it is difficult to believe, having seen me, that the Almighty made Adam in his own image.'

The man had recited this act of contrition in a single breath, like a practised speech, and Ballardieu had followed the tirade with regular shakes of his head and the synchronous movements of his lips.

The result appeared to satisfy him.

'Very good, lout. Here, take back your leg.'

'Thank you, monsieur.'

'But you forgot to mention your ugly mug, which is—'

'—so foul it turns milk into piss. I'm sorry, monsieur. Should I start again?'

'I don't know. Your repentance seems sincere to me, but . . .'

Ballardieu questioned Agnès with a look.

She simply stared at him, dumbstruck.

'No,' he said again. 'Madame la baronne is right: that will suffice. The punishment must be just and not cruel if it is meant to be a lesson.'

'Thank you, monsieur.'

Ballardieu rose, stretched, emptied his flagon of wine in two swallows and threw it over his shoulder. At the end of a beautiful arc through the air, the aforementioned flagon bounced off the pedlar's head, who was still sitting imprisoned in his wicker pannier.

'Good!' cried Ballardieu joyfully, rubbing his hands together. 'Shall we go?'

Behind him, the stunned pedlar tipped over onto his side like an overturned basket.

22

Alerted by her son, the woman appeared on the threshold of the thatched cottage to see the rider who had just arrived. With a word, she ordered her son to go and bring her something from inside. He was quick to obey, returning with a wheel-lock pistol which he handed to his mother.

'Go and hide, Tonin.'

'But mother—'

'Go and hide under the bed and don't come out unless I call you.'

The afternoon was drawing to close, with a faint warm breeze in the air. There were no other dwellings anywhere around the cottage for as far as the eye could see. The nearest village was a good mile away, and the road leading there passed by some distance away. Even pedlars and sellers of almanacs only rarely stopped off to visit them. In this lonely corner of the French countryside, the inhabitants were by and large abandoned to their own devices.

Remaining at the door alone, the woman checked that the pistol was loaded and that the gunpowder in the chamber was dry. Then she let the weapon hang at the end of her arm, slightly behind her body, out of the rider's sight as he entered the yard where a few hens pecked at the brown sun-beaten ground.

She barely nodded when Antoine Leprat greeted her from his mount.

'I should like to water my horse. And I would be glad to pay you for a glass of wine.'

She studied him for a long while without saying a word.

Badly shaven, grimy and bedraggled, he seemed exhausted

and hardly inspired either confidence or fear. He was armed: pistols were tucked in the holsters on his saddle and a curious white rapier hung at his side – his right side, as though he were left-handed. His night-blue doublet was open over a sweat-stained shirt and its sleeve, up by the shoulder, had a nasty gash through which a recent bandage could be glimpsed. Fresh blood had trickled over his hand, a sure sign that his wound had reopened.

'Where are you going?' asked the woman.

'To Paris.'

'By these roads, you won't reach Paris before nightfall.'

'I know.'

She continued to study him.

'You're wounded.'

'Yes.'

After his battle with Malencontre and his hired killers, Leprat had not immediately realised that he was bleeding. In the heat of the action, he had not noticed which of his adversaries had cut his arm. Nor had he felt any pain at the time. In fact, the wound had only begun to trouble him when he saw the threads of blood running from his sleeve and making his right hand sticky. It wasn't particularly dangerous, but the gash deserved medical attention. Leprat had simply applied a makeshift bandage and immediately returned to the road.

'An unlucky encounter,' he explained.

'With brigands?'

'No. Assassins.'

The woman didn't blink.

'Are you being followed?'

'I was being followed. I don't know if I still am.'

Since leaving the staging post Leprat had followed the minor roads which, although not the shortest route, reduced the risk of being ambushed. He travelled alone and his wound made him easy prey for ordinary brigands. But also he feared there was another ambush laid for him along the Paris road, set by those who had put the mercenaries on his trail.

'I will see to your wound,' said the woman, no longer

making any effort to conceal the pistol she held. 'But I don't want you to stay.'

'I ask only for a bucket of water for my horse and a glass of wine for myself.'

'I will see to your wound,' she repeated. 'I will look after you, and then you will leave. Come in.'

He followed her into the house, whose interior consisted of one large, dark and low-ceilinged room, poor but clean, with a few pieces of furniture on the hard-earth floor.

'You can come out now, Tonin,' the woman called.

While her son climbed out from beneath the bed and offered a timid smile to the stranger, she prepared a basin of water and clean linen cloth, all the while keeping the pistol close at hand.

Leprat waited until she pointed him to a bench before sitting down.

'My name is Leprat,' he said.

'Geneviève Rolain.'

'And I'm Tonin!'

'Hello, Tonin,' said Leprat with a smile.

'Are you a gentleman?' asked the boy.

'I am.'

'And a soldier?'

'Yes.'

'My father was a soldier, too. Of the Picardy regiment.'

'A very old and very prestigious regiment.'

'And you, monsieur? In which regiment do you serve?'

Predicting the reaction he would provoke, Leprat announced:

'I serve in a company of His Majesty's mounted musketeers.'

'With the King's Musketeers?' Tonin marvelled. 'Really? Did you hear, mother? A musketeer!'

'Yes, Tonin. You're shouting quite loudly enough for me to hear you —'

'Do you know the king, monsieur? Have you ever spoken to him?'

'A few times.'

'Go and water monsieur the musketeer's horse,' Geneviève interrupted, placing a basin of water on the table.

'But mother?'

'Now, Antoine.'

The boy knew it was never a good sign when his mother switched from 'Tonin' to 'Antoine'.

'Yes, mother . . . Will you still tell me about the king, monsieur?'

'We'll see.'

Delighted by this prospect, Tonin left the house.

'You have a lovely little boy,' said Leprat.

'Yes. He's at that stage where they dream of nothing but glory and adventure.'

'It is a stage which does not always pass with the coming of manhood.'

'And thus his father died.'

'I'm sorry to hear that, madame. He fell in battle?'

'Soldiers are quicker to die of hunger, cold or disease than a thrust from a sword . . . No, monsieur, it was the ranse which took my husband during a siege.'

'The ranse,' Leprat murmured, as though evoking an old and dreaded enemy . . .

It behaved like a virulent disease, and originated from dragons and their magic. The dragons – or more accurately their distant descendants of human appearance – suffered little from it, but the men and women who frequented their company for too long a period were rarely spared. The first symptom was a small mark on the skin, scarcely more alarming than a beauty spot, and which often went unnoticed in an age when people did not wash and never took off their shirts. The mark grew, becoming purplish in colour and rough to the touch. Sometimes it would slowly develop black veins and begin to crack open, oozing pus, while deeper tumours would develop underneath. This was known as the 'Great ranse'. Then the patient became contagious and felt the first pains, the first lumps, the first deformities, and the first monstrosities . . .

The Church saw this as clear proof that dragons were evil

incarnate, to the extent that they could not even be approached without mortal danger. As for seventeenth-century medicine, it was impotent to either fight or prevent the ranse, whether great or small. Remedies were sold, to be sure, and new cures appeared in the apothecaries' dispensaries and the smooth-talking vendors' stalls almost every year. But most of these were nothing but the work of more or less well-intentioned charlatans or practitioners. As for allegedly more serious medications, it proved impossible to measure their effectiveness objectively because those afflicted were not all equally susceptible to the ranse. Some passed away after two weeks, while others lived for a long time after the appearance of the first symptoms and suffered little. Meanwhile, you could still encounter other unfortunate victims in the final stages of the disease who, having been transformed into pitiable monsters, were reduced to begging on the streets to survive. They were obliged to wear a red robe and announce their presence by shaking a rattle, when they were not forcibly incarcerated in the recently founded Hospice des Incurables in Paris.

Shrugging away her bad memories, Geneviève helped Leprat remove his doublet. Then she unwound the bandage he had hastily wrapped around his bicep, over his shirt sleeve.

'Your shirt now, monsieur.'

'Rip the sleeve, that will suffice.'

'The shirt is still good. You just need to have the tear sewn up.'

Leprat reflected that the price of a new shirt was not the same for a gentleman as for a countrywoman forced to make economies.

'It is,' he admitted. 'But please, close the door.'

The woman hesitated, with a glance at her pistol, but finally went to shut the door which still stood open to the yard. Then she lent a hand to the musketeer, who was stripping to the waist, and understood immediately when he bared his muscular 'back.

Large, coarse and purplish splotches of the ranse spread across it.

'Do not fear, madame. My illness has not yet reached a

point where it could affect you. But it's a sight that I'd rather spare your son.'

'Do you suffer?'

'Not yet.'

23

Sitting at a table in an empty tavern whose keeper was sweeping the floor at the end of a very long day, the Gascon was glowering into the bottom of his glass when he realised someone was standing nearby.

'Captain.'

'Good evening, Marciac.'

'Please, take a seat.'

'Thank you.'

La Fargue pulled a chair towards him and sat down.

A second glass, as clean as one might hope for in such an establishment, was placed on the table. Marciac took and filled it for the old man.

It was the dregs of the jug. Barely a mouthful.

'Sorry, captain. It's all that's left.'

'It will do.'

La Fargue didn't touch his glass and, while the silence stretched out, noticed the crumpled letter which the Gascon had received in rue de la Grenouillère.

'The Blades are recalled to service, Marciac.'

The other nodded, pensive and sad.

'I need you, Marciac.'

'Mmh.'

'The Blades need you.'

'And who are they?'

'The same as before. Other letters have been sent. They will be arriving soon.'

'The same as before. That's to say: those who still live.'

'Yes.'

The silence fell again, thicker than before.

Finally, Marciac burst out:

'I have a life now, captain.'

'A life which pleases you?'

They exchanged a long glance.

'Which pleases me well enough.'

'And where is it leading you?'

'All lives lead to the cemetery, captain. What matters is to make the path pleasant.'

'Or useful.'

'Useful? Useful to whom?'

'We serve France.'

'From the sewers.'

'We serve the king.'

'And the cardinal.'

'It's the same thing.'

'Not always.'

Their conversation, sharp and delivered like a lethal clash of blades, ended with these words. Averting his eyes, Marciac drained his glass and asked:

'Will we be justly rewarded?'

'With neither honour nor glory, if that's your idea. In that respect, nothing has changed.'

'Let us speak of finances instead. If I accept I want to be paid handsomely. Very handsomely. On the day and hour specified. At the first delay, I hang up my sword.'

La Fargue, intrigued, blinked slowly.

'Agreed.'

The Gascon allowed himself a few moments of further thought while he examined his steel signet ring.

'When do we start?' he asked.

24

There were a dozen courts of miracles in Paris. All of them were organised according to the same hierarchy, inherited from the Middle Ages: they consisted of an enclosed area where the communities of beggars, criminals and other marginal elements could congregate. Scattered through the capital, they took their name from the professional mendicants – the kind with fake diseases and fake mutilations – who were 'miraculously' restored to good health after a hard day of begging, once they were far from the inquisitive eyes of outsiders. Cour Sainte Cathérine was one such refuge, situated in the Saint-Denis neighbourhood; another was to be found on rue du Bac; and a third near the Saint-Honoré market. But the most famous court, the one which had earned its status as the Court of Miracles – with capital letters and without further reference – was the one on rue Neuve-Saint-Sauveur, near the Montmartre gate.

According to a chronicler of the times, it was located in 'the worst-built, the dirtiest and the most remote district of the city' and consisted of a vast courtyard dating from the thirteenth century. It was rank, muddy, surrounded by sordid, rickety buildings, and hemmed in by the tangled and labyrinthine alleys behind the Filles-Dieu convent. Hundreds of beggars and thugs lodged here with their women and children, so that there were at least a thousand inhabitants in all, ruling as absolute masters over their territory, permitting neither intrusions nor strangers nor the city watch, and ready to repel them all with insults, thrown stones and bludgeons. When, eight years earlier, a new street was supposed to be laid nearby, the workers were attacked and the project had to be abandoned.

Jealous of its independence, the insubordinate little world of the Court of Miracles lived according to its own laws and customs. It was led by one man, the Grand Coësre, who Saint-Lucq was waiting to meet this afternoon. Through the slimy glass of a first floor window, from behind his red spectacles, he observed a large, sorry-looking and at this hour almost deserted cul-de-sac – it would only become animated at nightfall when the thugs and beggars returned from their day of larceny and mendicity in Paris. The décor had something sinister and oppressive about it. Those who ventured here unawares would sense that they were in enemy territory, and being spied upon, just before the inevitable ambush.

The half-blood was not alone.

An old woman dressed entirely in black kept him company, sitting in her corner she nibbled on a wafer like a rabbit chewing a chicory leaf, clasping it between the fingers of her emaciated hands, her eyes lost and vague. Tranchelard was there too, the thug Saint-Lucq had threatened earlier. The man endeavoured to make the atmosphere as unpleasant as possible with a heavy silence and a fixed black glare directed against the visitor, his hand on the pommel of his sword. Back turned, Saint-Lucq was unaffected. Minutes passed in this room, where the mottled and stained appearance of the floor, the walls and the door frames contrasted with the motley collection of luxurious furniture and carpets stolen from some mansion or wealthy bourgeois house. Nothing but the old woman's chewing disturbed the silence.

Eventually, preceded by a severe-looking individual with a noticeably receding hairline, the Grand Coësre arrived.

Slender and blond, the Grand Coësre was no more than seventeen years old, an age when one was already reckoned an adult in these times, but he seemed rather young to be leader of some of the toughest and most frightening members of the Parisian underworld. He nevertheless displayed all the self-assurance of a feared and respected monarch, whose authority was never disputed without blood and tears flowing from the challenge. His right cheek carried the scar from a badly-healed gash. His clear eyes shone with cynicism and intelligence. He was unarmed, certain that that no harm would befall him in his own stronghold where a mere glance on his part could condemn another to death.

While the Grand Coësre settled himself comfortably on the high-backed armchair reserved for his use, the man who had held the door for him moved to his side, standing straight and expressionless. Saint-Lucq knew him. His name was Grangier and he was an *archisuppôt*. Within the strict hierarchical organisation of the Cour des Miracles, archisuppôts ranked just below the Grand Coësre, along with the *cagoux*. The latter were responsible for organising the troops and training new recruits in the arts of picking pockets and eliciting compassion – and money – from strangers. The archisuppôts, in contrast, were often highly educated judges and advisors. A defrocked priest, Grangier had his master's ear due to his formidable perspicacity.

Saint-Lucq bowed his head, but did not remove his hat.

'I must admit you're not lacking in courage,' the Grand Coësre observed without preamble. 'If anyone but you behaved like this, I would think I was dealing with a cretin.'

The half-blood didn't respond.

'To come here after having manhandled two of my men and threatened to cut poor Tranchelard's throat—'

'I had to be sure he would not forget to pass on my message.'

'You realise that he now speaks of nothing but dis-embowelling you?'

'He's of no importance.'

Tranchelard bristled, visibly itching to draw his sword. As for his undisputed master, he burst out laughing.

'Well! You can always boast later of how you piqued my curiosity. Speak, I'm listening.'

'It concerns the Corbins gang.'

At hearing these words, the Grand Coësre's face darkened. 'And?'

'Recently, the Corbins have seized certain goods. Precious, fragile merchandise. Merchandise of a kind which, up until now, had never interested them. Do you know what I am referring to?'

'Perhaps.'

'I would like to find out where they stash their goods. I know the place is not in Paris, but nothing more than that. You, on the other hand . . .'

The master of the Cour des Miracles paused for a moment without speaking. Then he leaned towards Grangier and said a few words to him in *narquois*, a language which was incomprehensible to the uninitiated. The archisuppôt replied in the same idiom. Without reacting, Saint-Lucq waited for their secretive discussion to end. It was brief.

'Supposing I have the information you seek,' the Grand Coësre said to him. 'Why should I tell you?'

'It's information for which I'm willing to pay full price.'

'I'm already rich.'

'You're also a bastard without faith or morality. But above all, you are a shrewd man.'

'Which is to say?'

'The Corbins are making inroads into your territory. Because of them, your influence and your business revenues are shrinking. But, in particular, they don't take their orders from you.'

'This problem will soon be resolved.'

'Really? I can resolve it for you now. Tell me what I want to know, and I will deliver the Corbins a blow from which they will have trouble recovering. You can even take the credit if you want . . . We don't like one another, Grand Coësre. And no doubt, one day or another, blood will be spilt between us. But in this matter our interests coincide.'

The other stroked his well-trimmed moustache and goatee thoughtfully, although they were still not so much hair as down.

'This merchandise is precious to you, then?'

'To you, it's worth nothing.'

'And for the Corbins?'

'It is worth the price they have been offered. I think they are only hirelings in this business and soon they will deliver the goods to their employers. For my purposes, it will be too late to act once that occurs, and you will have lost a beautiful opportunity to give them a taste of their own medicine. Time is short.'

'Allow me an hour to consider it.'

The man and the half-blood exchanged a long glance, in which each delved into the heart of the other.

'One hour, no more,' Saint-Lucq stipulated.

Once Saint-Lucq had gone, the Grand Coësre asked his archisuppôt:

'What did you make of that?'

Grangier took a moment to reflect.

'Two things,' he said.

'Which are?'

'To begin with, it is in your interest to help the half-blood against the Corbins.'

'And then?'

Rather than replying, the archisuppôt turned towards the old woman who, he knew, had followed his chain of thought. Between nibbles of her wafer, her gaze still directed straight ahead like someone either blind or indifferent to the world, she said:

'The following day, he will have to be killed.'

25

Within the Cardinal's Guards, the troops received their pay every thirty-six days. This occasion demanded a roll call, which was also an opportunity to take a precise count of the Cardinal's manpower. The guards lined up. Then the captain or his lieutenant walked past with a list in hand. Each man in turn called out his name, which was immediately ticked off the list. Each ticked name was then copied out onto a list which was certified and signed by the ranking officer. This document was given to the paymaster, and the guards would go – in good order – to receive their due at his office.

Today, it had been decided that roll call would take place at five in the afternoon, in the courtyard of the Palais-Cardinal, since His Eminence was currently residing there. Unless they were excused, all the guards not currently on duty thus found themselves collected here. They were impeccably turned out – boots polished, capes pressed and weapons burnished. They waited to be called to attention and chattered amongst themselves, enjoying the idea of soon being a little richer. They might have been gentlemen in social rank, but most of them lacked fortunes of their own and lived on their pay. Happily, the cardinal paid well – fifty livres for a guard and up to four hundred for a captain. But above all, he paid punctually. Even the prestigious King's Musketeers were not remunerated so regularly.

Sitting by himself on a windowsill, Arnaud de Laincourt was reading when Neuvelle joined him. The young man, delighted to be taking part in his first roll call, was beaming.

'So, monsieur Laincourt, what will you do with your hundred-and-fifty-four livres?'

It was the pay grade of an ensign with the Cardinal's Guards.

'Pay my landlord, Neuvelle. And also my debts.'

'You? You have debts? That's not like you. Don't take this the wrong way, but I can't imagine you burning through money . . .'

Laincourt smiled amiably without replying.

'Let's see,' continued Neuvelle. 'I have observed that you don't drink and you scorn the pleasures of the table. You don't gamble. You're not vain. Do you have a hidden mistress? Rumour has it that you give all you have to good works. But you can't run into debt through acts of charity, can you?'

'My debts are with a bookseller.'

Neuvelle made a face while curling up the tips of his slender moustache, between his thumb and index finger.

'Myself, I read nothing but monsieur Renaudot's *Gazette*. You can always find a copy of it lying about somewhere. The news is sometimes a little dated, but I always find myself rather well informed.'

Laincourt nodded, his blue eyes expressing nothing other than an amiable and patient reserve.

It had been two years since Théophraste Renaudot began to produce – with royal dispensation – a highly popular news journal which was hawked on the streets. Every week his *Gazette* comprised thirty-two pages and two slim volumes – one dedicated to 'News from the East and the South', the other to 'News from the West and the North'. It also contained information pertaining to the French court. To this was added a monthly supplement which summarised and then enlarged upon the news from the preceding weeks. It was common knowledge that Cardinal Richelieu exerted tight control over everything which was printed in the *Gazette*. He had, on occasion, even taken up a pen himself and contributed to it under his own name. And, surprising as it seems, even the king did not scorn to comment on events which related closely to him in the *Gazette*.

'What are you reading at this hour?' asked Neuvelle to make conversation.

Laincourt offered him his book.

'Goodness!' said the young guard. 'Is that Latin?'

'Italian,' explained the officer, abstaining from further comment.

Like most gentleman of the sword, Neuvelle was almost illiterate. However, he could not hide his admiration of Laincourt's learning:

'I've heard that in addition to Latin and Greek you understand Spanish and German. But Italian?'

'Well, yes . . .'

'And what does this work speak of?'

'Draconic magic.'

A bell-tower, and a few others nearby, sounded three quarters of the hour, indicating to the assembled guards it was time to prepare for the roll call. Neuvelle returned the book as though it were some compromising piece of evidence and Laincourt slipped it beneath his cape and into his doublet.

At that moment, a lackey wearing the cardinal's livery walked towards them.

'Monsieur Laincourt, the service of His Eminence calls you before monsieur de Saint-Georges.'

'Now?' Neuvelle was astonished, seeing the troops being formed up.

'Yes, monsieur.'

Laincourt reassured the young guard with a glance and followed the lackey inside.

After climbing a staircase and a long wait in an antechamber, Arnaud de Laincourt saw, without real surprise, who awaited him beneath the high carved ceilings of the captain's office. The room was vast and impressive in length, its gold and its woodwork burnished to a high gleam in the daylight which shone in through two enormous windows in the rear wall. These windows opened onto the main courtyard and through them came the sound of roll call, now almost over.

Stiff and impassive, six guards renowned for their loyalty stood at attention, three to the right and three to the left, opposite each other, as though showing the way to the grand desk at which captain Saint-Georges was sitting with his back to the light. Stood close to him, and slightly further back, was Charpentier.

The presence, in this place and under these circumstances, of Richelieu's private secretary could only signify one thing, and Laincourt realised this immediately. He waited until the lackey had closed the door behind him, then took one slow step forwards between the guards. Old Brussand was one of their number and seemed to be struggling with his emotion; he stood more stiffly than the others and was almost trembling.

As all present held their breath, Laincourt pulled himself together and saluted.

'By your order, monsieur.'

Saint-Georges, his gaze severe, rose and walked around his desk.

And holding out his hand before him, he ordered in an irrevocable tone:

'Your sword, monsieur.'

At the same moment, the beat of a drum outside announced the end of the roll call.

26

'You know that it's not your fault, don't you?'

Agnès de Vaudreuil jumped as though she'd been poked in the kidneys with a blazing poker. She had been dozing and, startled by the voice, dropped the book which had been lying open on her lap. A feeling of surprise tinged with fear took hold of her, but a second was enough for her to realise that she was alone. Besides, the voice that she had heard or dreamed could only have been speaking from beyond the grave.

As soon as she returned from the inn with Ballardieu she had shut herself away in her favourite room in the manor, a very long hall almost devoid of furniture, where, when it fell, the silence seemed greater than anywhere else in the house. On one side, old suits of armour on their pedestals alternated with panoplies and racks of mediaeval weaponry. On the other side, through four tall windows with stone mullions, daylight fell in oblique rays – against which the armour seemed to be mounting a resolute guard. Two large chimneys opened their blackened brick mouths at each end of the hall originally intended to host banquets. But the chairs and the immense table had been removed, and the great iron chandeliers now looked down on empty flagstones.

Agnès was drawn to this room when times were bad, either alone or with Ballardieu. She liked to take refuge here to read, reflect or simply to wait until another day, or sometimes another night, was over. For this purpose she had arranged an area for her use around the one fireplace which could still serve against the early frosts. There was an old leather-covered armchair there, a table polished by age and use, a worm-eaten old chest, some shelves where she stored her treatises on fencing, and an old quintain.

Her entire world was here.

On this afternoon, Agnès was taking her ease with a book. She had hung her belt over the quintain, removed her boots and her thick red leather corset, and then she had ensconced herself comfortably in the armchair, legs stretched out and ankles crossed on the chest before her. But she was clearly more tired than she had thought. Sleepiness had won as she thumbed through a chapter dedicated to the comparative merits of quadruple and sextuple parries against a point lunge delivered by an adversary with the advantage of a longer reach.

Then there came the voice:

'You know that it's not your fault, don't you?'

Agnès' gaze fell on the quintain.

Before reaching the ultimate disgrace of becoming a porte-manteau, it had served as training mannequin for fencers for a long time. Its horizontal arms had been shortened by two-thirds and its bust – firmly fixed to a solid base which no longer allowed it to pivot – was covered with notches, the number of which increased in proportion to their proximity to the heart symbol engraved on the wood. It was Ballardieu, the soldier to whose care Agnès had been abandoned by her father, who had brought this worm-eaten device in from the field where it had then been serving as a scarecrow. At the time, still a child, the future baronne had to struggle, with both hands, in order to lift a rapier that was almost as tall as she. But she had refused to use any other.

The cry of a wyvern nearby tore through the silence.

Agnès pulled on her boots, rose, laced up her leather corset which fastened at the front, and, with her baldric slung over her shoulder and her sheathed rapier crossing her back, she headed for the courtyard on which the first shadows of the evening were beginning to encroach.

The wyvern rider was already climbing down from his white mount, its broad leathery wings now folded against its flanks. The beast's colour and the man's livery were unmistakable: he was a royal courier. He had evidently come straight from the Louvre.

After he had assured himself of the identity of the baronne de Vaudreuil and had saluted respectfully, the wyvern rider held out a letter drawn from the great reptile's saddle bags.

'Thank you. Is an immediate response expected?'

'No, madame.'

Seeing Marion appear on the kitchen threshold, Agnès directed the royal messenger to her so that he could partake of a glass of wine and whatever else he desired before setting out again. The man thanked her and left Agnès in the company of his wyvern which, calm and docile, twisted its long neck around to observe its surroundings with a placid eye.

Agnès broke the wax seal showing the Cardinal Richelieu's arms and, without expression, read the contents.

'What is it?' asked Ballardieu coming over for news.

She didn't reply at once, but turned her head and stared at him for a few moments.

And then, finally, for the first time in a very long while, she smiled.

27

That evening three riders passed through the Buci gate – or Bussy, as it was written then – entering the vast and peaceful faubourg surrounding Saint-Germain abbey. They rode down rue du Colombier at a slow walk, soon reached rue des Saints-Pères, passed Les Réformés cemetery and, in front of La Charité hospital, turned into rue Saint-Guillaume.

'Here we are,' said La Fargue, stepping down from his horse.

Marciac and Almades shared the same expression as they looked towards the huge gates before which they had stopped – these were massive and gloomy, with two carved, rectangular wooden panels fixed in place with large round-headed nails. They also dismounted and, as their captain rapped the wrought iron knocker three times, they observed the tranquil street which forked halfway along its length towards rue de Saint-Dominique. There were only a few people walking on its filthy paving stones beneath the golden and crimson skies at sunset, and its tradesmen were packing away their stalls. The vague odour of cooking mingled with the excremental scent of Parisian muck. Not far away, a fistful of knotted hay served as a sign for a local tavern.

'It's barely changed,' said the Gascon.

'No,' the Spanish master at arms replied laconically.

A door for pedestrians had been cut into one of the great panels of the carriage gate. This door was pushed open slightly and, from within, a voice inquired:

'Who's there?'

'Visitors,' replied La Fargue.

'Are they expected?'

'Their presence has been called for.'

This curious exchange made Marciac smile with nostalgia.

'Perhaps we should change the passwords,' murmured Marciac to Almades. 'It's been five years, after all . . .'

The other made a face: right now, all that mattered was whether the door would open for them. And it did.

La Fargue going first, they passed through the small door one by one, leading their mounts by their bits to make them lower their heads. As soon as they crossed the threshold the horses' shoes clattered loudly against the paving stones, filling the courtyard into which they emerged with echoes.

It was a massive old residence built in a severe architectural style, entirely out of grey stone, which a strict Huguenot had commissioned according to his specifications, following the massacre on the feast day of Saint-Barthélemy in 1572. It evoked the ancient fortified manors which still survive in some parts of the French countryside, whose walls are veritable ramparts and whose windows can be used as embrasures. A high wall separated the courtyard from the street. To the right, as one entered, rose the scabby, windowless wall of the neighbouring building. Opposite the gates were two coach doors leading into the stables, which were topped by a hay loft. Finally, to the left, the main building stood at an angle. Flanked by a turret and a dovecote, it comprised a tier of tiny attic windows embedded in its slate rooftop, two rows of stone-mullioned windows looking on to the courtyard, a protruding study and a ground floor which could be reached by a short flight of steps.

Abandoning his horse Marciac climbed these steps, turned towards his companions who had remained behind, and declared with affected pomposity:

'And so we have returned to Hôtel de l'Épervier, the House of the Sparrowhawk which, as you can see, has lost none of its charms . . . Damn!' he added in a lower tone. 'This place is even more sinister than I recalled, which I hardly believed possible . . .'

'This house has served us well in the past,' declared the

captain. 'And it will serve again. Besides, we are all familiar with it.'

Having closed the pedestrian door again, the person who had granted them admission now came to join them.

The old man limped on a wooden leg. Small, skinny, dishevelled, he had bushy eyebrows and his bald head was surrounded with a crown of long thin yellowish-white hair.

'Good evening, monsieur,' he said to La Fargue, holding a large bunch of keys out to him.

'Good evening, Guibot. Thank you.'

'Monsieur Guibot?' interrupted Marciac, coming closer. 'Monsieur Guibot, is it really you?'

'Indeed, monsieur, it's me.'

'I thought I recognised your voice but . . . have you really been guarding these sorry stones for the past five years?'

The man reacted as though someone had insulted his family:

'Sorry stones, monsieur? Perhaps this house is not very cheerful and no doubt you will find, here and there, a few cobwebs and some dust, but I assure you that her roof, her structure, her walls and her floors are solid. Her chimneys draw well. Her cellars and stables are vast. And of course, there is always the small door at the bottom of the garden which leads to a dead-end alley which—'

'And her?' Almades interrupted. 'Who is she?'

A young woman in an apron and white bonnet hovered on the threshold to the main building. Plump and blonde, with blue eyes, she smiled timidly while wringing her hands.

'This is Naïs,' Guibot explained. 'Your cook.'

'What about madame Lourdin?' inquired Marciac.

'She passed away last year, monsieur. Naïs is her niece.'

'Is she a good cook?'

'Yes, monsieur.'

'Can she hold her tongue?' asked La Fargue, who had his own sense of priorities.

'She is, so to speak, mute, captain.'

'What do you mean, "so to speak"?'

'She is so timid and bashful that she almost never utters a word.'

'That's not exactly the same thing . . .'

Naïs hesitated to approach, and La Fargue was about to beckon her closer when the knocker on the carriage gate was heard again. It took everyone by surprise and even made the young girl jump.

'It's him,' Guibot announced with a hint of worry in his voice.

The captain nodded, his silver hair touching the collar of his grey doublet.

'Let him in, monsieur Guibot.'

'"Him"?' asked the Gascon while the porter obeyed. 'Who is "he"?'

'Him,' said the captain lifted his chin towards the gentleman who entered the courtyard leading a bay horse by the bridle . . .

Somewhere between forty-five and fifty years old, he was tall, thin and pale, patently smug and self-assured, dressed in a crimson doublet and black breeches.

Marciac recognised him even before he caught sight of the man's well-groomed moustache and the scar on his temple.

'Rochefort.'

28

As was his habit, the young marquis de Gagnière dined at home, early and alone. An immutable ritual governed even the tiniest details of the meal, from the perfect presentation of the table to the silence imposed on the servants, as they presented a series of dishes prepared by a famous and talented rôtisseur who was accustomed to the tastes of the most demanding of his customers. The crockery laid out on the immaculate linen tablecloth was all made of vermeil, the glasses and decanters were all crystal, the cutlery silver. So luxuriously dressed that he would dazzle at court, Gagnière ate with a fork according to an Italian fashion which had not yet become commonplace in France. He cut small, equal pieces which he chewed slowly, emotionless and stiff, his gaze always directed straight ahead, and pausing between each dish he placed his hands flat to either side of the plate. When he drank he took care to wipe his mouth and moustache in order to avoid dirtying the edge of the glass.

He had finished a slice of pheasant pie when a lackey, taking advantage of one of the pauses between dishes, murmured a few words into his ear. The marquis listened without betraying any emotion or moving a muscle. Then he nodded.

A little later, Malencontre entered.

His manner was defeated; he was filthy and bedraggled, stank like a stable, had his hair stuck to his face and his left hand trussed up in a grimy bandage.

Gagnière accorded him one clinical glance.

'I gather,' he said, 'that all did not go according to plan.'

A stuffed quail was placed before him, which he proceeded to meticulously carve up.

'Your men?' he asked him.

'Dead. All of them. Killed to a man.'

'By one man?'

'Not just any man! It was Leprat. I recognised his rapier.'

Gagnière lifted a morsel of quail to his mouth, chewed, and swallowed.

'Monsieur Leprat,' he said to himself. 'Monsieur Leprat and his famous ivory rapier . . .'

'A musketeer!' insisted Malencontre as though that justified his failure. 'And one of the best!'

'Did you think the king would entrust his secret dispatches to comical lackeys . . . ?'

'No, but—'

'The letter?'

'He still has it.'

The marquis finished his quail while Malencontre watched his expressionless young face in silence. Then, having crossed his fork and spoon on his plate, he rang a small bell and said:

'You can go, Malencontre. And take proper care of your hand; you'll be less useful to me without it.'

A lackey entered to serve him and the assassin, in leaving, passed a servant who carried a sealed missive on a plate. He presented it to Gagnière, who carefully unsealed and opened it.

It was written in the vicomtesse de Malicorne's hand.

Your man has failed. The courier will arrive at the Saint-Denis gate before midnight. The letter must not reach the Louvre.

The marquis refolded the paper and allowed himself one last mouthful of wine.

At the same moment Leprat, travelling alone, was riding into the sunset on a dusty and empty road.

Lying against his heart, in the folds of his shirt, beneath his dust, sweat and dried blood stained doublet, he carried a secret piece of diplomatic mail which he had sworn to defend even at the cost of his life. Exhausted and wounded, weakened by the illness which patiently ate away at him, he galloped towards Paris and nightfall, unaware of the dangers which awaited him.

The Spanish Chevalier

1

Huge torches lit the Saint-Denis gate when the chevalier Leprat d'Orgueil arrived there an hour after nightfall. Tired, grimy, his shoulders slumped and his back in torment, he was scarcely in a better state than his horse. As for that poor beast, its head drooped, it was struggling to put one foot in front of the other, and was in danger of stumbling with every step.

'We're here, my friend,' said Leprat. 'You've certainly earned the right to a week's rest in the stable.'

Despite his own fatigue he held his pass out with a firm hand, without removing his plumed felt hat or dismounting. Distrustful, the city militia officer first lifted his lantern to take a better look at this armed horseman with a disturbing, dangerous air: unshaven cheeks, drawn features and a hard gaze. Then he studied the paper and upon seeing the prestigious signature at the bottom, he displayed a sudden deference, saluted and ordered the gate opened.

Leprat thanked him with a nod of the head.

The Saint-Denis gate was a privileged point of access to the city of Paris. Pressed up against the new rampart and fortifications to the west that now encircled the older faubourgs, it led into rue Saint-Denis which crossed the entire width of the city's Right Bank from north to south, stretching as far as Le Châtelet and the Pont au Change bridge. During the day this almost straight arterial road teemed with turbulent, noisy life. Once twilight fell, however, it became a narrow trench that was quickly filled with mute, menacing shadows. Indeed, all of Paris offered this dangerous visage to the night.

Leprat soon realised that he was being watched.

His instincts warned him first. Then the peculiar quality of an expectant silence. And, finally, a furtive movement on a rooftop. But it was only when he drew level with La Trinité hospital that he saw the barrel of a pistol poking out between two chimneys and he suddenly dug his heels into his mount.

'YAH!'

Startled, his horse found a last reserve of energy to surge forward.

Gun shots rang out.

The balls whistled past, missing their targets.

But after a few strides at full gallop, the horse ran straight into an obstacle which slammed into its forelegs. Neighing in pain the animal fell heavily, never to rise again.

Leprat freed himself from the stirrups. The shock of impact was hard, and a sharp pain tore at his wounded arm. Grimacing, he got to his knees—

—and saw the chain.

Parisian streets had capstans at either end which made it possible to stretch a chain across the roadway – an old mediaeval device designed to obstruct the passage of the rabble in the event of a riot. These chains, which could not be unwound without a key, were the responsibility of officers of the militia. They were big and solid, too low to stop a rider but high enough to oblige the horse to jump. And in the darkness, they had been turned into a diabolical trap.

Leprat realised then that the gunmen's main objective had not been to shoot him, and that this was the true ambush, on the corner of rue Ours, not far from one of the rare hanging lanterns lit by the city authorities at twilight, which burned until their fat tallow candles were extinguished.

Three men emerged in the pale glow and more were arriving. Gloved and booted, armed with swords, they wore hats, long dark cloaks and black scarves to hide their faces.

Leprat got to his feet with difficulty, unsheathed his ivory rapier and turned to face the first of the men charging towards him. He dodged one and let him pass, carried on by his momentum. He blocked the second's attack and shoved the third with his shoulder. He struck, pierced a throat, and recoiled *in extremis* to avoid a blade. Two more masked killers presented themselves. The chevalier d'Orgueil broke away and counterattacked at once. He seized one of his new assailants by the collar and threw him against a wall while continuing to defend himself with his sword. He parried, riposted and parried again, endeavouring to set the rhythm of the engagement, to repulse or elude one adversary in time to take on the next. Although being left-handed gave him a small advantage, the reopened wound on his arm handicapped him and his adversaries had the advantage of greater numbers: when one faltered, another took his place. Finally, he skewered the shoulder of one and with a violent blow of his pommel, smashed in the temple of another. This attack earned him a vicious cut to his thigh, but he was able to step back as the combatant with the wounded shoulder fled and his partner fell dead on the muddy pavement.

The two remaining assassins paused for a moment. They moved prudently, with slow gliding steps, to corner the chevalier. He placed himself *en garde*, his back to the wall, careful to keep both of them in his field of vision. His arm and thigh were giving him pain. Sweat prickled in his eyes. As the assassins seemed unwilling to take the initiative, Leprat guessed that they were expecting reinforcements, which were not long in arriving: three men were coming down rue Saint-Denis at a run. No doubt the same men who had fired on him from the rooftops.

Leprat could not afford to wait for them.

He altered his guard slightly, pretending to attack the adversary to his left and thereby offering an opening to the one on the right, only to abruptly change his target. The ivory caught a ray of moonlight before slicing cleanly through a fist which remained clenched around a sword hilt. The amputee screamed and beat an immediate retreat, clutching his stump which was bleeding in vigorous spurts. Leprat promptly forgot him and pivoted in time to deflect a sword thrust aimed at his face. Parrying twice, he seized an over-extended arm, pulled the man towards him and head butted him full in the mouth, then followed it with a blow of the knee to his

crotch and finally delivered a reverse cut with his sword that
slit the man's throat.

Letting the body fall into the blood-soaked mud, the
chevalier snatched a dagger from its belt and made ready to
face the three latecomers. He deflected the first thrust with his
white rapier, the second with the dagger and dodged the third
which, rather than slicing through his eye as far as his brain,
merely left a scratch across his cheek. Then he shoved one
brawler away with a blow from his boot, succeeded in stopping the blades of the two others with a high parry, and with
the ivory grating beneath the double bite of steel, heaved them
both back and to the side, forcing their blades downward. His
dagger was free: he stabbed it into one assailant's exposed
flank three times. Pressing his advantage, Leprat planted a
foot firmly on a boundary stone and, spinning into the air,
decapitated the man he had just kicked away before the latter
managed to fully recover his balance. A bloody scarlet spray
fell in a sticky rain over the chevalier d'Orgueil and his third,
final opponent. They exchanged a number of attacks, parries
and ripostes, each advancing and retreating along an ima-
ginary line, mouths drawn into grimaces and exchanging
furious glares. At last the assassin made a fatal error and his
life came to a swift end when the slender ivory blade slid
beneath his chin and its stained point exploded from the back
of his head.

Drunk from exhaustion and combat, weakened by his
wounds, Leprat staggered and knew he was in a bad way. A
violent retch doubled him over and forced him to lean against
a door as he vomited up long strands of black ranse phlegm.

He believed the fight was over, until he heard a horse
approaching at a slow walk.

Keeping one hand against the wall at whose foot he had
vomited, Leprat peered to one side, his tired eyes straining to
make out the rider advancing towards him.

He was a very young and very elegant gentleman with a
blond moustache, mounted on a lavishly harnessed horse.

'My congratulations, monsieur Leprat.'

All his limbs in agony, the chevalier made an effort to

straighten up, although he felt as if even a breath of wind would knock him over.

'To those with whom I am unacquainted, I am "monsieur le chevalier d'Orgueil".'

'As you wish, monsieur le chevalier d'Orgueil. I beg your pardon.'

Leprat spat out the remains of blood and bile.

'And you. Who are you?'

The rider offered a sympathetic smile and levelled a loaded pistol at the chevalier.

'It is of very little importance, monsieur le chevalier d'Orgueil, if you carry my name with you to your grave.'

The chevalier's eyes flared.

'A man of honour would face me with his feet on the ground and draw his sword.'

'Yes. No doubt he would.'

The marquis de Gagnière took aim and shot Leprat with a pistol ball straight to the heart.

2

In bed a little earlier than usual, Armand Jean du Plessis de Richelieu was reading when he heard the scratch at the door. Candles were burning and on this cold spring night a huge, greedy log fire burned in the hearth. Of the three secretaries who shared the cardinal's chamber, always ready to take down a letter by dictation or to provide the care which their master's failing health required, two slept on trestle beds arranged against the walls while the third stayed awake on a chair. This one rose, and after a nod from His Eminence, opened the door slightly, then wider still.

A Capuchin monk in his fifties entered. Dressed in a grey robe and shod in sandals, he silently approached the grand four-poster bed in which Richelieu was sitting, his back propped up against pillows to allay the pain in his back.

'This missive has just arrived from Ratisbonne,' he said, presenting a letter. 'No doubt you would like to read it before tomorrow.'

Born François-Joseph Leclerc du Tremblay, and known to the world as Père Joseph, he was of a noble family and had received a solid military education before joining the Capuchins at the age of twenty-two, by religious vocation. A reformer of his order and also founder of the Filles du Calvaire congregation of nuns, he had distinguished himself through his zeal and his sermons to the royal court. But above all, he was the famous 'Grey Eminence', the most intimate and influential of Richelieu's confederates, to whom His Eminence was prepared to entrust certain affairs of state. He sometimes took part in the deliberations of the king's Council and later became a minister of the Crown in his own right. A sincere friendship, a mutual high esteem and a shared view on the policies needed to counter Habsburg influence in Europe united the two men.

Closing his copy of Plutarch's *Lives*, the cardinal took the missive and thanked him.

'There is one other thing,' said Père Joseph.

Richelieu waited, then understood and ordered his secretaries out. When the one who was on duty had wakened and accompanied his colleagues into the next room, the monk took a chair and the cardinal said:

'I'm listening.'

'I would like to speak to you again about your . . . Blades.'

'I thought this matter was settled between us.'

'I yielded to you without being persuaded by all of your arguments.'

'You know that men of such temper will soon be necessary to France—'

'There are other men beside these.'

Richelieu smiled.

'Not so many. And when you say "these", you're thinking "him", aren't you?'

'It is true that I have little love for monsieur de la Fargue. He is inflexible and has disobeyed you too often.'

'Really?'

Père Joseph launched into a rapid inventory, ticking each item off on his fingers.

'To refresh your memory: in Cologne, in Breda, and in Bohemia. And I've not even mentioned the disaster at La Rochelle—'

'If La Rochelle was torn from the bosom of France to become a Protestant republic, I do not think that the responsibility can be laid at Captain La Fargue's door. After all, if the dam we built had resisted the force of the ocean tides for a few more days, the outcome would be quite different today . . . As for the other events you mention, I believe that La Fargue only "forgot" his orders when doing so increased the chances of his mission's success.'

'He will always be headstrong. He is one of those men who never change.'

'I certainly hope so.'

Père Joseph sighed, reflected a moment, and then returned to his argument:

'And what do you think will happen when La Fargue uncovers the secret motives behind the task we are about to confer on him? He will feel deceived and, in view of his grievances against you, he could be tempted to ruin everything. If he stumbles across the comte de Pontevedra's true identity—!'

'He would have to stumble across the comte's existence first.'

'He will, without question. Your Blades are spies as much as they are soldiers. They have no end of craftiness and imagination, and we have seen them unravel far more complicated knots than this.'

It was His Eminence's turn to utter a sigh.

'If it comes to that, we shall take the necessary measures . . . For the moment, what matters is that this mission is vital for France. And for reasons with which you are well acquainted, the Blades are the ones best able to carry it out successfully – as well as the ones who must be prevented from learning about this cabal . . .'

'A curious paradox.'

'Yesterday I told the captain that I do not always have a choice of weapons. It's very true. In this business, the Blades are the weapon which I must employ. Spain has set her conditions. I have preferred to give her some degree of satisfaction rather than seeing her harm us.'

Père Joseph nodded resignedly.

'You're tired,' continued the cardinal in a solicitous, almost affectionate, tone. 'Take some rest, my friend.'

In the Palais-Cardinal the monk's chamber was next to Richelieu's. Père Joseph glanced at the door leading to it.

'Yes,' he said. 'You're right.'

'And if it helps you sleep, remember that we are speaking of a ship that has already set sail and cannot be recalled to port.'

Père Joseph look puzzled.

'At this very moment,' explained the cardinal, 'Rochefort is briefing La Fargue on the details of his assignment.'

'So the dice are thrown.'

3

'Thank you,' Marciac said to Naïs as she placed a bottle of wine on the table. 'You should go and lie down, now.'

The pretty young servant thanked him with a smile and, looking truly tired, took her leave accompanied by an admiring glance from the Gascon.

He and Almades were in the main room of the Hôtel de l'Épervier, where Naïs had just served them an excellent dinner. The remains of their meal and several empty bottles stood on the long oak table around which the Blades used to meet and, so it seemed, would be meeting once again. For the time being, however, there were only the two of them and the immense room seemed bleak. The fire in the hearth was not enough to brighten it, any more than it was enough to warm it. It crackled, sang, groaned and seemed to throw itself fiercely into a battle already lost against the advancing shadows, and the silence and the cold of the night.

'She's lovely, that girl,' offered Marciac, to make conversation.

The Spanish master at arms didn't respond.

'Yes, quite charming,' Gascon tried again.

Less carefree than he wished to appear, he drew a pack of cards from his pocket and proposed:

'Shall I deal you a hand?'

'No.'

'Name your game. Or a throw of the dice?'

'I don't play.'

'Everyone plays!'

'Not me.'

Discouraged, Marciac fell against the back of the chair, which creaked ominously.

'You've always been dreadful company.'

'I am a master of arms. Not an exhibitor of bears.'

'You're an entirely dismal individual.'

Almades drank three small sips of wine.

'Always in threes, hmm?' said the Gascon.

'Excuse me?'

'Nothing.'

With a heavy sigh, Marciac rose and walked around the room.

He was one of those men whose roguish charm and nonchalance is emphasised by their neglect of their appearance. His cheeks bore a three-day stubble a shade darker than his blond hair; his boots were in need of brushing and his trousers of ironing; his unbuttoned doublet gaped open over his shirt; and he carried his blade with a studied but unforced nonchalance that seemed to say: *Don't be fooled, old chap. I have a good friend at my side whose weight is so slight that she's no burden to me, and upon whom I can always rely.* His eyes, finally, glittered with laughter combined with a mocking intelligence; the eyes of a man no more easily deceived by himself than by life's great comedy.

Almades, on the other hand, was severity incarnate. Fifteen years older than the Gascon, black-haired and with a grizzled moustache, he was as economical with his gestures as he was with his words, and even at the best of times his long angular face expressed nothing but an austere reserve. He was neatly dressed despite wearing an old mended doublet; the feather was missing from his hat, while the cuffs and collar of his shirt bore lace that had seen better days. It could thus be guessed that he was poor. But his state of destitution in no way altered his dignity: it was simply one more test in life that he faced with a stoicism as proud as it was unshakeable.

While Marciac paced fretfully, the Spaniard remained like marble, head lowered, his elbows on the table and his hands clasped together around the tin beaker he was turning round and round and round.

Three turns, then a pause. Three turns, a pause. Three turns . . .

'How long have they been in there, do you reckon?'

The fencing master directed a dark, patient eye towards the Gascon. With a thumb, Marciac indicated the door behind which La Fargue and Rochefort were closeted together.

'I don't know.'

'One hour? Two?'

'Perhaps.'

'I wonder what they're saying. Do you have any idea?'

'No.'

'And it doesn't intrigue you?'

'When the time comes, the captain will tell us everything we need to know.'

Marciac, thoughtful, ran his nails up his stubbled cheeks.

'I could press my ear against the door and listen.'

'No, you couldn't.'

'Why not?'

'Because I forbid you from doing so, and I shall also prevent you.'

'Yes, of course you would. That's an excellent reason.'

The Gascon returned to his chair like a scolded schoolboy.

He drained his glass, refilled it and, rather than say nothing, asked:

'So what were you doing, during the past five years?'

Perhaps with the intention of diverting Marciac's attention from the door, Almades made an effort to reply.

'I practised my trade. In Madrid to begin with. Then in Paris.'

'Ah.'

'And you?'

'The same.'

'Because you have a trade.'

'Err . . . In fact, no,' the Gascon admitted.

But he added quickly:

'That's not to say I have not been very busy!'

'I don't doubt it.'

'I have a mistress. That can keep you occupied, a mistress.

Her name is Gabrielle. I shall introduce you to her when she stops hating me. Very beautiful, nevertheless.'

'Prettier than little Naïs?'

Marciac was known for his many amorous adventures.

He caught the allusion and, a poor loser, shrugged his shoulders.

'The one has nothing to do with the other.'

A silence fell beneath the dark ceiling, which the sound of the fire was barely able to fill.

'They don't care much for one another,' said the Gascon finally.

'Who?'

'La Fargue and Rochefort.'

'No one likes Rochefort. He does the cardinal's dirty work. A spy, and no doubt also an assassin.'

'And what are we, then?'

'Soldiers. We fight in a secret war, but it's not the same thing.'

'Nevertheless, there's a feud between those two which goes far beyond the ordinary quarrel.'

'You think so?'

'I'm sure of it. You've seen the scar Rochefort bears on his temple?'

Almades nodded.

'Well, never mention it in front of Rochefort when the captain is present. Rochefort could take it as a mocking reference. He might think you know how it got there.'

'And you . . . you know?'

'No. But I act as though I do. It gives me a certain air.'

The Spaniard let this remark pass without comment, but said:

'I'd like you to shut up now, Marciac.'

The door opened and Rochefort crossed the room without sparing a glance for either of them. La Fargue appeared behind him. He walked to the table, sat down astride a chair and, preoccupied, began to pick at the remaining food on the plates.

'So?' asked Marciac innocently.

'So we have a mission,' replied the veteran of numerous wars.

'Which is?'

'Briefly put, it is a question of serving Spain.'

Spain.

The sworn enemy of France: Spain, and her Court of Dragons.

The news fell as heavily as an executioner's axe on the block, and even the exceptionally reserved Almades raised a wary eyebrow on hearing it.

4

Armed with the information that the Grand Coësre had given him, Saint-Lucq waited for dawn before springing into action.

The location proved to be perfect for his purpose: discreet, hidden from the road by the wood that surrounded it and less than an hour from Paris. It was on the farthest fringe of the faubourg Saint-Jacques, a short distance from a hamlet whose presence was indicated by a silent bell-tower. An old mill, whose large waterwheel no longer turned, had been built on the bank of the river. Its stones stood firmly in place, but its roof – like those of the other buildings in the vicinity: a woodshed, a granary, a miller's house – had suffered from years of exposure to the weather. A solid wall still enclosed the abandoned property. Its front porch opened on to the only road which passed by, not much travelled since the mill had stopped working.

How did the Grand Coësre know the Corbins – the Crows – had established one of their hideouts in this place? And how did he know that Saint-Lucq would find what he wanted here? Perhaps it was of minor importance. All that mattered, in the end, was that the information was accurate. The reasons that had persuaded the king of the Cour des Miracles to help the half-blood remained shadowy and unclear. Certainly, it would be in his interest if Saint-Lucq's plan succeeded and he made some mischief for the Corbins. The gang had held sway over the province and the faubourgs for the past two years and their attention had now turned to the capital. A battle for territory was brewing, which the Grand Coësre no doubt wished to forestall. But above all he feared that the Corbins' activities, even indirectly, would harm him to some greater or lesser extent in the long term. These highwaymen plundered, raped, were quick to use torture and often murdered. They terrorised the population and infuriated the authorities, who would ultimately react brutally and instinctively, mobilising a regiment out of necessity and erecting dozens of gibbets. The Corbins were running to their own destruction. However, not all of the blows directed against them would strike the gang. The Court of Miracles would also suffer the consequences and its leader wished to avoid them. Nevertheless, Saint-Lucq had played a dangerous game in going to find him in his fiefdom on rue Neuve-Saint-Sauveur and demanding information in such a challenging manner. Time was running short, to be sure, and the half-blood would stop at nothing to achieve his objectives. But one day he would pay the price for his audacity. The Grand Coësre's hand could not be forced with impunity.

A man was dozing in a chair in front of the miller's house, his sword hanging from the back of the chair and his pistol resting across his thighs. His hat was tipped down across his eyes, and he was wrapped up in one of the big black cloaks which were the gang's distinctive sign. He had been on guard, shivering in the cold, all night.

Another Corbin left the house. Dressed in leather and coarse cloth, he stretched, yawned, scratched his side with one hand and the back of his neck with the other, and then shook his accomplice by the shoulder. The guard sat up and stretched in turn. They exchanged a few words and then the man in leather walked away, undoing his belt as he went. He went into the woodshed where the horses were stabled, pulled down his trousers, squatted, urinated loudly with a sigh of ease and had begun to defecate when Saint-Lucq garrotted him from behind.

Unable to call for help, the brigand tried to seize the thin strap which bit into his flesh and stood up abruptly. The half-blood matched his movement without reducing the pressure on the strap and drew his victim with him as he backed up two steps. The Corbin's ankles were trapped inside his dropped breeches. His arms thrashing, he tipped over backwards but could not fall as Saint-Lucq held him suspended halfway to the ground, strangling him under his own weight. The man fought, struggling as much as he could. His heels frantically dug into the urine-saturated ground. A death rattle was torn from his chest as his face turned crimson. His fingernails scratched deeply into his tortured throat, clawing uselessly at the leather garrotte. Then he tried to strike back, his fists furiously pummelling the air in front of the half-blood's face. Saint-Lucq, impassive and focused, simply drew his shoulders back. Terror emptied the remaining contents of the unfortunate man's bowels. Brown, sticky faeces stained his thighs before falling to the ground with a soft squelch. With a final spurt of effort, the Corbin searched desperately for a foothold, for some support, for a rescue which was not coming. His struggles weakened. Finally, his windpipe collapsed and his sex released its last, smelly dregs. His tongue hanging out, his eyes rolling up, the man slowly collapsed into his own excrement, still held by his torturer.

The horses had barely stirred.

Dropping the soiled corpse, Saint-Lucq rewound his garrotte and pushed his red spectacles further up his nose before going to look outside.

The brigand on guard duty was still at his post. Legs stretched out and ankles crossed, fingers interlaced over his stomach and his hat covering his eyes, he was dozing in a chair, its back tipped against the wall of the house.

The half-blood drew his dagger and, advancing with a determined step which he meant to be heard, walked towards the man. The other heard his approach but mistook it for the return of his companion.

'So? Feeling better?' he asked without raising his nose.

'No.'

The Corbin jumped with a start and dropped the pistol resting across his thighs. Swiftly, Saint-Lucq slapped a hand against his mouth to both silence him and force him back down into his chair, and struck with his dagger, upwards from beneath his chin. The blade went home with a dry thump, pierced the brigand's palate and dug deep into his brain. He died in an instant, his eyes wide-eyed and full of pain.

The half-blood dried the dagger on the Corbin's shoulder and left the body slumped limply on the chair, its arms hanging. He had counted six horses in the woodshed. Six minus two. Four men remained.

He went to the front door and pressed an ear to it before gently pushing it open. Inside, two brigands who had just risen were talking while eating a frugal meal. Both had their backs turned to him, with one sitting on a small upturned barrel and the other on a wobbly stool.

'We'll be running out of wine soon.'

'I know.'

'And bread. And you wanted to feed him—'

'I know, I know . . . But we'll be finished with this business today.'

'You said that yesterday.'

'Today, I tell you. They can't be much longer.'

Saint-Lucq entered silently. As he passed, he picked up a poker which had been abandoned on the mantelpiece above a long-unused fireplace.

'In any case, I'm not spending another night in this ruin.'

'You'll do as you're told.'

'We'll see about that!'

'No, you'll see. You remember Figard?'

'No. I never knew him.'

'That's because he disobeyed an order before you arrived.'

Saint-Lucq was on them quicker and more silently than any ordinary assassin. The first collapsed, his skull split by the poker. The second only just had time to rise before falling in turn, his temple shattered.

Two seconds, two blows. Two deaths. No cries.

The half-blood was on the point of letting the bloody poker fall onto the stomach of one of the dead bodies when he heard the squeak of hinges.

'So, lads?' someone said. 'Already busy stuffing your faces, are you?'

Saint-Lucq about-turned and flung out his arm.

The poker hummed as it whirled through the air and drove itself, hook first, between the eyes of the Corbin who, hatless and dishevelled, had so casually entered the room. Stunned, the man staggered backward and crumpled onto the floor.

Four and one made five – the count was still short.

His right hand tightening around the hilt of his sheathed rapier, Saint-Lucq slipped into the room the dead brigand had just come from.

Makeshift beds had been set up in there and, Saint-Lucq found the last surviving Corbin lying on one of them, paralysed by absolute terror. He was young, an adolescent of perhaps fourteen or fifteen years old. His lip sported no more than blond fuzz and bad acne ate at his cheeks. Woken with a start, he seemed unable to tear his gaze from the corpse and the wrought iron rod embedded in its face. The poker began to tip over very slowly, its point spattered with viscous fluid and lifting up a piece of skull bone which tore through the skin. With a final cracking sound, it toppled and fell to the floor with a clatter.

The sound made the adolescent quiver all over and he suddenly directed his attention towards the half-blood wearing red spectacles. Looking deathly pale and distraught, his eyes already filled with tears, he vainly tried to force out a few words, vigorously shaking his head – a quiet, desperate supplication. Rising from his bedcovers, he retreated until his hands and heels touched the wall. He wore nothing but a shirt and a pair of breeches, breeches that were now stained with urine.

'Mer . . . Mercy—'

Saint-Lucq took a slow step towards him and drew his sword.

Lucien Bailleux shook with fear, cold and exhaustion. He wore nothing but a nightshirt and the hard ground on which he was lying proved as chilled as the stones against which he sometimes leaned.

It had been three nights since he had been surprised, unsuspecting, in his sleep at home, in the apartment where he lived above his notary's office. They had gagged him before pulling a hood over his head and knocking him senseless. What had they done with his wife, who had been sleeping at his side? He had woken here, bound hand and foot, in a location he could only guess at due to the hood. He was attached to a wall by a short, heavy chain that ran around his waist. He had no idea on whose authority he was held. All he knew for sure was that he was no longer in Paris, but somewhere in the countryside. The noises from his present surroundings, which also allowed him to keep track of the passing days, had made that much clear to him.

Initially believing he had been abandoned he had chewed away his cloth gag and shouted, yelling until his voice broke. He'd finally heard a door open, the footsteps of several men in boots approaching and a voice, at last, saying to him:

'It's just you and us, here. No one else can hear you. But your shouting annoys us.'

'What . . . what do you want with me?'

Rather than answering him, they had beaten him. In the stomach and kidneys. A kick had even dislodged one of his teeth. He'd swallowed it, as his mouth filled with blood.

'Not the head!' the voice had said. 'We must deliver him alive.'

After that, the notary had done nothing to draw attention to himself. And the hours and the nights had dragged by, filled with anguish and uncertainty about his fate, and without anyone troubling to give him something to eat or drink . . .

Someone pushed the door open and entered.

Bailleux cowered reflexively.

'I beg you,' he mumbled. 'I will give you everything I have.'

His hood was removed and, once he grew used to the light, he saw a man squatting close beside him. The stranger was dressed as a cavalier, with a sword at his side and strange red glass spectacles covering his eyes. Something dark and threatening emanated from him. The notary grew even more frightened.

'Don't hurt me, please . . .'

'My name is Saint-Lucq. The men who abducted you are dead. I've come to free you.'

'Me . . . To free me . . . Me?'

'Yes.'

'Who . . . who sent you?'

'It's not important. Did you talk?'

'I'm sorry?'

'You've been beaten. Was it to make you talk? Did you tell them what you know?'

'Good Lord! What is this all about?'

The half-blood sighed and patiently explained:

'You recently discovered and read a forgotten testament. The testament indicated where a certain document could be found.'

'So, this is about . . . that?'

'Well?'

'No. I didn't say anything.'

Saint-Lucq waited.

'I swear to you!' the notary insisted. 'They didn't ask me a single question!'

'Good.'

Only then did the half-blood unfetter Bailleux, who asked:

'And my wife?'

'She is well,' replied Saint-Lucq, who in truth had no idea.

'Thank God!'

'Can you walk?'

'Yes. I am weak but—' There was the sound of a horse neighing in the distance and they heard hoof beats approaching. Leaving the notary to complete the task of freeing his ankles, Saint-Lucq went to the door. Bailleux took note of his surroundings. They were on the ground floor of a disused, dusty old water mill, close to the enormous grindstone.

Having risked a glance outside, the half-blood announced:

'Six horsemen. No doubt those to whom you were to be delivered.'

'Lord God!'

'Do you know how to fight? Or at least how to defend yourself?'

'No. We are lost, aren't we?'

Saint-Lucq spotted an old, worm-eaten wooden staircase and raced up the steps.

'Up here,' he said after a brief moment.

The notary followed him to the next floor, where the central driveshaft, attached to the hub of the huge waterwheel, joined the vertical axle which, passing through the floor, had formerly powered the grindstone.

The half-blood forced open a skylight.

'We have to slip out through here and let ourselves drop into the river. The current will carry us away. With a little luck, we won't be seen. Although it's a shame, because I had horses waiting for us in the wood.'

'But I can't swim!'

'You'll learn.'

5

That morning, reclining on a long, low seat, the vicomtesse de Malicorne was savouring the tranquillity of her flowering garden when the marquis de Gagnière was announced. The strange globe filled with its shifting darkness was next to her, on its precious stand, and she caressed it nonchalantly – as she might have stroked the head of a sleeping cat. The turbulent interior of the Sphère d'Âme seemed to respond to each stroke. Gagnière, arriving on the terrace, made a conscious effort to look elsewhere. He knew the dangers that the soul sphere represented. He also knew the use to which it was destined to be put, and the casual manner with which the young woman was treating this relic, entrusted to her by the Masters of the Black Claw, both worried and astonished him.

'Good morning, monsieur le marquis. What have you come to tell me at such an early hour?'

'Leprat is dead.'

'Leprat?'

'The messenger Malencontre and his men failed to stop between Brussels and Paris. Using your information I laid an ambush for him yesterday evening, near the Saint-Denis gate.'

'Monsieur Leprat . . .' sighed the young woman with a thoughtful look. 'Is that so?'

'One of the King's Musketeers,' Gagnière hastened to explain.

'And formerly one of the Cardinal's Blades. I told you you would be hearing more about them, didn't I?'

'Indeed. However—'

'You killed him?'

'Yes. With a pistol ball to the heart.'

'My congratulations. And the letter?'

The elegant marquis took a deep breath.

'He didn't have it.'

For the first time since their conversation began, the vicomtesse lifted her gaze to look at her visitor. Her angelic face remained unreadable, but her eyes burned with fury.

'Excuse me?'

'He did not have it on him. Perhaps he never had it at all.'

'So he was simply playing with us while the true messenger travelled discreetly, by a different route and without mishap?'

'I believe so.'

'Yes,' said the vicomtesse de Malicorne, contemplating her garden anew. 'It's certainly possible, after all . . .'

They were silent for a moment and Gagnière did not know what to do with himself; his perfect manners forbade him from taking a seat without invitation so he was forced to remain standing, ill at ease, his beige deer-skin gloves in his hand.

'If the letter is at the Louvre—' he began.

'That indicates that the king and the cardinal now know we represent a threat to France,' finished the pretty young woman. 'I'll wager that the prospect of facing the Black Claw within their kingdom does not enchant them.'

From the little smile she displayed, however, one could guess that this development, upon reflection, did not truly displease her.

'It's no use crying over spilt milk,' she concluded. 'For the moment we have other matters to attend to . . .'

She suddenly rose and, taking the arm of the marquis, asked him to stroll with her in the garden. This initiative surprised Gagnière, until he realised that the vicomtesse wished to be out of range of any listening ears. Even here, in her own home.

'You will recall,' she said at last, 'that our Spanish brothers and sisters promised to send us a trustworthy man. And so they have: Savelda is here in Paris.'

'I still think we should not let him know of our plans.'

'Impossible,' interrupted the vicomtesse. 'On the contrary,

give him a warm welcome. Do not hide anything from him and employ him as usefully as possible. If it is understood, between you and I, that Savelda's mission is to keep us under surveillance, then we should not reveal our suspicions. We must show ourselves to be grateful of the honour the Grand Lodge of Spain does us by placing a man of his worth at our disposal . . .'

'Very well.'

This matter being settled, the vicomtesse turned to another subject:

'When will you capture Castilla?'

'Soon. Tonight, even.'

'And the girl?'

'Castilla shall lead us to her and we will abduct her.'

'Charge Savelda with the task.'

'What—!'

'It will keep him busy. And that will leave us with a freer hand to prepare our first initiation ceremony. Once that has taken place, a Black Claw lodge shall exist in France and our Spanish brothers, jealous as they may be, shall not be able to do anything against us.'

'You will then take the rank of Master.'

'And you, that of First Initiate . . . but do not cry victory just yet. Many have failed because they were too quick to believe they had succeeded and did not see danger coming. In our case, I do foresee that there is danger.'

At the bottom of the garden, in a verdant nook, was a stone bench. The vicomtesse took a seat, and indicated to Gagnière that he should join her.

'There is one matter,' she murmured, 'about which Savelda and our masters must be kept in ignorance: one of our agents at the Palais-Cardinal was caught yesterday.'

'Which one?'

'The best. The oldest. The most precious.'

'Laincourt!'

'Yes. Laincourt . . . I still don't know how it was done, but it has happened. Monsieur de Laincourt was unmasked. He is under arrest now, no doubt waiting to be interrogated.'

'Where?'

'Le Châtelet.'

'Laincourt won't talk.'

'That remains to be seen. You will need, perhaps, to make sure of it.'

6

A long night had gone by since Captain Saint-Georges had solemnly requested his sword and in so doing indicated to Laincourt that he was under arrest for treason. The prisoner had then been led to Le Châtelet under a firm escort, where his last personal effects were removed before he was anonymously locked up. In the eyes of the world, he might just as well have vanished into the bowels of the earth.

He no longer existed.

In 1130, Louis VI had ordered a small fortified castle – or *châtelet* – built to defend the Pont au Change, which connected the Right Bank of the Seine to Ile de la Cité. Rendered useless by the construction of King Philippe Auguste's ramparts, the Grand Châtelet – as it was sometimes called to distinguish it from the Petit Châtelet built on the Left Bank at the mouth of the Petit Pont – lost its military function. But King Louis IX enlarged it, Charles IV remodelled it and Louis XII restored it. In the seventeenth century, Le Châtelet was the seat of the legal courts under the jurisdiction of the provost of Paris, while its dungeon housed the prison cells. These cells, located on various levels, were given nicknames. On the upper level were the common halls where prisoners were packed together: Beauvoir, La Salle, Barbarie and Gloriette; below that, there were three areas with individual cells: La Boucherie, Beaumont and La Griesche; lower still: Beauvais, another communal hall; and finally, in the very foundations of the place, were the worst of all, without air or light: La Fosse, Le Puits, La Gourdaine and L'Oubliette.

Laincourt had been accorded the honour of La Gourdaine, where he was forced to endure its rotting straw overrun with vermin. At least he had been spared the horror of La Fosse, a pit into which the prisoner would be lowered through a trap door, on the end of a rope. The bottom of that most infamous gaol cell was swimming in stagnant water and took the shape of an inverted cone, so that a prisoner could neither lie nor sit down, and was even denied the relief of something to lean against.

Since the door had been closed on Laincourt, the hours had passed, stretched out and silent, in absolute darkness. In the far distance he heard the echo of a scream, that of a prisoner gone mad in solitude or of some poor wretch being subjected to torture. There was also the sound of water falling slowly, drop by drop, into deep brackish puddles. And the scratching of rats against the damp stone.

And then suddenly, in the morning hours, a key scraped in the lock. A gentleman with a greying moustache entered, with whom the gaoler left a lit lantern before closing the door again.

Laincourt stood and, blinking his eyes, recognised Brussand.

'You shouldn't be here, Brussand. I'm in solitary confinement.'

'For you,' replied the other, handing him a flask of wine and a piece of white bread. The former ensign of the Cardinal's Guards gladly accepted the victuals. He tore into the bread but forced himself to chew slowly. Then, having swallowed a mouthful of wine, he asked:

'How were you able to get in here?'

'The officer in charge of admissions owed me a favour.'

'Was the favour you did him as big as this one?'

'No.'

'So now you are in his debt . . . That is regrettable and entirely unnecessary on your part. Nevertheless, you have my thanks . . . Now go, Brussand. Go before you compromise yourself completely.'

'Our time is short, in any case. But I want you to tell me something.'

Beneath his unshaved cheeks and drawn features, Laincourt gave a faint, pale smile.

'I owe you that much, my friend.'

'Just tell me that all this is untrue,' the old guard demanded. 'Tell me they've made a mistake on your account. Tell me that you are not the spy they accuse you of being. Tell me that and, in the name of our friendship, I will believe you and defend you!'

The prisoner stared at the old guard for a long time.

'I don't want to lie to you, Brussand.'

'So it's true?'

Silence.

'My God!' Brussand exclaimed. 'You . . . ? A traitor . . . ?'

Demoralised, disappointed, misled, and still incredulous, he retreated a step. Finally, like a man resigned to facing the inevitable, he took a deep breath and cried out:

'Then talk! Talk, Laincourt! Whatever happens, you will be judged and condemned. But spare yourself being subjected to questioning . . .'

Laincourt searched for the right words and then said:

'A traitor betrays his masters, Brussand.'

'So?'

'I can only swear to you that I have not betrayed mine.'

7

He woke up washed and bandaged in the room that he rented under the eaves of a house on rue Cocatrix, and he recognised the familiar décor as soon as he opened his eyes.

'So you have finally returned to us,' said a deep male voice.

Although he was rather modestly dressed, the gentleman sitting at his bedside had a natural elegance that signalled his superiority to common mortals from a hundred paces. He carried a sword, had laid his hat down close to hand and was holding a book which he now closed. He looked to be forty years old and he served in the King's Musketeers.

'Good morning, Athos,' said Leprat.

'Good morning. How are you feeling?'

Leprat sat up against the pillows with caution and took stock of his wounds. His arm was carefully bandaged, as was, beneath the sheets covering his naked body, his thigh. He was not in much pain, felt rested and had a clear mind.

'Surprisingly well,' he replied. 'The letter?'

'Don't worry, it has reached its destination. The duty officer at the Saint-Denis gate, to whom you so prudently entrusted it on your arrival in Paris, made no delay in delivering it to monsieur de Tréville . . . Are you hungry?'

'Yes.'

'That's an excellent sign.'

Athos picked up a basket which he placed on the bed between them and lifted the red-and-white chequered cloth to reveal sausage, cheese, a pot of pâté, half a round loaf of bread, a knife, two glasses and three bottles of wine.

'And so,' said Leprat while the other spread a thick layer of pâté on a slice of bread, 'I am alive.'

'Indeed. Here, this is for you, eat.'

The patient bit into the slice and found it only stimulated his appetite more.

'And how is it that I am still for this world?'

'Thank the heavens in the first instance. And monsieur de Tréville in the second . . . But start by telling me what you remember.'

Leprat searched his memories.

'Yesterday evening, after nightfall . . . it was yesterday evening, wasn't it?'

'Yes.'

'So, yesterday evening, after nightfall, I was caught in an ambush at the corner of rue Saint-Denis and rue aux Ours. I beat off most of my attackers, but the last, a gentleman, got the better of me. I remember that he shot me with a pistol ball to the heart, and after that – nothing.'

'Did you know your would-be assassin?'

'No. But from now on, I would recognise him amongst a thousand others.'

Athos nodded, thoughtful. He knew neither the details nor the heart of this mission and, being a discreet man, refused to pose any questions on the subject. He suspected that the chevalier knew little more than he did. He twisted around on his chair, unhooked Leprat's baldric from its back and said:

'This is why you should thank the heavens in the first instance. They made you left-handed.'

Leprat smiled.

'Because you are left-handed, you carry your sword on your right. The baldric comes over your left shoulder, protected the left-hand side of your chest and stopped the ball which was meant to pierce your heart. It was the force of impact alone that knocked you down, and senseless.'

'Thank God my assassin did not aim for my head . . .'

'Such are the fortunes of war. They are not always against us.'

The wounded man nodded in agreement and accepted the proffered glass of wine. He had sufficient experience to know that those in battle often owed their lives to luck.

'Although I can guess at the reason,' he said as their glasses clinked together, 'now tell me why I must thank monsieur de Tréville.'

Athos drained his glass before replying.

'Despite being alerted by the sounds of your fight, the clowns who were guarding the Saint-Denis gate only reached you at the moment when you were shot. Their arrival forced the assassin to flee. Naturally they believed you were dead at first, but then realised that you were not – or not quite. Thanks to the pass you had shown at the gate they knew you were a musketeer; one of them ran to find monsieur de Tréville while the others carried you to a doctor. Monsieur de Tréville rushed to you at once, rescued you from the claws of that quack, brought you back here and entrusted you to the good care of his own surgeon. And that's all.'

'That's all?'

'That's all.'

'But how does that explain why you now play nurse-maid?'

Athos shrugged.

'I was on duty last night,' he explained.

Cutting the discussion short, he rose, picked up his hat, and announced:

'And now I must leave you.'

'Are you returning to rue du Vieux-Colombier?'

'Yes.'

'With your permission, I'll come with you.'

'Really?'

'I believe I'm fit enough and monsieur de Tréville is no doubt waiting to hear my report . . . Just give me time to dress.'

'Very well. I shall wait for you in the corridor.'

Antoine Leprat lived on Ile de la Cité.

Dressed in clean clothes but sporting an ugly three-day beard, he was quick to rejoin Athos but begged him to permit a short stop with a barber. The other accepted all the more readily as he would also benefit from the barber's attentions. Monsieur de Tréville required that his Musketeers be – at the very least – presentable. A barber on rue de la Licorne left their cheeks clean-shaven and furnished them with the opportunity to relax and talk a little more.

'One thing intrigues me,' said Athos.

'What is that?'

'You only remember the cavalier who shot you, is that right? But the archers posted upon the Saint-Denis gate spoke of seeing a second cavalier . . . A rider dressed in light grey or in white, on a horse with a white caparison, who sat facing the first while you lay sprawled on the ground. To hear them speak, this latecomer was almost ghostly in appearance . . . And he lingered no longer than the other to be recognised.'

'I told you everything I can remember, Athos.'

Later, around ten o'clock, they crossed the Petit Pont. Like most of the bridges in Paris, the Petit Pont was built up; on either side of the narrow roadway stood a row of houses which could in no way be distinguished from those on an ordinary street and which made it possible to cross the Seine without ever catching a glimpse of the river. On the Left Bank, they followed rue de la Harpe and then rue des Cordeliers as far as the Saint-Germain gate, where they were slowed by an impatient, agitated crowd. But such delays in passing through the city gates were an unavoidable ordeal for anyone wishing to leave Paris or reach its faubourgs.

The capital was indeed fortified in its fashion. Punctuated by turrets topped with conical 'pepper pots', the mediaeval walls measured over four metres in height and overlooked a series of ditches. They were supposed to protect the city in times of war, whether domestic or foreign. However, these defences did not seem at all warlike in this period. One would search in vain for the smallest cannon. The ditches were filled with rubbish. And the ramparts were falling into ruin despite the best efforts of the city authorities to rebuild them. Parisians, who could not be fooled, said that their walls were made of nothing more than potter's clay and that one shot from a musket could create a breach, while a drum roll would be enough to bring them tumbling to the ground. Nevertheless, it was not possible to enter Paris except through one of these gates. They were large buildings as outmoded as they were dilapidated, but they accommodated the Paris tax collectors, as well as the city's militia. The first levied taxes on all merchandise entering the city while the second examined foreigners' passports. Both groups carried out their duties zealously, which did nothing to speed the flow of traffic.

Once they reached the faubourg Saint-Germain, Athos and Leprat passed before the church of Saint-Sulpice and, taking rue du Vieux-Colombier, entered the gates to the Tréville mansion.

Monsieur de Tréville being the captain of the King's Musketeers, this building was more like a military encampment than a great man's residence. It was filled with a jostling crowd and one ran a constant risk of bumping shoulders with some proud gentleman of no fortune but with a murderous eye. Although lacking in wealth, all of His Majesty's Musketeers had hot blue blood. All were ready to draw swords at the first provocation. And all of them, whether they were on duty or not and whether they wore the blue cape with its silver fleur-de-lys cross or not, tended to congregate here in their captain's house. They gathered in the courtyard, slept in the stables, mounted guard on the stairs, played dice in the antechambers and, on occasion, even joyfully crossed blades in the hallways for entertainment, training or the demonstration of the excellence of a particular series of moves. This picturesque spectacle that visitors found so striking was by no means extraordinary. In these times, most soldiers were recruited only when war loomed and then dispersed, for reasons of economy, once their services were no longer required. As for the few permanent regiments that existed, they were not barracked anywhere . . . due a lack of barracks. As members of the king's own prestigious military household, the Musketeers were among these few troops who were always available and not disbanded in peacetime. Nevertheless, no particular arrangements were made for housing them, equipping them, or supplying their daily needs: the pay they received from the king's Treasury, as paltry and irregular as it was, was supposed to suffice for these provisions.

Within the Hôtel de Tréville, everyone had heard about the ambush into which Leprat had fallen. Rumour had said that he was dead or dying, so his return to the fold was warmly greeted. Without participating in the effusive cries of joy and other virile manifestations of affection, Athos accompanied Leprat as far as the great staircase littered with musketeers, servants and various seekers of favour. There, he took his leave.

'Remember to conserve your strength, my friend. You've received a hard knock.'

'I promise you I will. Thank you, Athos.'

Leprat was announced and did not have to wait long in the antechamber. Captain de Tréville received him almost immediately in his office, rising to greet him when he entered.

'Come in, Leprat, come in. And have a seat. I am delighted to see you, but I did not expect to see you on your feet again so soon. I was even planning to come and visit you at home this evening.'

Leprat thanked him and took a chair, while monsieur de Tréville sat down again at his desk.

'First of all, how are you?'

'Well.'

'Your arm? Your thigh?'

'They both serve me once again.'

'Perfect. Now, your report.'

The musketeer began, recounting how he had initially overcome Malencontre's henchmen but allowed the leader himself to escape.

'"Malencontre", you say?'

'That's the name he gave me.'

'I'll make a note of it.'

Then Leprat quickly outlined the ambush on rue Saint-Denis and the mysterious gentleman who had shot him down without a second thought. When he finished his recital the captain rose and, hands behind his back, turned towards the window. It offered a view of the courtyard of his private mansion, a courtyard full of the musketeers he adored, protected and scolded like a father. As undisciplined and unruly as they were, there was not one of them who was not prepared to risk a thousand dangers and give his life for the king, for the queen, or for France. Most of them were young and, like all young men, they believed they were immortal. But that was not enough to explain either their fearlessness or their extraordinary devotion. Although they might not look like much, they were an elite force equal to the Cardinal's Guards.

'You should know, Leprat, that the Louvre is well pleased with you. I saw His Majesty the king this morning. He remembers you and sends his compliments . . . Your mission has been a success.'

Turning his gaze from the courtyard, Tréville faced Leprat again.

'I have been charged with sending you on leave,' he said in a serious tone.

'Thank you.'

'Don't thank me. It is to be an unlimited leave of absence.'

The musketeer stiffened in shock and disbelief.

A few days or weeks of leave were a reward. But unlimited leave signified that, until given new orders, he was to hang up his cape.

Why?

8

Entering Paris through the Richelieu gate, a two-horse coach descended the street of the same name between the Palais-Cardinal gardens and Saint-Roch hill, followed the quays of the Seine and crossed the river over a recently built wooden toll bridge: the Pont Rouge, so-called because of the red lead paint with which it was daubed. And so the coach reached the faubourg Saint-Germain which was prospering in the shadow of its famous abbey and almost constituted a city in its own right.

A new neighbourhood had sprung up, just at the far end of the Pont Rouge. Before Queen Marguerite de Navarre decided, at the beginning of the century, to make the Pré-aux-Clercs her domain the area had been nothing but a muddy riverbank and a vast empty ground. Now it comprised a new quay, a luxurious mansion, a large park and the convent of Les Augustins Réformés. The queen, who was Henri IV's first wife, had borrowed money to finance her projects and had even gone as far as to misappropriate funds – from which, it was said, came the name of Malaquais quay, meaning 'badly acquired'. Upon her death in 1615 she left behind a magnificent property, but also 1,300,000 livres in debts and a host of creditors who were still anxious to collect. To satisfy them, the domain was put up for auction and sold off in lots to various entrepreneurs who laid out new streets and started building.

Guided by the sure hand of a solidly built grey-haired coachman who chewed at the stem of a small clay pipe, the coach followed the Malaquais quay and then took rue des Saints-Pères. At Hôpital de la Charité he turned the coach onto rue Saint-Guillaume and soon came to a halt before a large and sombre looking nail-studded door.

Within the coat of arms, worn away over time, a bird of prey carved from dark stone presided on the pediment above the gate.

Sitting at the bottom of the steps to the Hôtel de l'Épervier, Marciac was bored and playing dice against himself when he heard the heavy thud at the coach door. He lifted his head to see monsieur Guibot hobbling on his wooden leg across the courtyard to see who was knocking. At the same time, Almades leaned out of an open window.

A moment later a woman entered through the pedestrian gate. Very tall, slender, dressed in grey and red, she wore a dress whose skirt was hitched up on her right side to reveal male hose and the boots of a cavalier beneath it. Her wide-brimmed hat was decorated with two large ostrich feathers – one white and the other scarlet – and a veil which hid her face while protecting it from the dust to which anyone under-taking a long coach journey on the terrible roads was exposed. But the shape of her mouth could be discerned: pretty, with full, dark lips.

Without taking any interest in Marciac, who approached her, she looked up at the private mansion as if she were considering buying it.

'Good day, madame.'

She turned towards him, looking at him haughtily without replying.

But her mouth smiled.

'How may I help you?' the Gascon tried.

From the window, Almades chose that moment to intervene.

'You have a very poor memory, Marciac. You don't even recognise your friends.'

Disconcerted, Marciac shrugged and wrinkled his brow, then went from puzzlement to sudden joy when the baronne de Vaudreuil lifted her veil.

'Agnès!'

'Hello, Marciac.'

'Agnès! Will you permit me to embrace you?'

'I will allow that.'

They hugged in a friendly fashion, although the young woman had to restrain a hand that had gone wandering down the small of her back before they separated. But the happiness which the Gascon displayed on seeing her again seemed sincere and she did not want to spoil it.

'What a delight, Agnès! What a delight . . . ! So, you too, you're back in the game?'

Agnès indicated the steel signet ring she wore over her grey leather glove.

'By my word,' she said. 'Once in . . .'

'. . . always in!' Marciac completed for her. 'Do you know how many times I have thought of you over the past five years?'

'Really? Was I dressed?'

'Sometimes!' he exclaimed. 'Sometimes!'

'Knowing you, that's a very pretty compliment.'

Almades, who had left the window, emerged from the front door of the main building.

'Welcome, Agnès.'

'Thank you. I'm very pleased to see you. I've missed your fencing lessons.'

'We can continue them at your pleasure.'

During these effusions, Guibot had toiled to open the two great doors of the carriage gate. This done, the coach entered, driven by Ballardieu who jumped down from the seat and, pipe between his teeth, smiled broadly. Once again, the greetings were jubilant and noisy, in particular between the old soldier and the Gascon: these two shared quite a few memories of bottles emptied and petticoats lifted.

They had to unhitch the coach, tow it into the stables, unload the luggage and settle the horses in their stalls. This time everyone lent the porter a hand, all the while forbidding Agnès from lifting a finger to help. She wasn't listening, but happily made acquaintance with the charmingly shy Naïs who had been drawn from her kitchen by the sound of raised voices.

La Fargue, in his turn, arrived.

Without entirely putting a damper on their joyful mood, his presence did cause them to lower their tone slightly.

'Did you have a good journey, Agnès?'

'Yes, captain. We hitched up the horses upon receiving your letter and we have burned our way through the staging posts getting here.'

'Hello, Ballardieu.'

'Captain.'

'It's still a sad place,' said the young woman, indicating the sinister grey stones of the Hôtel de l'Épervier.

'A little less now,' said Marciac.

'Is that everyone, captain?'

Looking stern and proud, girded in his slate-grey doublet and with his hand resting on the pommel of his sheathed sword, La Fargue blinked slowly and paused before replying, his gaze drifting towards the carriage gate.

'Almost, now.'

The others turned and immediately recognised the man standing there, with a white rapier at his side, smiling at them in a way which might have been melancholic or simply sentimental.

Leprat.

9

On Sundays and feast days, when the weather was fine, Parisians were happy to travel beyond the capital for their pleasure. Once past the faubourgs the country villages of Vanves, Gentilly and Belleville, and the market towns of Meudon and Saint-Cloud offered hospitable inns where all could drink, dance, play bowls beneath the trees, or simply partake of the cool shade and fresh air. The atmosphere was joyful and people took liberties or, in the eyes of some, indulged in scandalous licence. And it is true that spontaneous revels of love-making at times took place there in the evenings, enlivened by wine and a desire to taste all of life's pleasures. There being fewer customers during the week, these establishments then became retreats which were visited mainly for their tranquillity and the quality of their table – such as *Le Petit Maure*, in Vaugirard, renowned for its peas and strawberries.

Saint-Lucq and Bailleux had temporarily found refuge in one of these inns. Having jumped into the river through a window in the water mill where the notary had been held captive, they successfully escaped the cavaliers who had come to collect their prisoner but were also carried far from their horses by the current. Rather than turn back towards their enemies Saint-Lucq had decided they would continue on foot. They therefore walked for several hours through woods and across fields, scanning the horizon on constant lookout for signs of pursuit, and arrived, exhausted, at a village with a hostelry standing by its entrance.

For the time being Lucien Bailleux found himself alone in a room on the first floor. Sitting at a table laid for the purpose, he ate with a ferocious appetite born of three days' captivity, poor treatment and fasting. He was still in his nightshirt – the same one he had been wearing when he was dragged from his bed in the middle of the night. But at least he was clean, after his forced bath in the river. Thin, his face drawn and his hair falling across his eyes, he looked exactly what he was: a survivor.

He gave a sharp, worried glance towards the door when Saint-Lucq entered without knocking. The half-blood brought a package of clothes which he threw onto the bed.

'For you. They belonged to a guest who left without paying.'

'Thank you.'

'I also found us two saddled horses,' continued Saint-Lucq, risking a quick glance out of the window. 'Can you ride?'

'Uh . . . Yes. A little . . . You think the cavaliers are still after us?'

'I'm sure of it. They want you and they've not given up the fight . . . The bodies of the brigands I killed at the mill were still warm when they arrived and as a result, these cavaliers know they only missed us by a tiny margin. And if they found the horses I had planned to use in our flight, they also know there are two of us, and that we are on foot. They are no doubt scouring the countryside for us at this very moment.'

'But we'll escape them, won't we?'

'We'll have a chance if we don't delay. After all, they don't know where we're going.'

'To Paris?'

'Not before we've reclaimed that document. Not before we've put it in a safe place. Get dressed.'

A little later, Bailleux was just finishing dressing when he broke down. He dropped onto the bed, put his face in his hands and burst into sobs.

'I . . . I don't understand,' was all he managed to say.

'What?' said the stone-faced half-blood.

'Why me? Why has all this happened to me . . .? I've led the most orderly of lives. I studied and worked with my father before inheriting his position. I married the daughter of a colleague. I was a good son and I believe I am a good husband. I'm charitable and I pray. I conduct my business with honour and honesty. And in return, I have asked for nothing but to be allowed to live in peace . . . So why?'

'You opened the wrong testament. And, what is worse, you let that fact be known.'

'But it was my duty as a notary!'

'Undoubtedly.'

'It's not fair.'

To that, Saint-Lucq did not reply.

From his point of view, there was no fairness in life. There were only strong men and weak ones, the rich and the poor, the wolves and the sheep, the living and the dead. That was how the world was, and how it would always be. Anything else was merely fiction.

He approached the notary in the hope of encouraging him to get a grip on himself. The notary rose suddenly and hugged him hard. The half-blood braced himself as the other spoke:

'Thank you, monsieur. Thank you . . . I don't know who you are, in truth. I don't know who sent you . . . But without you . . . My God, without you . . .! Believe me when I say that you have my eternal regard, monsieur. There is nothing, from now on, that I could refuse you. You saved me. I owe you my life.'

Slowly but firmly, Saint-Lucq moved away from him.

Then, his hands resting on Bailleux's shoulders, he gave him a shake and ordered:

'Look at me, monsieur.'

The notary obeyed and the crimson spectacles returned his gaze.

'Do not thank me,' continued Saint-Lucq. 'And do not trouble yourself any further with the question of who employs me, or why. I do what I do because I'm paid to. If I had been required to kill you, you would be dead. So never thank me again. My place is neither in sensational novels, nor in the chronicles of our times. I'm not a hero. I'm only a swordsman. Contrary to your opinion, I do not deserve anyone's esteem.'

Initially incredulous, Bailleux was visibly hurt by this declaration.

Finally, still looking dazed, he nodded and pulled on the beret the half-blood had brought him.

'We should hurry,' concluded Saint-Lucq. 'Each minute that passes is a minute lost.'

The notary left the room first and while he climbed gracelessly into the saddle in the courtyard the half-blood paused inside for a moment to pay the landlord and slip a few words into his ear. The man listened to his instructions attentively, then nodded and pocketed an additional piece of gold.

Less than half an hour after Saint-Lucq and Bailleux left, armed riders arrived. The landlord was waiting for them on the doorstep.

10

In the dining room of the Hôtel de l'Épervier, the Cardinal's Blades finished their lunch.

Seated at the head of the rough oak table, La Fargue spoke very seriously with Leprat and Agnès. Marciac listened, close by, and occasionally made an interjection but otherwise contented himself with rocking back and forth on his chair and shuffling a deck of cards which, inevitably, then turned out to have all four aces on top. Almades, silent, waited. As for Ballardieu, he digested his lunch while smoking a pipe and sipping the last of the wine, not without casting longing glances at Naïs' backside as she cleared the table.

'Pretty girl, isn't she?' Marciac said to him, seeing the old soldier ogling the comely young woman.

'Yes. Very.'

'But not very talkative. Almost mute.'

'I see an advantage there.'

'Really? What a strange idea . . .'

They had all been somewhat apprehensive of this meal, which, following the immediate and genuine rejoicing of their initial reunion, would force them to take the true measure of their friendship. What remained of the people they had been? One never knows what friends lost from sight for a long time may have become and the circumstances which led to the disbanding of the Blades during the siege of La Rochelle had laid a mournful veil over the memories of its members. This veil, however, soon lifted and the previous ties between them were quickly re-established.

As was entirely natural, the distribution of the Blades around the table indicated their affinities as well as the resumption of old habits. Thus the captain presided over the table, in close council with Agnès and Leprat whom he consulted with ease, the musketeer even acting as a lieutenant within the very informal organisation of the Blades. Marciac, remaining somewhat aloof, was one of those who knew their own value and abilities but preferred to stay on the margins, never showing himself to be unworthy and who would consider it an insult if he were ordered about. Serious and reserved, Almades waited to be called upon. And Ballardieu, accustomed to long preludes before battle, took advantage of any moment of peace.

Only three Blades, out of the original band, were missing. One of them had vanished as if the twisted shadows from which he had emerged had engulfed him once again after La Rochelle. The other had been a traitor and no one, yet, had dared to speak his name. And the last one, finally, had perished and his loss was a wound which continued to bleed in the memories of all present.

As Naïs left the room with the last plates, Agnès glanced with a question in her eye at La Fargue, who understood and nodded. The young woman rose and said with deep feeling:

'I believe, messieurs, that the time has come to raise our glasses in honour of he whom only death could keep from being here.'

They all stood, glasses in hand.

'To Bretteville!' said La Fargue.

'To Bretteville!' cried the others in chorus.

'To Bretteville,' Agnès repeated in a strangled voice, as if to herself.

The Blades re-seated themselves, divided between the joy of having known Bretteville, the pride of having loved this man and the sorrow of having lost him at the last.

'We have a mission,' La Fargue said after a moment.

They listened.

'It is a matter of finding a certain chevalier d'Ireban.'

'What has he done?' Agnès inquired.

'Nothing. He has disappeared and there is concern for his life.'

'People who have not done anything do not disappear,' Almades declared in a neutral voice.

'A Spaniard?' Marciac was surprised.

'Yes,' said the captain.

'So Spain will be busy trying to find him!'

'That is precisely what the Cardinal wishes to avoid.'

La Fargue rose, walked around his chair and leaned against the back, his hands folded.

'The chevalier d'Ireban,' he repeated, 'is the heir to a Spanish grandee. A secret and unworthy heir to the title. A corrupt young man who, under an assumed name, has come to Paris to spend his coming fortune.'

'What is his real name?' asked Almades.

'I don't know. It seems Spain would like to keep it a secret.'

'No doubt for fear of a scandal,' Ballardieu guessed. 'If his father is a grandee—'

'"If"!' Marciac interrupted. 'Should we take everything Spain says at face value?'

La Fargue silenced the Gascon with a glance and continued:

'His father is not well. He will soon be dead. And Spain has been seeking the safe return of the son since she first realised he had disappeared. Ireban seems to have vanished suddenly and it is feared he has met with some mishap in Paris.'

'If he was leading a life of debauchery,' noted Agnès, 'that's probable. And if he was keeping bad company, and they realised who he really is—'

'Once again, "ifs",' Marciac emphasised in a low voice.

'Via a special emissary,' La Fargue went on, 'Spain has explained the situation, her concerns and her intentions to our king.'

'Her "intentions"?' queried Ballardieu.

'Spain wants Ireban returned and to this end, not to mince words, she is threatening to send her agents into our kingdom if France is not prepared to do what is necessary. That is where we become involved.'

Leprat's self-restraint finally wore away.

Unable to hear any more he rose and paced a hundred steps in livid silence, his expression hard and a fire in his eyes. Firstly, he was displeased that Spain was imposing conditions upon France. But secondly, and more importantly, he had not intended to hang up his musketeer's cape only to discover, on the very same day, that he had done so in order to serve another country.

An enemy country.

La Fargue had been expecting this reaction from his Blades.

'I know what you're thinking, Leprat.'

The other stopped his pacing.

'Really, captain?'

'I know because I think just like you. But I also know that Richelieu is seeking a rapprochement with Spain right now. France will soon be at war in Lorraine and possibly in the Holy Roman Empire. She cannot allow herself to come under threat from the Pyrenees border at the same time. The cardinal needs to please Spain and so he's offering her tokens of friendship.'

Leprat sighed.

'Very well. But why us? Why recall the Blades? The cardinal does not lack for spies, as far as I know.'

The captain didn't respond.

'The mission is delicate,' Agnès began . . .

'. . . and we are the best,' added Marciac.

But as agreeable as this was to say and to hear, these explanations did not satisfy anyone.

It was a mystery which filled each of their minds.

The silence stretched out, until at last the Gascon said:

'We don't even know this chevalier d'Ireban's real name and Spain is unlikely to tell us anything more about him. Suppose he lives. Suppose he is in hiding or being held prisoner. The fact remains that there are some five hundred thousand souls in Paris. Finding one, even a Spaniard, will not be easy.'

'We have a trail to follow,' announced La Fargue. 'It is thin and no doubt cold, but it has the merit of existing.'

'What is it?' Agnès asked.

'Ireban did not come to Paris alone. He has a companion in vice. A gentleman of means, also a Spaniard. An adventurous duellist when it suits him and a great connoisseur of Paris at night. The man goes by the name Castilla. We shall begin with him. Almades, Leprat, you'll come with me.'

Those he'd named nodded.

'Marciac, stay here with Guibot and make an inventory of everything we're missing. Then this evening you will make the rounds of all the cabarets and gambling houses that Ireban and Castilla are likely to frequent.'

'Understood. But there are a lot of them in Paris.'

'You will do your best.'

'And me?' asked the baronne de Vaudreuil.

La Fargue paused for a moment.

'You, Agnès, must pay a visit. See to it.'

She already knew what he meant and exchanged a glance with Ballardieu.

Later, La Fargue went to see Leprat who was saddling horses in the stable.

'I know what this costs you, Leprat. For the rest of us, a return to service with the Blades is a benefit. But for you . . .'

'For me?'

'Your career with the Musketeers is well established. Nothing forces you to give it up and if you want my advice . . .'

The captain didn't finish.

The other man smiled warmly, obviously touched, and recalled what monsieur de Tréville had said on relaying the orders for his new mission:

'You are one of my best musketeers. I don't want to lose you, especially not if you wish to keep your cape. I will take your side. I will tell the king and the cardinal that you are indispensable to me, which is the simple truth. You could stay. You have only to say the word.'

But Leprat had not said the word.

'This mission does not inspire confidence in me,' La Fargue

continued. 'Spain is not being frank with us in this business. I fear that she intends to use us for her benefit alone, and perhaps even at the expense of France . . . At best, we shall gain nothing. But you, you have a great deal to lose.'

The former musketeer finished tightening a strap, and then patted his new mount on the rump. The animal was a beautiful chestnut, a gift from monsieur de Tréville.

'May I speak freely, Etienne?' he demanded of La Fargue.

He only spoke to the captain so personally in private.

'Of course.'

'I am a soldier: I serve where I'm told to serve. And, if that is not enough, I am a Blade.'

11

For Ballardieu, the moment of his true reunion with Paris took place on the Pont Neuf. For if the market at Les Halles was the city's belly and the Louvre was its head, then the Pont Neuf was the heart of the capital. A heart that pumped blood, giving the city life and movement, animating the great populous flow that ran through its streets. Everyone, after all, used the Pont Neuf. For convenience, primarily, since it permitted people to travel directly from one bank to the other without passing through Ile de la Cité and its maze of mediaeval alleyways. But also for the sake of entertainment.

The bridge was originally intended to support houses, as was only to be expected in a city where the tiniest building space was already utilised. But this plan was abandoned to avoid spoiling the royal family's view of the Cité from the windows of the Louvre. Of this original plan only two wide platforms survived, both six steps high and running the entire length of the bridge, on either side of the paved roadway. These platforms became pavements, the first in Paris, from which it was possible to admire the Seine and enjoy the fresh air without fear of being run over by a coach or a horse rider. Parisians soon grew to like going for a stroll there. Street artists and traders set up shop along the parapets and in the half-moon-shaped lookout points, and the Pont Neuf soon became a permanent fair, filled with jostling crowds.

'God's blood!' Ballardieu exclaimed, taking a deep breath. 'I feel like my old self again!'

More reserved, Agnès smiled.

They had come through the Nesle gate on foot and passed

in front of the Hôtel de Nevers before arriving at Pont Neuf. It was the shortest route to the Louvre, their destination.

'It is good to be here!' added the delighted old soldier. 'Don't you think?'

'Yes.'

'And nothing has changed! Look at that buffoon, I remember him!'

He pointed to a tall thin fellow in a moth-eaten cloak, mounted on the back of a poor old nag who was as gaunt as he was, boasting of a miraculous powder which he claimed would preserve your teeth. The fact that he had only one remaining tooth in his own mouth did not seem to weaken his conviction or bother his audience.

'And over there! Tabarin and Mondor . . . ! Come on, let's go hear them.'

Tabarin and Mondor were famous street entertainers who each had their own stage at the entrance to Place Dauphine. At that moment one of them was singing a bawdy song while the other, armed with an enormous enema bag, was playing at being a quack and offering all comers the chance to have 'their arseholes washed all clean and pink!' Their spectators were bursting with laughter.

'Later,' said Agnès. 'On our way back.'

'You've no sense of fun, girl.'

'You do remember that I am a baronne?'

'A baronne I knew when she had neither tits nor an arse, who rode on my shoulders and who I made drink her first glass of *eau-de-vie*.'

'At eight years old! What a handsome feat . . . I remember puking my guts out the whole night after.'

'That helps forge character. I was only six when my father did the same for me as I did for you, madame la baronne de Vaudreuil. Have you some objection about the education that my father saw fit to give me?'

'Come on, you old beast. Move along, now . . . On the way back, I tell you.'

'You swear?'

'Yes.'

The traffic of carriages, horses, wagons and handcarts on the roadway was so dense that one could barely advance, while the sidewalks were crammed solid with gawking pedestrians. Charlatans, traders, tumblers, exhibitors of trained dragonnets, teeth pullers ('No pain! And I replace the one I pull!') and street minstrels all put themselves on show or touted their wares to the crowd in Italian, Spanish, and even Latin or Greek to appear more learned. There were numerous booksellers, offering wrinkled, dog-eared and torn volumes at low prices, among which there were sometimes buried treasures to be found. Each of them had their own stand, hut, tent or stall. Places were dear and bitterly disputed. Those who had no right to a spot on the bridge put up signboards giving their names, addresses and specialities. Others – flower sellers, second-hand hatters and *eau-de-vie* vendors – hawked their goods loudly as they made their way from one end of the bridge to the other, carrying a tray on their bellies or pushing a cart before them. Anything could be bought or sold on the Pont Neuf. A lot was stolen there, too, for thieves like nothing better than an idle crowd.

Agnès was passing in front of a famous bronze horse – which, standing on its marble pedestal, would wait almost two centuries before being finally mounted by Henri IV – when she realised she was walking on her own. Retracing her footsteps, she found Ballardieu halted before a Gypsy woman playing a tambourine and dancing lasciviously with a metallic wriggling of her sequined skirt. Agnès dragged the old man away by his sleeve. He followed her backwards at first and tripped on the scabbard of his sword, before pricking up an ear at the call:

'*Hasard à la blanque!* With three tries, you can't miss! For one sou, you'll get six! *Hasard à la blanque!*'

The fellow who was shouting this at the top of his lungs was luring passers-by to place bets on the game of *blanque*, that is to say, the lottery. He was turning a wheel, while the prizes to be won were spread before him: a comb, a mirror, a shoehorn, and other ordinary bric-a-brac which wouldn't be nearly so attractive if anyone looked them over twice.

Ballardieu tried his luck, won, and took away a snuffbox with a lid that was only slightly chipped. He was endeavouring to show this prize to the increasingly impatient young baronne when a fanfare of trumpets resounded.

Intrigued and murmuring, the people in the crowd craned their necks uncertainly, seeking the source of the noise.

On the Left Bank, soldiers belonging to the regiment of French Guards were arriving to clear the bridge. They herded coaches and horse riders from the road across the bridge, pushed the pedestrians back onto the pavements and formed three rows on the steps, standing to attention with their pikes held straight up or with muskets on their shoulders. A line of drummers beat out a steady rhythm as the regiment's vanguard marched forward, followed by a group of elegant riders – officers, lords and courtiers. Pages dressed in royal livery came next on foot, while the famous hundred Swiss mercenaries with their halberds accompanied them on either side. Then came the golden royal coach, drawn by six magnificent horses and surrounded by an escort of gentlemen. Was it really the king whose profile could be glimpsed as it passed? Perhaps. Kept at a distance by the hedgerow of pikes and muskets, the people did not applaud or cheer. They remained respectful and silent, with bared heads. Other coaches went by. One of them lacked any coat of arms, and was pure white, like the team of horses harnessed to it. This coach belonged to the abbess of the Order of the Sisters of Saint Georges – the famous 'White Ladies' who for the past two centuries had protected the French royal court from the draconic menace.

Agnès had stopped, like everyone else on the bridge, standing speechless and hatless as the procession went by.

But the royal coach interested her far less than the immaculate white one from which she was unable to tear her eyes the moment she saw it. When it drew level with her, a gloved hand lifted the curtain and a woman's head appeared. The abbess did not need to search for what she sought. She immediately found Agnès' eyes and stared straight into them. The moment stretched out, as if the white coach had somehow slowed down, or time itself was reluctant to interrupt the silent exchange going on between these two beings, these two souls.

Then the coach passed on.

Reality reasserted itself and the procession moved away with a clattering of hooves on paving stones. In perfect order, the French Guards relinquished control of the pavements and marched off the bridge. The usual frantic activity resumed on the Pont Neuf.

Only Agnès, looking towards the Louvre, remained still.

'Now that was a pair of eyes I would not like to have staring at me,' said Ballardieu from nearby. 'And as for staring right back . . .'

The young woman gave a fatalistic shrug.

'At least now I don't have to go to the Louvre.'

'You won't speak with her?'

'Not today . . . What would be the point? She knows I'm back. That's enough.'

And determined to put the matter behind her, Agnès smiled at the old soldier.

'So?' she asked him. 'Shall we go?'

'Where?'

'But to listen to Tabarin and Mondor, of course!'

'Are you sure?'

'I made you a promise, didn't I?'

12

They arrived at the chapel in the middle of the afternoon

It sat in the middle of the countryside at a spot where a deserted road crossed a pebble-strewn track. A flock of sheep grazed nearby. A windmill whose sails turned slowly in the breeze looked out over a landscape of green hills.

'Here we are,' said Bailleux from the edge of the wood.

He and Saint-Lucq were side by side on horseback, but rather than watch the chapel the half-blood watched their surroundings.

He had just caught sight of a cloud of dust.

'Wait,' he said.

The cloud was approaching.

He could just make out riders trotting up the road. There were four, or perhaps five, of them, all armed with swords. It was not the first time that Saint-Lucq and the notary had spotted them since leaving the inn. Them, or others like them, in any case. But all of them had only one thing in mind: laying their hands on Bailleux and ripping his secret out of him.

'We'll let them go by,' said the half-blood, very coolly.

'But how could they know . . . ?' Bailleux worried.

'They don't. They're searching, that's all. Calm yourself.'

The riders halted for a moment at the crossing with the track. Then they split up into two parties, each taking a different direction. A short while later they had all disappeared off into the distance.

'There,' said Saint-Lucq before spurring his mount.

Bailleux caught up with him as they descended a grassy slope at a slow trot.

'I think the baptism was held here. That's why—'

'Yes, of course,' the half-blood interrupted.

They soon dismounted on a patch of ground in front of the chapel and then entered the building. It was low-ceilinged, cool, bare of decorations and the air was laden with dust. No one seemed to have visited for quite some time, although perhaps it served occasionally as a refuge for travellers caught in bad weather.

Saint-Lucq took off his spectacles in the dim light and rubbed his tired eyes with his thumb and forefinger before surveying their surroundings with a slow circular gaze. Almost at once, the notary pointed to a statue of Saint Christophe standing on a pedestal, in a niche.

'If the testament speaks truly, it's there.'

They approached and examined the statue.

'We'll need to tilt it,' said Bailleux. 'It won't be easy.'

The weight of the painted statue would indeed have posed a difficulty if Saint-Lucq had desired to preserve it intact. But he braced himself, pushed and simply tipped the effigy of Saint Christophe over, to fall heavily onto the flagstones and break into pieces. Bailleux crossed himself at this act of sacrilege.

Someone had slipped a slender document pouch beneath the statue, and the cracked leather now lay exposed on the pedestal. The notary took it, opened it, and carefully unfolded a page torn from an old register of baptisms. The parchment threatened to come apart at the folds.

'This is it!' he exclaimed. 'This is really it!'

The half-blood held out his hand.

'Give it to me.'

'But will you tell me, finally, what this is all about? Do you even know?'

Saint-Lucq considered the question, and reached the conclusion that the notary had a right to this information.

'This piece of paper proves a certain person's legitimate right to an inheritance. One which is accompanied by a ducal coronet.'

'My God!'

Bailleux wished to read the prestigious name which

appeared on the page, but the half-blood swiftly snatched it from him. At first taken aback, the other man decided to be reasonable.

'It's . . . It's no doubt for the best this way . . . I already know too much, don't I?'

'Yes.'

'So it's over now. I won't be troubled again.'

'It will be over soon.'

Just then, they heard riders arriving.

'Our horses!' gasped Bailleux, but keeping his voice down. 'They're bound to see our horses!'

The riders came to a halt before the chapel but did not seem to dismount. The horses snorted as they settled. Inside the chapel the long seconds flowed by in silence. There was no means of exit other than the front doors.

Panicking, the notary could not understand the half-blood's absolute state of calm.

'They're going to come in! They're going to come in!'

'No.'

With one sharp, precise move, Saint-Lucq stabbed Bailleux in the heart. The man died without comprehension, murdered by the man who had initially saved him. Before he died, his incredulous eyes found the emotionless gaze of his assassin.

The half-blood caught the body and laid it gently on the ground.

Then he wiped his dagger carefully and replaced it in its sheath as he walked towards the door with an even step and emerged into broad daylight. There, he put his red spectacles back on, raised his eyes to the heavens and took a deep breath. Finally, he looked over at the five armed riders who waited before him in a row.

'It's done?' one of them asked.

'It's done.'

'Did he really believe we were chasing you?'

'Yes. You played your part perfectly.'

'And our pay?'

'See Rochefort about it.'

The rider nodded and the troop left at a gallop.

Saint-Lucq followed them with his gaze until they disappeared over the horizon and he found himself alone.

13

It was early afternoon when they came for Laincourt.

Without a word, two of the gaolers at Le Châtelet took him from his dungeon cell and led him along dank corridors and up a spiral stairway. The prisoner did not ask any questions: he knew it would be futile. Both his ankles and his wrists had been unbound. Overly confident of their strength, the gaolers were only armed with the clubs tucked into their belts. But escape was not on the agenda as far as Laincourt was concerned.

They reached the ground floor and continued upwards, which told Laincourt that they would not be leaving Le Châtelet. On the next floor, the gaoler walking ahead stopped before a closed door. He turned to the prisoner and gestured to him to hold out his wrists while his colleague bound them with a leather cord. Then he worked the latch and moved away. The other gaoler tried to push him forward, but Laincourt shoved back with his shoulder the moment he felt the other man touch him and entered of his own accord. The door was shut behind him.

It was a cold, low-ceilinged room, with a flagstone floor and bare walls. Sunshine fell in pale, oblique rays from narrow windows, former embrasures now equipped with frames and dirty panes of glass. There was a fireplace, where a fire had just been lit and the heat was still struggling to dispel the prevailing damp. Candles were burning in two large candelabra on the table at which Cardinal Richelieu was sitting, wrapped up in a cloak with a fur collar. Wearing boots and dressed as a cavalier, he had kept his gloves on, while the wide hat he used to remain incognito outside the walls of the Palais-Cardinal was resting in front of him.

'Come closer, monsieur.'

Laincourt obeyed and stood before the table, at a distance which offered no threat to Richelieu's security.

The cardinal had not come alone. Without his cape or anything else that might reveal his identity or his function, Captain Saint-Georges, the commanding officer of the Cardinal's Guards, was standing to the right of his master and slightly behind him, wearing his sword at the side and a look on his face that expressed a mixture of hatred and scorn. One of Richelieu's innumerable secretaries was also present. He sat on a stool with a writing tablet on his lap, ready to transcribe the details of this interview.

'So,' said the cardinal, 'you've been spying on me . . .'

The secretary's goose quill began to scratch across the paper.

'Yes,' replied Laincourt.

'That's not good. For a long time?'

'Long enough.'

'Since your over-extended mission in Spain, I should think.'

'Yes, monseigneur.'

Saint-Georges quivered.

'Traitor,' he hissed between his teeth.

Richelieu immediately lifted a hand to command silence and, seeing that he was obeyed, addressed the prisoner again.

'I would say, by way of reproach, that I have honoured you with my trust but, of course, that is a prerequisite in the exercise of your profession. After all, what good is a spy if one is wary of him . . . ? However, it does seem to me that you have been well treated. So why?'

'There are some causes that transcend those who serve them, monseigneur.'

'So it was for an ideal, then . . . Yes, I can understand that . . . Nevertheless, were you well paid?'

'Yes.'

'By whom?'

'Spain.'

'But more than that?'

'The Black Claw.'

'Monseigneur!' Saint-Georges intervened, seething with anger. 'This traitor doesn't deserve your attention . . . ! Let us hand him over to the torturers. They'll know how to make him tell us everything he knows.'

'Now, now, captain . . . It's true that, sooner or later, their victims will tell an expert torturer everything. But they will also say anything . . . And besides, you can see for yourself that monsieur de Laincourt is not at all indisposed to answering our questions.'

'Then let him be judged, and be hanged!'

'As for that, we shall see.'

Richelieu returned his attention to Laincourt who, throughout this exchange, had remained unperturbed.

'You do not appear to be afraid of the fate that awaits you, monsieur. Yet I assure you that it is an unenviable one . . . Are you are a fanatic?'

'No, monseigneur.'

'Then enlighten me. How is it that you remain so calm?'

'Your Eminence knows the reason, or already guessed it.'

The cardinal smiled, while Saint-Georges could no longer contain himself, taking a step forward, hand on his sword.

'Enough of this insolence! Answer!'

Richelieu was once again forced to dampen his captain's ardour.

'I wager, monsieur de Laincourt, that you have a document that protects you hidden away somewhere safe.'

'Indeed.'

'It's a letter, isn't it? Either a letter or a list.'

'Yes.'

'There is always too much being written down . . . What would you require in exchange for it?'

'Life. Freedom.'

'That is a lot to ask.'

'Furthermore, there will not be an exchange.'

Saint-Georges was dumbstruck, while the cardinal frowned

and, elbows on the table, gathered his fingers to form a steeple in front of his thin lips.

'You won't exchange,' he resumed. 'Will you sell?'

'No, I won't sell either.'

'Then I don't understand.'

'The letter in question will cease to protect me once it is in your hands, and one does not remove one's armour when faced by the enemy.'

'The enemy can promise to make peace . . .'

'The enemy can promise all it likes.'

This time Richelieu lifted his hand even before his captain reacted. The secretary, on his stool, seemed hesitant to take down this retort. A log shifted in the hearth, and the fire gained new strength.

'I want this letter,' the cardinal declared after a moment. 'Given that you are not prepared to divest yourself of it, I could turn you over to the torturer. He will make you reveal where you have hidden it.'

'I have placed it in the care of a reliable person. A person whose rank and birth protects them. Even from you.'

'Such people are rare. Throughout the entire kingdom, they can be counted on the fingers of one hand.'

'A hand wearing a steel glove.'

'English steel?'

'Perhaps.'

'A clever move.'

Laincourt bowed slightly.

'I attended a good school, monseigneur.'

Richelieu dismissed the compliment with a vague gesture, as one might wave away an annoying insect.

'This person of whom we speak, do they know the nature of the paper you have entrusted to them?'

'Certainly not.'

'So what do you propose?'

'Monseigneur, you are misleading when you say you desire to find this letter.'

'Really?'

'Because instead you wish to destroy it, don't you? What

you desire, above all, is that this letter should remain unread by anyone, ever.'

The cardinal sat back in his armchair and signalled to the secretary to stop writing.

'I think I guess your intentions, monsieur de Laincourt. You want your life and your liberty, and in return you would pledge that this overly compromising letter remains where it is. And thus it would continue to guarantee your safety: if I were to incarcerate you for too long, or kill you, its secret would be revealed. But what guarantees can you offer me in return?'

'Nothing will protect me from you if I reveal the secret of this letter, monseigneur. And I know that wherever I go, it will never be far enough to escape you. If I want to live—'

'But do you want to live, monsieur de Laincourt?'

'Yes.'

'In that case, think instead of your masters. Think of the Black Claw. The lever that you employ with me will not work with them. On the contrary, the Black Claw has every interest in seeing the secret that binds us be revealed. So, who will protect you from them? I should even say: who will protect *us* from them?'

'Do not trouble yourself on that account, monseigneur. With respect to the Black Claw, I have also made certain arrangements.'

The cardinal then drew the secretary's attention and indicated the door. The man understood and went out, taking his writing tablet with him.

'You also, monsieur,' said Richelieu addressing Saint-Georges.

The captain at first thought he had misheard.

'Excuse me, monseigneur?'

'Leave us, please.'

'But monseigneur! You cannot seriously think I would leave you!'

'Never fear. Monsieur de Laincourt is a spy, not an assassin. Besides, I only need to call out to have you return, is that not so?'

Regretfully, Saint-Georges left the room and as he was closing the door, he heard:

'You are most decidedly a very prudent man, monsieur de Laincourt. Explain to me what this is all about . . .'

14

'He no longer lives here, messieurs.'

'Since how long?'

'Some time.'

La Fargue and Leprat were questioning the owner of an inn on rue de la Clef, in the faubourg Saint-Victor. While Almades guarded the horses outside, the other two had taken a table, ordered wine and invited the innkeeper to bring a third glass for himself.

'Have a seat, monsieur. We'd like to talk to you.'

The man hesitated for a moment. Wiping his big red hands on his stained apron, he looked around the room, as if making sure that he had nothing better to do. Then he sat down.

La Fargue knew that Castilla, the chevalier d'Ireban's companion in debauchery, had been lodging here. Unfortunately, that was no longer the case.

'Be more precise, if you please. When did he leave?'

'Let me see . . . It was about a week ago, I think. He took his things one night and never returned.'

'In a hurry, then.'

'I believe so, yes.'

'Had he been lodging here long?' asked Leprat.

'About two months.'

'Alone?'

'Yes.'

'No visitors?'

Suddenly wary, the innkeeper moved back in his chair.

'Why these questions, messieurs?'

The other two exchanged a look and La Fargue spoke again.

'Castilla has debts. He owes money, lots of money, to certain people. These people wish to recover what is owed them. They would prefer that their names not be mentioned but they are willing to be most generous. You understand?'

'I understand. Gambling debts, is it?'

'Indeed. How did you guess?'

The innkeeper had the satisfied smile of one who, without saying anything, wants to give the impression of knowing much.

'Bah . . . Just an idea, like that—'

'His room,' Leprat interrupted. 'We want to see it.'

'Well . . .'

'What? Have you let it to someone else?'

'No, but Castilla has paid for the month. Whether he uses the room or not, it is still his. Would you be happy to think I had opened the door to your room for strangers?'

'No,' conceded La Fargue.

'So what do I tell him if he returns tomorrow?'

'You shall tell him nothing. And what's more, you shall send word to me at the address that I shall indicate to you shortly . . .'

The captain drew from his grey doublet a purse – small but full – which he pushed across the table to the innkeeper. It was swiftly snatched up.

'Follow me, messieurs,' said the man as he rose.

They accompanied him upstairs where the innkeeper unlocked a door thanks to a ring of keys attached to his belt.

'This is the room,' he announced.

He pushed the door open.

The room was modest but neat, with walls daubed in beige and an unpolished wood floor. The sole furniture consisted of a stool, a small table upon which was placed a water pitcher and a basin, and a stripped bed whose straw mattress was folded back. A chamber pot was turned over on the sill of the window that opened onto the street.

The place had been tidied up and, perfectly anonymous, awaited a new lodger. The two Blades exchanged glances and sighed, doubting that they would find much of interest here.

Nevertheless, to allow Leprat a chance to inspect the room in peace, La Fargue kept the innkeeper busy in the corridor.

'You didn't tell us if Castilla had any visitors . . .'

'Only one, in truth. A very young cavalier, another Spaniard like him. Castilla addressed him as "chevalier", but they seemed to be close friends.'

'Do you remember his name?'

'Something like . . . Oberane . . . Baribane . . .'

'Ireban?'

'Yes! The chevalier d'Ireban. That's it . . . Does he also have debts?'

'Yes.'

'That doesn't surprise me. Between those two, it was often a question of whether to visit madame de Sovange. And why would they go to see madame de Sovange, if not to gamble?'

'What did he look like, this Castilla?'

Without shutting it completely, Leprat pushed the door until it was ajar, under the pretext of looking behind it. He then conducted a thorough search of the room.

He did not know what he was looking for, which didn't make the task any easier. He knocked on the walls and floor, looked in corners, prodded the straw mattress and examined its seams closely.

In vain.

The room concealed no secret. If Castilla had ever possessed anything of a compromising nature, he had taken it with him.

The former musketeer was about to give up when by chance he looked out the window and down into the street. What he saw there or rather who he saw there – made him instantly go still.

Malencontre.

Malencontre who, wearing his leather hat and a bandage on his left hand, was being directed towards the inn by a passerby. He gazed up towards the room's window, stiffened in surprise and promptly turned tail.

'Merde!' swore Leprat.

He knew that he would never catch the hired assassin if he

took the stairs. He shoved open the window, causing the chamber pot to smash on the floor, and jumped out into the air just as La Fargue – drawn by the noise – came into the room.

Leprat landed near Almades in front of the inn. But he had forgotten the wound to his thigh. Pain shot through his leg and he crumpled with a loud yelp that alarmed people in the street. Unable to stand, grimacing and cursing at himself, he nevertheless had the presence of mind to point out Malencontre to the Spanish master of arms.

'There! The leather hat! Quick!'

Malencontre was moving away, almost running, jostling people as he went.

As he set off in pursuit, Almades heard Leprat yelling at him from behind:

'Alive! We need him alive!'

The Spaniard had already lost sight of the assassin when he arrived at the corner of rue de la Clef and rue d'Orléans. He climbed onto a cart that was being unloaded and, paying no heed to the protests he was raising, looked further down the street. He spotted the leather hat just as Malencontre was turning into an alley. He leaped into the crowd, banging his hip into a stall which tipped and spilled its vegetables onto the paving stones. He did not stop, pushing aside anyone who did not get out of his way quickly enough, provoking shouts and raised fists in his wake. Finally, he reached the alley.

It was deserted.

He drew his sword.

La Fargue left the inn with his rapier in his fist, only to find Leprat twisting in agony on the ground, clenching his teeth and holding his thigh with both hands. Some kind souls came over to help him, but they hung back upon seeing the captain.

'Blast it, Leprat! What the hell . . . ?'

'Malencontre!'

'What?'

'Leather hat. Bandaged hand. Almades is after him. I'll explain later. That way! Quick!'

La Fargue took a pistol from the saddle of his horse and dashed off down the street.

Step by cautious step, Almades inched his way through silent alleys as narrow as corridors in a building. He had left the noises of the crowded streets behind him and he knew his prey had stopped running. Otherwise he would have heard his footsteps. The man was hiding. Either to escape from his pursuer, or to set an ambush for him.

Careful . . .

The attack came suddenly, from the right.

Emerging from a recess, Malencontre struck with a log he had taken from a woodpile. Almades raised his sword to protect himself. The log hit the rapier's hilt violently, dislodging the weapon from the Spaniard's grip. The two men immediately shifted to hand-to-hand fighting. Each held the right wrist of the other, grunting as they wrestled, bouncing off the walls of the alley, both of them receiving jarring blows as their backs collided with the rough stone. Then Almades drove his knee hard into the assassin's side. Malencontre lost his hold but succeeded in landing a sharp blow with the log to the temple of his opponent. Stunned, the Spaniard reeled and then stumbled backward. His vision blurred while his ears filled with a deafening buzz. The universe seemed to lurch dizzily about him.

Dimly, he perceived Malencontre unsheathing his rapier.

Dimly, he perceived him preparing to deliver the fatal stroke while he himself slid down the wall to a sitting position on the ground, vanquished.

And as if wrapped in some woolly dream, he scarcely heard the detonation at all.

Malencontre fell in a heap.

At a distance of ten metres, La Fargue was pointing a pistol with a smoking barrel.

15

There were three riders waiting at Place de la Croix-du-Trahoir, which was a modest square in the neighbourhood near the Louvre, where rue de l'Arbre-Sec met rue Saint-Honoré. Silent and still, they sat on their horses near the fountain with an ornamental cross which gave its name to the square. One of them was a tall gentleman with a pale complexion, who had a scar on his temple. Not many passers-by would have recognised the comte de Rochefort, the cardinal's henchman. But his sinister bearing never failed to disturb those who saw him.

Drawn by a handsome team, a coach without any coat of arms pulled up.

Rochefort descended from his horse and gave his reins to the closer of the two other riders, saying:

'Wait for me.'

And then he climbed into the coach which immediately drove off.

The leather curtains were lowered, so that the interior of the vehicle was bathed in ochre shadow. Two white wax candles were burning in wall holders fixed to either side of the rear bench of the coach. A very elegant gentleman had taken a seat on this bench. With thick long hair and greying temples, he wore a brocade doublet with braids embellished by gold and diamonds. He was in his fifties, a respectable age for these times. But he was still robust and alert, and even exuded a physical charm that was enhanced by maturity. His moustache, as well as his royale beard, was perfectly trimmed. A thin scar marked his cheekbone.

By comparison, the man sitting to his right was rather undistinguished.

Short and bald, he was modestly dressed in a brown outfit with white stockings and buckled shoes. His manner was both humble and reserved. He was not a servant, yet one perceived him to be a subordinate, a commoner who had risen above his state by dint of zeal and hard work. He was perhaps thirty or thirty-five years in age. His features were of a type that did not attract much notice and were easily forgotten.

Rochefort was seated opposite these two persons, with his back to the direction of travel.

'I'm listening,' said the comte de Pontevedra in perfect French.

Rochefort hesitated, glancing at the little man.

'What? Is it Ignacio who worries you? Forget him. He does not matter. He is not here.'

'So be it . . . The cardinal wishes you to know that the Blades are already at work in this matter.'

'Already?'

'Yes. Everything was prepared. It only remained for them to answer the call.'

'Which they did promptly, I suppose . . . And La Fargue?'

'He is in command.'

'Good. What does he know?'

'He knows that he is searching for a certain chevalier d'Ireban, whose disappearance upsets Madrid because he is the son of a Spanish grandee.'

'And that is all?'

'Just as you wished it.'

Pontevedra nodded and took a moment to reflect, the candlelight highlighting his forceful profile from the side.

'La Fargue must remain unaware of the true under-pinnings of this affair,' he said finally. 'It is of the utmost importance.'

'His Eminence has seen to that.'

'If he should discover that—'

'Do not be concerned about this, monsieur le comte. The secret you evoke is well guarded. However . . .'

Rochefort left his sentence unfinished.

'Well, what?' said Pontevedra.

'However, you should know that the success of the Blades is by no means certain. And if La Fargue and his men should fail, the Cardinal is anxious to know what—'

The other interrupted:

'It is my turn to reassure you, Rochefort. The Blades shall not fail. And if they do, it will be because no one could succeed.'

'And so Spain . . .'

'. . . will keep its word, come what may, yes.'

Once again, Pontevedra looked away.

He suddenly seemed struck by great sadness, and in his eyes there was a flicker revealing a profound worry.

'The Blades shall not fail,' he repeated in a strangled voice. But rather than asserting a sense of conviction, he seemed to be addressing a prayer to Heaven.

16

By the time they reached the Hôtel de l'Épervier, Leprat was barely hanging on to his saddle and Malencontre was laid over Almades's horse. La Fargue called out, summoning everyone into the courtyard. They took care of Leprat first, Agnès helping him walk while Guibot closed the gate. Then Ballardieu and the Spaniard carried Malencontre into the house. Following the captain's instructions, they stretched him out on an unused bed, tucked away in a windowless cubbyhole.

'What happened?' asked Marciac when he returned from his bedroom with a dark wooden case.

'Later,' replied La Fargue. 'See to him first.'

'Him? What about Leprat?'

'Him first.'

'Who is he?'

'He's called Malencontre.'

'And . . . ?'

'And he must live.'

The Gascon sat down on the bed facing the unconscious wounded man, and set the case down at his feet. Bound in iron, it took the shape of a small chest that could be carried easily using a leather grip nailed to its curved lid. It was a surgeon's kit. Marciac opened it but did not touch any of the sinister-looking instruments – blades, saws, hammers, pincers – it contained. He leaned over Malencontre and began, with a great deal of care, to remove the bloody bandage wrapped about the assassin's skull.

'What happened to him?'

'I fired a pistol ball into his head,' explained La Fargue.

With a smirk, Marciac turned towards the captain.

'And he must live? Would it not have been better to not bash his head in, for starters?'

'He was going to kill Almades. And I wasn't aiming at his head.'

'No doubt that will console him and help him to heal.'

'Do your best.'

Marciac was left alone with the patient.

He rejoined the others in the main room a little later.

'Well?' asked La Fargue.

'He will live. Your pistol ball only scraped across the bone, and the man has a hard head . . . But I don't think he will be up to answering questions for a while. In fact, he still hasn't regained his senses.'

'Merde.'

'Indeed. May I take care of Leprat now?'

The captain nodded, looking troubled and preoccupied.

Leprat had been installed as comfortably as possible in an armchair, with his leg stretched out and resting on a footstool. A large rip in his breeches exposed his wounded thigh, which Naïs was finishing washing with warm water and fresh linen.

'Naïs, let me take your place, please.'

The pretty servant got up, looked at the surgeon's kit curiously and gave the Gascon a searching glance.

'I'm a doctor,' he explained. 'Well, almost . . . It's a long, complicated story . . .'

This revelation astonished Naïs even more. She turned to Agnès, who nodded in confirmation.

As he busied himself examining the wound, the others explained how Leprat managed to reopen it. Then they told him of the pursuit, the fight between Almades and Malencontre in the alley and La Fargue's timely intervention.

'Rest and a crutch,' the almost-doctor prescribed when he finished bandaging the wound. 'This is what happens when a patient plays at being an acrobat.'

'I overdid things a bit,' apologised Leprat.

'I suspect you forgot to think before you leaped . . . For the next few days, I suggest you eat your meat rare and drink a decent quantity of unwatered red wine.'

'So tell us, what the devil got into you?' intervened La Fargue. 'Who is this Malencontre exactly? And what did you want with him?'

They all drew closer to listen, except Naïs and Guibot who left the room, and Ballardieu who remained leaning against a wall nibbling on sugared almonds out of a large cornet that he had purchased on the Pont Neuf. Only Agnès had been invited to share them.

'Until this morning,' said Leprat, 'I was still with the Musketeers. And yesterday, I carried out a secret mission . . . For some time now, the King's couriers have been attacked, robbed and murdered on the roads between Brussels and Paris. The first time it occurred, it was thought the courier had merely run into brigands. But there was a second time, then a third, and finally a fourth, despite changes in the itinerary. It was as if the assassins not only knew when couriers were leaving, but also which routes they would take . . . A diligent inquiry was conducted by the Louvre. In vain. So it was decided to lay a trap for the enemy.'

'And you were the bait,' guessed Agnès.

'Yes. After arriving in Brussels incognito I came back carrying a letter from our ambassador to the Spanish Netherlands. And it worked: I was ambushed on the border, then in Amiens, and finally at a staging post a few leagues from Paris I was caught and attacked by a group of hired assassins. Only one of them escaped me. Their leader. It was Malencontre.'

'And that's all?' asked La Fargue.

'Almost . . . I didn't reach Paris until yesterday, during the night. Since my horse was tired and I wasn't feeling too strong myself, plus as a precaution, I had been taking minor roads. I think Malencontre reached the capital before me. Be that as it may, I rode into an ambush on rue Saint-Denis. And I would have been killed if the pistol ball aimed at my heart had not been stopped by my leather baldric.'

'So where did you acquire the wound to your thigh?' inquired Marciac.

'Rue Saint-Denis.'

'And the one on your arm?'

'At the staging post.'

'And having been fortunate enough to survive a pistol ball, the following day you jumped out of a window . . .'

Leprat shrugged.

'I didn't stop to think . . . Malencontre saw me the moment I saw him. He was already fleeing when—'

He cut himself short and turned to Almades.

'I'm sorry, Anibal.'

Head bare, the Spaniard was holding a cool, damp cloth against his temple.

'I let myself be taken by surprise,' he said. 'It was my own fault. I'm lucky to get away with just this handsome bump . . .'

'Let us return to the matter at hand,' said La Fargue. 'What else do you know about Malencontre?'

'Nothing. I know his name, which he told me. And I know that he works for the enemies of France.'

'Spain,' suggested Marciac. 'Who else but Spain would wish to know the content of France's dispatches from Brussels?'

'The whole world,' retorted Agnès. 'England, the Holy Roman Empire, Lorraine. Perhaps even Holland or Sweden. Not to mention supporters of the Queen Mother in exile. The whole world. Friends or enemies . . .'

'Yes, but the whole world isn't looking for the chevalier d'Ireban . . .' said Ballardieu between sugared almonds.

'Malencontre,' explained Leprat, 'did not find rue de la Clef by chance. He was being pointed in the direction of Castilla's inn when I recognised him. It can't have been a coincidence.'

There was silence, punctuated only by the sound of Ballardieu munching, while each of them reflected on what had been said. Then La Fargue placed his hand on the table and said:

'It is useless to lose ourselves in conjecture. This business is more complex than it seems, that's plain. Let us hope that we learn more from Malencontre when he comes round. But for the moment we have a mission to accomplish.'

'What's the next step?' asked Agnès.

'It all depends on Marciac.'

'Me?' the Gascon was astonished.

'Yes, you . . . Do you know a certain madame de Sovange?'

17

Urbain Gaget was speaking to one of the handlers who worked for his flourishing enterprise when he received word that his merchandise had arrived at the Saint-Honoré gate. The information was transmitted to him by a gangling adolescent who came rushing into the courtyard.

'Finally!' snapped Gaget.

Evening was falling and the Paris gates would soon be closed.

Gaget gave a coin to the boy, went over the final preparations one last time with the handler and called for his lackey. He was trading his shoes for a pair of clean boots to protect his stockings from the ravages of Parisian muck when Gros François joined him.

'Take a stick,' he told him. 'We're going out.'

Thus escorted by a solid-looking lackey armed with an equally solid stick, he hastened to go and make his payment to the tax collectors.

As he had taken care to add a few pistoles to the tax, the formalities were dealt with swiftly. Soon he was watching the heavy cart enter the queue of travellers and suppliers granted permission to enter the capital. A dense crowd blocked the area around the gate and stretched almost as thickly along rue Saint-Honoré. This had been one of the main Paris roads even before the city's recent enlargement. Still as busy as ever, it had now been extended as far as the new fortified city wall – called 'Yellow Ditches' by Parisians because of the colour of the earth that had been dug from the site – and was so full that it was difficult to make any progress here, with a noisy, restless multitude trying to advance up and down the street.

Loaded down with a dozen cages, each of which sheltered a dragonnet, the cart moved forward at a slow but steady pace behind the oxen pulling it. A peasant held the reins; his partner had given his place on the driver's bench up to Gaget and was guiding the beasts forward by their bits while Gros François walked ahead and opened a path through the tightly packed mob with some difficulty. Fortunately, their destination spared them from having to follow rue Saint-Honoré into the twisted, populous maze of the old heart of Paris. Instead, they turned onto rue de Gaillon and continued along the street for almost its entire length until they came to the porch of a building opposite rue des Moineaux. In the shadow of Saint-Roch hill with its windmills, it was one of the most attractive areas on the Right Bank – that is to say, the *Ville*, as it was designated by way of contrast to the *Université* on the Left Bank and the *Cité* on its island between them. This new neighbourhood was still under construction in the spring of 1633, but it had already been divided up and was criss-crossed with regular streets and punctuated by numerous gardens as well as a vast esplanade that served as a horse market. As further proof of its success, many beautiful and prosperous-looking private mansions were now being built there.

If it had been located elsewhere in the capital, Urbain Gaget's property would easily have occupied an entire block. Several stone buildings were arranged around a cobbled courtyard that was strewn with straw. These included a round, slender tower capped with a conical slate roof that was pierced with several rows of semi-circular openings. It resembled a dovecote – an oversized one, for inmates who made meals out of doves. Dragonnets could be heard moving around inside, mewling and sometimes spitting, accompanied by the brusque flapping of wings.

It was thanks to these small winged reptiles that Gaget would soon be a very rich man and was already a very busy one. He had started out with his father's business selling ordinary dragonnets in the city markets. Then he turned his attention to the luxury end of the trade, selling creatures with pedigrees or with spectacular physical characteristics to his wealthier customers. But the idea that would make his fortune only came to him later, when he hit upon a method of using dragonnets for a new purpose: a messenger service. Whereas a homing pigeon could only transport a minuscule roll of paper, a dragonnet was powerful enough to carry letters, or even a small package, faster and further than any bird.

The problem was that while dragonnets could be trained to travel between two given points in the same city, they lacked the predispositions of homing pigeons: they went astray or escaped when the distances they covered became too great. His solution was to take advantage of the females' maternal instinct, an instinct that always brought them back to their egg regardless of the difficulty or length of the journey. Gaget began to displace the females just after they laid their eggs, substituting the real eggs with simulacra when necessary to which the dragonnets would became equally attached and to which they would inevitably return, along with the mail they carried, once they were released. All that was left, after that, was to transport the females back to their point of departure by road.

Without abandoning the retail trade of buying and selling the dragonnets themselves, the breeder was soon able to carry out his new trade with a royal licence granting him a monopoly within Paris and surrounding towns. His messenger service very quickly thrived, linking the capital with Amiens, Reims, Rouen and Orléans. With the help of relay stations, it was even possible to send mail by air as far as Lille, Rennes, or Dijon.

A slender and rather handsome grey-haired fellow, not lacking in charm, Gaget supervised the unloading of the cart and watched as his employees carried the cages into a building where the dragonnets would remain confined and alone for a few days, until they settled down after the stress of their journey and became accustomed to their new environment. The result of a strict selection process, these particular specimens were destined to be sold and each one was worth a small fortune. They had to be treated with care, for fear that they might injure one another or damage themselves.

Satisfied, the breeder left his handler to examine the reptiles and returned to his office, where tedious paperwork awaited him. He removed his cloak and his boots, realised that he had gone out without wearing a hat, and then gave a start when he became aware of another presence in the room when he had believed he was alone. His heart beating fast, he gave a sigh of relief when he saw who it was. He had quickly discovered that along with the royal licence he held came the expectation of certain discreet services. He owed his new privileges to the cardinal's intervention and could of course refuse nothing to such a benefactor, especially when he was so honoured to have his trust. Thus the Gaget messenger service became a favoured means of transmitting secret dispatches.

And much else besides.

'I frightened you,' said Saint-Lucq.

He was sitting in an armchair, his hat lowered over his eyes, legs stretched out and crossed and his heels resting on a window sill.

'You . . . You surprised me,' explained the breeder. 'How did you get in here?'

'Does it matter?'

Quickly recovering his composure, Gaget went to lock the door and close the curtains.

'I've been waiting for you to show up for three days,' he said in a reproachful tone.

'I know,' said the half-blood lifting his felt hat.

With a casual air, he began to clean his spectacles with his sleeve. His reptilian eyes seemed to glow in the shadows.

'I received a visit from the comte de Rochefort,' said the breeder.

'What did he want?'

'News. And to tell you that there is some concern about your progress.'

'They are wrong to be concerned.'

'Will you succeed before it is too late?'

Saint-Lucq replaced the spectacles upon his nose and took time to weigh his reply.

'I was unaware that there was any other option . . .'

Then he asked:

'When will you see Rochefort again?'

'This evening, no doubt.'

'Tell him that the business which worries him so greatly is now settled.'

'Already?'

Saint-Lucq stood, smoothed the front of his doublet and adjusted his leather baldric, ready to leave.

'Add that the paper is in my possession and I simply wait to learn who I should deliver it to.'

'That I do know. You are to deliver it in person to the cardinal himself.'

The half blood paused and gave Gaget a curious glance above his red glasses.

'In person?'

The dragonnet breeder nodded.

'As soon as possible, I was told. This very evening, therefore. At the Palais-Cardinal.'

18

The carriage reached the faubourg Saint-Jacques at dusk and followed rue des Postes, to rue de l'Arbalète before passing through the gates of a large private mansion. Although still useless at this hour, torches were burning in the courtyard where, one by one, passengers were already alighting from their coaches while sedan chairs arrived and elegant horse riders left their mounts in the care of stable boys. Three storeys of tall windows were brightly illuminated from within. Guests were conversing with one another on the front steps as they waited to pay their respects to the mistress of the house. The latter, madame de Sovange, smiled and had a pleasant greeting ready for each of them. Dressed in an elegant court gown she made friendly reproaches to those who did not come often enough, complimented others and flattered everyone's sense of vanity with consummate skill.

Then it was Ballardieu's turn to halt their carriage at the bottom of the stairs. A lackey opened the door and Marciac emerged, elegantly dressed and holding out a hand for Agnès. Coiffed, powdered and beautifully attired, the baronne de Vaudreuil was stunning in a gown of scarlet silk and satin. It was a somewhat unfashionable dress, however, as no one here failed to notice. Agnès was also aware of this, but she'd had no time to convert her wardrobe to the current fashion. Moreover, she knew she could count on her beauty see her through, and this faux-pas in fact corresponded with the character she was playing.

'They only have eyes for you,' Marciac murmured as they waited patiently on the front steps.

In fact, she was attracting a number of sideways glances.

Wary and sometimes hostile looks from the women, interested and often charmed ones from the men.

'It's simply justice, isn't it?' she said.

'You are superb. And what about me?'

'You're not embarrassing, at least . . . To be honest, I wasn't sure you knew how to shave . . .'

The Gascon smiled.

'Try not to stand out too much. Remember who you are this evening . . .'

'Do you take me for a debutante?'

They ascended several steps.

'I only see the great and the worthy here,' observed Agnès.

'Only the most worthy. Madame de Sovange's gaming academy is one of the best frequented in Paris.'

'And they let you in?'

'You are cruel. The important thing is, if Castilla's landlord told the truth, the chevalier d'Ireban and Castilla liked coming here often.'

'Who is she, by the way?'

'Madame de Sovange? A widow whose dear departed husband left her nothing but debts and who resolved to support herself by opening her salons to the biggest gamblers in the capital . . . But her house is not restricted to gambling. There is much intrigue as well.'

'Of what kind?'

'Of every kind. Gallant, commercial, diplomatic, political . . . You can't imagine all the things which can be secretly arranged in certain antechambers, between two games of piquet, with a glass of Spanish muscatel in one's hand . . .'

They arrived before madame de Sovange, a dark, plump woman lacking in any real beauty but whose smile and affable manner provoked a sympathetic response.

'Monsieur le marquis!' she exclaimed.

Marquis?

Agnès resisted the temptation to look around for the marquis in question.

'I am delighted to see you, monsieur. Do you know how much we have missed you?'

'I am the first to regret my absence,' replied Marciac. 'And do not think I have been unfaithful to you. Important business kept me far from Paris.'

'Has this business been resolved?'

'But of course.'

'How fortunate.'

Still addressing madame de Sovange, Marciac turned slightly towards Agnès.

'Allow me to present madame de Laremont, a cousin of mine who I am showing around our beautiful capital.'

The mistress of the house greeted the so-called madame de Laremont.

'You're most welcome, my dear . . . But tell me, marquis, it seems that all of your cousins are ravishing . . .'

'It runs in the family, madame.'

'I will speak more with you later.'

Agnès and Marciac passed through a brightly lit vestibule with all its gilded décor and walked on into a series of salons whose communicating doors had been left wide open.

'And so, you are a—'

'My word,' replied the Gascon, 'if Concini was made maréchal d'Ancre, I could very well be a marquis, couldn't I?'

Neither of them took any notice of a very young and very elegant gentleman who was watching them, or rather, was watching the baronne de Vaudreuil – no doubt attracted by the dazzling beauty of this unfamiliar woman. If he had been present, Leprat would have recognised the cavalier who had fired a pistol ball into his heart on rue Saint-Denis. It was the marquis de Gagnière, who was discreetly approached from behind by a valet who whispered a few words into his ear.

The gentleman nodded, left the salons and found his way to a small courtyard used by servants and suppliers. A hired sword waited for him there. Booted, gloved and armed, both his clothes and his hat were of black leather. A patch – also made of leather and covered with silver studs – masked his left eye, but not enough to hide the rash of ranse that spread all around it. He had an olive complexion and angular features. Dark stubble covered his hollow cheeks.

'Malencontre has not returned,' he said with a strong Spanish accent.

'We will worry about that later,' Gagnière decreed.

'So be it. What are your orders?'

'For the moment, Savelda, I want you to gather some men. We will act tonight. This business has already gone on too long.'

19

The riders reached the old water mill as sunset bathed the landscape in flaming golds and purples. There were five of them, armed and booted, all them belonging to the Corbins gang, although they did not wear the distinctive large black cloaks. They had been riding for some distance since leaving the forest camp where most of the gang was currently to be found and they preferred not to be recognised as they made their way here.

The first body they saw was the lookout's, lying in front of the miller's house, stretched out close to the chair he'd been sitting in when Saint-Lucq had surprised and stabbed him.

One of the riders dismounted and was immediately copied by the others. A stocky man in his fifties, he owed his nickname Belle-Trogne, or 'handsome mug', to his battered, scarred face. He took off his hat, wiped away the sweat beading his completely bald skull with leather-gloved hand and said in a rough voice:

'Search everywhere.'

As the men scattered, he entered the house and found two lifeless corpses close to the fireplace, then a third lying a little further away. They were lying in congealed puddles that offered a feast to a swarm of fat black flies. The smell of blood was mixed with that of dust and old wood. Nothing could be heard except for the buzzing of insects. The evening light came through the rear windows at a low angle that cast long sepulchral shadows.

The Corbins who had gone to inspect the rest of the property soon returned.

'The prisoner has gone,' said one.

'Corillard is with the horses in the shed,' announced another.

'Dead?' Belle-Trogne asked to put his mind at rest.

'Yes. Strangled while he shat.'

'God's blood, Belle-Trogne! Who could have done such a thing?'

'A man.'

'Just one? Against five?'

'There was no fight. They were all murdered in cold blood. First Corillard in the shed, then Traquin in front of the house. After that, Galot and Feuillant in here, while they were eating. And Michel last of all . . . One man could have done that . . . If he were good . . .'

'I don't want to be the one who tells Soral . . .'

Belle-Trogne didn't reply, instead going to squat near the last body he had mentioned. The man called Michel was lying in the open doorway to the room where the Corbins had been sleeping – pallets and blankets attested to the fact. Feet bare, shirt outside his breeches, his forehead had obviously been split open by the poker that had fallen close by.

'It happened early in the morning,' confirmed Belle-Trogne. 'Michel had just woken.'

He stood back up and then something caught his attention. He frowned, counting the pallets.

'Six beds,' he said. 'One of ours is still missing . . . Have you looked everywhere?'

'The kid!' exclaimed one Corbin. 'I forgot all about him, but don't you remember? He insisted on taking part and Soral finally—'

He didn't finish.

Muffled thumps could be heard and the brigands, by reflex, all drew their swords.

The thumping came again.

Belle-Trogne in the lead, the brigands went back into the common room, cautiously approaching a cupboard. They opened it suddenly and found the sole survivor of the massacre.

Gagged, bound, eyes reddened and wet, a boy aged about fourteen looked up at them with an expression that was both imploring and scared.

20

Night had fallen, but at madame de Sovange's house fires and candles provided a warm light that reflected off the gold, the crystal and the mirrors. The women looked radiant in their elaborate attire and the men were almost equally resplendent. All of them were dressed as if making an appearance at the royal court. Indeed, some of those present had come straight from the court, avid for the distractions and conversation that Louis XIII would not tolerate at the Louvre. But here, at least, away from their dull, timid king who only had a taste for the pleasures of the hunt, one could find amusement in agreeable company. It was possible to converse, pay court, laugh, gossip, dine, drink and, of course, gamble.

There were billiard tables upstairs, upon which madam de Sovange's guests tapped at ivory balls with curved canes. Here and there were chess sets, chequers and trictrac boards left at the guests' disposal. Dice were being rolled. But above all, cards were being played. *Piquet*, *hoc*, *ambigu*, *impériale*, *trente et un*, *triomphe* – all of these games involved gambling on an ace of hearts, a nine of clubs, a wyvern of diamonds, or a king of spades. Fortunes were lost and won. Inheritances could disappear with an unlucky hand. Jewels and acknowledgements of debts were snatched up from the felt mat, along with piles of gold coins.

Abandoned by Marciac at the first opportunity, the so-called madame de Laremont wandered through the salons for a while, and turned away a few presumptuous seducers before allowing one old gentleman to court her. The vicomte de Chauvigny was in his sixties. He still maintained a handsome bearing but he was missing several teeth, which he tried to hide by holding a handkerchief to his mouth when he spoke. He was friendly, amusing and full of anecdotes. He wooed Agnès without any hope of success for the sole pleasure of gallant conversation, of which he was a master and which no doubt summoned up memories of his many past conquests as a dashing cavalier. The young woman willingly let him continue, as he spared her from having to endure less welcome attentions and was unknowingly providing her with precious pieces of information. She had already learned that the chevalier d'Ireban and Castilla had indeed been made welcome at the Hôtel de Sovange, that Ireban had not made an appearance here for some time, but that Castilla, even if he never remained for long, continued to visit almost every evening.

Trying in vain to catch a glimpse of Marciac, Agnès saw a dumpy little woman whose austere manner, surly glance and plain black gown jarred with the setting. She skulked about, pillaging the plates of pastries, and kept a watchful eye on the proceedings as if she were searching for something, or someone. No one seemed to notice her and yet everyone avoided her.

'And her? Who is she?'

The vicomte followed the glance of his newfound protégée. 'Oh! Her . . . ? That's La Rabier.'

'Who is . . . ?'

'A formidable moneylender. Permit me, madame, to give you some advice. Sell your last gown and embark for the Indies in your nightshirt rather than borrow money from that ghoul. She will suck your blood down to the very last drop.'

'She doesn't look so terrible . . .'

'That is an error in judgment that others have repented from too late.'

'And she is allowed to carry on?'

'Who would stop her . . . ? Everyone owes her a little and she is only cruel to those who owe her a lot.'

Casting a final wary glance over her shoulder, La Rabier left the room.

'Would you like something to drink?' asked Chauvigny.

'Gladly.'

The vicomte left Agnès but was quick to return with two glasses of wine.

'Thank you.'

'To you, madame.'

They clinked glasses, drank and the old gentleman said in a conversational tone:

'By the way, I just saw that Spanish hidalgo you were asking me about a short while ago . . .'

'Castilla? Where?'

'There, at the door. I think he's leaving.'

'Please excuse me,' said Agnès handing her glass over to Chauvigny, 'but I simply must speak with him . . .'

She hurried over to the door and recognised Castilla from the description given by the innkeeper from the rue de la Clef. Slender, handsome, with a thin moustache and very dark eyes, he was descending the front steps, greeting a passing acquaintance in his strong Spanish accent.

Agnès hesitated to accost him. Under what pretext? And to what end?

No, it would be better to follow him.

The problem was that Ballardieu was nowhere to be found and she could not imagine herself trailing Castilla around Paris at night in her slippers and evening gown. If only Marciac deigned to reappear!

Agnès cursed silently.

'Is there a problem?' madame de Sovange asked her.

'No, madame. None at all . . . Isn't that monsieur Castilla who is just leaving?'

'Yes, indeed it is. Do you know him?'

'Would you happen to know where the marquis is?'

'No.'

Masking her anxiety, the young woman returned to the salon, ignoring Chauvigny who smiled at her from afar, searching for Marciac. She passed before a window and caught sight of Castilla, crossing the porch. At least he was on foot . . .

The Gascon, finally, appeared at a door.

Given the circumstances, Agnès paid no heed to the grave expression on his face.

She caught him by an elbow.

'Good grief, Marciac! Where have you been?'

'Me . . . ? I—'

'Castilla was here. He just left!'

'Castilla?' replied Marciac as if hearing the name for the first time.

'Yes, Castilla! Damn it, Marciac, pay attention!'

Eyes closed, the Gascon took a deep breath.

'All right,' he finally replied. 'What do you wish from me?'

'He left the mansion on foot. If no one is waiting for him in the street with a carriage or a horse, you can still catch him. He was dressed as a cavalier with a red plume on his hat. See where he goes. And don't let him get away!'

'Understood.'

Marciac headed off, watched from behind by Agnès.

The young baronne remained pensive for a moment. Then, seized by a doubt, she pushed open the door through which the Gascon had just emerged. It led to a windowless antechamber, lit by a few candles.

Busy nibbling from a plate of almond paste sweets, La Rabier greeted Agnès with a polite, reserved nod of her head.

21

The same night, Saint-Lucq saw Rochefort in an antechamber within the Palais-Cardinal. They exchanged a brief nod of the head, each taking note of the other's presence without further ado. It was a salute between two professionals who knew one another but were otherwise indifferent to each other.

'He's waiting for you,' said the cardinal's henchman. 'Don't bother to knock.'

He seemed to be in a hurry, no doubt on his way to another errand. The half-blood stepped past him, but waited until he was alone to remove his red spectacles, adjust his attire and open the door before him.

He entered.

The room was high-ceilinged, long, silent, sumptuous, and almost completely plunged into shadow. At the far end of the vast study lined with precious books, beyond the chairs, desks and other furniture whose shapes and lacquered surfaces could barely be discerned, the candles of two silver candelabra cast an ochre light over the worktable at which Richelieu was sitting, his back to a splendid tapestry.

'Come closer, monsieur de Saint-Lucq. Come closer.'

Saint-Lucq obeyed, crossing the hall to reach the light.

'It has been a while since we last saw one another, has it not?'

'Yes, monseigneur.'

'Monsieur Gaget is a very capable intermediary. What do you make of him?'

'He is both discreet and competent.'

'Would you say he is loyal?'

'Most men are loyal for as long as they have no interest in betrayal, monseigneur.'

Richelieu smiled briefly.

'Inform me, then, of the progress of your mission, monsieur de Saint-Lucq. The comte de Rochefort is concerned that the days are passing by. Days which, according to him, are running short for us . . .'

'Here,' said the half-blood, holding out the page torn long ago from an old register of baptisms.

The cardinal took it, unfolded it, drew it closer to a candle in order to decipher the faded ink, and then carefully placed it in a leather satchel.

'Have you read it?'

'No.'

'You have succeeded in just three days when I believed the task impossible. Please accept my congratulations.'

'Thank you, monseigneur.'

'How did you manage it?'

'Does Your Eminence wish to know the details?'

'Just the essentials.'

'The Grand Coësre told me where and by whom the notary Bailleux was being held captive. I freed him and led him to believe we were being hunted by those who had ordered his abduction.'

'Which was, strictly speaking, only the truth . . .'

'Yes. But the riders who were searching the countryside in our vicinity and who constantly seemed to be on the verge of catching us, those riders were solely intended to intimidate Bailleux to the point of losing his better judgment.'

'So that was the purpose of the men you requested from Rochefort.'

'Indeed, monseigneur.'

'And the notary?'

'He won't talk.'

On that point, the cardinal demanded no further explanation.

For a moment, he looked at his little dragonnet, which,

inside its large wrought iron cage, was gnawing at a thick bone.

Then he sighed and said:

'I shall miss you, monsieur de Saint-Lucq.'

'I beg your pardon, monseigneur?'

'I made a promise that I must keep. To my great regret, believe me . . .'

Entering discreetly, a secretary interrupted them to whisper a few words into the ear of his master.

Richelieu listened, nodded and said:

'Monsieur de Saint-Lucq, if you would wait next door for a few moments, please . . .'

The half-blood bowed, and by means of a concealed door, departed in the wake of the secretary. Shortly after, La Fargue appeared, in a manner suggesting that he was responding to an urgent summons. Left hand on the pommel of his sword, he saluted by removing his hat.

'Monseigneur.'

'Good evening, monsieur de La Fargue. How does your mission fare?'

'It is too soon to say, monseigneur. But we are following a trail. We have learned that the chevalier d'Ireban and one of his close friends frequented madame de Sovange's establishment. At this very moment, two of my Blades are there incognito, gathering information.'

'Very good . . . And what can you tell me about your prisoner?'

La Fargue twitched.

'My prisoner?'

'Today you captured a certain Malencontre with whom monsieur Leprat had a dispute recently. I want this man to be released to my custody.'

'Monseigneur! Malencontre has still not even regained his senses! He has not spoken a word and—'

'Anything this man could tell you would be of no consequence to your business.'

'But how can we be sure? The coincidence would be enormous if—'

The cardinal imposed silence by lifting his hand.

His sentence allowed no appeal, as the ageing captain, with clenched teeth and a furious look in his eye, was finally forced to admit.

'At your command, monseigneur.'

'You are about to discover, however, that I am not a man who takes without giving in return,' Richelieu murmured.

And in a voice loud enough to be heard in the adjoining room, he ordered:

'Ask monsieur de Saint-Lucq to come in.'

22

Castilla led Marciac through dark deserted streets to the nearby faubourg Saint-Victor. They crossed rue Mouffetard and proceeded up rue d'Orléans, passing the rue de la Clef where the Spaniard had so recently been a lodger, before finally turning into the small rue de la Fontaine. There, after glancing around without spotting the Gascon, Castilla knocked three times on the door of a particular house. It opened almost at once and as the man entered, Marciac caught a glimpse of a female silhouette.

The Gascon waited for a moment, and then crept forward. He approached the windows, but with the curtains closed all he could see was that there were lights burning within. He went up the alley to one side of the house and noticed a small window too high and too narrow to warrant such protection. He jumped up, gripped the sill and lifted himself by his arms until he could rest his chin on the stone. While he was unable to hear what they were saying, he could see Castilla and a young woman speaking in a clean and tidy room. The unknown woman was a slender, pretty brunette, wearing her hair in a simple chignon, with soft curls gracing her temples. She wore a rather ordinary dress, of the kind the daughter of a modest craftsman might own.

Castilla and the young woman embraced in such a way that Marciac was unable to decide if they were friends, lovers, or brother and sister. His arms torturing him, he had to finally let go and landed nimbly. He heard a door open on the garden side of the house and then other hinges squeaked. A horse snorted and, moments later, the Spaniard came riding down the alley at a slow trot. Marciac was obliged to flatten himself in a recess to avoid being seen or run over. He then dashed out after Castilla, but his quarry was already disappearing around the corner of rue de la Fontaine.

The Gascon bit back on an oath. He knew that it would futile to try and follow a man on horseback.

So now, what should he do?

Standing guard here all night would probably serve no useful purpose and, besides, sooner or later he would need to report back to the Hôtel de l'Épervier. It would be better to find the other Blades now in order to organise a continual watch on the house and its charming occupant. In any case, La Fargue would decide.

Marciac was about to leave when he detected suspect noises coming from the direction of rue du Puits-l'Hermite. He hesitated, turned back in his tracks and risked taking a peek around the corner of a house. A little further down the street a group of hired thugs had gathered around a rider dressed in black leather and wearing a patch with silver studs over his left eye.

These devils are up to some mischief, Marciac thought to himself.

He wasn't close enough to hear them and he sought in vain a means of approaching them discreetly at street level. He spied a balcony, climbed to it and then up onto the roofs and then, silently, his left hand holding the scabbard of his sword so it would not knock into anything, he passed from one house to another. His movements were fluid and as-sured. The gaps that he sometimes had to stride across did not frighten him. He crouched down and finally crawled forward before completing his journey at the tiled roof edge.

'It's on rue de la Fontaine,' the one-eyed man with a Spanish accent was saying. 'You'll recognise the house, won't you . . . ? The girl is alone, so you won't run into any problems. And don't forget that we need her alive.'

'You're not coming, Savelda?' asked one of the thugs.

'No. I have better things to do. Don't fail me.'

Without waiting for a reply, the man in black spurred his horse and left, while Marciac, still undetected, abandoned his observation post.

23

Laincourt emerged, dirty and unshaven, from Le Châtelet at nightfall. His clothes, hat and sword had been returned to him, but his guards had relieved him of the contents of his purse. That did not surprise him and he had not sought to make a complaint. Honesty was not one of the criteria in the selection of gaolers. Nor was it demanded of the archers in the city watch or among the lower ranks of those who served the king's justice. Clerks, halberdiers, scriveners, and turnkeys, all of them found ways of supplementing their ordinary pay.

His stay in prison had left him in a weakened state.

His back, his kidneys and his neck ached. A migraine lanced through his temples with each beat of his heart. His eyes glittered in pain. He felt the beginning of a fever coming on and dreamed of finding a good bed. He was not hungry.

From Le Châtelet, he could easily reach rue de la Ferronnerie by walking a short distance up rue Saint-Denis. But he knew that his apartment there had been visited – and no doubt ransacked – by the cardinal's men. Perhaps those assigned with this task even wore the cape. They would have arrived by horseback, broken down the door, made a great deal of noise and alerted the entire neighbourhood to their activities as they kept the curious at bay. No doubt his neighbours were talking of nothing else right now. Laincourt did not fear their attention. There was nothing to attach him to rue de la Ferronnerie anymore, since Ensign Laincourt of His Eminence's Guards no longer existed.

He rented another dwelling in secret, where he kept the only possessions that had any importance to him: his books.

Despite everything, he resolved not to go there at once and, by way of rue de la Tisseranderie, he went to a square near the Saint-Jean cemetery instead. Out of fear of being followed he made various detours, taking obscure passages and crossing a maze of backyards.

This was the ancient heart of Paris, formed of winding alleys where the sun never shone, where the stinking air stagnated and where vermin thrived. There was muck everywhere, and in thicker layers than anywhere else. It covered the paving stones, was smeared on the walls, spattered pedestrians' clothing and stuck to their soles. Black and foul, it was a mixture of turds and droppings, earth and sand, rot and garbage, of manure, of waste from latrines, of organic residues from the activities of butchers, tanners and skinners. It never completely dried, ate away at cloth fabrics and did not even spare leather. According to one very old French proverb, '*Pox from Rouen and muck from Paris can only be removed by cutting away the piece.*' To protect their stockings and breeches pedestrians were forced to wear tall boots. Others travelled by carriage, or in sedan chairs, or, according to their means, on the back of a horse, a mule, or . . . a man. When they did their rounds, the few dustmen in Paris only managed to collect a certain amount before dumping their carts at one of the nine rubbish tips, or *voieries*, situated outside the city. The peasants from the surrounding areas knew the value of Parisian muck, however. They came each day to harvest it and spread it on their fields. Parisians couldn't help noticing that these tips were cleaner than the capital itself.

Laincourt pushed a tavern door open and entered an atmosphere thick with smoke from pipes and poor-quality candles made of tallow. The place was dirty, foul-smelling and sordid. All of the customers were silent and despondent, seeming to be crushed by the weight of the same contagious sadness. An old man was playing a melancholy air on a hurdy-gurdy. Dressed in moth-eaten rags and wearing a miserable-looking hat whose folded brim at the front boasted a bedraggled feather, he had a gaunt, one-eyed dragonnet sitting on his shoulder, attached to a leash.

Laincourt took a seat at a table and found himself served, without asking, with a goblet filled with a vile cheap wine. He wet his lips, refrained from grimacing at the taste and forced himself to drink the rest in order to buck himself up. The hurdy-gurdy man soon ceased playing, to the general indifference of his audience, and came to sit in front of Laincourt.

'You're a sorry sight, boy.'

'You'll have to pay for the wine. I don't have a brass sou to my name.'

The old man nodded.

'How do matters stand?' he asked.

'I was arrested yesterday and released today.'

'Did you see the cardinal?'

'At Le Châtelet, in the presence of Saint-Georges and a secretary who noted everything down. The match has begun.'

'It's a match in a dangerous game, boy. And you don't even know all the rules.'

'I didn't have any other choice.'

'Of course you did! And there may still be time to—'

'You know that's impossible.'

The hurdy-gurdy player stared into Laincourt's eyes, then looked away and sighed.

The dragonnet leaped from his master's shoulder onto the table. It lay down, stretched out its neck and scratched playfully at a pile of wax that had solidified on the grimy wood.

'I see you are determined to see this whole affair through to the end, boy. But it will cost you, believe me . . . Sooner or later, you will be caught between the cardinal and the Black Claw, as between the hammer and the anvil. And nothing you—'

'Who is Captain La Fargue?'

The question caught the old man short.

'La Fargue,' Laincourt insisted. 'Do you know who he is?'

'Where . . . Where did you hear this name?'

'He reappeared at the Palais-Cardinal.'

'Really? When was this?'

'The other night. His Eminence received him . . . Well?'

The hurdy-gurdy player waiting before saying, as if with regret:

'It's an old story.'

'Tell me.'

'I don't know all the details.'

Laincourt grew all the more impatient as he didn't know the reasons for such reluctance.

'I'm not in the mood to drag this out of you. You're supposed to keep me informed and serve me, aren't you?'

But the other man still seemed hesitant.

'Tell me everything you know!' ordered the young man, raising his voice.

'Yes, yes . . . All right . . .'

The hurdy-gurdy player drank some wine, wiped his mouth on the back of his sleeve and, giving Laincourt a reproachful look, said:

'A while ago, La Fargue commanded a group of men who—'

'—carried out secret missions for the cardinal, yes. This much, I already know.'

'They were called the Cardinal's Blades. There were no more than ten of them. Some would say they did the cardinal's dirty work for him. Personally, I would say that they were both soldiers and spies. And at times, it's true, assassins—'

'"Assassins"?'

The hurdy-gurdy player made a face.

'The word is perhaps a little strong. But not all of France's enemies fight on the fields of battle, nor do all of them advance to the beat of drum and preceded by a banner . . . I don't need to tell you that wars can also be waged behind the stage and that many deaths take place there.'

'And for there to be deaths, someone has to cause them '

'Exactly. But I remain convinced that the Blades have saved more lives than they have taken. Sometimes you have to cut off a hand to preserve the arm and the man that comes with it.'

'What happened at the siege of La Rochelle?'

Once again surprised, but now on guard, the old man lifted an eyebrow at Laincourt.

'If you're asking that question, boy, then you know the answer . . .'

'I'm listening to you.'

'The Blades were given a mission that, no doubt, was meant to hasten the end of the siege. But don't ask me the nature of it . . . Whatever it was, La Fargue was betrayed.'

'By who?'

'By one of his own men, by a Blade . . . The mission failed and another Blade lost his life there. As for the traitor, he managed to flee . . . And as for the siege, you know how it ended. The dam that prevented the besieged forces in the town from being reinforced by sea suddenly broke, the king had to recall his armies rather than risk the financial ruin of the realm, and La Rochelle became a Protestant republic.'

'And after that?'

'After that, there was no longer any question of the Blades.'

'Until today . . . What do the Blades have to do with the Black Claw?'

'Nothing. Not to my knowledge, at least . . .'

The dragonnet had fallen asleep. He snored softly.

'La Fargue's return no doubt signals the return of the Blades,' Laincourt declared in a low voice. 'It must have something to do with me.'

'That's by no means certain. The cardinal always has several irons in his fire.'

'Be that as it may, I would prefer not to have to watch my flanks as well as my rear . . .'

'Then you chose the wrong path, boy . . . entirely the wrong path . . .'

Later, as Laincourt ventured back out into the night, a black dragonnet with golden eyes discreetly took flight from a roof nearby.

24

La Fargue was galloping through Paris at Almades's side. He had just come out of the Palais-Cardinal and found the master of arms waiting for him with their horses. They rode along the École quay and crossed a deserted Pont Neuf at full speed.

'His Eminence wants Malencontre?' the captain was saying loudly enough to be heard over the hoof beats. 'Very well. I can only bow to his demand. But nothing prevents me from dragging the truth out of the villain before I hand him over!'

'If the cardinal is asking for him, it's because Malencontre is more valuable than we imagined. No doubt he knows a lot. But about what?'

'Or about who . . . ? If we believe the cardinal, whatever Malencontre knows has nothing to do with the affair that concerns us. We'll see about that . . .'

A short distance from Pont Neuf, they were forced to halt at the Buci gate.

They went forward at a slow walk between two crenellated towers, beneath a wide vaulted ceiling which made the horses' hoof beats echo against the paving stones like shots from a musket. The pikemen of the city militia called their officer over, who examined the riders' passes in the lantern light and saw a seal – that of the cardinal – which opened gates everywhere in France.

The portcullis was already raised and the drawbridge lowered. But the enormous doors themselves still had to be opened and the sleepy militia soldiers were taking their time to remove the chains, lift the bar and push the heavy iron-bound panels. They were wasting time that La Fargue knew to be precious.

He grew impatient.

'HURRY UP, MESSIEURS!'

'Malencontre was still doing poorly when we left,' Almades said to him. 'He had barely regained his spirits and wasn't—'

'That doesn't matter . . . I will make him spill what he knows in less than an hour. By force if necessary. Whatever the cost.'

'But, captain—'

'No! I did not agree to hand this devil over in good condition, after all. He doesn't even have to be alive, come to think of it . . .'

At last they were able to pass and spurred their horses on to cross the foul muck-filled ditch before riding quickly through the streets of the faubourg. They burst into rue Saint-Guillaume just as Guibot was closing the gates to the Hôtel de l'Épervier. Almades slowed down, but not La Fargue. He entered at a full gallop, obliging the old porter to jump aside while pushing one of the panels of the coach gate back open. La Fargue's horse had to pull up abruptly in the courtyard as the captain jumped down from the saddle and rushed over to the main building . . .

. . . and found Leprat sitting, or rather sprawled, on the front steps.

Bare-headed, with his doublet open and his shirt untucked, his wounded leg stretched out before him, the former musketeer was leaning back, supported by his elbows against the last step. He was drinking, without thirst, straight from a wine bottle. His rapier, still in its scabbard, was lying nearby.

'Too late . . .' he spat. 'They took him away.'

'Malencontre?'

Leprat nodded.

'Who?' insisted La Fargue. 'Who took him away?'

The other man swallowed a last mouthful, noticed that his bottle was empty and threw it against a wall where it shattered. Then he picked up his rapier and heaved himself up.

'It looks rather as if, in summoning you, the cardinal only wished to draw you away, doesn't it?' he replied in a bitter tone.

'Spare me that, will you? And answer my question.'

'Rochefort and his underlings, of course . . . They just left. They had an order signed by His Eminence. An order that Rochefort seemed particularly pleased to wave under my nose.'

'I couldn't have foreseen that! I couldn't know—'

'Know what?' Leprat flared. 'Know that nothing at all has changed? Know that the cardinal continues to play his own game with us? Know that we are puppets with him pulling the strings? Know that we count for so little . . . ? Go on, captain, did the cardinal even tell you why he was taking Malencontre from us? No, I think not. On the other hand, he was careful not to announce his decision until you were powerless to do anything about it . . . That should wake some familiar memories in you. And it stirs up just as many questions . . .'

Disgusted, Leprat limped back inside the house.

He left La Fargue behind, who was joined by Almades leading their horses by their bridles.

'He . . . He's right,' murmured the captain in a tight voice.

'Yes. But that's not the worst news . . .'

La Fargue turned towards the Spaniard.

'Guibot,' explained Almades, 'just told me Rochefort and his men brought a coach in which to carry Malencontre off. That means the cardinal not only knew we were holding him, but also that he was not in a fit state to ride a horse.'

'So what?'

'We were the only ones who knew that Malencontre was wounded, captain. Just us. Nobody else.'

'Which means one of us is informing Richelieu on the sly.'

25

After making sure the front door was shut, the young woman extinguished all of the lights except one on the ground floor and, candlestick in hand, walked upstairs protecting the wavering flame with her palm. The candle illuminated her pretty face from below and set two golden points aglow in the depths of her eyes, while the creak of the steps was the only sound to be heard throughout the house.

Once she reached her bedroom, she set down the candlestick on a table and, undoing the chignon that held up her long dark hair, went over to close the window which had been left ajar behind the curtains. She had started to undo the lacings of her dress when someone seized her from behind and placed a hand against her mouth.

'Don't cry out,' murmured Marciac. 'I won't harm you.'

She nodded, felt his grip on her relax, and broke free with a vicious blow of her elbow. She rushed to her bedside table and turned around brandishing a stiletto.

Marciac, who suffered less from his painful ribs than from hurt pride, stretched out his hand in an appeasing gesture and, keeping his distance, said in a voice that he also hoped was calming:

'You really don't have anything to fear from me. On the contrary.'

He was worried that she might injure herself.

'Who . . . Who are you?'

'My name is Marciac.'

He stepped cautiously to one side, but the young woman, on her guard, followed the movement with the point of her stiletto.

'I don't know you . . . ! What are you doing in my home?'

'I have been hired to protect you. And that's exactly what I'm trying to do.'

'Hired? Hired by whom?'

The Gascon was willing to gamble here.

'The man who just left you,' he ventured. 'Castilla.'

That name caused the wary gaze directed at Marciac to falter.

'Castilla . . . ? He . . . He said nothing to me.'

'He was afraid of worrying you unnecessarily. He paid me and told me to stay out of your sight.'

'You're lying!'

With a swift gesture, he reached out and seized the young woman's wrist and, without disarming her, forced her to turn around against him. He now had her firmly in his grasp, but he was trying not to hurt her.

'Listen to me closely, now. Time is short. Some hired swordsmen are preparing to abduct you. I don't know who they are. I don't know exactly what they want with you. All I know is that I won't let them have their way. But you must trust me!'

As he said these words, there was a sinister squeak of hinges, coming from the ground floor.

'Do you hear that? They're already here . . . Do you understand, now?'

'Yes,' replied the young woman in a lifeless voice.

He released her, spun her around again and, placing his hands on her shoulders, looked straight into her eyes.

'What's your first name?'

'Cécile.'

'Do you have a weapon, other than this toy?'

'A pistol.'

'Armed and loaded?'

'Yes.'

'Perfect. Get it, and put on a cloak.'

Without waiting, he left the bedroom and went to the stairs. He listened carefully, and could pick out the sounds of men coming up the steps in single file, as silently as possible. He waited until the first arrived on the landing and, emerging from the shadows, struck him a blow full in the face with a stool.

The man tumbled backward, knocking over his accomplices and provoking a debacle. Cries rose as the thugs struggled with one another on the stairs. For good measure, Marciac threw the stool down at them blindly and scored a hit, adding to the confusion.

By now Cécile was there with him, wearing a large cloak with a hood. He led her towards a window which he opened. It looked out over a side alley, less than a metre away from a balcony. The Gascon passed the young woman over to the other side before joining her. From the balcony, he climbed onto the roof just above, then stretched his hand down. Cécile caught hold of it and he brusquely pulled her up just as one of the swordsmen reached the window. The man attempted to seize her dress, but his fingernails only clawed at the fabric. The young woman cried out. Carried by the momentum of his violent heave, Marciac fell backwards and Cécile collapsed on top of him.

'Are you all right?' he asked.

'Yes.'

They picked themselves up.

One of the thugs had already leaped onto the balcony. He was climbing up when the Gascon surprised him with a powerful kick of his boot which smashed his jaw and sent him tumbling six metres to the ground below.

With Marciac keeping hold of Cécile's hand, they fled together across the tangled maze of abutting rooftops. A shot rang out and a pistol ball crashed into a chimney as they disappeared behind it. They heard the assassins hailing one another and organising the pursuit – some on the roofs, some down on the streets. They climbed up to another roof, their figures standing out for a moment against the starry sky and offering a perfect shot to an eager marksman, but Marciac was able to get a general idea of their situation from this vantage point. He knew they would have to come down again eventually. Rather than wait until they were backed up against an impassable drop, he headed towards a deep dark hole that marked the position of an inner courtyard.

There they found an immense scaffold, the vestiges of an abandoned work site, attached to the three storeys of a condemned building. Their pursuers approaching, As Marciac lowered Cécile and let her drop onto the temporary framework a swordsman appeared out of nowhere. The Gascon drew his sword and a duel ensued. The combatants confronted one another on the ridge of the rooftop. As they crossed swords, they moved back and forth to the rhythm of their strikes and counterstrikes between the sky and the waiting depths. The tiles which they dislodged with their feet fell in a cascade and bounced against the scaffolding before shattering in the courtyard, fifteen metres below. At last, parrying a cut and seizing his opponent by the wrist, Marciac attempted to throw him over his shoulder by pivoting suddenly. But his hold was poor and he lost his balance, dragging the thug who still held him along as he fell. The two men rolled and toppled off the roof. Before Cécile's eyes – who stifled a cry of horror – they crashed through the highest catwalk of the scaffold and landed on the next one down. The impact shook the entire structure, which swayed for a long moment. Boards and beams groaned. Cracking noises could be heard, indicating further sinister developments to come.

Although he was still tottering, Marciac was the first one on his feet. He searched for his rapier, realised that it was now at the bottom of the courtyard and, with a kick beneath the chin, finished off his adversary when he had barely begun to rise. Then he told Cécile to join him by sliding down the catwalk that had broken in the middle. He took her hand again, reassured her with a glance and, together, they climbed down several flights of shaky steps, fearing that the old tormented scaffold would come down around their ears at any second.

Finally on the ground, they discovered that the courtyard had only one exit: a shadowy passage from which three thugs suddenly materialised. One of them pointed a pistol at the fugitives. Marciac immediately clasped the young woman by the waist and turned his back to the shooter. The detonation rang out. The ball gashed the Gascon's shoulder, and he clenched his teeth and pushed Cécile behind a cart filled with wine barrels. He rushed over to his rapier which was lying in the mud and, just in time, turned to face his assailants. Concentrated and relentless, he fought without ceding an inch of terrain or letting himself be outflanked, for fear of exposing his young charge to danger. Then, when he seemed unable to press home his advantage against one swordsman without another forcing him to break off his attack immediately, he initiated a lightning counterattack. He slit the throat of his first opponent with a reverse cut, struck the second with a blow of the elbow to the temple, kicked the third in the crotch and then planted his rapier in the man's chest, all the way to the hilt.

He hoped that it was finished, but Cécile called out to him, pointing to the last floor of the rickety scaffold: with rapiers in their fists, two men who had come down from the roofs were venturing onto the platform with cautious steps. At the same time, a latecomer was emerging from the dark passageway and the entire neighbourhood was starting to awaken. Tired and wounded, the Gascon guessed that he was no longer in any condition to eliminate three additional opponents. Would he have the strength and the time to vanquish one before the other two arrived?

He retreated towards Cécile and the two-wheeled cart behind which she had sought shelter. Impassive, he waited as the first swordsman advanced and his two accomplices reached the second storey of the scaffold. Then suddenly, raising his rapier high with both hands, he struck with all his might at the stretched rope which, passing through rings rooted in the paving stones of the courtyard, kept the cart horizontal. Cut clean through, the rope cracked like a whip out of the rings. The cart leaned sharply, lifting its shafts into the air and freeing its pyramid of barrels, which rolled out like an avalanche.

The swordsman in the courtyard hastily backed up and was brought to bay beneath the scaffold, although he managed to avoid being crushed by the barrels. Some of them burst against the wall, releasing floods of wine. But others slammed into the unstable beams that propped up the enormous framework. These beams gave way and the entire three-storey structure collapsed with an incredible racket which drowned out the cries of the unfortunate souls doomed by the huge falling wooden beams. Pieces of masonry were torn off the façade along with wide plaques of plaster. Thick clouds of dust rose into the air, swallowing the entire courtyard and swelling until they climbed up past the surrounding roofs . . .

. . . and then they fell back onto a courtyard which was turned completely white with dust, and to silence.

Marciac was still for a moment, contemplating the disaster. As the neighbourhood began to fill with worried calls from its residents, he sheathed his sword and walked towards Cécile. Covered in dust like him, she was curled up in a corner.

He squatted, turning his back to the wreckage.

'It's over, Cécile.'

'I . . . I . . . Those men,' stammered the young woman . . .

'All is well, Cécile . . .'

'Are they . . . dead?'

'Yes. Here, take my hand . . .'

She seemed to neither hear, nor comprehend.

He insisted in a gentle voice.

'We need to leave, Cécile. Now . . .'

He was going to help her up when he read a sudden terror in her eyes and realised what it meant.

One of the swordsmen had survived.

He could feel the killer's presence behind him, ready to strike. He knew he didn't have time to stand and turn, and still less to unsheathe his rapier.

He looked deeply into the young woman's eyes, praying that she would understand, even thought he saw her give a very slight nod . . . And then he dove to one side.

Cécile lifted her pistol with both hands and fired.

The Sphère d'Âme

His legs dangling, the man's entire weight hung from his bound wrists. He swayed gently and his toenails scraped the hard-earth floor. He was wearing only breeches and a torn, bloody shirt. More of the same blood – his own – soaked his tangled hair, spattered his swollen face and glistened on his bruised torso beneath the torchlight. The man still lived, but was barely breathing: a hoarse rasp escaped from the painful depths of his chest and pink bubbles formed at the nostrils of his broken nose.

He was not alone in this cellar that had been converted into an antechamber of Hell. With him was the obese, sweating giant busy torturing him with heavy blows from a chain, delivered in a brutal but skilful manner. Then there was the one-eyed man who spoke to the prisoner, asking questions in Castilian. With olive skin and a sharp-featured face, he was dressed entirely in black leather, including his gloves and a hat which he never removed. A black patch with silver studs masked his left eye but failed to disguise the fact that it was eaten away by the ranse. Indeed, the disease had ravaged the entire area surrounding the socket and spread towards the man's temple and cheek, the tumour extending in a star-shaped tracery of dark violet ridges.

The one-eyed man went by the name of Savelda and served the Black Claw. In a calm voice, he had promised his prisoner a thousand torments if he did not obtain the answers he was seeking.

He had not been lying.

Patient and determined, Savelda conducted the interrogation without ever becoming too concerned about his victim's obstinate refusal to give up his secrets. He knew that time, pain and despair were all working on his side. He knew that the prisoner would talk eventually, just as the most solid of castle walls will eventually crumble under a barrage of cannon balls. It would happen suddenly, with little or no warning. There would be one impact too many and then a great, liberating collapse.

With a gesture, he halted the rain of blows from the chain. Then he said:

'Do you know what never ceases to amaze me . . . ? It is when I see the degree to which our bodies are attached to life.'

Inert but still conscious, the victim remained silent. His swollen lids were half-shut over his glassy, bloodshot eyes. Seeping clots encrusted his ears. Threads of mixed drool, bile and blood ran from between his cracked, puffed lips.

'Take you, for example,' continued Savelda. 'At this very moment, your only desire is for death. You desire it with your entire will, with all your soul. If you could, you would devote your last remaining strength to dying. And yet it won't happen. Life is there, within you, like a nail driven deep into a solid block of wood. Life doesn't care what you might want. It doesn't care what you're suffering, or the service it would do you if it would just abandon your body. It's stubborn, it persists, it finds secret refuges within you. It's growing tired, to be sure. But it will still take some time to dislodge it from your entrails.'

Savelda tugged on his gloves to tighten them, making the leather creak as he clenched and unclenched his fists.

'And that's what I'm depending on, you see. Your life, the life instilled in you by the Creator, is my ally. Against it your courage and loyalty count for nothing. Unfortunately for you, you are young and vigorous. Your will to resist speaking will give up long before life decides to leave you and death carries you away. That's just how things are.'

The victim made an effort to speak, murmuring something. Savelda bent close and heard:

'*Hijo de puta!*'

At that moment, a hired swordsman came down the stairs

into the cellar. He halted on the steps and, leaning over the railing, announced in French:

'The marquis is outside.'

'Gagnière?' the one-eyed man said in surprise, pronouncing the French name with a strong Spanish accent.

'Yes. He wants to speak with you. He says it's urgent.'

'All right. I'm coming.'

'And me?' asked the torturer. 'What should I do? Shall I continue?'

Shirt open over his wide torso which was streaming with sweat, he rattled the bloody chain. The victim stiffened on hearing the sound.

'No. Wait,' replied the one-eyed man as he went up the stairs.

After the damp warmth of the cellar Savelda welcomed the cool evening breeze that gently blew through the ground floor. He crossed a room where his men slept or idled away the time playing dice and went out into the night to breathe the fragrant air. A flowering orchard surrounded the house.

Extravagantly elegant as always, the handsome young marquis de Gagnière was waiting on horseback.

'He still hasn't talked,' reported Savelda.

'That isn't what brings me here.'

'A problem?'

'That's one way to put it. Your men failed on rue de la Fontaine. The girl escaped.'

'Impossible.'

'Only one of your men returned, with a broken leg and jaw. From his mutterings, we understood that the girl was not alone. There was someone else with her. And this single person sufficed to rout your entire team.'

Disconcerted, Savelda was at a loss for words.

'I will take it upon myself to inform the vicomtesse,' continued Gagnière. 'For your part, do not fail with your prisoner. He must be made to talk.'

'He'll talk. Before tomorrow.'

'Let's hope so.'

The gentleman dug in his spurs and trotted off in the moonlight between two rows of trees, following a path covered with white petals which swirled beneath his horse's hooves.

2

'She's resting,' said Agnès de Vaudreuil as she left the room. 'Keep her company, would you? And come and find me the moment she wakes.'

Shyly avoiding the baronne's eye, Naïs nodded and slipped through the half-open door which she closed behind her without making a sound.

Agnès waited a short while and then, almost groping her way, went to the stairs. She could barely see anything in this gloomy corridor of the equally gloomy Hôtel de l'Épervier. All of it was built from the same bare, funereal grey stone; the windows were low and far between, often occluded by shutters and always defended by stout iron bars. Elsewhere, along the passageways and stairs, there were narrow embrasures, veritable arrow slits, which at this hour only admitted small slivers of the pale glow of dawn. Moreover, it was usual to carry a light when moving about the house at night, rather than allow a flame to burn alone; out of a natural fear of fire, but also for the sake of economy – even tallow, as nasty smelling as it was, cost money, and the better-quality white wax candles were an expensive luxury. But Agnès had left her candle in the room.

She was about to descend the dark stairs carefully when someone called to her.

'Agnès,' said Captain La Fargue.

She had not noticed him standing there, hidden by silence and shadow. Added to the imposing stature of a body that had been hardened by combat and other trials, his patriarchal air demanded respect: his proud martial bearing and grim face whose features had been sharpened by the years, the closely shaven beard and eyes full of wisdom and strength. He was still wearing his boots and his doublet, with the top button undone. But he did not have his sword or his hat and his thick silver hair almost glowed in the dim light.

He approached Agnès, took her gently by the elbow and invited her to sit with him on the first step of the stairs. She agreed, intrigued, understanding that he wished to speak to her before they rejoined the other Blades, whose faint voices rose from the ground floor. The old captain and the young baronne were separated by gender and three decades. And they also had to overcome a natural reserve on his side and a reluctance to confide in others on hers. But a special bond of friendship and mutual respect united them despite their differences and sense of proprieties. A bond almost akin to the love between father and daughter.

'How is she?' asked La Fargue.

He spoke in a low voice, as if they found themselves in the house of someone recently dead.

Looking over her shoulder, Agnès darted a brief, instinctive glance towards the door of the room where the young woman saved by Marciac had just fallen asleep.

'Her adventure last night has severely shaken her.'

'Did she confide in you?'

'Yes, if she is to be believed, she—'

'Later,' La Fargue cut her short. 'For now, I would simply like to know what you make of her.'

Agnès had not yet had time to change and was still wearing the elegant gown of scarlet silk and satin that she had donned before going out with Marciac to madame de Sovange's mansion. With a rustle of skirts, petticoats and hoop, she drew back from the captain to look at him squarely.

'What a strange question,' she remarked.

Leaning forward, elbows on his thighs and hands clasped, he stared out at a distant point in front of them.

'Among other talents, you are better at delving into people's souls than anyone else I know. So what do you make of her?'

Agnès turned away from the captain, sighed and took the time to collect her thoughts and sum up her impressions.

'I believe . . .' she started to say. 'I believe that she lies a little and hides much.'

Inscrutable, La Fargue nodded slowly.

'I would also guess that she was born in Spain,' Agnès continued. 'Or has at least lived there for many years.'

She watched him from the corner of her eye and caught his expression. He frowned, straightened up and asked:

'How do you know that?'

'Her Spanish origins cannot be detected from her inflexions. But a few of her turns of phrase could be directly translated from Castilian.'

He nodded again, this time with a worried, resigned air.

A silence ensued.

'What exactly is it that you want to know, captain?' the baronne finally asked in a quiet voice. 'Or rather, what do you already know . . . ? I was next to you when Marciac returned with the girl. I saw how you reacted. You went completely white . . .'

On her return from the gambling house, Agnès had found the lights still burning at the Hôtel de l'Épervier despite the late hour and the Blades in turmoil following the abduction – at the cardinal's orders – of Malencontre by the comte de Rochefort. Frustrated and humiliated, Leprat in particular would not calm down and drank more than was reasonable. Then Marciac had arrived with a woman he had managed to rescue after an epic struggle and they were suddenly faced with other matters of concern.

'I am not yet sure of anything,' La Fargue said. 'Go rejoin the others, will you? And do not speak to them of our conversation. I will be with you shortly.'

Agnès hesitated, then rose and went downstairs.

Once he was alone, the old captain withdrew a medallion from his doublet, opened the small carved lid and lost himself in the contemplation of a miniature portrait. If it had not been painted twenty-five years earlier, it might have been that of the new, mysterious guest at the Hôtel de l'Épervier.

After removing her gown and washing her face, Agnès joined the rest of the Blades in the main room, where the torches provided more light than the faint glimmer of day that entered through the small lozenge-shaped window panes.

Sitting in an armchair by the fireplace, Leprat, with his wounded leg propped on a stool before him, was silently drinking from a bottle. To one side, Almades was sharpening his rapier with a whetstone – three strokes along one edge, three strokes along the other, over and over. At the table, Ballardieu and Marciac partook of a light but solid repast that Guibot, hobbling about on his wooden leg, had served at their request. They drank, but the Gascon, still excited by his recent adventure, spoke more than he ate while the veteran nodded vigorously and polished off his meal with an appetite that nothing could discourage.

'I thought I was lost,' Marciac was saying. 'But I threw myself to the side, she brandished her pistol with both hands and – bam! – she fired. And her aim was dead on . . . ! The assassin who was about to run me through from behind collapsed with a ball right in the middle of his forehead.'

'That was damned good piece of luck,' Ballardieu commented before washing down a mouthful of *pâté en croûte* with a swallow of wine.

'It was destiny, my friend. Destiny. "*Audaces fortuna juvat!*" '

His lips greasy and his mouth full, the other man looked at him with wide eyes.

'The saying,' Marciac explained 'is more or less borrowed from Virgil: "Fortune smiles upon the brave".'

Ballardieu was about to ask who Virgil was, but held his tongue as the Gascon, seeing Agnès, asked anxiously:

'How is she?'

'Well. She sleeps.'

'I'm glad to hear it.'

'And you? Your shoulder?'

In addition to a girl who was still trembling from fright, Marciac had returned from his eventful evening with the air of a conquering hero, his hair full of plaster, a few bruises and

– not that he paid much notice to it – a nasty wound to the shoulder.

'Oh, it's just a scratch,' he said, with a vague gesture towards the bandage hidden beneath the sleeve of his clean, unwrinkled shirt. 'It scarcely bled at all.'

'You were lucky,' Leprat said from his armchair, with just a hint of bitterness.

'No one succeeds without a bit of luck,' said Agnès as she sat down at the big table.

She took a plate and, after poking around in the dishes, loaded it with cold meats and cheeses, gratefully accepting a glass of wine that Ballardieu poured for her. La Fargue arrived, sat astride a backward-turned chair, and immediately launched a general discussion:

'You first, Marciac. Tell us what you know about this girl.'

'Her name is Cécile.'

'And what else?'

'That's all. I followed Castilla, who Agnès and I spotted leaving madame de Sovange's gaming salons. Castilla led me to Cécile's house in rue de la Fontaine. He did not stay long and left on horseback. By chance, I then came upon some men who I overheard preparing to abduct Cécile – although at the time, I didn't know that was her name. Be that as it may, I told myself that I could not let them succeed in their plan. And there you have it.'

'Who were these men?'

'Just some hired swords, like others of their kind. But they took their orders from a Spaniard, a one-eyed man in black leather who was so sure of their success that he did not remain with them.'

'Would you recognise him?' asked Leprat.

'Of course.'

'But you'd never seen him before.'

'No.'

La Fargue mulled over this information and then turned to Agnès.

'Now you.'

The baronne emptied her glass before speaking.

'She says her name is Cécile Grimaux. Last year she was living with her father and mother in Lyon. Both of them are now dead, the father from illness and the mother from grief, shortly after him. With no other resources, Cécile went to join her elder sister, Chantal, a seamstress who was living modestly in Paris but who was glad to take her in—'

' "Was living"?' Leprat interrupted.

'I'm coming to that . . . she occasionally worked for a glove maker and it was through him that Chantal made the acquaintance of two Spanish adventurers, the chevalier d'Ireban and his friend Castilla. She fell in love with the first and became his mistress. They trysted in secret in a little house in the faubourg Saint-Martin, living their perfect love while hidden from the eyes of the world. It lasted for a few weeks until they both disappeared suddenly. Since then, Castilla has been searching for them and Cécile awaits news. It seems that this ordeal has drawn them together.'

'How closely has it drawn them together?' asked Marciac.

Cécile being a very pretty girl, the others immediately guessed the reason for his interest.

'I believe you have a rival for her affections,' indicated Agnès with a quirk of her lips. 'But no doubt your chivalrous exploits last night plead in your favour—'

'That's not at all what I was thinking about!'

'Come, now . . .'

'That's enough!' La Fargue ordered with a rare display of temper.

But he recovered his calm quickly, pretending not to notice the wary looks being exchanged by the others.

'Nevertheless,' said Ballardieu, 'it's a strange tale.'

'But it matches pretty well with what Rochefort has told us,' noted Leprat almost regretfully.

Resuming the discussion, the Blades' captain asked Agnès:

'What does Cécile know of Ireban?'

'Almost nothing. According to her, her sister was not very forthcoming on the subject.'

'And of Castilla?'

'We hardly spoke of him. I only know that he has taken up

residence at the love nest in the faubourg Saint-Martin, in case Chantal or the chevalier shows up there.'

'Do you know where it is?'

'Yes.'

'Give Almades the directions: he will accompany me there in the hope of finding Castilla, who may help us get to the bottom of things. You will stay here, Agnès, and learn everything you can from Cécile once she wakes. As for you, Marciac, you've earned the right to rest for a bit.'

Since it went without saying that wherever Agnès was, one would also find Ballardieu, it only remained to assign Leprat. For a brief moment, out of respect, La Fargue tried to think of a task for him. But the former musketeer came to his rescue:

'Don't trouble yourself, captain. I know that I'll be useless until this blasted leg is healed. Let's just say that I am holding the fort in your absence.'

Everyone nodded, slightly embarrassed, before heading off on their various errands.

As preparations were being made, La Fargue went to his room and wrote a short letter which he carefully sealed. Agnès saw him a little while later, scratching at the door to Cécile's room and exchanging a few words with Naïs through the narrow opening, before giving her the missive. The baronne slipped away unnoticed and went to find Ballardieu.

'Get ready,' she said, once she was sure they were out of earshot of the rest of the company.

'For what?'

'Naïs will be going out, no doubt after the captain and the others have left. I want you to follow her.'

'Naïs? Why?'

'You'll see.'

'Ah . . . right.'

3

Arriving by way of rue Beauregard, the marquis de Gagnière dismounted in front of Notre-Dame-de-Bonne-Nouvelle church and hitched his horse to a ring. It was still very early in the morning and not many people were up and about. But the elegant gentleman still found it prudent to entrust his mount to the watchful eye of one of the vendors of *eau-de-vie* who, in the early hours of the day, went around Paris – crying '*Vi! Vi!* Drink! Drink!' – selling little cups of alcohol which were bought and eagerly drunk on the spot by people of the lower classes before their hard day of labour.

The church was silent, dark, damp and empty. As was usual in churches there were no pews, but chairs were stored in a corner ready to be rented out during services by the porter, who was also charged with ensuring the tranquillity of the premises, chasing away any beggars or stray dogs who attempted to enter with equal zeal. Gagnière advanced between the columns and placed himself in front of the high altar, near a thin young man with smooth cheeks and crystalline blue eyes. The young man did not react until they stood almost shoulder-to-shoulder. He wore an ochre doublet that matched his breeches, boots, and was carrying a sword at his side. If he was not praying then he seemed at least meditative, with his eyes shut and his hat in his hand.

'I am rather surprised to see you here this morning,' said the marquis after a moment.

'Have I ever missed one of our appointments?' Arnaud de Laincourt replied, opening his eyes.

'No, to be sure. But, until now, you had never been arrested.'

For a few seconds, the former ensign of His Eminence's Guards did not respond.

'So you know,' he said at last.

'Naturally. Did you believe that such news would escape our attention?'

'No, I didn't. But so quickly—'

'We are everywhere, Laincourt. Even at the Palais-Cardinal. You, better than anyone, should know that.'

'And at Le Châtelet, marquis? Are you present there, too?' Gagnière pulled a face.

'The walls there are, shall we say . . . thicker.'

They remained silent for a moment in the sinister refuge of this deserted church where their secret meetings took place, always at dawn.

Notre-Dame-de-Bonne-Nouvelle had begun its life as a chapel, which was destroyed by soldiers of the Catholic League when the king of Navarre – and future Henri IV of France – laid siege to Paris in 1591. The existing church had been built in its place, with the first stone laid by Queen Anne d'Autriche. As the city absorbed its faubourgs, so the church now found itself at the extreme limit of the Saint-Denis district, right by the new city wall; only the narrow width of a newly laid street lined with building sites separated it from the bastions between the Poissonnière and Saint-Denis gates. This was the very edge of Paris.

'I am still a faithful servant of the Black Claw,' announced Laincourt in a calm voice. 'My loyalty remains unchanged.'

'Permit me to doubt that. Your liberation scarcely argues in your favour. By all rights, at this moment you should be locked away in Vincennes castle waiting to be put to the question. But here you are, having been found guilty of treason, free to come and go as you please. You must admit that the extraordinary clemency the cardinal has shown you offers ample grounds for suspicion . . .'

With a conciliatory shrug, Laincourt indicated that he understood. He explained:

'I possess a document which protects me; it contains a secret the cardinal fears will be divulged.'

Perplexed, Gagnière frowned. Then, almost amused, he said:

'A document that you have therefore taken pains not to transmit to us. A shining example of loyalty!'

'I am loyal, but also cautious,' Laincourt replied unmoved. 'I knew that a day like today would come.'

This time it was the turn of the marquis to accept the other's argument: he was forced to recognise that a 'day like today' had indeed come.

'Very well. What is this document?'

'It's a list naming France's secret correspondents in the Spanish royal court. It is in reliable hands and will be released if ever I delay too long in giving signs of life. The cardinal had no choice. He and I agreed that I should remain alive and free as long as this list remained secret.'

'You are very naïve if you imagine Richelieu will be satisfied with such an arrangement for long. He will deceive you at the very first opportunity. He may already be working to do so as we speak. He will find your list and have you murdered.'

'That is precisely why I am turning to you rather than galloping towards the nearest border.'

'Where is this list?'

'In reliable hands, as I told you. And they will remain anonymous.'

Gagnière's tone became menacing.

'It is a secret which we could tear out of you.'

'Not before the list would be brought to the knowledge of all.'

'So? We do not share the cardinal's fears. On the contrary, we would be delighted to see relations between France and Spain deteriorate even further.'

'To be sure,' allowed Laincourt. 'However, information concerning the Black Claw itself would be revealed at the same time. And believe me, this information could be most damaging.'

Gagnière greeted this news calmly, measuring what Laincourt knew about the Black Claw and the danger it might pose.

'Another list?' he suggested.

'Another list.'

'You are playing a very dangerous game, monsieur de Laincourt . . .'

'I have been employed as a professional spy for some time now, Gagnière. Long enough to know that servants of my type are sacrificed just as easily as the foot soldiers on a field of battle.'

The marquis sighed, no doubt annoyed not to have the upper hand.

'Let us cut to the chase. You would not be here if you had nothing to offer me. Speak.'

'I offer to deliver both lists to you as a token of my loyalty. You will destroy the one and do as you see fit with the other.'

'These papers protect you and yet you would separate yourself from them? Doesn't that run contrary to your interests?'

'I will separate myself from them, even though I'll risk incurring the cardinal's wrath. But, in return, I want to be assured of the Black Claw's protection.'

Gagnière was beginning to understand where this was leading, but nevertheless asked:

'How?'

'I want to join the circle of initiates to which you belong. Besides, I believe I have already earned that right on merit alone.'

'It is not up to you to be the judge of that.'

'I know. So take this proposal to the person who is.'

4

Barely distracted this time by the noisy, colourful crowd that milled about on the Pont Neuf, Ballardieu followed Naïs discreetly. He was in a foul mood and, with an angry look in his eye, talked to himself as he pushed through the throng.

'Ballardieu, you're not a complicated man,' he grumbled. 'You're not a complicated man because you don't have very much in the way of wits and you know it. You have loyalty and courage but not much wit, and that's simply the way of things. And you do as you're told, usually without protest. Or without protesting too much, which is the same thing. You are a soldier, even a good soldier. You obey orders. But I know you would greatly appreciate it if someone did you the honour of explaining, just once in a while, for the sole pleasure of breaking with old habit, the orders they gave you . . .'

At this point in his monologue, keeping an eye on Naïs' white bonnet, Ballardieu repeated Agnès' words and his own, hastily exchanged at the Hôtel de l'Épervier.

' "I want you to follow her." "Naïs? Why?" "You'll see." "Ah . . . right." A fine explanation! And what did you reply to it? "Ah . . . right." Nothing else . . . ! Ballardieu, you might have even less wit than you imagine. Because, in the end, there's nothing preventing you from demanding an explanation, is there? Well, granted, the girl had that look in her eye and you know very well that she wouldn't have explained anything at all. But at least you'd have tried instead of meekly following orders . . .'

Now getting himself worked up, Ballardieu shook his head.

'Good soldier! Good faithful dog, more like it . . . ! And where will the first blows land when things go wrong? On the dog, not on the mistress, by God! Because have no doubt about it, Ballardieu, this business will go wrong and it'll do so at the expense of yours truly. No one acts behind the captain's back and gets away with it. Sooner or later, you—'

Lost in his thoughts, he had bumped into a lampoonist who fell backwards in an explosion of printed papers.

'What?' flared Ballardieu angrily and in perfectly bad faith. 'Can't you watch where you're going? Is this the new fashion in Paris?'

The other man, bowled over in both the literal and figurative senses, took some time to recover himself. He was still wondering what had happened to him, and gaped with amazement and fear at this bull of a man who had come out of nowhere and charged into him as he was haranguing the crowd and brandishing his sheets which – as he was unable to blame the king directly – accused Richelieu of crushing the people beneath the weight of taxes. The individual who had so abruptly entered the life of the lampoonist was not someone with whom he would wish to seek a dispute. Without being particularly tall, he was wide, heavy and massive, and in addition to being red in the face and fuming, he was armed with a good-sized rapier.

But Ballardieu, to the great relief of his innocent victim, passed almost at once from anger to compassion and regret.

'No, friend. Forgive me. It's my fault . . . Here, take my hand.'

The lampoonist found himself catapulted upwards rather than simply raised.

'I offer my apologies. You'll accept them, won't you? Yes? Good man! Nothing broken, I hope . . . Good, I would happily pay for the brushing of your clothes but I'm short of time. I promise to buy you a drink when next we meet. Agreed? Perfect! Good day, friend!'

With these words, Ballardieu went on his way, while the other man, still tottering and dazed, an idiotic smile on his lips, bade him farewell with a hesitant wave.

Far ahead of him, Naïs had fortunately taken no notice of the incident and he had to quicken his pace in order not to lose sight of her. After Pont Neuf she followed rue Saint-Denis, then rue de la Vieille-Cordonnerie, came out on rue de la Ferronnerie and went up rue Saint-Honoré, which Ballardieu had never known to seem so long. They passed in front of the scaffolding of the Palais-Cardinal and went as far as rue Gaillon, into which Naïs turned. Recently absorbed by the capital by the construction of wall know as 'Yellow Ditches', this former faubourg was foreign territory to Ballardieu. He was about to discover its layout, its houses and its building sites.

Opposite rue des Moineaux, Naïs crossed a large porch that opened onto a courtyard full of people and animation, overlooked by a strange tower that stood at the end, like an oversized dovecote. A sign hung over the entrance where one could read the words: 'Gaget Messenger Service'.

'"Gaget Messenger Service"?' muttered Ballardieu with a frown. 'What's this, then?'

Seeing a passer-by, he asked him:

'Excuse me, sir, what is this place of business?'

'There? Why it's the Gaget Messenger Service, of course!'

And the man, in a hurry like all Parisians and as lofty as most of them, walked away.

Feeling his temper rise, Ballardieu sucked in his cheeks, took a deep breath in the vain hope of controlling the murderous impulses that had entered his head and caught up with the passer-by in a few strides, gripping him by the shoulder and forcing him to spin round.

'I know how to read, monsieur. But what is it exactly?'

He was breathing hard through his nose, was red-faced again and his eyes were glaring dangerously. The other man realised his mistake. Turning slightly pale, he explained that the company owned by Gaget offered customers a postal service using dragonnets, that this service was both rapid and reliable, although somewhat expensive, and . . .

'That's enough, that's enough . . .' said Ballardieu, finally releasing the Parisian to go about his business.

He hesitated for a moment over whether or not he should enter and then decided to take up a position at a discreet distance in order to wait and to observe – after all, Naïs might go elsewhere next. It wasn't long before the old soldier saw a familiar figure come out of Gaget's establishment.

It was not Naïs.

It was Saint-Lucq.

5

La Fargue and Almades had no trouble finding the house Cécile had indicated, which stood at the fringe of the faubourg Saint-Denis where the buildings faded away into open countryside. It was surrounded by an orchard enclosed by a high wall, in the middle of a landscape of fields, pastures, small dwellings and large vegetable gardens. The spot was charming, peaceful and bucolic, yet was less than a quarter-league from Paris. There were peasants working in the fields and herds of cows and sheep grazing. To the east, beyond some leafy greenery, the rooftops of the Saint-Louis hospital could be seen.

Along the way they had encountered a band of riders coming in the other direction at full gallop, forcing them to draw aside towards the ditches. In normal circumstances they would have taken little notice of them. But the band was headed by a one-eyed man dressed in black leather who strongly resembled the individual Marciac had surprised the night before, organising the abduction of the young Cécile Grimaux.

'I don't believe in coincidences of this kind,' La Fargue had commented as they watched the riders disappear towards Paris.

And, after a meaningful look in reply from Almades, they both promptly spurred their mounts in an effort to arrive at their destination as quickly as possible.

They did not slow down until they reached the gate. It was opened wide onto the path that led straight through the orchard to the house.

'Are your pistols loaded?' asked the old captain.

'Yes.'

Riding side by side, all their senses alert, they advanced up the path between rows of blossoming trees. The air was sweet, full of delicate fruity fragrances. A radiant morning sun dispensed a light that was joyfully greeted by birdsong. The foliage around them rustled in the gentle breeze.

There were two men standing in front of the small house. On seeing the riders approaching at a walk, they came forward, curious, craning their necks to see better. They were armed with rapiers and wearing doublets, breeches and riding boots. One of them had a pistol tucked in the belt that cinched his waist.

'Who goes there?' he challenged in a loud voice.

He took a few more steps, while the other stood back and placed the sun behind him. At the same moment a third man emerged from doorway to the house and remained close to the threshold. La Fargue and Almades observed these movements with an appreciative eye: the three men were perfectly positioned in case of a fight.

'My name is La Fargue. I've come to visit a friend of mine.'

'What friend?'

'The chevalier de Castilla.'

'There is no one by that name within.'

'Yet this is his dwelling, is it not?'

'No doubt. But he just left.'

The man with the pistol was trying to appear at ease. But something was worrying him, as if he was expecting something irremediable to happen at any minute. His companions shared his anxiety: they were in a hurry to finish whatever they were doing and wanted these untimely visitors to turn round and leave.

'Just now?' asked La Fargue.

'Just now.'

'I'll wait for him.'

'Come back later, instead.'

'When?'

'Whenever you please, monsieur.'

Almades was leaning forward like a tired rider, his wrists

crossed over the pommel of his saddle, hands dangling just a few centimetres from the pistols lodged in his saddle holsters. His glance sweeping out from under the brim of his hat, he observed his potential opponents and knew which of them – taking into account, among other things, the layout of the place – he would have to take on if things went badly. With his index, middle and ring fingers he idly tapped out a series of three beats.

'I would be obliged,' said La Fargue, 'if you would inform the chevalier of my visit.'

'Consider it done.'

'Will you remember my name?'

'La Fargue, was it?'

'That's right.'

The hired swordsman at the doorstep was the most nervous of the three. He kept glancing over his shoulder, seeming to watch something going on inside the house which was likely to be coming out soon. He cleared his throat, no doubt signalling to his accomplices that time was running short.

The man with the pistol understood.

'Very well, messieurs,' he said. 'Goodbye, then.'

La Fargue nodded, smiling, and pinched the felt brim of his hat in farewell.

But Almades sniffed: a suspect, alarming odour was tickling his nose.

'Fire,' he muttered from the corner of his mouth to his captain.

The latter looked up at the chimney of the house, but could see no plume of smoke rising from it. On the other hand, in the same instant he and the Spaniard caught sight of the first curls of smoke obscuring the windows from within, on the ground floor.

The house was burning.

The assassins realised their secret was discovered and re-acted instantly. But Almades was faster still, seizing his pistols, extending his arms and firing simultaneously to the right and the left. He killed both the man on the doorstep and the other man who had been hanging back with two balls that drilled into the middle of their respective foreheads. The detonations startled his horse, which whinnied and reared, forcing La Fargue's steed to take a step to one side. The last man had meanwhile drawn his pistol and was taking aim at the captain. But his shot missed La Fargue who, struggling to control his mount, had to twist round in his saddle in order to return fire. He hit his target nevertheless, lodging a ball in the neck of his opponent who collapsed in a heap.

Silence returned to the scene just as suddenly as the previous violence had been unleashed. With La Fargue removing a second pistol from its holster, he and Almades dismounted, taking cover for a moment behind their horses, observing the house and its surroundings for signs of any other enemies.

'Do you see anyone?'

'No,' replied the Spanish master of arms. 'I think there were only three in all.'

'No doubt they stayed behind to make sure the fire took good hold.'

'That means there's something inside that must disappear.'

Rapiers in their fists, they rushed into the house.

Fires had been set at several points and thick black smoke attacked their eyes and throats. But the danger was not yet significant, although it was too late for there to be any hope of extinguishing the conflagration. While Almades rushed up the stairs to the floor above, La Fargue took charge of inspecting the ground level. He went from room to room without finding anything or anyone, until he spied a small, low door, just as the Spaniard came back down.

'There's a room up there with a chest full of clothing for both a man and a woman. And there are theatre face paints.'

'Let's look in the cellar,' decided the captain.

They opened the small door, went down some stone stairs and there, in the dim light, found Castilla half-naked and bloody, still suspended by his wrists, having been left to perish in the blaze that was beginning to ravage the entire house. At his feet lay the heavy chain that had served to torture him.

La Fargue supported his weight while Almades cut him down. Then they carried him, hastily crossing the ground floor where flames were already licking at the walls and attacking the ceilings. They stretched the unfortunate wretch out on the grass at a safe distance from the house.

Castilla was agitated, moaning and mumbling in spite of his weakened state. Something urgent was forcing him to call upon his last reserves of strength. La Fargue leaned over him and brought his ear close to the man's swollen lips.

'What is he saying?' inquired Almades.

'I don't know exactly,' answered the captain, straightening up on his knees. 'Something like . . . "garanegra"?'

'*Garra negra*,' murmured the Spaniard, recognising his mother tongue.

La Fargue shot him an intrigued look.

'The Black Claw,' Almades translated.

6

It didn't take Saint-Lucq long to spot Ballardieu.

His instinct, initially, had led him to suspect that he was being watched from rue des Moineaux as he left the Gaget Messenger Service. To confirm this, the half-blood entered a bakery nearby. When he reappeared in the street he was nibbling innocently on a little tart, but took the opportunity to survey his surroundings from behind the red lenses of his spectacles. Without seeming to do so, he took careful note of Ballardieu's round, weathered face among the ordinary passers-by.

The presence of the old soldier surprised him but was not a cause for worry. Obviously, Ballardieu had latched onto his trail after following Naïs, the servant from the Hôtel de l'Épervier. This could only be at Agnès' request. All that remained was to find out why.

The previous evening, on returning from a delicate mission, Saint-Lucq had learned both that the Blades had resumed service and that he would be rejoining them under the direct command of La Fargue. The captain, however, had wished to keep the half-blood in reserve and it was agreed that he would await his orders at the Gaget Messenger Service. This idea had not displeased him. It indicated that the captain wished to keep a card up his sleeve, and that he was to be this card. But to be played against whom, and to what end? Did La Fargue mistrust someone within the Palais-Cardinal, or even among the Blades themselves? Saint-Lucq had not deemed it necessary to ask the question. Nevertheless, there was something fishy going on and Agnès de Vaudreuil, evidently, had not taken long to come to the same conclusion. Hence the appearance of Ballardieu on the half-blood's heels.

With La Fargue's letter in his pocket, thanks to Naïs, Saint-Lucq proceeded at a steady, tranquil pace as far as the quays along the Seine, which he then followed upstream. Then, by way of the Pont Neuf and the elegant Place Dauphine he arrived at the Palais de la Cité. He had concluded that he needed to shake Ballardieu from his tail without seeming to do it on purpose, in order not to arouse his suspicions and, above all, those of Agnès, who seemed to be dancing a strange *pas de deux* with La Fargue. The half-blood's loyalty was to his captain first, and the Palais de la Cité was ideally suited for an impromptu game of hide-and-seek. At one time the seat of royal power, it was now, among other things, the most important court of law in the French kingdom, housing fourteen of the twenty-nine jurisdictions in Paris within a jumble of buildings dating back to the Middle Ages.

Saint-Lucq entered via rue de la Barillerie, and then through a gate flanked by two turrets. Beyond were two courtyards to either side of the Sainte-Chapelle. The court-yard on the left was that of the Chamber of Accounts: full of horses, carriages and shops spilling over from the neighbour-ing streets, its walls were hung with signboards displaying the names and portraits of criminals at large. The Mai courtyard lay to the right, giving access to a staircase and then a gallery leading to the Salle des Pas Perdus. This immense, high-ceilinged, dusty and noisy waiting room had been rebuilt in stone after a fire in 1618. It was swarming with people – lawyers, prosecutors and clients who chattered and argued, often shouting and sometimes even coming to blows in a heated atmosphere aggravated by all the legal chicanery. But the plaintiffs and the men of law in their long black robes were not the only individuals haunting the place. It was also invaded by a multitude of curious onlookers and customers of the two hundred and twenty-four shops which occupied the galleries and passageways within the Palais. All sorts of trifles were sold in these small shops whose keepers called out to potential buyers: silks, velvets, lace, bibelots, jewellery, fans, precious stones, hats, gloves, cravats, books and paintings. They were favoured as meeting-places, elegant ladies strolled here and handsome messieurs gave the glad eye to all of them.

Saint-Lucq had little trouble losing Ballardieu in this populous maze. After wandering about in an apparently innocent fashion, he suddenly found a hiding place and watched from afar as the old soldier hurried straight on. The half-blood quickly left the Palais, feeling quite pleased with himself.

He was then free to return to the mission which La Fargue had entrusted to him. He crossed the Seine by the Petit Pont and went to rue de la Fontaine in the faubourg Saint-Victor. There he found a house that he was supposed to first search and then keep an eye on. It was the dwelling of a young woman – a certain Cécile Grimaux – whom the Blades were protecting after some hired swordsmen had tried to abduct her the previous night. Marciac had foiled their attempt, proof that the years had not changed him in the least and that he was still as gifted as ever at playing the valiant knight rescuing demoiselles in distress. Whatever anyone thought of this, such occasions were rare and when they did present themselves, they always seemed to favour the Gascon.

The house was small, modest, and discreet; on the side facing the street, only the shutters and windows distinguished it from its neighbours on this weekday morning. After a quick and unobtrusive look at the place, Saint-Lucq went around to the rear, into the garden and found a window that had already been broken into and left open. He entered cautiously, subjected the ground floor to a rigorous examination, found signs of a fight – or at least a violent upheaval – in the stairway, continued up to the next floor, noted a certain disorder and the wide-open window through which Marciac and his protégée had no doubt made their escape to the rooftops.

Nothing indicated that Cécile's rooms had been searched. Saint-Lucq therefore performed this task with some hope of success, starting with the more obvious hiding places before narrowing his focus. Fortune smiled upon him. In a jewellery box, among various rings, necklaces and earrings of no great value he found a curved nail that caught his interest. He then had only to guess at what this nail might be used to dislodge. As it turned out, it was a small stoneware tile in a corner of the bedroom, beneath a small table which – having been moved too often – had left some faint scuff marks on the floor.

Saint-Lucq sighed upon discovering this cache, half-pleased to exhume the handwritten documents within, half-disappointed by the trivial ease of this paltry treasure hunt.

He was worth better than this.

7

At the Hôtel de l'Épervier, Marciac had slept for less than two hours when he rejoined Leprat in the main room. The musketeer was still sitting in the same armchair near the fireplace, now gone cold, his wounded leg stretched out before him with his foot propped on a stool. Restless from inactivity, he continued to mope, but at least he had ceased drinking. He was still a little inebriated, however, and feeling drowsy.

Marciac, in contrast, seemed full of energy. He smiled, his eyes shone and he displayed a vitality and *joie de vivre* that quickly exasperated Leprat. Not to mention the unkempt – but artfully maintained – state of his attire. The Gascon was every bit the perfect gentleman, dressed in a doublet with short basques and a white shirt, with his sword in a baldric and boots made of excellent leather. But he wore it all in a casual manner that betrayed his blind faith in his personal charm and his lucky star. The doublet was unbuttoned from top to bottom, the collar of his shirt gaped open, the sword seemed to weigh nothing and the boots were desperately in need of a good brushing.

'Come on,' said Marciac in a lively tone as he drew up a chair. 'I need to look at your wound and perhaps change the bandage.'

'Now?'

'Well, yes. Were you expected somewhere?'

'Very funny . . .'

'Grumble as much as you like, you dismal chap. I have sworn an oath that obliges me to treat you.'

'You? An oath . . . ? In any case, my leg is doing quite well.'

'Really?'

'I mean to say that it is doing better.'

'So you aren't downing bottle after bottle to dull the pain . . . ?'

'Haven't you anything better to do than count bottles?'

'Yes. Treat your leg.'

Sighing, Leprat surrendered and with ill grace allowed Marciac to get on with it. In silence, the Gascon unwound the bandage and inspected the edges of the wound, making sure it wasn't infected. His touch was gentle and precise.

At last, without lifting his eyes towards his patient, he asked:

'How long have you known?'

Leprat stiffened, at first surprised and then upset by the question.

'How long have I known what?' he said defensively.

This time, Marciac looked into his eyes. He had a grave, knowing expression that spoke louder than any words. The two men stared at one another for a moment. Then the former musketeer asked:

'And you? Since when have you known?'

'Since yesterday,' explained the Gascon. 'When I first treated your leg . . . I noticed the obatre mixed in with your blood. There was too much for you to be unaware that you have the ranse.'

According to Galen, the Greek physician of ancient times whose theories provided the basis of all Western medicine, human physiology was derived from the equilibrium of four fluids – or humours – that impregnated the organs: blood, yellow bile, black bile and phlegm. The predominance of each of these humours determines the character of an individual, resulting in sanguine, choleric, melancholic and phlegmatic temperaments. Everything is for the best when the humours are present in their proper amounts and proportions within the organism. People fall ill whenever one of these humours is in excess or is tainted. Then it becomes necessary to drain off the malignant humour by means of bleeding, enemas and other purgings.

Avant-gardist for their time, the doctors at the University of Montpellier – where Marciac had studied – believed that the disease transmitted by the dragons came from contamination by a fifth humour peculiar to that race, called obatre. This substance, they claimed, perturbed the balance of human humours, corrupting them one by one and finally reducing victims to the pitiful state observed in terminal cases of ranse. Their colleagues and traditional adversaries at the University of Paris would not hear of any talk about obatre as it was not mentioned by Galen, and his science could not be questioned. And the quarrels between the two schools, although unproductive, went on and on.

'I have been ill for the past two years,' said Leprat.

'Have there been any symptoms of the Great ranse?'

'No. Do you think I would even let you come near me if I thought I was contagious?'

Marciac avoided answering.

'The Great ranse has perhaps not yet set in,' he declared. 'Some people live with the lesser version until their death.'

'Or else it will set in and make me a pitiful monster . . .'

The Gascon nodded sombrely.

'Where is the rash?' he asked.

'All across my back. Now it's beginning to spread to my shoulders.'

'Let me see.'

'No. It's useless. No one can do anything for me.'

As a matter of fact, whether the doctors of Montpellier were wrong or right, whether obatre actually existed or not, the ranse was incurable by any known medicine.

'Do you suffer?'

'Only from fatigue. But I know there will eventually be pain.'

Marciac found he had nothing further to add and redid the bandage on the musketeer's thigh.

'I should be grateful if . . .' Leprat started to say.

However, he did not finish.

The Gascon, standing up, addressed a reassuring smile at him.

'Don't worry,' he said. 'I never actually took the Hippocratic oath, since I never became a physician, but your secret is safe with me.'

'Thank you.'

Then, firmly planted on his legs and smiling again, Marciac declared:

'Well! Now I'll go and make sure that our protégée lacks for nothing. But since Naïs has gone out, I can also make a trip to the kitchen and bring you back anything you like . . .'

'No, leave it. I believe I shall sleep for a bit.'

Upon reflection, Marciac told himself that in fact he was somewhat hungry and went to the kitchen. He found it empty, but searched out a dish of pâté and half a loaf from the bread bin, and made himself a small repast at the corner of the table. Leprat's potentially fatal disease concerned him, but, aware that he could do nothing, he forced himself not to think about it. He could only hope to offer the musketeer some comfort by sharing his secret. If he desired to speak of his illness, he now knew who he could turn to.

The Gascon was drinking straight from a bottle when Cécile entered and greeted him.

'Good morning, monsieur.'

He almost choked, but managed a charming smile instead.

'Good morning, madame. How are you feeling, today? Can I be of service?'

She was looking pale and drawn, but nevertheless remained exceedingly pretty. And perhaps her weakened state and large sad eyes even added to her fragile beauty.

'In fact, monsieur, I was looking for you.'

Marciac hastened to pull out a chair for the young woman and sat in front of her attentively.

'I am listening, madame.'

'I beg you, call me Cécile,' she said in a timid voice.

'Very well . . . Cécile.'

'I want, first, to thank you. Without you, last night . . .'

'Forget that, Cécile. You are now safe within these walls.'

'Indeed, but I know nothing of you and your friends. I

cannot help but ask questions which no one will answer for me.'

She put on a desolate expression that was almost heart-breaking to see.

The Gascon took her hand. She did not withdraw it. Had she leaned forward slightly to encourage him? Marciac presumed so and was amused by this little game.

'By paths I cannot reveal to you without betraying secrets that are not mine to divulge,' he explained, 'my friends and myself have been led to meet you. Nevertheless, rest assured that we are your allies and that your enemies are also our own. In fact, anything that you can tell us will aid your cause, whatever that may be. Have faith in us. And if that is too difficult for you, have faith in me . . .'

'But I have already told madame de Vaudreuil everything,' Cecile replied sulkily.

'In that case, you have no further cause for concern, because we will take care of the rest. I swear to you that if the thing is humanly possible, we will find your sister Chantal.'

'My profound thanks, monsieur.'

'I am entirely at your service.'

'Truly, monsieur?'

He looked deeply into her eyes, this time taking delicate hold of both her hands, with his fingertips.

'Most assuredly,' he said.

'Then, perhaps . . .'

Leaving her sentence unfinished, she turned away, as if she already regretted having said too much. The Gascon pretended to fall into her snare:

'I beg you, Cécile. Speak. Ask what you will of me.'

From beneath her eyelashes, she gave him a timid glance whose effectiveness she had no doubt tested in the past.

'I should like, monsieur, for you to accompany me to my home.'

'Now?'

'Yes. I left there some personal effects that I miss and should like to recover.'

'That would be most imprudent, Cécile . . .'

'Please, monsieur.'

'On the other hand, tell me what you lack and I shall go fetch them for you.'

'It concerns personal effects that a woman cannot go long without . . . Or speak about to a man . . .'

'Ah . . . Well, see about that with the baronne. Or with Naïs . . . Be that as it may, it is out of the question for you to return to your home. The danger is still too great.'

The young woman realised that she would not win this argument. Defeated, she nodded sadly and said:

'Yes. No doubt you are right.'

'And I'm sincerely sorry, Cécile.'

She rose, thanked him one last time, indicated that she was returning to her room and left the kitchen.

Marciac remained pensive and still for a moment.

Then he asked:

'What do you make of that?'

Agnès emerged from behind the door where she had been standing for some time now. She had witnessed the conversation without being seen or heard by Cécile. But the Gascon had noticed her presence, she knew.

'She almost tried everything,' Agnès said. 'For a moment, I even thought you might fall for it.'

'You do me an injustice.'

'Nevertheless, the demoiselle seems most promising.'

'What do you think she wants to collect from her home?'

'I don't know, but I shall go and see.'

'Alone?'

'Someone needs to stay here, and neither Leprat nor old Guibot will prevent Cécile from giving us the slip.'

'At least take Ballardieu with you.'

'He's not here.'

'Wait for him.'

'No time.'

8

Wearing a blue silk and satin gown, with a grey mother-of-pearl unicorn pinned close to her neckline, the vicomtesse de Malicorne was amusing herself by feeding her dragonnet. From a vermilion and silver plate, she was tossing bloody shreds of meat one by one to the little reptile, who plucked them out of the air from his perch and gulped them down. It was a superb animal with gleaming black scales and shared an intimate bond with its mistress. She had sometimes been seen talking to it as if it were an accomplice, a confidant, perhaps even a friend. But the strangest thing was that the dragonnet understood her, a glow of intelligence would pass through its golden eyes before it flew off with a flap of its wings, usually on some nocturnal mission.

When the marquis de Gagnière entered the salon, the young and pretty vicomtesse set down the plate of meat, licking – delicately but with relish – the tips of her slim fingers. She did not accord much attention to the visitor, however, pretending to be interested only in her sated pet.

'Savelda has just returned from the little house in the orchard,' Gagnière announced.

'The refuge of the so-called chevalier d'Ireban?'

'Yes. Castilla finally talked.'

'And?'

'Our Spanish brothers were mistaken.'

The young woman's glance shifted from the dragonnet to the elegant marquis. The news he had just delivered obviously delighted him: a satisfied smile caused his thin lips to quirk upwards.

Among all the more or less well-intentioned individuals

who served the Black Claw, rare were those who did so knowingly. Those who did were known as affiliates. But, generally unaware of the exact nature of their missions, they took their orders from initiates, who occupied the highest rank to which anyone without the blood of dragons running in their veins might aspire. An aristocratic adventurer without land or fortune, Castilla was one of these affiliates whose loyalty had not yet been firmly established. Therefore he had hitherto only been given missions that one wished not to see fail, but which did not require full knowledge of their purpose to be carried out. Intelligent, competent and capable of taking initiatives, he had never given cause for complaint.

At least until he had suddenly gone missing.

' "Mistaken", marquis? What do you mean by that?'

'I mean that Castilla was not running away from the Black Claw.'

Castilla's disappearance had been worrying. Had he betrayed them, and if so, had he taken with him enough secrets to harm the Black Claw? They needed to find him in order to shed light on this affair and, if need be, eliminate him. Their spies discovered that Castilla had left Spain by ship and that he had disembarked at Bordeaux in the company of a certain chevalier d'Ireban – or at least the latter had signed the ship's register under that name. Had they met during the crossing or were they fleeing together? It mattered little in the short run, for the Black Claw then lost trace of them. From Bordeaux, they could just as easily have travelled by sea to another continent as gone by road to a neighbouring country. But they were soon seen again in Paris. Without delay, the Black Claw in Spain had demanded that madame de Malicorne do everything in her power to track them down. In a capital of five hundred thousand souls, that was all the more difficult as she had other business at hand. Nevertheless, she was in no position to refuse and, against all expectations, she had succeeded where some had perhaps hoped she would fail, her first exploits in France having already provoked jealousy in Madrid.

Castilla being too frequent a visitor to a certain Parisian

gambling house, he was the first to be located. Then it was the turn of a young woman he often met, who proved to be none other than the dashing chevalier d'Ireban. No doubt in an effort to remain discreet, she still sometimes disguised herself as a cavalier. But whenever she wore a woman's dress, she had invented for herself the identity of a modest orphan from Lyon. As soon as it was possible, Gagnière – who also had much else to do – organised the capture of the couple with the assistance of Savelda, a henchman recently arrived from Spain. But the young woman escaped, thanks to a miraculous rescue, while Castilla was taken and tortured.

'Come to the point, marquis. And tell me what secrets Savelda extorted from Castilla last night.'

'As we suspected, Castilla and the lady were lovers. However, it was not the Black Claw they wished to escape by fleeing Spain, but the demoiselle's father.'

'Am I to understand that we have spent all this time and effort to find two eloping lovers?'

'Yes.'

'And that Castilla never sought to harm us?'

'Never. And perhaps not even to abandon us.'

The vicomtesse stifled a laugh.

'In other circumstances,' she said, 'I would be furious. But here we have the means of putting our Spanish brethren in their place and, if necessary, teaching them a lesson in humility. Besides, they won't be able to deny it when it is their own envoy, Savelda himself, who uncovered the full facts behind this story.'

'I doubt that the more jealous of our rivals will appreciate the irony when the news reaches Madrid,' said Gagnière in an amused tone.

'Henceforth, they will appreciate whatever we choose to serve them.'

Smiling with pleasure, the young vicomtesse de Malicorne dropped into an armchair.

'But who is this father that Castilla wanted to flee from so badly, even when it meant incurring the wrath of the Black Claw?'

'That's the best part of the story, madame. The father is none other than the comte de Pontevedra.'

The young woman's eyes sparked with sudden interest.

Pontevedra was a foreign aristocrat with a troubled past who, in less than two years after appearing at court, had become a friend of the comte d'Olivares and a favourite of King Felipe IV, thus winning both fortune and renown in Spain. The man was influential, powerful and feared. And he was presently in Paris, on a mission as an ambassador extraordinary. For the past week he had been engaged in secret negotiations at the Louvre, no doubt with the aim of fostering a rapprochement between France and Spain.

A rapprochement that the Black Claw did not want at any price.

'Everything now becomes clear,' said the vicomtesse. 'At least until the Cardinal's Blades entered the scene . . .'

Gagnière forced himself to contain his scepticism on the subject.

His associate's obstinate tendency to see Richelieu's agents everywhere was becoming worrisome. Granted, her magic might be informing her of more than she was telling. But it was almost as if there were an old dispute between her and the Blades that obsessed and blinded her.

'Madame . . .' he started to say in a reasonable tone. 'Nothing indicates that—'

'And just who, according to you, rescued Pontevedra's daughter last night?' she interrupted. 'Her saviour did not fall from the Moon, so far as I know. . And he was able enough to carry her off in the face of numerous opponents . . . ! Courage, audacity, valour: the very mark of the Blades . . . What? You still have doubts . . . ?'

She had become uselessly worked up, as the gentleman's cautious silence made her realise. In order to calm and perhaps reassure herself, she opened a precious-looking casket set on a table beside her. It contained the Sphère d'Âme, which she caressed with the tips of her fingers, her eyelids half-closed.

She drew in a breath and then carefully explained:

'Do me the favour of thinking the matter through. You are the comte de Pontevedra and you know that your daughter has fled to Paris – where she is perhaps under threat from the Black Claw. Now, there is nothing that France would refuse you, given the importance of the negotiations that you are conducting with her. Would you not seek help from the cardinal? And would you not demand that he mobilise his very best men?'

'Yes,' Gagnière admitted reluctantly.

'The very best, meaning the Blades.'

'I believe you.'

'It's about time . . . ! But what a shame that Pontevedra's daughter managed to evade us! What a lever she would have provided us against him!'

'All is perhaps not lost on that score. I sent Savelda to the girl's house, in rue de la Fontaine. He may find something there and, if not, it will at least keep him busy.'

'Excellent initiative. We will thus have our hands free to prepare the ceremony this evening. Is everything ready at the castle?'

'We are applying ourselves to the task.'

'Nothing must disturb our very first initiations, marquis. The Grand Lodge will not forgive us if there is the slightest sour note.'

'I know that. However . . .'

Gagnière, hesitant, left his sentence unfinished.

But as the vicomtesse was looking at him with a frown on her face, he continued:

'We need now to discuss a delicate case, madame.'

'Which is?

'Laincourt.'

9

Agnès de Vaudreuil cursed between her teeth when she discovered the empty cache in the bedroom floor.

Suspecting that Cécile wanted to recover something compromising from her home, Agnès had quickly and discreetly gone there to search the small house from top to bottom. To do so, she had hailed an empty sedan chair that was passing on rue des Saints-Pères and asked the bearers to carry her to rue d'Orléans in faubourg Saint Victor, by way of rue de la Fontaine. She had paid in advance, climbed into the little cabin through the door at the front, between the two handles, and, as soon as the curtains were drawn, felt herself being lifted before she let herself be cradled by the steady rocking of the bearers' walking pace. As they passed along rue de la Fontaine, she had opened a curtain slightly to identify the house Marciac had described and inspect its surroundings without being seen. She had seen nothing disquieting. Descending from the vehicle in rue d'Orléans, she had circled round to enter the premises from the rear, through the garden, remaining out of view of any watchers.

And now Agnès had to face up to two obvious facts. Firstly, she had indeed guessed correctly about Cécile's intentions: she had been hiding something in her bedroom, something valuable enough to her that she wanted to return to the house despite the danger, even attempting to use her charms on Marciac to convince him to accompany her. And secondly, someone had pipped Agnès at the post and seized the prize before her.

But who?

The same men who had tried to abduct Cécile, no doubt . . .

Makeshift as it was, the cache in the floor was not large and offered no clues as to what it had contained. The best thing to do, therefore, would be to seek information from the principal interested party, Cécile herself. In any case, Agnès felt that the Blades – at La Fargue's request – had been too gentle with her. Granted, the young woman had been the victim of a brutal attempt to kidnap her and she did not seem prepared to face this sort of adventure. But the gratitude which she displayed towards her new protectors did not extend as far as laying her true cards on the table. Now convinced of Cécile's duplicity, Agnès was determined not to tolerate it any longer.

To set her mind at rest, she continued to search the entire house. In vain. And when she pushed open the little door leading to the garden, Agnès suddenly found herself standing nose-to-nose with an armed, one-eyed man in black who – initially as surprised as Agnès – smiled at her in a sinister manner.

'Well, well!' he exclaimed with a strong Spanish accent. 'So the little bird has returned to its nest . . .'

Agnès immediately understood.

She wore a plain dress, a thin brown coat and a matching short cape with a hood. The modesty of her attire had been calculated: not knowing that she would have the luxury of making her journey in a sedan chair, the young baronne had left the Hôtel de l'Épervier thinking that she would have to walk to her destination, then loiter near the house while she scouted the surroundings. She had thus wished to go unnoticed and, to that end, the best thing was to seem neither too rich nor too poor. But Cécile could very well have been dressed in similar fashion. She and Agnès also had their beauty, their long, dark hair and their youth in common, being only a few years apart. If the one-eyed man had never met either of them and had been given only a brief description of Cécile, he was entirely likely to mistake one woman for the other.

Agnès promptly adopted a fearful attitude, as one would

expect of a defenceless young woman who had just fallen into the hands of a menacing enemy. Besides, the one-eyed man was not alone. Some hired swordsmen with an evil look accompanied him.

'As Heaven is my witness,' said the Spaniard, exhibiting the cruel signs of the ranse that had destroyed his eye and was ravaging his cheek, 'I could never have hoped for so much in coming here . . . My name is Savelda, Cécile.'

'What do you want from me?'

'I don't know what's wanted of you and it isn't for me to decide. I can only promise that no harm will come to you if you follow us without making a struggle or noise. So, Cécile? Will you be reasonable?'

'Yes.'

A few minutes later, Agnès found herself back on rue de la Fontaine, closely hemmed in by the hired swordsmen, with Savelda leading the way. It was there that she saw and recognised Saint-Lucq; wearing dark clothing and a sword at his side and discreetly positioned at the entrance to an alley-way, he observed the scene from behind his ever-present red spectacles.

Agnès' astonishment was such that she almost betrayed her emotion. All they needed was the half-blood for the Cardinal's Blades to be complete, but La Fargue had not announced his recruitment to anyone. Yet . . . his presence here could not be mere chance? No doubt he was watching the house. Perhaps it had even been Saint-Lucq who had searched the premises and emptied the cache inside. It was ironic that it was her own fault they had missed one another: he could not have guessed that she was in the sedan chair that had passed by in the street and then she had entered the house by the rear while he had been keeping his eye on the main façade out front.

Seeing Agnès being led away, Saint-Lucq was already taking a step towards her and reaching for his sword – if he hadn't lost any of his skills the matter would doubtless be quickly settled. Only Savelda could perhaps pose a problem.

But the false captive stopped the half-blood in his tracks with a glance that she hoped he would comprehend.

Sometimes, throwing yourself into the lion's jaws was the only means of finding its den.

10

La Fargue and Almades returned around noon covered in sweat, soot and blood, the hooves of their horses suddenly filling the walled, cobbled courtyard with loud echoes that woke the Hôtel de l'Épervier from its sad torpor. They turned the care of their mounts over to old Guibot, who came hurrying as quickly as his wooden leg would allow, while they dashed up the front steps.

'War council, now!' shouted the captain as he burst into the main room of the house.

Leprat, trapped in his armchair by his wounded leg, was already there. Marciac joined them and for a brief moment there was expectant silence. Obviously, there had been an urgent new development, about which Leprat and the Gascon were both anxious to learn the nature, while La Fargue paced back and forth before finally asking:

'And the others?'

'Agnès has gone out,' said Marciac.

'Ballardieu?'

'Here,' announced the old soldier, entering the room.

He had just arrived himself – he had even seen La Fargue and Almades pass him in the street at a rapid trot as he was returning from Palais de la Cité, where Saint-Lucq had shaken him off his tail.

' "Gone out"?' asked the captain, thinking of Agnès. 'Gone out where?'

Receiving the same questioning look as Marciac, Leprat shrugged his shoulders: he didn't know anything about it.

'She's gone to search Cécile's house,' explained the Gascon.

'Alone?' inquired Ballardieu in a worried tone.

'Yes.'

'I'm going over there.'

'No,' ordered La Fargue, visibly upset. 'You stay.'

'But, captain . . .'

'You're staying right here!'

Ballardieu was going to protest further but Almades placed a reassuring hand on his shoulder.

'Agnès knows what she's doing.'

Reluctantly, the old man subsided.

'Marciac,' said La Fargue. 'The doors.'

Nodding, the Gascon closed all the exits to the room and when he finished the captain announced:

'We found Castilla. Tortured and left for dead.'

'Is he dead now?' Leprat wanted to know.

'No. But he's hardly better off for being alive. His tormenters spared him nothing. Almades and I rescued him at the last minute from a fire set to make him vanish. We took him straight to the Saint-Louis hospital which, fortunately, was close by.'

'Did he speak?'

'Two words only,' interjected Almades. '*Garra negra*. The Black Claw.'

Everyone went quiet: they all knew what that meant.

The Black Claw was a secret society that was particularly powerful in Spain and its territories. It was not secret in the sense that its existence was unknown, but in that its members did not reveal their identities. And for good reason. Directed by dragons who were avid to acquire power, the society stopped at nothing to further its ends. For a time, it had been thought to serve Spain. However, even although its most active and influential lodge was to be found in Madrid its ambitions were not always in harmony with those of the Spanish crown. Sometimes they were even opposed. The masters of the Black Claw in truth wanted to plunge Europe into a state of chaos that would aid their plans to institute an absolute draconic regime. A state of chaos that, in the end, would not spare the Spanish Court of Dragons.

Tentacular in nature, the Black Claw was nowhere as

powerful as it was in Spain. It was nevertheless at work in the Netherlands, in Italy and in Germany where it had established lodges which remained subordinate to the oldest and most dreaded of them all, the Grand Lodge in Madrid. As for France, so far she had eluded the society's clutches. Although the Black Claw sometimes hatched schemes within the French kingdom, it had never succeeded in implanting a lodge there.

'If the Black Claw is involved,' said Leprat, 'it explains why the cardinal suddenly called us back to service. It also means that the danger is great. And imminent.'

'So this whole affair could just be a pretext to put us on the trail of the Black Claw?' ventured Marciac.

'I doubt that,' answered La Fargue. 'But the cardinal may know more than he has let on.'

'So what are we to believe? And who?'

'Ourselves. We only believe in ourselves.'

'That's a tune I've heard sung before . . .'

'I know.'

'Back to the matter at hand,' prompted Leprat, seeing that the company was rehashing its shared bad memories. 'If the Black Claw is, like us, searching for the chevalier d'Ireban, it is no doubt because he is something more than the debauched son of a Spanish grandee.'

'That much, we already guessed,' interjected Marciac.

'So then, who is he?'

'Perhaps he and Castilla belonged to the Black Claw. If they betrayed it, they had every reason to flee Spain and seek refuge in France, where the Black Claw still enjoys little influence.'

'If the Black Claw were after me,' observed Almades in a grim tone, 'I would not stop running until I reached the West Indies. And even then, I would stay on my guard.'

'Castilla and Ireban might have less good sense than you, Anibal . . .'

'I'll grant you that.'

'We still need to know,' said Leprat, 'what information the Black Claw wanted from Castilla and whether or not they obtained it.'

'If he hadn't talked we would have found a dead body,' asserted La Fargue. 'Judging by his sad state, he resisted as long as he could. He therefore had some important secrets to hide.'

'Perhaps he was trying to protect Ireban.'

'Or Cécile,' suggested Ballardieu, who until then had remained quiet.

His remark gave rise to a pause. To some degree or other, all of them had noticed the curious attitude La Fargue seemed to have adopted with regard to the young woman. Anyone else in similar circumstances would have been closely questioned by the Blades. But it was as if the captain wished to spare her for some obscure reason.

La Fargue understood the silent reproach being directed at him by his men.

'Very well,' he said, assuming his responsibilities. 'Where is she?'

'As far as I know,' said Marciac, 'she's still in her room.'

'Fetch her.'

The Gascon was leaving by one door when Guibot knocked at another. Almades opened it for him.

'Monsieur de Saint-Lucq is waiting in the courtyard,' said the old man.

11

There was a coach in the courtyard of the Hôtel de Malicorne, waiting to depart, when Gagnière arrived at a gallop.

'Madame!' he called out as the vicomtesse, dressed in a travelling cloak with a short cape, was about to climb through the coach door held open for her by a lackey. 'Madame!' Surprised, the young woman paused. She had the casket containing the Sphère d'Âme under her arm. She proffered it to a man sitting inside the vehicle, of whom the marquis saw no more than his gloved hands, saying:

'Don't open it.'

Then turning to Gagnière, she asked:

'Where are your manners, marquis . . . ?'

The gentleman dismounted, and unsure who was inside the coach, said in a confidential tone:

'I beg you to forgive me, madame. But circumstances demand that I forgo the usual formalities.'

'I am listening, monsieur.'

'We have Pontevedra's daughter.'

Gagnière's eyes shone with excitement. The vicomtesse, on the other hand, manifested nothing more than a cautious wariness.

'Really?'

'She fell into our hands by returning to her home at the very moment when Savelda happened to be there as well. The souls of the Ancestral Dragons are watching over us, madame!'

'No doubt, yes . . . Where is she at present?'

'With Savelda.'

The vicomtesse winced.

As the ambassador extraordinary of the king of Spain, the comte de Pontevedra was negotiating a rapprochement with France which the Black Claw opposed. With that in mind, his daughter constituted a choice prey. A prey that should be preserved intact.

'When the Grand Lodge of Spain learns that Pontevedra's daughter is in our hands,' said the young woman, 'it will lay claim to her. We must therefore hide her in a secure place, outside Paris; somewhere no one will be able to reach her without passing through us.'

She thought for a moment and decreed:

'Have Savelda conduct her without delay to the Château de Torain.'

'Today?' asked Gagnière, alarmed. 'But, madame—'

'Do it.'

The man in the coach then spoke up, still without revealing himself:

'It was at Pontevedra's express request that the cardinal called up the Blades . . .'

The vicomtesse smiled.

She privately reflected that it was in her power to, sooner or later, wreck Pontevedra's diplomatic mission by threatening his daughter's life. But the same means could be used to a different, more immediate, end. It would, moreover, be an opportunity to measure the depth of the ambassador's paternal feelings.

'Let us send word to Pontevedra that we hold his daughter and that if he wishes to see her again alive, he must provide us with some tokens of his good will. The first is to persuade Richelieu to recall his Blades as of today. That will remove a thorn from our foot.'

'And who shall carry this news to Pontevedra?' asked Gagnière.

The vicomtesse thought for a moment and an idea came to her.

'Monsieur de Laincourt wishes to be initiated this evening, does he not? Well, let him show his mettle. If he carries out this mission successfully then he shall have what he wants.'

After Gagnière's departure, the vicomtesse climbed into the coach which immediately set out. She sat facing the person the marquis had been unable to see and to whom she had entrusted the precious reliquary.

'It's the Sphère d'Âme, isn't it?' asked the man as she took the casket from him.

'Yes. Without it, nothing that will take place this evening would be possible.'

'I am anxious to see that.'

'I believe you. But the experience is painful. And sometimes, fatal.'

'I don't care!'

Full of confidence in him, the young woman smiled at monsieur Jean de Lonlay, sieur de Saint-Georges . . . and captain of the Cardinal's Guards.

If he survived, there was no question at all that he would become an initiate of the first order in the Black Claw's French lodge.

12

As La Fargue had not informed anyone that he'd recruited Saint-Lucq, the half-blood's entrance on the stage took the others off guard but was not altogether surprising. Firstly, because the Blades could not claim to be complete without him. And secondly, because Saint-Lucq had always been an irregular soldier who was most effective when he was off on his own, operating in the shadows. The news that he brought, moreover, took priority in their minds. He announced it at once, without pausing for preliminaries, in the courtyard of the Hôtel de l'Épervier.

'Agnès has been abducted.'

' "Abducted"?' Ballardieu roared.

Bursting with anger, he took a menacing step towards Saint-Lucq, who did not make any gesture, either to defend himself or to retreat. It took more than this to impress him.

La Fargue, on the other hand, moved to interpose himself between the two Blades.

'Let him explain what happened, Ballardieu.'

Impassive, the half-blood recounted his tale.

'I was watching this house according to your orders . . .'

'Cécile's house,' the captain clarified for the others.

'I suppose that Agnès entered around the back because I didn't see her beforehand. And the same for the men who came out with her and took her away.'

'But what men, by God?!' shouted Ballardieu.

'Hired swordsmen,' replied Saint-Lucq calmly.

'And you did nothing!'

'No. Agnès didn't want me to intervene. She wanted these men to take her away.'

'How do you know that?'

'Agnès saw me in the street. She threw me a glance and I understood.'

'You're very clever . . . !'

'More than you.'

'WHAT?'

Ballardieu, red in the face, seemed to expand in volume. Saint-Lucq looked at him disdainfully, without so much as a quiver, and said:

'You heard me.'

'That's enough!' intervened La Fargue in a loud voice.

Leprat, who had come down into the courtyard despite the wound in his thigh, forced Ballardieu to move back, taking him by the arm. Only Marciac was missing, having gone to find Cécile in her room just as the half-blood was announced.

'Go on, Saint-Lucq. What happened next?'

'Next? Nothing . . . I followed them for as long as I could, but they soon mounted horses. I was on foot.'

'What's going on?' demanded Marciac, coming out of the stables and passing Leprat who was still trying to calm Ballardieu. 'Well! Hello, Saint-Lucq.'

'Agnès has been abducted,' explained La Fargue.

'Oh? By whom?'

'By hired swordsmen led by a one-eyed man afflicted by the ranse,' said the half-blood.

'My one-eyed man with the ranse?' asked the Gascon. 'The one from last night?'

'And the same man as this morning,' added Almades. 'The riders we passed on the road, they were also led by a man whose eye was ruined by the ranse.'

'That means that Agnès is in the hands of the Black Claw,' concluded La Fargue. 'She allowed herself to be taken in order to unmask our adversaries, but she couldn't guess that—'

'I'm afraid I have another piece of bad news to announce,' declared Marciac. 'Cécile has disappeared. She has run away.'

'*Merde!*'

The captain's profanity rang out like a musket shot in the courtyard.

The Blades searched the Hôtel de l'Épervier from top to bottom and, when Cécile's disappearance was no longer in any doubt, they gathered in the main room. The young woman had almost certainly slipped out through the garden, where they discovered the gate ajar – from there, she would have had no difficulty losing herself in a maze of alleys and passageways. A wider search would thus have proved futile.

'I think she must have been listening at the door during our meeting,' said Marciac. 'No doubt wishing to avoid answering the questions that we intended to ask her, she preferred to duck out. We were too trusting of her. She wasn't the poor orphan that we believed, mixed up against her will in a dark intrigue. I would even wager that her sister, who supposedly disappeared at the same as the chevalier d'Ireban, never existed.'

'She and Ireban are one and the same,' announced Saint-Lucq, throwing a small bundle of documents on the table. 'I found these in her home. Reading them, you'll discover that Cécile is the daughter of a great Spanish lord, that she and Castilla are lovers, and that they fled Spain together, Cecile disguising herself as a man to fool any spies. You'll also see therein that Cécile and Castilla not only feared the wrath of her father, but also that of another mysterious enemy.'

'The Black Claw,' guessed Leprat.

'Must I remind you that Agnès is in the Black Claw's hands?' Ballardieu interjected in tight voice that barely concealed his contained anger. 'Isn't that the most important thing?'

'Yes,' said La Fargue. 'However, it is perhaps only by getting to the bottom of this whole story that we will find a way to rescue Agnès . . .'

'And I tell you that we need to do everything in our power to save her. Starting right now!'

'Agnès voluntarily placed herself in the lion's jaws,' Leprat reasoned, 'but she may not have known which lion was involved.'

'She passed right in front of me,' Saint-Lucq pointed out. 'I heard the one-eyed man talking to her as they took her away, and by all appearances, they mistook her for Cécile. That won't last. Ballardieu is right: time is running short.'

'Who can help us?' the old soldier asked. 'The cardinal? Castilla?'

'I doubt that Castilla is in any state to talk,' said Almades. 'As for the cardinal . . .'

Silence fell upon them, heavy with worry compounded by a sense of impotence.

'Malencontre,' said Leprat after a long moment.

The others stared at him, while Almades explained briefly to Saint-Lucq who this Malencontre was. That done, Leprat continued:

'Malencontre belongs to the Black Claw; otherwise we would not have surprised him beneath Castilla's windows. And he must know a great deal, or the cardinal would not have taken him from us.'

'But if I follow the chronology of events correctly,' said Saint-Lucq, 'this man can't know where Agnès is being held today, because he was arrested yesterday—'

'He certainly knows enough to put us on the right track!'

'Yes!' exclaimed Ballardieu. 'Yes! That's an excellent idea!'

He turned towards La Fargue and solicited his opinion with a glance.

'The idea is a good one, yes . . . But—'

'But, we don't know were he can be found at present,' Marciac filled in for his captain. 'Moreover, we will not be able to reach him without permission from the cardinal. And, lastly, he won't talk unless we can offer him something in return.'

'Freedom,' said Almades. 'Malencontre knows he is lost. He will not talk in return for anything less than his liberty.'

'We'll persuade Richelieu to offer Malencontre his freedom!' declared Ballardieu. 'If he knows that Agnès' life hangs in the balance . . .'

He wanted to believe it, but the others were less confident. What price did the cardinal currently place on the life of one of his Blades? He had never hesitated to sacrifice them on the altar of political necessity in the past.

'I can arrange a meeting with His Eminence quickly,' proposed Saint-Lucq.

'Then let us try that,' concluded La Fargue.

They all rose and Marciac took the captain to one side.

'With your permission, I would like to go in search of Cécile.'

'Do you know where she went?'

The Gascon smiled.

'If Agnès were here, she would tell you that you do not know women very well, captain.'

'That may be. Go ahead, follow your idea. But we will have need of you soon.'

'I won't be long.'

13

In 1607 Concino Concini, an Italian adventurer who, together with his wife, enjoyed such influence over Queen Marie de Médicis that she made him marquis d'Ancre and a marshal of France, built a vast mansion on rue de Tournon. Greedy and incompetent he was hated by the population, who pillaged his mansion for the first time in 1616 and then again, after his death in 1617. Louis XIII resided there from time to time, and then gave it to one of his favourites, only to buy it back later. From then on, and up until 1748, the beautiful house in rue de Tournon became a residence for visiting ambassadors extraordinary.

The creation of permanent ambassadors was not yet a widespread practice. With rare exceptions, European kingdoms only employed ambassadors extraordinary to conduct particular negotiations or represent their monarchs on grand occasions – princely baptisms, betrothals, marriages, and other important ceremonies. These envoys – always great lords expected to maintain appearances at their own cost – would return to their country once their mission was completed. Diplomacy was yet to become a career.

Thus, in Paris, ambassadors and their retinues were the guests of the king in the marquis d'Ancre's former mansion. Having been appointed by King Felipe IV of Spain, the comte de Pontevedra had been lodging there for several days and would no doubt remain there as long as was necessary to ensure the completion of a mission that was surrounded by the greatest secrecy. What were the comte and Richelieu discussing during the course of their long daily meetings – meetings at which even the king himself made appearances?

The royal court was filled with rumours on this subject and everyone either claimed to know or made educated guesses. The truth, however, went beyond any of their expectations. It involved nothing less than preparing, if not an alliance, then at least a rapprochement between France and Spain. Was such a thing even possible? If it was, it would represent an enduring upheaval in European politics and would affect the destinies of millions of souls.

On this day, the comte de Pontevedra returned rather earlier than usual from the Louvre. He rode in a luxurious coach, surrounded by twenty gentlemen in arms whose role was both to protect him and enhance his prestige with their numbers and their elegance. At the mansion in rue de Tournon he hurried alone to his apartments, sent his servants away and even refused his valet's assistance to remove his brocade doublet and his gold-trimmed baldric. He poured himself a glass of wine and settled down in an armchair. He was preoccupied, eaten away by worry. But it was not the difficulty of the delicate diplomatic negotiations he was engaged in that spoilt his days and haunted his nights.

A door creaked.

The ambassador rose, furious, ready to drive away the unwelcome visitor and then suddenly froze. He glanced around for his sword which, unfortunately, he had abandoned out of easy reach.

'That would be suicide, monsieur,' said Laincourt, emerging from an antechamber. 'I am not an assassin. I am a messenger.'

'Who sent you?'

'The Black Claw.'

In his fifties, tall, dignified, with greying temples and a fine scar decorating his cheekbone, the ambassador was still a handsome man. He was not trembling, but he had grown pale.

'I see,' added Laincourt, 'that you have guessed the reason for my visit . . .'

'Speak, monsieur.'

'We have your daughter.'

Pontevedra remained expressionless.

'You don't believe me,' inferred Laincourt after a moment.

'On what grounds should I believe you? I await your proofs. Can you show me a jewel that could only belong to her? Or perhaps a lock of her hair?'

'Neither jewel, nor hair. But I could return with an eye . . .'

There was another silence, during which the two men exchanged stares, each trying to probe the other.

'What do you want? Money?'

Laincourt gave a faint but amiable smile.

'Why don't you sit down, monsieur? In this armchair. That will place you away from the table you are edging towards and the letter opener that rests upon it.'

Pontevedra obeyed.

In turn, the Black Claw's envoy also took a seat, but one a good distance from the ambassador, while constantly covering him with his pistol.

'Once upon a time,' said Laincourt, 'there was an adventurous French gentleman who became a great lord in Spain. This gentleman had a daughter who, one day, wished to remove herself from his company. The gentleman did not want this to happen. So his daughter fled, crossing the border disguised as a cavalier and finding refuge in Paris. The gentleman received word of this. And he soon learned, through his spies, that one of his most powerful enemies was threatening, or at least also pursuing, his daughter. The gentleman, understandably, became worried . . . What do you think of my story, monsieur? Is it accurate enough that I should continue?'

Pontevedra nodded.

'In that case, I'll go on . . . At the same time, an ambassadorial mission was being prepared in Madrid. Did our gentleman engage in a few little intrigues to have this mission entrusted to him, or did fate serve him by happenstance? It matters little. What does matter is that he was named ambassador extraordinary and came to Paris to negotiate with the king of France and his most eminent minister. His political mission was of the utmost importance, but he merely regarded it as the means of saving his daughter. Using all the influence he was able to wield, he obtained a promise from France, via

Cardinal Richelieu, that she would endeavour to search for his daughter. Or rather, to search for the chevalier d'Ireban, since it was under this name and this disguise that she had secretly reached Paris. Our gentleman gave the chevalier prestigious origins, so that the cardinal might believe that he was rendering a service to the Spanish crown rather than to its ambassador . . . Does my tale still have the ring of truth?'

'Yes.'

'Good . . . This gentleman, in fact, did more than simply demand that France search for his daughter. He wanted France to use her best men for this delicate mission. He wanted the Cardinal's Blades . . . When Richelieu asked him why, he answered that Spain wished to assure herself that France was doing everything in her power to succeed: she would therefore show the best possible goodwill by having recourse to the Blades. Careful not to give offence to Spain on the eve of crucial negotiations, the cardinal no doubt agreed to this demand with fairly good grace. After all, for him it was simply a question of recruiting men who had already demonstrated their worth and could soon prove useful once again. And so it was arranged . . . But I see with regret that my tale has started to bore you . . .'

'It is a tale whose subject matter is already familiar to me.'

'I am coming now to precisely those elements of which you are perhaps ignorant.'

'Very well. Continue.'

'I said earlier, our gentleman was worried that a particular enemy of his was pursuing his daughter. He was indeed worried, but was not surprised by this. It must be said that his daughter had become bound by ties of affection to a handsome adventurer who was in the pay of the enemy in question. That is to say, the Black Claw. The daughter was unaware of this fact. But the gentleman knew. And it was no doubt in seeking to separate her from her dangerous admirer that he provoked her anger and subsequent flight. Because the girl was of an age when people are willing to sacrifice everything for love—'

'You promised to speak of developments that are unknown to me.'

'And here they are: your daughter's lover is dead, but before he died he told us who she is, which we did not know until then. You must recognise that she constitutes a significant prize for us . . . But it remains the case that your manoeuvres have placed the Blades on our trail. This must cease. As of today.'

'What guarantees do you offer me?'

'None. You have persuaded Richelieu to deploy his Blades against us. See that he henceforth employs them for another purpose and your daughter shall live.'

'Richelieu will refuse if he suspects something.'

'Richelieu already suspects something. His suspicions began the instant you demanded he involve the Blades in this matter. Don't forget that he knows who you really are. But does your daughter know? And if she doesn't, do you want her to remain ignorant of the facts?'

14

Escorted by riders, the coach had all its curtains lowered and was travelling at a rapid pace along a dusty, rutted road that subjected its creaking axles to constant torment. Inside, shaken by the bouncing of the cabin, Agnès did not utter a word. She was sitting in front of the one-eyed victim of the ranse who had abducted her. Savelda pretended to pay her no attention, but he discreetly kept his eye on her, watching her slightest movement.

After surprising her at Cécile's dwelling, Savelda and his henchmen had taken Agnès to the courtyard of a nearby inn where their horses were waiting for them. She was placed on the rump of one of their mounts and, still led by the Spaniard, the riders left the faubourg Saint-Victor at a trot, depriving Saint-Lucq of any chance of following them. Their destination was an isolated house where Agnès was kept under guard for a while, no doubt just long enough for news of her capture to be transmitted and for orders to come back. Finally, she had been forced to embark in this coach, which had been on the move ever since. But where was it going?

No one had questioned her yet. For her part she did not speak, remained docile and tried to appear anxious and overwhelmed by all these events. She wanted to lull her guardians into a false sense of security until the moment came for her to act and, until then, she did not wish to say or do anything that risked compromising the misunderstanding that had led to her abduction. These men – Savelda at their head – mistook her for Cécile. Agnès wanted that to last until she was able to discover who she was dealing with and what their motivations were. As they seemed to attach great value to their hostage,

Agnès did not feel actually threatened. But the problem remained that she herself did not know Cécile's true identity. She was playing a dangerous game, trying to impersonate someone about whom she knew almost nothing. The best she could do was to adopt a low profile in order to avoid making any blunders. She didn't fancy her chances if her deception was revealed.

If her story were to be believed, Cécile was an innocent young woman searching for her elder sister who had disappeared at the same time as her lover, the chevalier d'Ireban. Agnès was convinced that she had been lying to the Blades, at least in part. Therefore, Cécile no doubt knew more than she was prepared to say about the hired swordsmen Marciac had saved her from the previous night: she must have some idea what they wanted and why. If it was simply a question of their wishing to eliminate an overly curious sister, then they would have tried to murder her, not abduct her. Rather than merely an awkward witness, she was in their eyes a bargaining token, or perhaps a means of applying pressure on someone.

But for the young baronne de Vaudreuil, the real cause for worry lay elsewhere. She suspected La Fargue knew some of Cécile's secrets. Secrets that he had not shared with anyone.

This was both abnormal and disturbing. It was completely unlike the captain, who, with his frankness and absolute loyalty, had always shown himself worthy of the blind faith invested in him by his Blades. Where had this mistrust come from? Had the years changed him to such an extent? No, time alone did not cause well-tempered souls to bend. But the betrayal of a friend, perhaps . . .

Since Saint-Lucq was also in the game, the Cardinal's Blades were now, arguably, complete. Complete except for two, that is. Those two would never return. One of them, Bretteville, was dead. The other, Louveciennes, had betrayed them. He had been La Fargue's companion-in-arms, his oldest and his best friend, with whom he had founded the Blades and recruited all the others. As brutal as it was unexpected, his treason had first led to the death of Bretteville during the siege of La Rochelle and then brought about the infamous disbanding of the Blades as a whole. La Fargue had witnessed the shattering of his life's work at the hands of a man he had considered as a brother and who, rich from the fortune that this crime had earned him, had found refuge – it was said – in Spain.

The wound was deep. It had probably never healed and no doubt explained why La Fargue distrusted everyone, including the men under his command. Agnès understood this to a certain degree, but her resentment of it remained sincere and profound. The Blades were a citadel in which La Fargue was the central keep. Without the certainty of being able to find refuge there in case of need, Agnès could not imagine herself fighting for long upon the ramparts.

Having almost reached the end of its journey, the coach slowed as it climbed a winding and stony track.

Then it pulled to a halt.

Savelda descended first and, holding the door open, signalled for Agnès to follow him. Beneath a sun which, after the darkness inside the cabin, dazzled her for a moment, she found herself surrounded by the partially crumbled ruins and ramparts of a fortified castle whose imposing keep dominated a courtyard which had long been invaded by weeds and shrubs. Isolated on top of a rocky and wooded height overlooking the Chevreuse valley, the place was a scene of bustling activity at odds with its ancient sleeping stones. Men and dracs were busy planting torches, building woodpiles for bonfires, and erecting three tiers of benches on either side of an open air stage. Wagons loaded with materials were entering the site. Riders came and went. Overseers gave orders and assigned tasks, hurried by a sense of urgency. A wyvern and its rider circled in the sky. A second, saddled, waited in the shelter of a covered enclosure.

Savelda seized Agnès by the elbow and led her into a small building of which only the exterior walls remained standing, its interior being overgrown with brush. He made her descend a stairway carved into the rock, at the bottom of which a hired swordsman was already posted. Upon seeing them he opened a door and Agnès entered an underground chamber filled with dusty debris. There was an old oven for baking bread in one corner. Daylight entered through a small semicircular window which looked out on the courtyard.

A fat woman rose from her seat, abandoning her knitting.

'Keep an eye on her,' Savelda ordered.

Then, turning to the prisoner, he warned her:

'Don't try anything. If you obey us, no harm will be done to you.'

Agnès nodded and the one-eyed man departed, closing the door behind him and leaving her alone with her female guardian. After a moment, as the fat woman did not seem to be overly concerned about her, she went towards the window, whose bars she gripped with both hands in order to raise herself on tiptoe and, while verifying the solidity of the iron, gazed outside.

Something important was about to happen here and, despite the risks she was taking, Agnès knew she had been right to let herself be brought here.

15

Because it was designed to take in plague victims, the Saint-Louis hospital had not only been built outside Paris, it also resembled a fortress. Its first stone had been laid in 1607, after the serious epidemics which the Hôtel-Dieu, the only big hospital the capital possessed at the time, had been unable to cope with. Its four main buildings, each formed of a single storey above a ground floor with taller structures at their centre and extremities, surrounded a square courtyard. Two rings of walls separated it from the rest of the world. Between them, symmetrically distributed, were the dwellings of the employees, nurses and nuns who worked there. The pantries, kitchens, storerooms and bakeries were built against the outer wall. Around them spread the gardens, fields and pastures bordering the faubourg Saint-Denis.

Having shown his pass several times, Marciac received directions to the immense ward where, among the moans and murmurs of the other patients, he found Castilla lying on one of the beds aligned in rows. Cécile was sitting near him. Pale, her eyes red, she caressed his forehead with a light touch. The wounded man was clean and bandaged, but his face was swollen and horribly deformed. He was breathing but showed no reaction to his surroundings.

'Leave me be,' said the young woman on seeing Marciac. 'Leave us both.'

'Cécile . . .'

'That's not my name.'

'It's of little importance.'

'Oh, but it is . . . ! If I wasn't who I am, if he who claims to

315

be my father wasn't who he is, none of this would have happened. And this man here, he would live.'

'He isn't dead.'

'The sisters say he won't live through the night.'

'They don't know anything. I've seen many men survive wounds that were believed to be fatal.'

The young woman did not reply, seeming to forget the Gascon and, leaning over Castilla, continued to caress his brow.

'What should I call you?' asked Marciac after a while.

'Ana-Lucia . . . I believe.'

'You want this man to live, don't you, Ana-Lucia?'

She glared at him with damp eyes, as if this question were the worst possible insult.

'Then you should leave here,' Marciac continued in a gentle voice. 'The men who tried to abduct you are no doubt still after you. And if they find you here, they'll also find him . . .'

She stared at him and a new worry caused her drawn features to look even more distraught.

'You . . . You really think so?'

'I know so, Ana-Lucia. Please come. You will need to be brave. I promise you that we'll return tomorrow.'

Back in Paris an hour later, the beautiful Gabrielle, mistress of a brothel located in rue de la Grenouillère, heard knocking at her door. As no one in the house answered and the knocking continued, she wondered why she bothered paying her porter and, more resigned than angry, leaned from her window.

Outside, Marciac lifted a grave-looking face toward her, which worried her because the Gascon tended to be one who smiled in the face of adversity.

'I need you, Gabrielle,' he said.

He was holding a tearful young woman's hand.

16

The coach picked Rochefort up at Place de la Croix-du-Trahoir and, after a short conversation with the comte de Pontevedra, it left him in front of the scaffolding covering the façade of the Palais-Cardinal. The ambassador extraordinary of Spain had demanded this discreet meeting urgently. He had promised that he had important news and he had not been lying.

La Fargue and Saint-Lucq were waiting in an antechamber of the Palais-Cardinal. They were silent and pensive, aware of what was at stake during the interview His Eminence was about to grant them. Their chances of rescuing Agnès lay with Malencontre, a man Richelieu was keeping locked away and was not likely to give up to them easily – and they had no guarantee of success if he did.

After some considerable hesitation, Saint-Lucq rose from a bench and went to join La Fargue who stood gazing out a window.

'I found this at Cécile's house,' he said in a confidential tone.

He held out an unsealed letter on a yellowed piece of paper.

The old gentleman lowered his eyes to the missive and finally took it with a doubtful air.

'What is it?'

'Read it, captain.'

He read, looking stiff and grim, haunted by old torments that he refuse to show on his countenance. Then he refolded the letter, slipped it into his sleeve, and said:

'You also read this.'

'It was open and I had no way of knowing its contents.'

'Indeed.'

'I haven't said anything to the others.'

'Thank you.'

La Fargue resumed looking out at the cardinal's gardens, where workers were finishing digging the basins. Trees rooted in large sacks of earth were arriving in carts.

'Captain, did you know you had a daughter?'

'I knew it.'

'Why did you hide it?'

'To protect her and safeguard her mother's honour.'

'Oriane?'

Oriane de Louveciennes, the wife of the man who – until his act of treason at the siege of La Rochelle – had been La Fargue's best friend.

Saint-Lucq nodded, impassive behind his spectacles' round, red lenses.

'Why do you think Oriane wrote this letter so many years ago?'

'No doubt so that Anne might one day know who her real father was.'

'Perhaps your daughter came to Paris in the hope of meeting you.'

'Yes. Perhaps.'

A door creaked and Rochefort passed through the ante-chamber with a quick step without seeming to pay them any notice. Unlike them, he did not have to wait before being received by the cardinal.

'I don't like the look of that,' said the half-blood.

In his large and luxurious study, Richelieu was discussing matters with Père Joseph when Rochefort entered and interrupted them. They were speaking of Laincourt, of whom they had heard nothing.

'Please forgive my intrusion, monseigneur. But I have some important news.'

'We are listening.'

'The comte de Pontevedra has just informed me that the chevalier d'Ireban is in Madrid. Although he was thought to have disappeared here in France, in fact he decided to return to Spain by his own means and without letting anyone know.'

The cardinal and Père Joseph exchanged a long look: they did not believe a word of what they had just heard. Then Richelieu settled back into his armchair with a sigh.

'Whether it's true or not,' said the Capuchin monk, 'the mission entrusted to your Blades no longer has any reason to continue, monseigneur . . .'

Richelieu nodded thoughtfully.

He nevertheless took time to reflect before declaring:

'You are right, father. Have Captain La Fargue come in.'

17

Back at the Hôtel de l'Épervier, where Marciac had returned just a quarter of an hour before them, La Fargue and Saint-Lucq found the rest of the Blades gathered together in the main room.

'Richelieu refused,' announced the captain upon entering.

Dismayed, they all fell silent as La Fargue poured himself a glass of wine and emptied it in one gulp.

'Does he know . . .' Ballardieu started to say in a voice buzzing with anger. 'Does he know that Agnès is in danger? Does he know that she is being held prisoner by the Black Claw? Does he know—?'

'He knows!' said La Fargue sharply.

Then he added in a quieter tone:

'He knows all that because I told him.'

'And despite that, he still refuses to return Malencontre.'

'Yes.'

'This time, it has not taken His Eminence long to desert us,' said Leprat whose dark gaze was lost in a limbo where he saw the outline of La Rochelle standing before him.

'But there's more, isn't there?' guessed Almades, standing in a corner where he leaned with his arms crossed. 'Richelieu was not simply satisfied with refusing to allow you to speak with Malencontre . . .'

'No,' admitted the Blades' captain.

He paused for a moment and then said:

'Our mission has been cancelled. The chevalier d'Ireban has supposedly turned up recently in Madrid. Therefore we no longer have any reason to continue searching here in Paris.'

'But Ireban does not exist!' exclaimed Marciac. 'He and

Cécile were always one and the same person! How can he be back in Spain now?'

'Nevertheless, this is the case. At least, if one believes the ambassador extraordinary of Spain.'

'It's absurd!' objected Leprat. 'The cardinal can't be taken in by this lie—'

'It was at Spain's request that Richelieu entrusted us with this mission, and it is once again at her request that he has called us off. The stakes of the negotiations that are currently taking place in the Louvre go well beyond us. It was a matter of pleasing Spain. Now it is a matter of not displeasing her . . .'

'And we are suddenly asked to forget all about the existence of Ireban,' said Marciac. 'And about Malencontre. And about the Black Claw which is scheming in the very heart of the kingdom!'

'Those are our orders,' insisted La Fargue.

'Are we also to forget about Agnès?' Ballardieu demanded.

'There is no question of that.'

Leprat rose and, despite his wounded leg, could not stop himself from pacing back and forth.

'Malencontre remains our best hope of finding Agnès quickly,' he said, thinking out loud.

'The cardinal only deigned to tell us that Malencontre was being held at Le Châtelet, awaiting transfer to the prison in the Château de Vincennes,' indicated Saint-Lucq.

Leprat stopped pacing to and fro.

'I will go and speak with Malencontre,' he declared.

'But he's being held in solitary confinement!' the half-blood pointed out. 'No one can see him without a signed order.'

'I am only on leave from the Musketeers. I can still wear the cape and monsieur de Tréville will not refuse to help me.'

They all fell silent while they considered this idea.

'All right,' said La Fargue. 'Let's suppose that you manage to reach Malencontre. Then what? You have nothing to propose in exchange for his information.'

'Just let me have two words with him,' suggested Ballardieu, balling his fists.

'No,' replied Leprat. 'Malencontre and I are almost old acquaintances by now. Let us do this my way . . .'

Later, while the Blades were getting ready, La Fargue took Marciac by the elbow.

'Did you find Cécile?'

'Yes. At the Saint-Louis hospital, at the bedside of the man she loves, just as I guessed. She was listening at the door when you announced that he was dying there. She fled the house in order to be with him.'

'Is she in a safe place at present?'

'She is in rue de la Grenouillère. No one will go looking for her in a brothel and Gabrielle and the girls will take good care of her.'

'I thought you and Gabrielle had . . . ?'

'A falling out . . . ?' said the Gascon with a grin. 'Yes, we did, for a while . . . Let's just say that she did not particularly appreciate the fact that I was returning to active service under your orders. She remembers how things ended the last time only too well.' He fell silent, thinking, and then with a shrug concluded: 'Bah! She can always marry a haberdasher, if that's what she wants.'

He was turning away in a fairly good mood, when the captain called him back:

'Marciac!'

'Yes?'

'Thank you.'

Puzzled, the Gascon frowned but said nothing.

18

At Le Châtelet, the guards and other personnel were relieved at five o'clock in the evening. Wearing his blue cape with its silver fleur-de-lys cross, Leprat presented himself twenty minutes before the hour at the admissions counter with an authorisation signed by the hand of monsieur de Tréville, captain of His Majesty's Musketeers, and was led to Malencontre's place of detention. The man was being held in Le Puits, or the Well, one of the individual cells in the gaol's lower depths. There reigned a dark and putrid dankness that would have undermined the health and courage of even the most solid of men.

The gaoler left his lantern with Leprat, saying that he would remain within earshot at the other end of the corridor and then shut the door. The light it gave off was dim, barely illuminating the miserable hole, but it sufficed to dazzle the prisoner. Filthy and tired-looking, stinking of urine and refuse, he was sitting on a carpet of rancid straw, back towards the wall to which he was chained by the wrists. His position forced him to keep his arms raised, his long pale blond hair hanging before his face.

'Leprat?' he asked, squinting. 'Is that you, chevalier?'

'It's me.'

'You are very kind to pay me a visit. Would you like some foul water? I think I also have an old crust of bread that the rats haven't carried off yet . . .'

'I came to speak with you.'

The musketeer swept his ivory rapier back, crouched before Malencontre and set the lantern down between them.

'Do you know what awaits you?' he asked.

'I wager that I will soon be asked lots of questions.'

'And will you answer them?'

'If that can save my life.'

'Then talk to me. If you talk to me, I will help you.'

Malencontre stifled a small chuckle and made a grimacing smile that highlighted the scar at the corner of his thin lips.

'I doubt that you have anything to offer me, chevalier.'

'You're wrong. Those who will come after me will ask you the same questions, but in a different manner. Le Châtelet has no lack of torturers . . .'

'The cardinal will not send me a torturer right away. He will first seek to learn if I am disposed to talk. I will reply that I am and I will be treated well. I am no hero, Leprat. I am quite ready to collaborate and only ask for some small consideration.'

His crouching position becoming too uncomfortable due to his wounded thigh, Leprat stood up and, spying a stool in a corner, sat down on it, leaving the lantern where it was.

'You work for the Black Claw,' he said.

'Not really, no. I work for a gentleman who may, perhaps, work for them . . . You serve one master, I serve another.'

'Except that I happen to be free to come and go . . .'

'True.'

'Which gentleman?'

'A very good question.'

'The cardinal's agents will not make the distinction. For them, you belong to the Black Claw.'

'That only increases the value of my modest person, wouldn't you say?'

'You will never see the light of day again.'

'That remains to be seen.'

The musketeer sighed, searching for some means of gaining the upper hand with a man who had already lost everything and to whom he had nothing to offer. If he failed to make Malencontre speak of his own free will, the only solution that remained revolted him.

But the life of Agnès was at stake.

'The cardinal knows nothing of your visit to me, is that not so?' the prisoner remarked. 'So tell me, what brings you here?'

'I am going to offer you a deal that you cannot refuse.'

Outside, in front of Le Châtelet, La Fargue and Almades were waiting. They were on foot, the other Blades guarding the horses a short distance away at the entrance to rue Saint-Denis.

'Do you think Leprat will succeed?'

'Let us hope so.'

Those were the only words they exchanged, both of them anxious as they remained there, keeping track of the time and observing who was coming out of the enormous, sinister-looking building.

As the half hour tolled they saw the large felt hat and cape of a limping musketeer appear at last.

'He's favouring the wrong leg,' noticed Almades.

'What does it matter?'

They hastened to flank Malencontre as closely as possible on either side, without attracting attention.

'You will not be set free until you have told us everything we wish to know,' La Fargue told him in a firm voice.

'And who says that you won't do me an evil turn after-wards?'

'I do. But if you try anything at all . . .'

'I understand.'

They moved quickly towards the other Blades and their horses, fearing that at any moment someone would call after them from the doors of Le Châtelet.

'Who are you?' asked Malencontre. 'And how did you manage this?'

'We took advantage of the changing of the guards,' explained La Fargue taking a discreet look all around them. 'Those who saw Leprat enter were not the guards who let you leave. The hat, the musketeer's cape, the pass from Tréville and the white rapier did the rest. You will return that rapier to me, by the way.'

'And Leprat? Aren't you worried about him?'

'Yes.'
'How will he be freed?'
'It's possible he never will be.'

19

It must have been around eight o'clock in the evening and night was falling.

Still held prisoner, Agnès had seen enough to understand what was going on in the great fortified castle. The preparations were now complete. On either side of the open air stage, the three tiers of benches had been erected and covered with black cloth. On the stage itself, an altar had been placed before a thick velvet cushion. Tall banners had been raised that now floated in the wind, bearing a single golden draconic rune. Torches already illuminated the scene and bonfires waited to be lit. The men and dracs who had installed everything were not workers but hired swordsmen commanded by Savelda and under the direction of a very young and very elegant blond cavalier whom Agnès did not know but who was addressed as marquis: Gagnière. Their task finished, the swordsmen who were not on watch were now gathered around campfires, away from the stage they had set up, near the makeshift stable and the enclosure for the wyverns, and at the foot of the partly collapsed ramparts.

For the past hour, the places along the benches had been filling with men and a few women, most of them sumptuously dressed, whose horses and coaches had been left by the main castle gates. They wore black eye masks embellished with veils of red lace covering their mouth and chin. They waited, visibly anxious and saying little to one another.

Agnès realised why.

She had never taken part in the ceremony that was about to occur, but she had learned something of its nature during her years as a novice with the White Ladies, the religious order devoted to preserving the French kingdom from the draconic contagion. The Black Claw – whose sinister emblem decorated the banners and was even carved into the wood of the altar – was no mere secret society. Led by dragon sorcerers, its power was founded upon ancient rituals that ensured the unfailing loyalty of its initiates by spiritually uniting them with a superïor awareness: that of an Ancestral Dragon who came to impregnate their being. A Black Claw lodge was much more than a meeting of conspirators avid for wealth and power. It was the product of a rite that permitted a fanatical assembly to offer itself as the instrument and receptacle of an Ancestral Dragon's soul – thus bringing the dragon back to life through those who had sacrificed a part of themselves, and allowing it to once again exercise power over a land it had been driven from in the distant past. The ceremony could only be performed by a dragon – one who was thoroughly adept in the higher arcana of draconic magic. In addition, it required an extremely rare relic, a Sphère d'Âme, from which the Ancestral Dragon's soul would be freed at the most propitious moment.

A little while before, Agnès had seen a black coach arrive. An elegant woman in a veil, wearing a red-and-grey gown, had descended from it in the company of a gentleman. The latter had paused for a moment to adjust his mask and Agnès, incredulous, had the time to catch a glimpse of his face. It was Saint-Georges, the captain of the Cardinal's Guards. He and the woman had watched the completion of preparations before being joined by Gagnière and Savelda, with whom they exchanged a few words before turning towards the ruin in whose cellar Agnès was being held captive. The prisoner quickly withdrew from the window where she was spying on them and feared for a moment that they would come to see her, but the coach left with all of them except Savelda, driving off in the direction of the keep, which it entered by means of a drawbridge over a ditch filled with bushes.

As she knew that the ceremony would not take place until night, Agnès had resolved to wait until dusk before acting, and thus take advantage of the evening shadows.

*

The moment had come.

In the now darkened cellar, she turned towards the dirty obese woman charged with keeping watch over her, but who in fact almost never lifted her nose from her knitting. The fat woman was the first obstacle Agnès needed to overcome. The next was the closed door and the sentry that Savelda had prudently left behind it.

'I'm thirsty,' she complained, having noticed her guard's red nose, a clear sign of a fondness for drink.

The fat woman shrugged her shoulders.

'Can't we even have a pitcher of wine?' Agnès wheedled in an innocent voice.

The other woman reflected, hesitated, thought about the pitcher and ran the tip of her tongue over her lips, eyes filled with longing.

'I'd give anything for a cool glass of wine. Here, this is for you if you want it . . .'

Agnès removed one of her rings and held it out. In the fat woman's eyes, greed was now combined with longing. But still she hesitated.

'We deserve a little wine, don't you think? After all, we've been shut away down here for hours now.'

Narrowing her eyes, the fat woman licked her lips, her mouth dry. Then she set down her knitting, murmured something that sounded like assent, stood up and went to knock on the door.

'What is it?' ask the sentry on the other side.

'We're thirsty,' grumbled the woman.

'So what!'

'Go find us a bottle.'

'Out of the question.'

'Then let me go find one.'

'No.'

Although furious, the fat woman was about to give up when Agnès approached and showed her the ring again.

'The girl can pay.'

'With what?'

'A ring. Made of gold.'

After a short instant, Agnès heard the bar blocking the door being removed.

And smiled to herself.

'Let me see,' said the man as he opened up.

A few minutes later, Agnès came out beneath a sky of ink and fire, wearing the sentry's clothes and equipped with his weapons. Their owner was lying in the cellar, a knitting needle planted in his eye as far as his brain. The fat woman was stretched out nearby, a second needle sticking out of the back of her neck.

Agnès carefully surveyed the surroundings, pulled the hat down on her skull and, keeping her head slightly lowered, moved away praying that no one would hail her. She saw a masked rider approach who spoke with Savelda without descending from his mount and then spurred the horse towards the keep.

She went in the same direction.

20

Arriving as night fell, Laincourt discovered the old castle lit by torchlight and lanterns. He observed the stage where the first initiation ceremony would take place, had a look at the future initiates – wearing masks like him – waiting there, saw Savelda and directed his horse towards him.

'You're late,' said the Spaniard upon recognising him.

'They must be waiting for me.'

'Yes, I know. Over there.'

Savelda pointed at the impressive keep and Laincourt thanked him with a nod of the head before continuing on his way, not noticing that he was being followed.

If he was late it was because he had, after presenting the conditions set by the Black Claw to the ambassador of Spain, waited in vain for his contact to show up. The hurdy-gurdy player had not appeared at the miserable tavern in the oldest part of Paris where they ordinarily met and, running short of time, Laincourt had been finally forced to leave. Consequently, no one at the Palais-Cardinal knew where he was at present.

The castle keep was in fact made up of three massive towers, joined by ramparts as high as they were and enclosing a steep-sided, triangular courtyard. It was a castle within a castle, to which one gained access by means of a drawbridge, and where there was an immediate feeling of oppression.

Leaving his horse in the courtyard near a harnessed black coach, Laincourt entered the only tower whose embrasures and openings were illuminated. The marquis de Gagnière was waiting for him.

'So the grand evening is here at last,' he said. 'Someone wishes to see you.'

Laincourt still did not know whether or not he was going to be initiated in accordance with his demands.

He nodded before following Gagnière up a spiral staircase that rose up into the tower, its bare walls illuminated by the flames of a few torches. They climbed three storeys filled with flickering shadows and silence to arrive in a small windowless room lit by two large candelabra standing on the floor. The marquis knocked on a door, opened it without waiting and entered ahead of Laincourt. Located at the very top of the tower, the hall within had two other doors and three arched windows looking out over the inner courtyard far below. A curtain closed off an alcove to one side and on a chair in front of more large candelabras sat a young blonde woman, wearing a mask and a red-and-grey gown. She had a superb black dragonnet with golden eyes with her, sitting on the back of her chair. Richly attired, Captain Saint-Georges was standing to her right and Gagnière placed himself to her left, while Laincourt instinctively remained near the closed door at his back, between the two swordsmen on duty as sentries.

He removed his mask in the hope that the woman would imitate him, but she chose not to do so.

'We meet for the first time, monsieur de Laincourt,' declared the vicomtesse de Malicorne.

'No doubt, madame,' he replied. 'I can only say that the sound of your voice is unfamiliar to me.'

'It is rather unfair,' she continued without acknowledging his remark, 'because I know how highly I should regard you. At least if I am to believe monsieur de Saint-Georges . . . And even monsieur de Gagnière, normally so circumspect, tells me that you are, shall we say, a rare find.'

On hearing the compliment, Laincourt placed his left hand on his chest and bowed slightly. But this preamble did not sit well with him. He sensed a threat coming.

'However,' said the vicomtesse, 'your ambitions might seem overweening. Because you are demanding nothing less than to become an initiate, aren't you?'

'My situation is extremely delicate, madame. I believe I have always displayed perfect loyalty and I must now count on the help of the Black Claw against the cardinal.'

Laincourt knew he was risking his all at this precise instant.

'So in a manner of speaking, monsieur, you now wish to be repaid . . .'

'Yes.'

'So be it.'

The vicomtesse made a sign with her hand and Saint-Georges threw open the curtain that had hidden the alcove from view, revealing the hurdy-gurdy player. He was half-naked, covered in blood and possibly even dead. Chained to the wall, his head slack, the old man in his rags was slumped in a squatting position, suspended by his arms.

This vision transfixed Laincourt. In a fraction of a second, he understood that he had been unmasked, that the hurdy-gurdy player had confessed under torture and that the Black Claw no longer believed in the deception Richelieu had created to counter its activities.

A deception of which Laincourt had been the instrument, and now risked becoming the victim.

He smashed the throat of one of the swordsmen with a violent blow of the elbow and suddenly spun to drive his knee into the crotch of the other, then took the man's head between both hands and broke his neck with a brusque twist. Saint-Georges drew his sword and lunged at him. Laincourt avoided his rapier, ducked under his other arm, rose and seized the captain's wrist to bring it high up behind his back, then finished immobilising him by placing a dagger against his throat. The vicomtesse had stood up by reflex and Gagnière protected her with his own body, brandishing a pistol. Irritated, the dragonnet spat and flapped its wings, still gripping the back of the chair.

'I will slit his throat if either of you makes the slightest move against me,' Laincourt threatened.

The young woman stared at him . . .

. . . then invited Gagnière to take a step back. Nonetheless, he continued to keep his pistol aimed at Laincourt and his human shield.

Saint-Georges sweated, trembled and hesitated to swallow. On the floor, the swordsman with the smashed throat finished choking out his series of horrible death rattles. By a common accord, everyone waited for him to die and for silence to settle over the scene.

It seemed to go on for an eternity.

It had all started in Madrid where, already in the service of the cardinal, Arnaud de Laincourt had been appointed private secretary and trusted aide to an expatriate aristocrat through whom France had unofficially communicated with the Spanish crown. An agent of the Black Claw had approached him during this two-year mission and, understanding with whom he was dealing, Laincourt had informed Richelieu immediately by secret dispatch. The cardinal had ordered him to let matters take their course, without compromising himself too seriously: it was better at this stage to let the adversary keep the initiative and move his pieces as he saw fit. Laincourt thus gave a few tokens of goodwill to the Black Claw which, for its part, no doubt out of fear of discouraging a potential and very promising recruit, did not ask him for much. Things hardly went any further until his return to Paris.

Having entered the service of His Eminence's Guards, Laincourt very soon rose to the rank of ensign. He never entirely knew if this swift promotion rewarded his loyalty or was destined to excite the interest of the Black Claw. Whatever the case, after a long silence, the organisation contacted him again through an intermediary: the marquis de Gagnière. The gentleman told him – as if it were a revelation – the nature of those who had been receiving the small bits of information he had shared in Spain. He'd led Laincourt to understand that he had already done too much to back out now. He must continue to serve the Black Claw, but henceforth in full knowledge of his actions. He would not regret it, and he only had to say the word.

With Richelieu's accord, Laincourt pretended to accept and

for months thereafter had provided his so-called masters with carefully selected intelligence, all the while gaining their trust and rising within their hierarchy in the shadows. His objective was to uncover the person behind this dangerous embryo of a Black Claw lodge in France. He was to prevent them from succeeding and also unmask another spy, one who seemed to be working at the highest level within the Palais-Cardinal. As a precaution, Laincourt did not communicate with Richelieu through the habitual secret channels – even Rochefort did not know about him. His only contact was an old hurdy-gurdy player whom he met in a shabby tavern and about whom he knew almost nothing, except that he was trusted by the cardinal.

But this comedy could not continue. Because he was sharing information that always turned out to be less pertinent than it seemed at first, or which hurt France less than it did her enemies, the Black Claw would eventually work out that he was playing a double game. He needed to hurry matters along, and all the more quickly as the French draconic lodge was on the point of being born . . .

Together with Père Joseph, who was also in on the secret, Richelieu and Laincourt sketched out a bold plan. They arranged for the ensign to be caught in the act of spying, and, after that, they allowed a carefully prepared scenario to unfold. Convicted of treason, Laincourt was captured, locked up and then freed on the pretext that he had threatened to reveal explosive documents. These documents did not exist. But they seemed to have enough value to convince the Black Claw to grant Laincourt what he demanded: to become an initiate, as the reward for his work and skills.

The plan, however, did not expect him to actually go this far. The important thing was to identify the true master of the Black Claw in France and learn the date and place of the grand initiation ceremony. He would inform the cardinal as soon as possible, via the hurdy-gurdy player, to allow His Eminence to organise a vast operation to haul in all the conspirators.

But the hurdy-gurdy player had not shown up for the final meeting.

And with good reason . . .

The vicomtesse lifted an indifferent gaze from the dead body of the swordsman and smiled at Laincourt.

'And now?'

Still threatened by Gagnière's pistol, the cardinal's spy hesitated, tightening his hold on Saint-Georges, and then motioning towards the hurdy-gurdy player with his chin.

'Is he dead?'

'Perhaps.'

'Who betrayed him?'

This question haunted Laincourt. Except for himself, only Richelieu and Père Joseph were supposed to know of the role played by the hurdy-gurdy player in this affair. Even the traitorous Saint-Georges had been kept in the dark.

'No one did,' replied the young woman.

'Then how——?'

'I'm not as naïve as you seem to believe, monsieur. I simply had you followed.'

Laincourt frowned.

'By whom?'

'Him.' She pointed to her dragonnet. 'I saw your most recent meeting with the old man. Through his eyes. You can guess the rest . . . By the way, I must thank you for persuading the comte de Pontevedra to keep the Cardinal's Blades away from us. But I'm afraid it will be the last service you ever render us . . .'

Understanding that he could do nothing but try and save his own life, Laincourt used his heel to hook his hostage's ankles out from under him and abruptly shoved him. Saint-Georges tripped forward and collapsed in Gagnière's arms. But the marquis fired at the same time and hit the cardinal's spy in the shoulder as he was rushing out of the room and slamming the door behind him.

Gagnière took some time in untangling himself from his burden and the door resisted him when he sought to launch himself in pursuit of the fugitive. He turned around to address a helpless look at the vicomtesse.

Very calmly, she ordered:

'Let Savelda take charge of searching for monsieur de Laincourt. We three have better things to do. The ceremony cannot be delayed any longer.'

21

Holding a lantern in one hand and his sword in the other, Savelda kicked open the door to an empty, dusty room, dimly lit by the nocturnal glow coming from its sole embrasure. He examined the premises from the threshold, while hired swordsmen came and went behind him on the stairway.

'No one here!' he called out. 'Keep looking. Search the keep from top to bottom. Laincourt can't be far.'

Then he closed the door.

Silence returned and a moment went by before Agnès let herself drop from the ceiling beams she had been clinging to. Stealthily, she went to press her ear to the door and, reassured, returned to place herself at the embrasure. She did not know who this Laincourt was and the news that Savelda was hunting for someone other than her was only a small comfort. Granted, her escape had so far gone undiscovered. But the freebooters combing through the keep were still very much a threat to her.

Outside, in the lower part of the ruined castle, about fifty metres from the keep, the ritual was proceeding.

It had started at moonrise, led by Gagnière who officiated bare-headed, dressed in a ceremonial robe. He chanted in the ancient draconic tongue, a language which his audience did not understand but whose power, beyond its actual meaning, resonated in the depths of their being. Their souls aquiver, the candidates for initiation listened, taken over by a sacred fervour.

Then the vicomtesse, still masked, solemnly entered the

pool of warm light from the torches and bonfires, and took up her place behind the carved altar. There was a heavy silence while Gagnière stepped back to her side and, with lowered head and hands crossed upon his belly, adopted a meditative pose. She then began, also using the draconic tongue, the long litany of Ancestral Dragons, invoking their true names and asking for their protection. This took some time, as each Ancestral Dragon had to be addressed by its title and its closest family ties. And the names she pronounced before each panegyric were moreover repeated by Gagnière in his role as First Initiate, and then taken up in chorus by the entire audience.

Finally, the vicomtesse opened a casket placed on the altar and took out the Sphère d'Âme which she brandished in her outstretched arms. Still speaking in the draconic language, she called upon Sassh'Krecht, the Ancestral Dragon whose primordial essence haunted the globe with its black turmoil. Now, she recited all of Sassh'Krecht's parents and descendants, titles, legendary exploits and, as she declaimed them, the atmosphere around her filled with a presence that was as exalting as it was frightening, originating from the beginning of time and soon to be resurrected in defiance of the laws of nature.

At this point, beginning with Gagnière and with Saint-Georges just behind him, the faithful filed past the altar in good order, each knelt at the vicomtesse's feet, placed their lips upon the Sphère d'Âme which she had lowered to their height and then went to stand in a long row. By their kiss, they had signified their assent. Ready to sacrifice a part of themselves, they waited for Sassh'Krecht to manifest itself and impregnate their soul.

In a trance, the vicomtesse de Malicorne raised the globe towards the moon. She shouted a command. Whirlwinds lifted around her. Above the castle, the clouds in the sky suddenly dispersed, as if driven away by a centrifugal force. Black and grey plumes escaped from the paling Sphère d'Âme. They rose in long ribbons as a dull noise filled the night and, little by little, they formed the shape of a giant spectral dragon which reared up, deployed its wings and occupied an immense span of the sky. Sassh'Krecht had survived death for centuries now, a prisoner of the Sphère d'Âme where all of its power had been concentrated. It gloried in the freedom which it had now almost completely recovered, only its tail still attached to the relic the vicomtesse gripped in her hands, her body traversed by ecstatic shivers. It simply needed to take possession of the souls that its disciples were offering freely.

No one heard the shot, but all of them saw the Sphère d'Âme, now milky white, burst into shatters.

The vicomtesse screamed and collapsed. The entire gathering suffered an enormous shock that left it reeling and Sassh'Krecht emitted a cavernous howl that shook the members of the Black Claw to the core. Detached from the Sphère d'Âme before it had managed to become fully incarnate, the Ancestral Dragon contorted like an animal trapped in a blazing fire that was devouring it.

Gagnière was the first to react.

He rushed over to the unconscious vicomtesse, crouched down, lifted her up slightly, saw that she was still breathing and, at a complete loss, looked about him in an effort to comprehend.

Had the ritual failed?

The skies grew dark. Still howling, the spectral dragon twisted in pain as shreds were torn from its ghostly silhouette like wisps of mist. Stormy rumblings were heard. Gold and crimson flashes ripped through the night sky as Sassh'Krecht liberated energy that had to find an outlet.

Gagnière saw the vicomtesse's dragonnet flapping in the air around them. It hissed at him furiously, and then flew off towards the keep. He followed it with his eyes and saw the thin stream of smoke that filtered from an embrasure.

Pistol still smoking in her hand, Agnès dashed down the steps of the tower from where, both hidden herself and able to observe every detail of the ceremony, she had opened fire. Aware of what was at stake and doubting she would live to see the dawn, she had resolved that as she had nothing to lose she would wreak as much havoc as possible and wait for the ritual to reach its critical point before she intervened.

Now, she had to make an effort to survive and, perhaps, even to escape.

She descended one floor, then two, and had reached the first floor when she heard hurried steps climbing towards her from the ground floor below. She cursed, tore down an old drapery from a wall and hurled it like a fishing net over the first swordsman who presented himself, delivering a kick that broke his jaw. Her victim fell backwards, toppling his comrades who became tangled up with him and the dusty piece of cloth, which they ripped at without managing to free themselves. Those jostling with one another behind them were forced to retreat back down the stairs and Savelda's angry voice could be heard shouting.

Agnès immediately reversed course and climbed the steps two by two. Her only hope was to reach the top of the tower and the walkway along the keep's ramparts. She suddenly came face-to-face with a lone freebooter. She drew her sword to block his blade, violently drove the butt of her pistol upwards into his crotch and sent her opponent tumbling down the stairs, breaking his neck in the process.

With Savelda's men now at her heels, she arrived on the last floor of the tower when a hand on her shoulder drew her behind a wall hanging and through the little doorway which it hid. Agnès found herself in a narrow, shadowy corridor, pressed up against someone who murmured to her:

'Silence.'

She closed her mouth and remained still, while on the other side of the door, the Black Claw's hired swordsmen ran over to the keep's walkway without stopping.

'My name is Laincourt. Don't be afraid.'

'And of what would I be afraid?'

At which point, Laincourt felt the nip of a dagger that had reached high up between his thighs.

'I am in the cardinal's service,' he whispered.

'They are searching for you, monsieur.'

'So we have something in common. What's your name?'

'Agnès. I thought I heard a shot just before the ceremony began. Was that you?'

'In a manner of speaking. Come, it won't take them long to figure things out.'

They advanced silently down the dark corridor, passing before a triple-arched window.

'You're wounded,' said Agnès noticing the Laincourt's bloody shoulder.

'I didn't fire the shot.'

'Can you move it?'

'Yes. It's not broken and the pistol ball passed clean through. Nothing serious.'

They pushed a little door open and then followed a passage lit in the distance by some square openings looking out into the courtyard. The ceiling was so low that they could only progress bent double.

'This passage runs beneath the walkway. It will take us to the next tower. They're probably yet not looking for us there.'

'You seem to know the premises well . . .'

'My knowledge is newly gained.'

At the end of the passage they came to another door.

They listened, opened it cautiously and emerged behind a sentry. Laincourt slit his throat and held him as he sagged. They heard a great commotion on the lower floors, found only locked doors and were forced to climb some very steep steps in order to raise a hatch that gave them access to the roof.

They were fortunate it was deserted, although they could see torches and silhouettes moving about on one of the other towers, the one where Savelda and his men were finishing their search. Beyond, in the tormented sky, the spectral dragon had been replaced by a fury of uncontrolled magical energy. The red and golden flashes had redoubled in intensity. Interspersed by thunderclaps, a deep roar rumbled above them that could be felt in the gut and increasingly threatened to unleash itself upon the castle itself.

'Quick!' yelled Laincourt.

Seeking cover behind the crenellations, they took the walkway towards the third tower. They went as fast they could without running upright and started to believe that they might make good their escape when a strident cry rang out nearby: the vicomtesse's dragonnet was beating its wings level with them and giving away their position. Heads turned their way. A hue and cry was raised.

Laincourt brandished his pistol and shot the reptile down with a single ball that ripped off its head.

'A wasted shot,' commented Agnès.

'Not entirely,' replied the cardinal's spy, thinking of the hurdy-gurdy player who had been captured thanks to the dragonnet.

They were halfway between the second and the third tower, towards which Savelda's swordsmen were already hurrying. They ran under sporadic and badly aimed fire, reached the tower before their enemies and tried to open the hatch.

Locked.

'*Merde!*' Laincourt swore.

Agnès took stock of the situation. Savelda and his freebooters were coming towards them from the first tower by the walkway. Others were already emerging from the second tower and blocked any possibility of retreat. The ground was fifty metres below. They did not have time to force the hatch.

They were trapped.

Agnès and Laincourt placed themselves *en garde*, back to back . . . and waited.

Cautious now, the hired swordsmen slowed down and surrounded them, while Savelda, calm and smiling, walked up to them.

A circle of blades closed in the fugitives, who were resolved to die rather than allow themselves to be captured.

'Usually,' Agnès muttered to herself, 'they show up about now . . .'

Laincourt heard her.

'What did you say?' he asked over his wounded shoulder.

'Nothing. Delighted to have met you.'

'Same here.'

And then rescue came from the sky.

22

Outside the keep, the castle was plunged into a state of chaos that was dominated by the roiling storm of energies released by the destruction of the Sphère d'Âme. Sizzling lightning bolts fell from the ragged night sky, igniting trees and bushes, raising sprays of earth, pulverising stones and knocking down sections of wall. One of them split the altar open and set it ablaze as Gagnière fled from it, now rid of his ceremonial robe and carrying the unconscious vicomtesse in his arms. People were screaming and panicked horses whinnied. Followers of the Black Claw and its hired swordsmen were running in every direction, not knowing where to seek refuge or even who or what, exactly, they needed defending against.

Because the Cardinal's Blades had gone on the offensive.

Using Malencontre's information, La Fargue and his men were quietly surrounding the keep when Agnès interrupted the ceremony in such dramatic fashion. As desperate as it was, her initiative proved invaluable in diverting the attention of everyone present to the torments of the great spectral dragon. La Fargue, who was moving alongside a sunken path bordered by a low wall, hastened towards the enclosure where the two wyvern riders, who had been idle since the end of the day, were guarding their beasts. With a pipe in his mouth and a heavy sack slung round his shoulders in a bandolier, Ballardieu climbed to the top of a rampart, broke the neck of a lookout and discreetly took his place directly above the main gate and its sentries. Further off, Saint-Lucq stepped over another sentry's dead body and approached a campfire around which five swordsmen had gathered, all of them gaping up at the extraordinary display taking place in the night skies. At the same time, Marciac was slipping towards the stable.

In the keep, Agnès and Laincourt were moving from one tower to the next in an effort to stay ahead of Savelda's search parties when, outside, the first lightning bolt struck the ritual site. At first paralysed in terror, the Black Claw's followers scattered, ducking their heads as more bolts came down, while the hired swordsmen watching over the ritual finally began to react to the alarm.

Ballardieu judged that this was the right moment to take action. Digging into his bag, he took out a grenade and lit its fuse from his clay pipe before hurling the object blindly over the parapet against which he was crouching. A second and a third immediately followed, their explosions ringing out amidst the screams and the roar of the supernatural storm. He risked a glimpse at the scene below, was satisfied to see the bodies of sentries lying there and then spied a wyvern rising from the enclosure. Standing, he began bombarding the milling crowd with more grenades.

The freebooters gathered around a campfire saw the grenades exploding in the distance, grabbed their weapons and—
—froze.

A man dressed in black, his eyes hidden by red glasses that reflected the flames, was standing before them. He waited and pointed his outstretched rapier at them. He seemed both relaxed and determined. Apparently he had been there for some time. They realised they would have to get past him. And in spite of all their experience of suffering, fighting and massacres, a feeling of dread came over them.

Their guts clenched with fear; they knew for certain that they were going to die.

Panicked by the dazzling flashes of lightning and deafening thunder, the Black Claw's followers and their hired swords-men were running towards the stable when its doors opened wide to reveal the fire ravaging the interior and a stampede of horses that Marciac had freed. The terrified steeds knocked down and trampled the first arrivals, and shoved the rest aside, whinnying in fear before they dispersed.

The silhouette of the Gascon was outlined against the blaze as he emerged in turn, gripping his rapier. He rapidly dispatched the few disoriented freebooters who remained, slitting one man's throat, running his blade through the chest of another and splitting open the face of a third.

Taking advantage of a moment's respite, he lifted his gaze to the sky which seemed to have gone mad, and then noticed Saint-Lucq dashing off, barely slowing down to eliminate the men who brandished swords in his path. At the end of one assault, the half-blood turned toward Marciac and pointed to the dark mass of the castle keep, which was where he was headed. The Gascon understood and nodded, thought of following him, but was immediately distracted by defending himself against two more opponents.

Surrounded at the top of the tower, Agnès and Laincourt believed they were doomed when, thrown from above, grenades with blazing fuses bounced among the stupefied swordsmen who were threatening them, provoking panicked pushing and shoving before the missiles exploded one after another in clouds of fiery powder, their burning shards ripping through those who had not been able to retreat towards the keep's walkway.

Rearing up and flapping its wings to slow its approach, a wyvern set down on the tower.

'Captain!' Agnès exclaimed in relief when she saw who was riding the reptile.

'Hurry!' yelled La Fargue.

He held out a gloved hand to her, but the young woman pointed instead to Laincourt.

'He's coming too!'

'What? No! Too heavy!'

'He's coming too!'

It was not the time or the place for an argument: around

347

them, the hired swordsmen were beginning to rally themselves.

Agnès and Laincourt climbed onto the reptile's rump behind La Fargue, who dug in his spurs to launch the wyvern. The beast took a few lumbering steps towards the parapet. Seeing his prey escaping, Savelda ran towards them, taking aim with his pistol while yelling at his men to move out of the way. He fired and the pistol ball passed through the wyvern's long neck at the very instant when it was taking to the air. The reptile flinched. Its surprise, pain and the over-heavy load on its back toppled it over the edge, and it fell. It opened its wings as the ground approached and La Fargue hauled with all his might on the reins . . . and the wyvern pulled out of its dive at the very last second. Its belly brushed against the cobblestones and its claws scraped over them, raising a spray of sparks. It was moving too fast across the small courtyard to have any chance of climbing again. La Fargue barely succeeded in turning its head towards the keep's gate. The reptile swept at full speed beneath the vault. But its span was too wide and the impact broke its leathery wings. The wyvern screamed. Moving like a rock down a hillside, it crossed the lowered drawbridge, rolled over in a whirlwind of dust and blood, and threw off its passengers before finally crashing into one of the great bonfires that had been lit for the ceremony.

Ballardieu saw the wyvern burst forth from the keep and three bodies flying through the air.

'AGNÈS!' he screamed as the reptile with its broken wings smashed into the flaming pyre and vanished beneath it.

He vaulted over the parapet, landed six metres below and began to run without paying any heed to the pain from a sprained ankle. Two drac swordsmen attacked him. He did not slow down or even draw his sword. Instead, taking his sack, weighed with a few remaining grenades, by its bandolier, he swung it round, crushing a temple and dislocating a scaly jaw. Still running, shoving aside everyone in the terrified crowd who stood in his way, he yelled at the top of his lungs:

'AGNÈS . . . ! AGNÈS . . . !'

He saw La Fargue picking himself off the ground and went to him.

'Agnès! Where is Agnès?'

The captain, in a daze, was staggering on his feet. He blinked and almost tripped over. Ballardieu had to steady him.

'Captain! Where is she? Where is Agnès?'

'I . . . I don't know . . .'

Marciac arrived.

'What's going on?' he asked, trying to making himself heard over the din of thunder that accompanied the magical lightning bolts.

'It's Agnès!' explained the old soldier anxiously. 'She's here! Somewhere! Help me!'

Grimacing, with a dazed look in his eye, Laincourt struggled to drag himself from the ground, remaining for a moment on his hands and knees. He coughed and spat out a mixture of dirt and blood.

Then he stood up.

Around him the chaos of the battle drawing to a close blended with that of the incredible storm above, whose windy moans were rising to a high-pitched screech. The destructive bolts of lightning gained in intensity and the furious roaring shook the entire castle to its very depths, dislodging its stones. No one thought of fighting any longer, only of escape. The surviving followers and mercenaries of the Black Claw pressed toward the gate which Ballardieu no longer defended with his grenades.

Laincourt, too, should have been fleeing without delay.

But he had one last task to accomplish.

Still holding the unconscious vicomtesse in his arms, Gagnière arrived in the courtyard of the keep at the same time as Savelda and his men, coming down from the upper floors.

'We're under attack!' said Gagnière sweating.

'Yes,' replied the one-eyed Spaniard. 'And we've already lost . . . Give her to me.'

Without waiting for a reply, he seized hold of the vicomtesse.

The marquis let him take her, too stunned by the turn of events to even protest.

'We must flee!' he said. 'By the passageway. Quickly, while there's still time!'

'No.'

'What?'

'Not you. You stay.'

'But why?'

'To protect our retreat . . . Against him.'

Gagnière turned around.

Saint-Lucq was entering from beneath the vault, armed with a rapier in his right hand and a dagger in his left.

'You and you, with me,' ordered Savelda. 'The rest of you, with the marquis.'

And, followed by the two men he had selected, he disappeared through a door leaving the gentleman and four swordsmen in the courtyard.

Gagnière went over and tried to open the same door, only to find it had been locked from within. He then stared at the half-blood who met his glance and smiled at him from beyond the row of freebooters, as if they were an insignificant obstacle separating the two of them. This idea wormed its way into the mind of the marquis and he became frightened.

Gathering up a sword from a dead body that had fallen from the walkway above, he cried: 'ATTACK!'

Themselves unnerved by Saint-Lucq's predatory calm, the hired swordsmen flinched and then rushed forward. The half-blood parried two blades with his rapier, planted and then left his dagger in the belly of his first opponent, spun round and slit the throat of the second with a reverse thrust. In one smooth motion he ducked down in front of a drac who was preparing to strike high, slipped under his arm and stood up, throwing the reptilian over his shoulder. The drac fell heavily on his back and Saint-Lucq lunged to pierce the chest of the remaining mercenary, whom he disarmed. Then, completing his murderous choreography, he brought the rapier he had just acquired to a vertical position, and without looking, pinned the drac to the ground with it.

Expressionless, the half-blood turned to stare once again at Gagnière.

There was still a wyvern in the enclosure, although no doubt it would have fled earlier if it had not been chained up. Saint-Georges struggled to saddle it and he already had one boot in the stirrup when, amidst the racket of the storm, he heard distinctly:

'Step back.'

Bruised, wounded, bleeding; Laincourt stood a few metres behind him, pointing a pistol. He was a sorry sight, but there was an almost fanatical light in his eyes.

'Obey,' he added. 'I'm just waiting for an excuse to blow your brains out.'

Without making any sudden moves, Saint-Georges set his foot back on the ground and stretched out his arms. He did not turn round, however. Nor did he move away from the wyvern and the pistols tucked into its saddle holsters. Pistols that Laincourt, behind his back, could not see.

'We can still reach an understanding, Laincourt.'

'I doubt that.'

'I am rich. Very rich . . .'

'Your gold is the reward for your treachery. How many men have died because of you? The latest of your victims were no doubt the couriers from Brussels, whose itineraries you gave to the Black Claw. But before them?'

'Gold is gold. It shines everywhere with same brightness.'

'Yours will be worthless where you're going.'

Saint-Georges suddenly spun about, brandishing a pistol.

A shot rang out.

And Laincourt watched the traitor fall, his eye burst and the back of his skull torn out by the ball.

Then he gazed at the saddled wyvern.

The storm was now at its height. Whirlwinds of energy had formed at ground level and lightning bolts fell from the sky every second, digging craters wherever they landed. The castle looked as if it were being battered by a cannonade that was determined to destroy it.

'OVER HERE!' La Fargue yelled suddenly.

He was crouching near Agnès whom he had just found and was raising her head. The young woman was unconscious. Her hair was sticky with blood at her temple. But she was still breathing.

'IS SHE . . . ?' asked Ballardieu, who had come running, fearing the worst.

'NO. SHE LIVES.'

A rider appeared from a breach in a rampart. It was Almades, who towed the Blades' mounts behind him. They were good warhorses, fortunately, and thus did not panic in the din of battle.

'AGNÈS IS IN NO FIT STATE TO RIDE!' declared La Fargue.

'I'LL CARRY HER!' replied Ballardieu.

A lightning bolt struck nearby and showered them with smoking earth.

'LOOK!' cried the Gascon.

The vicomtesse's black coach was coming from the keep, driven by Saint-Lucq.

'Bless you, Saint-Lucq,' murmured Ballardieu.

The half-blood pulled up the coach in front of them. He had great difficulty controlling the team of horses. They whinnied and reared at each explosion, making the vehicle lurch backward and forward. Marciac seized the animals by their bits to settle them.

La Fargue managed to open the door and saw a form inside.

'THERE'S SOMEONE IN HERE!'

It was Gagnière. Fainted away, after receiving a sword wound in the right shoulder.

'A NEW FRIEND!' joked Saint-Lucq. 'COME ON! HURRY!'

Ballardieu climbed aboard holding Agnès in his arms. La Fargue closed the door for them, then mounted the horse whose reins the Gascon, already in his saddle, held out for him.

'COME ON! ALL HELL IS GOING BREAK LOOSE!'

Saint-Lucq cracked the lunges against the rumps of the harnessed horses. The riders spurred their own mounts and opened the way for the coach and they were all soon moving at a full gallop. Miraculously spared by the explosions whose blasts lashed their faces with various bits of debris, they crossed through the gate just before a violent flash brought it tumbling down. The convoy hurtled down the winding road, pitilessly running down any escapees in their path, leaving the ruined castle behind them in the grip of the full destructive fury of ancestral energies.

There was a second of tremendous silence and then a dazzling force broke forth from the sky. It swept away the last vestiges of the castle in an apocalyptic blast whose brightness drowned out the silhouette of a lone wyvern and its rider winging their way from the scene.

At the same moment, a quarter of a league away, a gate was pushed open in a thicket of undergrowth. Savelda came through first, battling with the thorns, soon followed by the two men carrying the vicomtesse. Drained of the draconic energy which had sustained her youth, she had regained her true age, becoming a haggard and ancient-looking old woman: her face was hollow and wrinkled, her complexion had lost its freshness and beauty, her long blonde hair had shrivelled into grey locks and her pretty lips had dried and thinned. A thick black bile ran from her mouth and nostrils, and she breathed with difficulty, moaning and hiccupping.

But she lived.

IV

A New Day

Two days went by and then, in the morning, Rochefort came seeking La Fargue. Less than an hour later, La Fargue was received alone by Richelieu. Sitting at his desk, elbows placed on the arms of his chairs and his fingers gathered into a steeple against his lips, the cardinal stared at the impassive old captain for a long while.

Finally he said:

'Monsieur de Tréville displayed great kindness in liberating monsieur Leprat from Le Châtelet, did he not? If it were up to me . . .'

Sitting stiffly and keeping his gaze fixed straight before him, La Fargue did not reply.

'If one is to believe monsieur de Tréville,' Richelieu continued, 'the man known as Malencontre duped your man, stole his things and escaped his prison cell in disguise, taking advantage of the changing of the guards. If monsieur Leprat were not the man that he is, this might be believable . . .'

'No one is infallible, monseigneur.'

'Without a doubt, indeed . . . Naturally, the most regrettable aspect, beyond monsieur Leprat's hurt pride, is the loss of Malencontre. Do you have any idea of where he is to be found?'

'None at all. But it seems to me that the capture of the marquis de Gagnière compensates for his loss. Malencontre served Gagnière. And the master always knows more than his creature.'

'So we have come out ahead in this exchange.'

'Yes, monseigneur. Considerably.'

'We shall see . . .'

The cardinal turned his gaze to the window.

'How is the baronne de Vaudreuil?'

'She is recovering.'

'And the others?'

'They're all in the best of form. These last few days of rest have been very beneficial for them.'

'Good, good . . . But there still remains the fact that I ordered you not to interfere.'

'That's true.'

'Père Joseph warned me about your insubordination. Do you have anything to say in your defence?'

'Yes. I believe that Your Eminence did not wish to be obeyed.'

'Really?'

'I believe that Your Eminence knew that I would not abandon one of my . . . one of your Blades. I believe that Your Eminence had foreseen that I would be led to confront the Black Claw. Finally, I believe that Your Eminence could not do other than to give me the orders that he gave me, out of fear of displeasing Spain. But despite all that, Your Eminence wanted me to pursue matters.'

'And from where do you draw this sentiment, captain?'

'First of all, from the concern you have for the welfare of France, monseigneur.'

'Very well. And then?'

'Nothing obliged you to tell me where Malencontre was being detained. In doing so, you gave me the means to take the next step without risk of annoying the ambassador extraordinary of Spain. Thus, appearances were saved.'

The cardinal smiled. His eyes crinkled and shone with an unspoken satisfaction.

'You will understand, captain, that I can only deny all this.'

'Indeed, monseigneur.'

'Know then that I condemn your initiative . . .'

La Fargue nodded.

'. . . and that I congratulate you.'

The old gentleman betrayed a hint of a sly smile.

He realised that he would probably never know what

358

Richelieu had or had not known since the beginning of this affair, what he had chosen to say or had preferred to keep silent, or what he had pretended to believe or had secretly guessed. The Blades were a weapon that the cardinal used as he pleased.

Richelieu rose and, a signal honour, accompanied La Fargue to the door.

'I should like, captain, for you to reflect on the proposal that I am about to make to you . . .'

'Monseigneur?'

'It concerns a certain young man of great worth who has served me well. Unfortunately, things turned out in a manner that prevents him from regaining his position among my Guards. Nevertheless, I do not wish to lose him. But if you should deign to accept him among the Blades . . .'

'His name?'

'Laincourt.'

'Is he the man who—'

'One and the same, captain.'

'I promise you that I shall think upon it, monseigneur.'

'Excellent. Think upon it. And give me your accord soon.'

2

'It's me,' announced Leprat after knocking on the door to Agnès' bedroom.

'Come in.'

The young woman was still in her bed, more out of laziness, however, than necessity. She looked well and the scratches on her face would not spoil her beauty. The platter Ballardieu had brought her was set down next to her. Leprat noticed with satisfaction that it was almost empty.

'I came to see how you were feeling,' said the musketeer.

Then pointing to a chair:

'May I?'

'Of course.'

Agnès closed her book, looked at Leprat as he sat down, taking care with his wounded leg, and waited.

'So?' he asked after a moment.

'So what?'

'Are you feeling well?'

'As you can see . . . I'm resting.'

'You deserve it.'

'I believe I do, yes.'

There was an awkward silence during which Agnès became amused by Leprat's embarrassment.

But she finally took pity on him and said:

'Go ahead. Say it.'

'You were reckless in letting yourself be abducted by those men.'

'I didn't know who they were, in fact, and that was precisely what I was counting on finding out. Furthermore, there were five or six of them and I was unarmed.'

'Nevertheless. When you saw Saint-Lucq in the street, you could have . . . Between the two of you, with surprise on your side . . .'

'I know.'

'Things could have turned out very badly.'

'Yes. The Black Claw could have established a lodge, here, in France.'

'That's one way of looking at it. But why did you go there, to begin with?'

'To Cécile's house?'

'Yes.'

'You know very well. To find out what she was hiding there. To find whatever Saint-Lucq managed to find before me, acting on his secret orders from the captain. If I had known that . . .'

Leprat nodded, with a distracted gaze.

Agnès narrowed her eyes and leaned forward to look at him squarely.

'That's what you've come to speak to me about, isn't it?'

'He's changed. He's not the same as he was . . . I . . . I think he's distrustful of us.'

And with an ill-tempered gesture, his voice vibrant with impotent anger, Leprat added:

'Of us, damn it! Of his Blades!'

The young woman, sympathising with him, laid her hand upon his wrist.

'We have Louveciennes to blame for that. When he betrayed us at La Rochelle, he might as well have stabbed La Fargue in the heart. He was his best friend. His only friend, perhaps . . . And that's not even including the death of Bretteville and the shameful dissolution of the Blades. That memory must be branded by a red-hot iron in his mind, and it burns him still.'

Leprat stood up, limped towards the window and let his gaze wander over the rooftops of the faubourg Saint-Germain.

'The worst part . . .' he finally admitted, 'the worst part is that I think he's right to be wary of us.'

'What?'

'Of one of us, in any case.'

'Who?'

'I don't know.'

He turned towards Agnès and explained:

'We were the only ones to know that we were holding Malencontre. But that didn't prevent Rochefort from coming to claim him after a few hours. So the cardinal knew we had him as well. Who told him?'

Sensing a feeling that she did not like at all come over her, the young baronne played devil's advocate:

'There's Guibot. And Naïs, who we don't know from Adam and Eve, after all . . .'

'And you really believe that?'

'Do you suspect me?'

'No.'

'So then, who? Saint-Lucq? Marciac? Almades? Ballardieu . . . ? And why couldn't it be you, Leprat?'

He stared at her without anger, looking almost hurt:

'It's anyone's guess . . .'

3

The comte de Rochefort was waiting in one of the confessionals in the Saint-Eustache church when, at the appointed hour, someone sat down on the other side of the opening occluded by tiny wooden crossbars.

'His Eminence,' Rochefort said, 'reproaches you for not having warned him about La Fargue's plans.'

'What plans?'

'The ones that permitted Malencontre to escape from Le Châtelet.'

'I didn't know about them.'

'Really?'

'Yes.'

'That's difficult to believe. So where is Malencontre hiding?' the comte demanded.

'La Fargue gave him his liberty in exchange for the information that allowed them to rescue Agnès. And, in the process, to strike a blow at the Black Claw. If he has an ounce of good sense, Malencontre has already left the kingdom.'

'That's regrettable.'

'I had rather imagined that defeating the Black Claw would be cause for rejoicing . . .'

'Don't be clever with me. That's not what we're paying you for . . . Did you know that this so-called Cécile was in fact La Fargue's daughter?'

There was an eloquent silence.

'No,' the man said finally.

'Well, now you do. His Eminence wishes to know where she is.'

'In a safe place.'

'That's not what I asked you.'

'Cécile, or whatever her name may be, is simply a victim in this whole affair. She deserves to be left in peace.'

'No doubt. But you haven't answered my question.'

'And I won't answer it.' The man's tone led Rochefort to understand that it would futile to insist.

'As you will,' the comte said resignedly. 'But I have to tell you, Marciac, you're hardly earning your wages.'

4

In the courtyard of the splendid Hôtel de Tournon, an escort of gentlemen sat on their horses near a luxurious coach. They were waiting for the comte de Pontevedra, who was about to take the road back to Spain. The secret negotiations had lately taken an unexpected turn, and having been prematurely interrupted, failed to reach any conclusion. It only remained for the ambassador to return to Madrid in order to inform the king and his minister Olivares.

Pontevedra was finishing preparing for his journey when a last visitor was announced. He displayed a certain astonishment on learning his name, hesitated, thinking, and then indicated that he would receive him unattended in a salon.

La Fargue was already standing there when he entered.

The two men stared at one another for a long time. They were roughly the same age, but one had become a gentleman of court and intrigue while the other remained a gentleman of war and honour. It was not, however, the comte de Pontevedra, ambassador extraordinary of Spain and favourite of His Majesty Felipe IV, that the old captain regarded so impassively. It was Louveciennes, his former brother-in-arms and in bloodshed, the sole true friend that he had ever had and the man who had betrayed him.

'What do you want?'

'I came to tell you that Anne, my daughter, is safe and well. It seemed to me that you deserved to know that.'

Pontevedra gave a twisted, mocking smile.

' "Your daughter"?'

'She is my daughter and you know it. Indeed, you have

always known it. As have I. As did Oriane. And now Anne knows it as well. Just as she knows who you are.'

A hateful mask disfigured the ambassador's face.

'What have you told her?' he spat.

'Nothing. I am not that kind of a man.'

'So how does she know?'

'A letter from her mother. Oriane, who you never loved as much as she deserved . . .'

'A reproach that cannot be made of you,' retorted the comte.

He had venom on his lips and a flame in his eyes.

'I have long regretted our conduct that night,' admitted La Fargue.

'A handsome excuse!'

'Oriane also regretted it as well. But that was before La Rochelle, before you revealed your true nature, before you turned traitor.'

'I made a choice. The right one. And to convince myself of that all I need to do is look at you. You have nothing. You are nothing. While as for me . . .'

'You are merely rich. And Bretteville is dead because of you, Louveciennes.'

'I am the comte de Pontevedra!' shouted the former Blade.

'We both know who you are,' said La Fargue in a calm voice.

Turning away, he already had his hand on the doorknob, when Pontevedra, crimson-faced, cried out:

'I will find Anne. Wherever you are hiding her, I will find her!'

The captain spared a thought for his daughter, whom he did not know and even dreaded meeting. For now, she was where no one would be looking for her, in rue de la Grenouillère, entrusted thanks to Marciac to the good graces of the beautiful Gabrielle and her comely lodgers.

That, however, could not last.

'No,' declared La Fargue. 'You will not find her. You are going to forget about her.'

The ambassador burst out laughing.

'How are you going to force me? You can't do anything against me, La Fargue! Nothing!'

'Oh, but I can. You have used your post as ambassador to pursue a personal ambition. You have schemed and you have lied. In doing so, you have seriously compromised your mission and betrayed the trust placed in you by your . . . king. You have even, in demanding that the Blades and I search for the so-called chevalier d'Ireban, gathered together men who will soon, no doubt, be a source of complaint for Spain. You wanted us because we are the best? Well, here we are. Do you believe that Richelieu will now wish to deprive himself of our services? No, Louveciennes. The Cardinal's Blades are back, a development that your masters will have cause to regret before long . . . So, think about it. Do you really want this to become known?'

'Don't threaten me.'

'I exchange my silence for my daughter. You have no choice . . . Oh, and one last thing . . .'

'Which is?'

'The next time we meet, I will kill you. Have a safe journey back to Spain.'

La Fargue left without closing the door.

Epilogue

Night had fallen when La Fargue returned to the Hôtel de l'Épervier that evening.

He led his horse to the stable, unsaddled it and carefully rubbed it down, then crossed the courtyard to the main building. The sound of laughter, snatches of song and joyful conversations reached his ears as he went up the front steps. He smiled, entered and, from the shadows in the front hall, watched the spectacle that presented itself to him through a wide open doorway.

The Blades were gathered around a meal that wine and enjoyment had prolonged. They were all there. Ballardieu and Marciac were standing on chairs and singing off key. Agnès, radiant, was laughing. Leprat was clapping his hands and joining in on the chorus. And even the austere Almades could not help laughing at the clowning of the first two, the Gascon playing at being drunk with only a little effort. Sweet Naïs was serving without losing the least bit of their performance. Delighted, old Guibot tapped out the rhythm with his wooden leg.

Ô charmante bouteille!
Pourquoi renfermes-tu
Dans un osier tordu
Ta liqueur sans pareille?
Pourquoi nous caches-tu
Sous tes sombres habits
Ton ambre et tes rubis?

Pour contenter la vue,
Ainsi que le gosier,
Dépouille ton osier,
Montre-toi toute nue.
Et ne nous cache plus
Sous tes sombres habits
Ton ambre et tes rubis.

They seemed happy and La Fargue envied their joy, their carefree attitude and their youth. He could have been the father of most of them and, in a certain sense, he was.

Or he had been.

In former times, he would have joined in. And he was hesitating over whether or not to do so now when Naïs, in order to pass by, shut the door and left the tired old captain plunged in darkness

He preferred to go to his room without being seen or heard.

Once there, far from the noise and the warmth of the party below, he stretched out, still fully dressed, on his bed, crossed his fingers beneath the back of his neck and waited, eyes wide open but staring blankly ahead.

Soon the Saint-Germain abbey bell-tower tolled midnight.

Then La Fargue got up.

From a small casket, whose key he always kept on his person, he took out a precious silver mirror that he placed before him on a table.

In a meditative pose, with lowered eyelids, he quietly recited a ritual formula in an ancient, dread and almost forgotten tongue. The mirror which at first sent back nothing but his own reflection responded to the call. Its surface rippled and, slowly, as if emerging from a layer of living mercury, appeared the slightly translucent head of a white dragon with red eyes.

'Good evening, master,' said La Fargue.

Ballardieu and Marciac's song

Oh charming bottle!
Why do you enclose
In twisted wicker
Your peerless liqueur?
Why do you hide from us
Beneath your dark apparel
Your amber and your rubies?

To satisfy the eye,
As well as the throat,
Shed thy wicker
And bare yourself
No longer hide from us
Beneath your dark apparel
Your amber and your rubies.

Turn the page for a sneak preview of
the sequel to *The Cardinal's Blades*

The Alchemist
in the
Shadows

Coming soon from Gollancz

JUNE 1633

It was that uncertain hour just before dawn, when the wind dies down and mists begin to rise, the morning still a pale promise at the edge of night. A veil of dew already covered the countryside around the solitary manor, standing close to the border between Alsace and Lorraine,. A great silence reigned beneath the long tattered clouds which lazed across a sky pricked with fading stars.

An elegant gentleman observed the manor from the edge of the nearby wood, watching the few lights that glowed within it. A mere shadow among the other shadows beneath the branches, he stood straight as a blade, feet slightly spread, with his thumb tucked into his belt and one hand curled around the pommel of his sword. He was a tall handsome man. His name was François Reynault d'Ombreuse.

And today, in all likelihood, he would either kill a dragon or the dragon would kill him.

Behind the wall which protected the ruined manor and its outbuildings, mercenaries with tired, heavy eyes waited impatiently for the sun to rise. They leaned tiredly on their muskets or held lanterns up as they peered out into the lightening darkness, envying their sleeping comrades. They were soldiers of fortune, part of a band of thirty freebooters, who had fought and pillaged under various banners during the fifteen terrible years of war that had raged throughout the German principalities of the Holy Roman Empire. Now they had been hired to escort a quiet pallid gentleman whose looks and manner impressed them more than they cared to admit. They knew nothing of him except that he paid well. As his entourage, they had crossed the Rhineland without ever pausing long enough to unsaddle their horses, until they reached this manor. It had been abandoned for some time, but the thick outer wall and solid gate remained defensible. They had been camped here for two days now, at a safe distance from the roads and, above all, hidden from the Swedish and Imperial armies fighting for control of Upper and Lower Alsace. It seemed they would soon be secretly entering nearby Lorraine. Perhaps they would even visit France. But to what end? And why this halt?

François Reynault d'Ombreuse did not turn around when he heard someone come up behind him. He recognised the footstep of Ponssoy, a comrade-in-arms.

'They've even posted sentries out here, in this isolated place,' Ponssoy said after counting the lanterns in the distance. 'That's more than just cautious . . .'

'Perhaps they know we're on their trail.'

'How would they know that?'

Pursing his lips doubtfully, Reynault shrugged.

The two men served in the prestigious guards company of Saint Georges. They wore a half-cuirass for protection and were kitted out entirely in black: wide-brimmed black hats with black plumes, black cloth doublets and breeches, black gloves and boots made of tough leather, black belts and scabbards and, last of all, black alchemical stones made of shaped draconite which decorated the pommels of their rapiers. The sole exception to this martial mourning attire was the white silk sash tied about Reynault's waist, proclaiming his rank as an officer.

'It's almost time' Ponssoy finally said.

Reynault nodded and they turned away from the old manor, plunging back into the wood.

In a clearing, the twenty-five guards forming Reynault's detachment prayed beneath the stars. They each placed one knee on the ground and one hand on the pommel of their sword, the other pressing their hat against their heart. They held a rapt silence, gathering their spirits before battle. They knew that not all of them would live to see the sun set, but the prospect of such a sacrifice did not weigh heavily upon their souls.

Soeur Béatrice, also on her knees, faced the men. She belonged to the religious order they had sworn to serve, dedicated to defending France from the draconic menace. She was a Sister of Saint Georges, or a *Chatelaine*, as members of the order founded by Saint Marie de Chastel were commonly known. Tall, beautiful and solemn, she was not yet thirty years of age. Although dressed in white, with a veil, her attire looked as much like a young horseman's as that of a nun. The heavy cloth of her immaculate robe concealed sturdy knee-boots and she had a leather belt cinched around her waist. She even wore a rapier at her side.

After a final amen, the assembly stood and dispersed just as Reynault and Ponssoy emerged from the trees. Ponssoy went over to join the guards, who wordlessly busied themselves with their final preparations: checking their weapons, helping one another with the straps of their breastplates, making sure the horses were correctly saddled, adjusting this, tightening that, taking all of the hundred precautions that prudence dictated, but which also kept their minds occupied.

Meanwhile Reynault conferred with Soeur Béatrice. They had become well-acquainted with one another over the past month, tracking the man now returning to France with the mercenaries he had recruited in the Holy Roman Empire. Their consultation was brief.

'He must not be allowed, at any cost, to regain his primal form,' the Chatelaine emphasised. 'Because if that happens—'

'If everything goes according to plan, he won't have time.'

'Then . . . may the grace of God be with you, monsieur d'Ombreuse.'

'And with you, sister.'

*

A coughing fit woke the Alchemist.

Curled up on his straw mattress, he continued coughing until his lungs were raw. The fit was painful and it was some time before he could finally catch his breath and stretch out on his back, arms extended, his face glistening with sweat. The Alchemist – not his real name, just the one by which certain people knew and feared him – felt worn out. His natural form was that of a dragon and his human body was causing him more and more suffering. He was struggling to keep the pain in check. He knew that he was a monster, a monster whose flesh was tormented precisely because his true nature was rebelling against it. It was making regaining his primal form almost impossible for him. Each time it was an ordeal, a slow torture that threatened to kill him and whose aftermath left him feeling weaker still.

Outside, dawn was breaking.

The Alchemist sat up in his bed, letting the blanket slip down his bony chest.

He was tall and thin, with an emaciated face of morbid-looking pallor. His eyes were icy grey and his lips were vanishingly thin. He had slept in his clothes, in the room he had taken for his personal use when he and his mercenaries had installed themselves in this abandoned manor. They had already been encamped here for two days and nights, wasting precious time. Through his own fault. Or rather, the fault of the exhaustion and pain which prevented him from riding further. But he had recovered somewhat. Today they would resume their journey, tomorrow they would be in Lorraine and soon after they would reach France where the Alchemist could pursue matters left neglected for far too long.

But right now . . .

Wracked by nausea, he felt cold, then warm, and started to shiver.

The symptoms of deprivation.

For his apparent recovery was deceptive. He owed it entirely to the abuse of a certain liqueur, which caused him to burn with an evil fire which energised him even as it devoured him from within.

But wasn't the important thing to hold on and endure, whatever the price?

He turned on his side and, leaning on an elbow, stretched out a hand to a casket hidden beneath an old rag near his boots. He opened it to reveal four large flasks made of glass and metal, each secured by leather straps. The first flask was already empty. The three others – one of which was already partly consumed – contained the precious liqueur distilled from henbane, a thick substance that resembled liquid gold.

As always, the first swallow was a delight.

The Alchemist let himself fall back onto the bed, a small smile on his lips. Eyes closed, he savoured the moment as much as possible. A warm, gentle feeling of well-being flowed into him, easing his suffering, lulling his soul . . .

But loud cries suddenly broke the spell. The sentries outside had raised an alarm and their comrades were already responding to the threat. The Alchemist rose and went to the window, which was nothing more than a gaping hole that looked out over the manor courtyard and the surrounding countryside.

Horsemen. They were coming up the track leading to the manor at a gallop. Armed horsemen, led by a figure dressed in white.

The Alchemist immediately knew who he was dealing with. He also understood he was trapped in this manor, and it would not resist an assault for long.

He turned to the casket that lay next to the straw mattress.

Three flasks of golden henbane.

Enough to kill a man.

Enough to awaken a dragon.

The guards in black charged flat out, raising a cloud of dust that caught the first rays of the rising sun. The thunder of hooves made the ground shake. Reynault and Soeur Béatrice led the column. They rode side by side, their eyes fixed on the manor ahead, whose defence was being hurriedly organised. Signs of movement, hats and musket barrels appeared along the wall enclosing the courtyard. The Chatelaine unsheathed her sword and brandished the shining black blade, a blade made of draconite, high in the air.

The mercenaries shouldered their muskets and took aim. They knew their weapons had a range of one hundred and twenty paces and that it was best to let the enemy draw near before firing. So they waited.

The horsemen came on at a gallop, following the dusty track, three or four abreast. But what would they do when they arrived? It was almost as though they saw an open gate before them. Yet both the heavy doors were closed tight and an old cart loaded with barrels full of earth had even been pushed behind them as reinforcement. Nevertheless, the guards came on at the same mad pace.

They were only two hundred paces away. At sixty, the mercenaries would start firing.

A hundred and fifty paces. The track ahead was a straight line. Her black sword still held aloft, the Chatelaine chanted an incantation in the draconic tongue.

A hundred paces. At any moment a hail of lead would mow down the front ranks of riders, felling both men and beasts whose bodies would in turn force those behind them to tumble.

Seventy-five. Soeur Béatrice was still chanting.

Sixty. The mercenaries were about to open fire . . .

But at the very last second, the Chatelaine screamed a word full of power. Her blade shone with a sudden light and the twin doors of the manor gate shattered into splinters. The explosion was tremendous. It shook the walls, made the ground vibrate and flung the cart and its barrels into the air. It killed, wounded or stunned the mercenaries posted to either side of the gate and left the remaining defenders in shock, deafened by the blast and blinded by the cloud of dust.

The riders did not slow. They burst into the courtyard, firing their short muskets. Some of their enemies' responded with their longer guns.

Musket balls whizzed back and forth, striking at their targets. One of them ricocheted off Reynault's breastplate. Another ripped off his hat. He dismounted, drew his sword and shouted curt orders to his troops. All around him, close-quarters combat broke out. Socur Béatrice remained close by his side.

'WHERE?' he asked loudly, over the din of yelling men and clashing weapons.

She seemed to search around and then pointed to the main building.

'THERE!' she cried.

'WITH ME!' Reynault commanded as he leapt forward.

He was immediately followed by Ponssoy and a few others who surrounded the Chatelaine. She knew how to fight, but it was her powers that could save them all as a last resort. Her survival was crucial.

Muskets appeared at the windows of the large manor house and began to blast away. One of the guards crumpled. Despite his loss, Reynault and the rest of his group nonetheless managed to reach the main entrance. It was barricaded shut – they would have to force their way inside. Someone found a beam to use as a battering ram and with each successive blow the twin doors shivered and then began to crack a little more every time. But they still held.

'Faster!' urged the Chatelaine, a fearful expression on her face. 'Faster!'

The doors gave way at last. Reynault and his men rushed inside, charging straight into the mercenaries who greeted them with a murderous volley of musket fire. Several guards fell. Ponssoy was seriously injured and Reynault's thigh was pierced right through, although he paid it no heed. A furious melee broke out, in which even the Chatelaine took part. She and Reynault attempted to force a passage through the combatants, until she finally placed a hand on the lieutenant's shoulder.

He turned to her.

'Too late,' she said in a quiet voice which he nonetheless heard perfectly clearly.

A dull rumble came from somewhere within the house. The stone floor slabs in the great manor hall began to tremble.

Reynault realised what was happening.

'RETREAT!' he shouted. 'RETREAT! RETREAT!'

Carrying their wounded and fending off the mercenaries still pressing them, Reynault and his group hastily withdrew. The whole building was now vibrating, as if shaken by an earthquake. Its foundations began to sag. Tiles fell from the roof. The stones in the walls came loose.

And suddenly a whole section of the façade collapsed.

'Lord God, have mercy on us!' the sister murmured.

Around her, guards and mercenaries were locked in a confused mass, all of them speechless with terror.

A great black dragon emerged from the manor amidst a cloud of plaster and a cascade of debris. Immense in size, it reared up and unfurled its leathery wings with a tremendous roar. A surge of power swept through the courtyard, a wave that churned the earth, toppling the men and causing the horses to bolt.

Only the Chatelaine, her white clothing flapping in the storm, managed to stay on her feet. Holding her black-bladed rapier in her right hand she spread her arms wide and began chanting again. The dragon seemed intrigued by this insignificant creature, somehow capable of summoning a power comparable to its own. It lowered its enormous head to peer at the sister, who continued without faltering. She chanted words in a language which found an echo in the dragon's brain – a brain dominated by brutal, primitive impulses, but not entirely devoid of intelligence.

Soeur Béatrice knew it was too late. She had failed. Now that it had recovered its primal form there was nothing she could do to vanquish – or even restrain – the most powerful adversary she had ever encountered.

But there was one last card she could play.

Looking straight into the terrible depths of the dragon's eye, she gathered her remaining strength and plunged into the huge creature's tormented mind. The effort she had to make was both colossal and perilous. But after several false attempts, she finally found what she was searching for. The vision struck her soul like a fist.

For the space of one brief yet seemingly eternal moment, the Chatelaine could see.

She saw the cataclysm threatening France, her people and her throne, a cataclysm that would soon become reality beneath torn skies. It left her

terrified, awed and gasping, while the dragon –
having been defeated in the very core of its being
– screamed with rage before taking to the air and
escaping with a few mighty beats of its wings.